T0304866

Last Stop on the Murder Express

Also by C. J. Farrington

Death on the Trans-Siberian Express

Blood on the Siberian Snow

Last Stop on the Murder Express

An Olga Pushkin Mystery

C. J. Farrington

CONSTABLE

CONSTABLE

First published in Great Britain in 2023 by Constable

1 3 5 7 9 10 8 6 4 2

Copyright © C. J. Farrington, 2023
Hedgehog illustration © Anna Morrison, 2021

The moral right of the author has been asserted.

All characters and events in this publication, other than those clearly in the public domain, are fictitious and any resemblance to real persons, living or dead, is purely coincidental.

All rights reserved.
No part of this publication may be reproduced, stored in a retrieval system, or transmitted, in any form, or by any means, without the prior permission in writing of the publisher, nor be otherwise circulated in any form of binding or cover other than that in which it is published and without a similar condition including this condition being imposed on the subsequent purchaser.

A CIP catalogue record for this book
is available from the British Library.

ISBN: 978-1-47213-319-9 (hardcover)
ISBN: 978-1-47213-320-5 (trade paperback)

Typeset in Caslon Pro by SX Composing DTP, Rayleigh, Essex
Printed and bound in Great Britain by Clays Ltd, Elcograf S.p.A.

Papers used by Constable are from well-managed forests
and other responsible sources.

Constable
An imprint of
Little, Brown Book Group
Carmelite House
50 Victoria Embankment
London EC4Y 0DZ

An Hachette UK Company
www.hachette.co.uk

www.littlebrown.co.uk

For Irah and Claire –
Good things come in threes.

Prologue

'How many have you got for me?' said the woman.

'As many as you want,' said the man, shrugging. 'You can have twenty, if you like.'

'I don't *need* twenty,' said the woman, with a touch of steel that belied her sing-song tone. 'I need the number I told you on the phone, and by the date I told you. No more, no less.'

'Well, as I said, you can have 'em – if you can pay!'

The woman laughed, a cold, mirthless bark that fitted well – thought the man – with the rather wolfish cast of her features.

'Don't worry about that,' she said. 'This isn't my first time around the *dacha*, believe me.'

And he did believe her: she was clearly an experienced customer, with who-knew-what kinds of horrors under her expensive-looking belt. He knew almost nothing about her, barring her air of slightly faded glamour and her unusual tastes when it came to off-the-books purchases.

Unusual? Bizarre, even – but then again, who was to say what was normal any more? Perhaps it was just to be expected these days that one might at any moment receive a call offering to buy things that were not, strictly speaking, for sale – things that weren't, indeed, really just things at all, and whose transfer, paid or unpaid, would break a host of laws both federal and local. The man was risking a great deal by entertaining the sale – but then again, he would risk even more by turning it down.

The woman looked around her, first to her left up the alley that led towards Ulitsa 40 Let Oktyabrya and the centre of Tayga, and then to her right, down the narrow pathway that led back towards the railway station. But it was a cold Tuesday afternoon in early November, and most Taygans had more sense than to brave the chill wind on foot. Seeing nobody, the woman took an envelope from her jacket and slapped it against her wrist.

'So,' she said, 'do we have a deal?'

The man looked down at the envelope, a basic, no-frills A5 affair of the kind they sold in the stationery kiosk by City Hall on Lermontov. It was strange to think that such an everyday item could start a chain of events that could land him in jail, or worse. But what choice did he have?

He lifted his head and nodded, a single yellow streetlight throwing his hollow, unshaven cheeks and black-bagged eyes into sharp relief. Then he stretched out a hand, a slash of worn blue fabric appearing briefly at the end of his sleeve, and took the envelope from her gloved fingers.

She nodded in turn, a faint smile playing around the corners of her lips and conveying (thought the man) an unpleasant sense of expected triumph.

'I'll be in touch to arrange the handover and transportation,' she said. 'Don't forget the – ah – special requirements I mentioned. You'll need to stage everything yourself.'

'Don't worry about that,' he said, tucking the envelope into his pocket. 'My operations always go to plan.'

The woman opened her mouth as if to add something, but turned at the sound of footsteps. 'I'll be in touch,' she said again, and stalked away up the alley and into the darkness that lay beyond the streetlight's fitful glow.

The man's route lay in the opposite direction, past the pedestrian now walking up the narrow path, so he pulled his collar up around his face and marched rapidly on, averting his eyes as he passed. He had deliberately dressed in the most nondescript clothes he could lay his hands on, and barely a scrap of his flesh was visible to the casual glance. But the pedestrian stopped and looked after him, nonetheless, standing and watching until he moved out of view.

She could have recognised me, said the man to himself as he strode along, bare hands balled into angry fists in his pockets. *Yes, she could have . . .*

He saw a bin by the side of the path and kicked it in frustration, then came to a halt, resting against a concrete fencepost with his head in his hands.

'I can't – I can't risk it,' he muttered to himself. 'If she did, she's got to go.

'Yes,' he went on, lifting his hands from his face. 'It's her, or them. It's her – or them.'

He repeated this to himself again and again, each time speaking in softer tones, as if he were uttering a calming mantra. Finally he nodded to himself, put his hands back in his pockets, and moved on, walking more slowly now and with his head raised above his collar. Behind him, the bin lay still on the damp earth, its contents spilled upon the ground.

1

Cold Counsel

Night was falling when Olga Pushkin arrived at the rendezvous, the building's half-familiar outline softened by twilight as if its edges were anything less than hard concrete. The failing light stole the bright red of the canopy over the door and turned it to grey, as if the owners had tried to match the interior with a more fitting livery in the first place. And though Olga had passed the location many times on trips to Tayga, she moved now along its rain-soaked flank as if her very life depended upon the maintenance of secrecy.

'Just a little more,' she muttered, struggling to catch her breath as she scurried along. 'Just a little – ah!'

She had caught her knee on an unseen drainpipe, the impact swinging her shoulder hard into the wall on her right. She swore without thinking, but clamped a gloved hand over her mouth. Now, more than ever, she had to be silent, for just a little longer – for just long enough to get there unobserved, do what she had to do, and come away again, as if she'd been in her little rail-side hut all along.

'Pushkin, is it?' came a voice, a very loud and very male voice, from the doorway under the canopy.

Olga hushed him energetically, and for good measure flapped her hands at him, too, to indicate the need for silence.

'Pushkin – I thought so,' continued the voice loudly, which Olga now saw belonged to the overweight middle-aged man with whom her rendezvous had been arranged. 'What's the problem? Why are you shushing me? Relax! Come inside! Get a vodka!'

'So what if someone saw you?' said the man, after they had sat down together a few minutes later, shrugging his camo-clad shoulders, and unfurling his meaty hand in a gesture of unconcern.

'Well, obviously I – I didn't want to be seen coming here, to be seen by someone who might know me,' said Olga Pushkin, leaning forward and glancing from side to side as if to convey the need for discretion. 'My meeting you here – well, it could be a bit embarrassing, couldn't it?'

'Embarrassing?' said the man, bald head wrinkling with incredulous lines. '*You* are embarrassed by *me*? You should take a look in the mirror. Maybe it's the other way round!'

Olga blinked, glancing down at her sensible outfit of winter jumper, waterproof trousers, and sturdy walking boots, before running a self-conscious hand over her tied-back hair. Had he expected her to doll herself up for the meeting, she wondered – to turn up in a cocktail dress and full warpaint? She knew he was an old army man, and therefore likely to be traditional in some ways – but on the other hand she'd thought his current occupation would place certain limits on the classic chauvinism of the Russian male at large, deriving, perhaps, from a bookish personality forced into the ranks and regiments at the behest of some old-school patriarch. And yet here he was, openly disparaging his newest client in the very public surroundings of the Rising Sun, Tayga's half-hearted effort at a Japanese restaurant.

So far, the conversation wasn't going quite as she had expected. In fact, if she were being truthful – and she tried hard to be as truthful as possible, these days – she'd have to admit it was almost the exact opposite of what she'd envisaged when Ekaterina Chezhekhov had arranged the meeting with Slava Sergeivich Kirillov, accredited counsellor and self-trained occupational, physical, marriage and karate therapist.

'Oh, he's the best, Olga,' Ekaterina had said the week before, squinting at her through the usual blue-grey cloud of cigarette smoke as they stood together on the platform at Tayga station. 'He's helped so many people round here – Grigory Pavlov, and Igor Babanin, and that signal engineer, too, I forget his name. You know, the one with the long beard.'

'All men, though, Ekaterina, are they?'

'Well, yes, but he works with women, too – I'm sure he does. Oh, he's just what you need, Olga – a no-nonsense outsider to talk things over with, get some closure on Vassily and Rozalina, and all those other situations you've had to deal with, too. Nevena, Ivanka, the lot. And you've still got the Roslazny gang on your hands – Papa Mikhail, and Aunt Zia, and old man Solotov, to boot. And don't forget your book!'

'Don't worry about my book,' Olga had said, secure in the knowledge that her masterpiece, *Find Your Rail Self: 100 Life Lessons from the Trans-Siberian Railway*, would soon be profitably distributed to bookstores from St Petersburg to Saratov. 'My book can look after itself!'

'If you say so,' Ekaterina had replied, but casting a troubled look at her friend all the same. Olga was certainly an accomplished railway engineer (second class), and had also shown a deft hand in managing her way out of some tricky – and indeed downright dangerous – circumstances over the past year, but Ekaterina worried that she expected altogether too much from publication day. Ekaterina was a little older than Olga, and had had enough experience of the world to doubt Olga's confident belief that books-on-shelves would automatically equal roubles-in-pocket – roubles that Olga desperately needed to quit her track-maintenance job and go to Tomsk State University, the Stanford of north-western Russia, to study literature and become a professional, full-time writer at last. 'Look, I'm sure you're right – but even so, it can't hurt to get another perspective, *da*? And it's only a thousand roubles, for the first meeting.'

'That's quite enough, when you've got a whole household to feed on a Russian Railways salary,' Olga had replied, thinking of her brother Pasha, recently discharged from the army, and her friend Anna Kabalevsky and her three small children – not to mention Olga's Siberian white-breasted hedgehog, Dmitri, all of whom depended on Olga's slender earnings for their sustenance and shelter.

'But nothing's more important than your happiness, Olga Mikhailova Pushkin,' Ekaterina had replied, 'and you haven't been happy since Rozalina came back, have you? Well then,' she'd nodded, when Olga confirmed that indeed she hadn't, 'you've got to do something about it. Nobody expected her back,' she'd continued, squeezing Olga's arm. 'I don't think even Vassily really thought he'd ever see her again. And arriving just at that moment, too, when you'd got past all the dangers at last – oh, Olga, it must be the hardest thing you've ever had to bear.'

Not quite, Olga had thought, remembering the death of her beloved mother, Tatiana, long ago – but it was still true that she hadn't felt quite herself since Vassily's lost wife had returned out of the blue barely a month ago. She'd tried everything she could think of – burying herself in her rail-side hut and working round the clock, scribbling down ideas for a sequel to *Find Your Rail Self*, helping Anna with the kids, even engaging with Fyodor Katin's crazy schemes for the improvement of Russia – but nothing had yet managed to dispel the gloom. Rozalina's return might not be the hardest thing she'd ever endured, but it had certainly come close. And Ekaterina was right: her happiness was important – so important that uncomfortable things like appointments with counsellors might have to be borne, even when those same counsellors insisted on meeting in a public space, on drinking vodka during the consultation, and now insulting his prospective client by suggesting that her appearance embarrassed him.

She opened her lips, intending to change the topic and keep things constructive, but Slava Sergeivich Kirillov barged on regardless. 'I mean, look at you . . . I've got a reputation to consider, you know! I've got men coming to me from the army, from the police, from security operations – from the FSB, for God's sake. So a lady engineer, by comparison . . .'

'I'm not a *lady* engineer,' said Olga, tight-lipped and angry. 'I'm an *engineer*, second class. I'd love to see somebody like you survive a day – no, an hour – in my shoes.'

'I wouldn't be caught dead in civvy shoes like that,' said Kirillov, darting his cigarette tip downwards. 'There's only one type of thing for this weather: standard-issue army boots. Look at that quality!'

He lifted a heavy foot sideways so Olga could see, then moved it back under the table, kicking its leg in the process. Kirillov swore as his glass toppled sideways over his plate, dousing his fish-filled *pelmeni* in a pool of clear vodka, and signalled for a cloth to a waitress dressed half-heartedly in a replica kimono.

'Not bad, this place, *nyet*?' muttered Kirillov, as the waitress helped him clear up the mess. 'I always have my meetings here – best food in Tayga. But, you know,' he said, in a lowered voice, leaning forward as the waitress left, 'we've still got unfinished business with Japan. 1905. Always remember 1905!'

Olga looked at him incredulously: was her counsellor-to-be suggesting Russia might once more go to war with Japan to avenge defeats of more than a hundred years ago?

'Oh, yes,' he went on, 'once we've taken care of business to the west, there's a whole list of people the other way who'll need to go carefully. This is only the beginning. So now can you see? My job's to help prepare us for that – I owe that much to my old regiment. I've got to sort out all the men who come to me, so they can fight, if need be. That's honest work. But I don't have time for a heap of old maids coming to me with a heap of made-up problems.'

'They're not—' began Olga loudly. But then she noticed several pairs of eyes swivelling in her direction, and proceeded more quietly: 'They're not made-up problems! I told you I've spent the past two weeks digging out an ancient siding because of some order filtering down from Kemerovo – look at these blisters!'

'And why shouldn't you dig out a siding, if your superior asked you to?' replied Kirillov. 'Aren't you paid by the state to do the state's bidding? Looks like you could do with losing a few pounds, too,' he went on. 'As for the rest – I reckon that sergeant's better off with his wife, after all, if this is what you're like. Oh, yes, Ekaterina brought me up to date. Classic female hysteria! And your book? Well, it sounds like the kind of rubbish only women would read, anyway, so what's the difference?'

Olga felt the blood rushing to her cheeks. She balled a fist under the table to contain her rage, and with the other hand gathered up her handbag prior to leaving – but Kirillov was still speaking.

'Listen,' he said, 'it's simple, *da*? Toughen up! Do your work without complaining, like a soldier! And forget about this book nonsense, too – you'll never get anywhere with that, or nowhere worthwhile, anyway. Stick to hammers and nails, wood and steel – that's the Russian way. And this Rozalina woman? Just find a way to make life uncomfortable for her. Get her to leave of her own free will, and *vualya*! Problem solved. And last of all, don't worry about what other people think! Who cares if some fancy man saw you coming here to meet with me? Just go your own way and the hell with everyone else.

'There,' he went on, knocking the table with his fist and looking at her with a satisfied smile. 'Consider yourself counselled! That'll be a thousand roubles.'

A thousand roubles, thought Olga, as she strode out of the café – enough to buy several meals for the household she'd sworn to support back in Roslazny. A thousand roubles – and for what? For a few words of idiotic advice that she could have extracted free, gratis and for nothing from any number of the bullet-headed has-beens that she saw on the trains and at Tayga station, flocking like swarming Kirillovs in identikit military gear, and with identical opinions to match.

And, of course, Kirillov had her over a barrel, since she'd been foolish enough to tell him some of her troubles before she realised what kind of 'counsellor' he really was. She'd only told him things in outline, admittedly, but with enough substance to be embarrassing if he chose to spread them around. Her father Mikhail, who earlier that year had unceremoniously ejected Olga and her brother Pasha from the family home, would fall on such juicy details like manna from Heaven, as would Zia Kuznetzov, Mikhail's sister-in-law and Olga's aunt, and their associate, Vladimir Solotov – not to mention the village gossips like Igor Odrosov, who presided over Café Astana, Roslazny's sole destination. So Olga had really had no option but to dig into her handbag and stump up the required cash, which Kirillov had gathered with satisfaction, before rolling it into a little tube and sticking it in the top of his combat-trousers pocket.

Oh, but he was really a thief, thought Olga, as she walked quickly back towards the station, wondering how on earth Ekaterina Chezhekhov could have recommended him in the first place. A stupid man filching money from honest people in exchange for unmitigated nonsense . . . Surely other countries didn't allow things like this to happen. Surely, in France or Germany or England, the authorities would stop unqualified people like Kirillov setting up as counsellors or therapists or life coaches! But things were different in Russia, where the authorities let people do what they like in exchange for upward payment. They hadn't stopped the aristocrats from working their serfs to death, in the old days, any more than they stopped the modern-day oligarchs stripping the country of oil and cash and blood. They started wars to expand their empire abroad and distract from problems at home. And meanwhile the people froze and starved and suffered, in small ways and big. In Russia, life itself was the thief, seizing youth and love and all good things, and turning them to bad. Yes, life was the thief, in Russia.

Olga walked through the streets of Tayga in the falling night, thinking how quiet it was everywhere, and how unlucky she'd been to see someone en route to her ill-fated meeting – someone who might well have recognised her, and later hear that she and Kirillov had been seen at the Rising Sun, and put two and two together . . . If she ever ventured to see a counsellor again, which seemed rather unlikely to her at that moment, she swore it would be somewhere much farther away from Roslazny than Tayga.

After a few minutes she stopped outside the Volkovs' shop, where she'd planned to stock up on a few groceries for dinner, and rolled her eyes as she saw yet another murder mystery poster pasted in the window.

JOIN RASPUTIN & THE ROMANOVS ON THE MURDER EXPRESS, ran the headline, and below, surrounding a colourful illustration of an old-fashioned locomotive powering through the Siberian snow:

Come to Roslazny (nr Tayga) and experience the DRAMATIC EVENT of the CENTURY! Meet the Tsar and Tsarina, Imperial Captains, and the Maddest Monk in history – all on board a specially adapted Russian Railways P36 steam train. Amid sabres, tsarinas, and sordid goings-on, can you solve the mystery and find the killer?

14–21 November incl. matinee performances at 3 p.m. and evenings at 8. Tickets 500R. For sale at Tayga station and at all good shops in the area. Don't miss out – buy today!

Olga sighed and glanced down at her hands, flexing her fingers and wincing at the sharp pains in her joints. The Murder Express did sound quite entertaining, she grudgingly admitted, but she wished it hadn't come along all the same. It was because of the Murder Express that she'd spent the last fortnight working with the Tayga maintenance crews to clear an old siding near Roslazny, carrying out endless hours of gruelling toil alongside her everyday duties in the rail-side hut. And as soon as tomorrow, she'd have the train itself to look after, too, on the express orders (as he put it) of Boris Andreyev, the red-star-wearing foreman at the Tayga depot and Olga's immediate superior, in title if not in nature. It was because of Boris that Olga had almost been unceremoniously shipped off to Mongolia earlier that year, and it was because of Olga that Boris's wings had been clipped so decisively not long afterwards, prompting a grudge that had clearly gone nowhere in the intervening months. He had assigned Olga's extra duties with such undisguised glee that even the other railwaymen, who normally found such things amusing, had frowned in disapproval – but disapproval was to Boris as a four-foot snowdrift was to the Trans-Siberian: the merest trifle to be tossed aside and immediately forgotten.

'I wish I didn't have to do this,' he'd said unconvincingly, smirking beneath his Ushanka hat, 'but this is from on high. Arkady Nazarov himself,' he continued, naming the new Mayor of Kemerovo. 'I think he must have invested a bit in the show . . . So you see, Pushkin, we need all hands on deck. Even ladies' hands – assuming you can put off your next manicure for a week or two?'

Olga had never had a manicure, barring the odd night when she and Anna Kabalevsky had had a few too many vodkas and ended up painting each other's nails in outlandish colours – but it hadn't seemed worth mentioning to Boris on that particular occasion. Unfortunately, Olga had never been privy to the secrets that her putative replacement, Polina Klemovsky, had used to blackmail Boris into letting her take Olga's spot on the Mongolian exchange, so Olga could hardly try to manipulate him herself. For the moment, her best option was to keep moving forwards, like a Luhanskteplovoz 2TE116 diesel locomotive barging ice and slush aside on the Tomsk–Irkutsk route. If she just stuck to doing what she knew, and doing it well, good things would surely come – or so she kept telling herself, when times were tough.

Olga brushed aside the inconvenient thought that this was more or less what Kirillov had advised, and gazed instead at the small pile of books that Madame Volkov had on display. The Volkovs were quite a literary family, by Tayga standards, and each month ordered in the most popular books from the Tomsk suppliers in the hope of selling a few to passers-by. Olga had often dreamed of her own book featuring in the small but tasteful displays of Madame Volkov, and half closed her eyes as if she could see her own title, *Find Your Rail Self*, nestling at the top of the carefully arranged heap of bestsellers.

But then she opened them wide, staring in horror at the glossy hardback that Madame Volkov had placed prominently on a stand surrounded by cardboard cut-outs of railway track, stations and locomotives, with several copies set out at artful angles.

The book itself was called *All on the Line*, by one Inessa Ignatyev, whose name was scrawled in improbable fonts across the base of the cover, beneath a colourful (if inaccurate) painting of a Russian Railways diesel shunter at work. But the thing that made Olga's breath catch in her throat was the subtitle, running from side to side as if to steal her life's work in a few well-chosen letters: *Eighty Life Learnings from a Trackside Engineer.* She staggered back in horror, reeling at this new and most unexpected blow. Was everything going to go wrong today, she asked herself, or only the most important things?

'But don't you see, Ekaterina?' cried Olga twenty minutes later, waving a copy of Inessa Ignatyev's book – unwillingly purchased from Madame Volkov – from side to side. 'It's *my* book! Somebody's stolen my idea and written it up. *All on the Line? Find Your Rail Self. Eighty Life Learnings? 100 Life Lessons.* It's the same bloody book. I don't know who this Inessa Ignatyev is, but she's about to find out who I am!'

Ekaterina Chezhekhov took a drag of her cigarette and handed it to Olga, then took the book from her hands and inspected it closely. 'Inessa Ignatyev – a TV journalist, with a couple of books under her belt already . . . And it's published in Novosibirsk – isn't that where your publisher's based? Well, then,' she went on, handing back the book and taking her cigarette again, 'there you go.'

'There I go – what?'

'It's your publishers. They liked your idea, but wanted to make sure it sold. So they roped in an established author, knocked off a copy, and banged it out before yours to ensure Inessa gets all the credit. But then, if it takes off, your book would be a nice little extra – picking up on the trend and hoovering up the interest.'

Olga stared at Ekaterina, wondering where on earth she could have got such ideas. 'But the publishers – I've signed a contract with them. I've signed a contract with them,' she repeated, much louder, to be heard over the gentle strains of a 3TE25K2M getting up speed at the head of thirty heavy-laden goods wagons.

'Olga, Olga,' said her friend, when the noise had died down, smiling sadly at her through a cloud of smoke. 'You've signed a contract with Russian Railways, too, but do you think that would stop them hanging you out to dry if it served their purpose?'

Olga glanced around her, taking in the well-worn sights of Tayga station but also viewing them with a different eye, seeing not just shunters and sidings but the remorseless efficiency and ruthlessness of a giant corporate machine that would indeed, as Ekaterina had said, sacrifice an Olga Pushkin without missing a step. She turned back to Ekaterina with a sigh, and raised the book once more, intending to comment on the poverty of invention and style displayed by the supposedly brilliant Inessa – but the words died on her lips as Ekaterina stepped forward and took her arm.

'Look, Olga, I'm sorry to add another burden to your shoulders, but there's something else you should know.'

'What now?' snapped Olga, feeling she couldn't bear it if another single thing went wrong that day.

'Oh, it's Boris,' said Ekaterina, rolling her eyes as if to soften the blow. 'You know how he is – and you know how he is about you.'

'I do,' said Olga, drily.

'Well, I happened to overhear him talking earlier on – when I was getting rid of my receipts. By chance, I chose a bin near Boris's office –'

'By chance, of course!'

'– and I didn't like what I heard at all. He was talking about how Russian Railways should adopt new technologies, adapt to the modern world – the usual *der'mo*. But then he started talking about you in particular, and how your hut was a relic from the last century –'

'Just like him!'

'– and how they could easily replace you with a drone, inspect the track from the air and call in the standard rail-mounted crews for repairs.'

'Replace me with – with a *drone*? You mean – one of those little helicopters that boys play with?'

'I know, Olga, I know – it's ridiculous. No drone could do what you do.'

Olga shook her head. 'But if Boris puts his mind to it . . . Oh, Ekaterina, I can't lose my job yet, especially if this other book takes away all my sales. What am I going to do?'

Ekaterina gripped her arm again. 'Look, Olga, you've beaten Boris before, and I'm sure you can do it again. Besides, I don't know if he could even get it past the inspectors – they still like boots on the ground, Pavel tells me. I can't see some spotty kid with the latest gadgets replacing someone like you, Olga – a strong, independent woman, an experienced engineer. No, Pavel would never allow it. I'd see to that!'

Olga smiled despite herself: Pavel Veselov was the latest in a long line of Ekaterina's romantic conquests, and as a member of the Kemerovo railway inspectorate he was definitely a step up from the usual engineers, drivers and signalmen.

'Well, I just hope you're right, or we'll all be out in the snow again with nowhere to go.' She reached out a gloved hand and took another of Ekaterina's cigarettes. 'What? Am I not allowed to smoke now? Am I not allowed to ease the tension, just a little, even if it is on Russian Railways property?'

Ekaterina shrugged. 'Of course, Olga. The more customers I have, the better.' Then she added: 'Oh, I almost forgot – how was Kirillov?'

Olga gazed back at her friend, short, round and vivid in one of her memorable dresses, topped with a heavy coat and multi-coloured scarf against the November twilight, and with sharp eyes that twinkled as brightly as the tip of her ever-present cigarette – an ongoing drain on her profits, since she was a cigarette vendor by profession, and had spent the best (or the worst) part of the last decade selling Primas and Belamorkanals to railwaymen and passengers, tourists and policemen, soldiers and bored housewives and nervous teenagers alike. And Olga had known Ekaterina for even longer than that, having made her acquaintance via an early boyfriend when Olga was still studying at the Irkutsk Institute of Railway Engineering – or, rather, its under-funded outpost at the Tayga Community College. She'd known her for so long, indeed, that she could hardly believe Ekaterina had thought Slava Kirillov was the right man to help with her undoubted challenges. Nobody ever really knew you, she thought, and you never really knew anybody. Or – better still, for Olga was always on the lookout for proverbs she could bestow on the Russian language – one woman's *pelmeni* was another's poison.

'Oh, he was . . .' she searched for the *mot juste* '. . . he was – er – enlightening. I definitely learned something. But I don't think I'll need to see him again.'

'Did it in one session, did he? Well, that's Kirillov,' said Ekaterina, beaming at her. 'That's Kirillov!'

It certainly was Kirillov, thought Olga, as she walked back out of the station and towards the road where she'd parked the car, Prospekt Kirova. Olga couldn't think of anyone, counsellor or otherwise, who could have put her off future meetings so effectively and in such a short period of time – anyone apart from her father Mikhail, that is, and his cronies, Zia Kuznetsov and old man Solotov.

She walked up to the car, a rusty Lada Granta, and dug in her handbag for the keys. She'd borrowed the car from Nonna, who occasionally babysat Anna's boys Boris, Gyorgy and Ilya, while Anna was out on her never-ending, ever-fruitless search for work. Nonna was a hotel maid by profession, but her jobs were always quite short-lived and she seemed permanently hard up – too hard up, at least, to take her car to the washer-men by the petrol station in Tayga, so the Lada was filthy inside and out. Olga stepped in gingerly, to avoid her coat skimming off the surface layer of mud on the door, and tried once again to clear the rear windscreen with ever-diminishing gouts from the windscreen spray. She sighed, opened her window and stuck her head out to look behind as she began to reverse.

'Want a hand, *devushka*?' said a brusque voice that belonged, she realised, to the Roslazny butcher, Nikolai Popov. A large, rotund man, Popov was standing on the pavement with his wife Nadya, who was looking at Olga with narrowed, unfriendly eyes.

'Oh, it's you, Olga,' went on Popov. 'Didn't recognise you with that scarf on your head!'

'Hello, Nikolai – Nadya,' she said, rather reluctantly, and then, feeling that more was expected, she added: 'I'm just in town to see Ekaterina Chezhekhov and – and to pick up some shopping,' she concluded, holding up the despised book by Inessa Ignatyev.

'Look, you're doing it wrong,' said Popov, stepping forward and grabbing the wheel through the open window. 'Left hand down and back, then right hand down and forward, and Bogdan's your uncle!'

'Oh – well, thanks, Nikolai,' said Olga, striving to hide her annoyance. 'Yes – yes, I can see what you mean. See you back in Roslazny!'

She rolled up the window so that Popov had to withdraw his hand, reversed quickly – a little too quickly, with the back wheel grinding against the kerb – and then took off at speed along Prospekt Kirova, angry with herself for breaking her resolution to be truthful at all times.

She'd made the promise to herself earlier that year, when she'd finally plucked up the courage to leave the house she'd shared with her father Mikhail – and it had seemed even more important after Rozalina had come unexpectedly back into their lives, like a character suddenly reappearing in a TV soap, robbing her of Vassily Marushkin just as things had seemed about to change at last. This final heartbreak had convinced Olga that life, in the end, was nothing more than a short and brutal fairground ride – a ride too short, and too brutal, to allow for any prevarication. She'd spent her whole life dancing around other people's feelings, but it was too late for that now. And yet there she was, simpering and thanking the ridiculous Roslazny butcher for his condescending driving advice as if she were a twenty-year-old debutante straight out of some tsarist-era finishing school!

She pushed her boot down hard on the pedal and accelerated towards the end of the road, feeling a fierce satisfaction as the engine revved and the Lada approached the upper reaches of its possible speed, slowing only at the last moment and turning into the narrow road that led to Roslazny. Why did everything have to be so difficult? she asked herself, bumping and swaying along the road at a higher rate than was strictly advisable at this time of year. And why did her life feel so cursed? A lost wife turning up like a bad kopek, a rival author worming out of the woodwork, a disastrous visit to a counsellor, witnessed by all and sundry – and now a renewed threat to her job, too, on top of weeks of hard labour clearing the siding, all so that some wandering troupe of puffed-up theatrical has-beens could perform a heap of nonsense about the last days of the Romanovs . . . It just didn't seem fair. But, then, who ever said life would be fair?

A few minutes later, Olga pulled up at Nonna's house in the same black mood, slamming on the brakes until she skidded to a halt outside the low breeze-block building with peeling-off white paint and a few half-hearted strokes of graffiti on one corner – the work of the teenage Petrovs, probably, who liked to pretend they lived in an edgy district of St Petersburg rather than on the outskirts of a half-empty village in Siberia. Vassily's bowl-headed son, Kliment, was far too kind-hearted to damage another person's property like that, however dilapidated or ramshackle it was in the first place – wasn't he? Olga was sure he was.

She got out and slammed the door, then marched up to Nonna's door, a sagging blue number on rust-red hinges, and banged on it with her gloved fist. She heard a faint cry from within, and the sound of breaking glass, and sighed at the inevitable delay. Could anything go right – anything at all?

She squatted down and leaned back against the wall to wait, plucking out her new pack of cigarettes and lighting one with a faint frisson of forbidden fruits, knowing that the small jet of pleasure was bad for her, but enjoying the moment nonetheless. She gazed at the ground beneath her feet, speckled with gravel and mud and dead leaves and shreds of cast-off plastic bags shifting in the breeze, until she saw a spider make its way across the little patch of ground. Then her deep-set eyes became deeper still, assuming a faraway look that ranged beyond the house by her side and the aggregate upon which she stood – for she was thinking of her mother, Tatiana, and the far-off days when she'd lived in Roslazny with Olga and Pasha and their father, Mikhail.

'You think this is empty ground?' she'd said to Olga once, sitting on the dry earth one summer day when the trees swayed, dreaming, in the heated air. 'Just look for a while,' she'd gone on, when the six-year-old Olga had nodded in response. 'Look, and wait, and things will come – you'll see. Just like people: if you wait, they will come. If you can open your eyes, you'll see – unlike most people, who only see what they expect, or what they want to see.' And indeed, a worm, and then a tiny moth, and then another spider had appeared as if by magic, and more after that, populating the little space with teeming life as if it were a great forest seen from afar.

Her mother had left something out of the picture, though, thought Olga, a few minutes later, as she finally handed over the keys to a flustered, red-wine-stained Nonna, turned on her heel, and set off homewards. Her mother Tatiana had left out the giant military-issue boots favoured by people like Kirillov – boots that would come along at the worst moment and plonk themselves down on the middle of the miniature world, squashing it to oblivion. Or it might be a pair of the expensive Italian leather shoes worn by the politicians and the oligarchs, which – though more delicate – were just as effective at wiping out everything in their path.

Olga hurried past the road that led to the police station, whose familiar outline brought an unsettling mix of memories surging to the surface: Vassily's posting there earlier in the year, resurrecting the abandoned building from its slow, cold sleep in the snow; the detective work they'd carried out together, narrowly avoiding death but also discovering Vassily's long-lost son, Kliment; the more recent excitement prompted by the return of Olga's old friend Nevena Komarov, and Olga's own brief imprisonment in the crumbling cells; and lastly the evanescent hope that Vassily might return Olga's love, before Rozalina miraculously resurfaced and dashed her hopes for ever. Despite herself, she glanced down the road, seeing a faint gleam of warm yellow light spilling out of the low windows and casting dim bars across the potholed street towards the trees opposite, the source of yet more remembrance: omens of breaking branches and heavy early snowfall.

The snow, thought Olga. I wish the snow would return and blanket us all in white nothingness. Then perhaps I could forget. Then perhaps I could stop imagining them in there together, sharing vodka and gherkins and the heat thrown by Vassily's gap-toothed, Soviet-era fireplace with the missing tiles. Then perhaps I could stop hating myself for hating Rozalina.

She hurried on homewards, pausing at Café Astana and peering in at the windows to see if Anna Kabalevsky or her brother Pasha might be there. They weren't, as it happened, but the bar was busy – unusually so for a Tuesday evening, in fact, and with several customers that Olga didn't recognise. Or so she thought at first – but didn't one or two of them look oddly familiar? There, drinking together in a group by the end of the counter, with a bottle of Odrosov's Rocket Fuel vodka to share between them – that man in his forties with long hair and a beard, and the woman he was talking to, a little younger and glamorous with glossy red hair and a tight-fitting dress, and next to them an athletic man in his late thirties – weren't they faces Olga had seen before somewhere?

The faint sense of recognition danced at the edge of her consciousness, but yielded no firm results in her tired mind. No doubt she'd remember at three in the morning, when she'd been woken by Anna's youngest crying for his night-time feed, when Olga would lie and stare at the ceiling, thinking of the past and of a future that might have been.

She shrugged, and turned away, but as she did so one of the group – the lithe figure in his thirties – strode rapidly across the bar, phone in hand, and came out just as Olga passed the door, almost walking into her in the process.

'Sorry,' he muttered, behind a hand, and rolled his eyes as if to communicate his annoyance at having to answer the call. He was good-looking, in a rather obvious way, and his smile was charming. Olga found herself smiling in return, and shrugging to dismiss the supposed inconvenience. Again she had the feeling that she had seen him somewhere before. He clearly wasn't a railwayman, though, which didn't leave her with many avenues to explore.

'Thanks for calling back,' said the man, who had turned and was walking in the same direction as Olga, who hung back a little out of politeness. 'It's Rodion. Rodion Rultava.'

Olga frowned: now she was absolutely sure that she'd come across him before. Where on earth had she heard that name?

But Rodion was still talking.

'*Da, da*. From the show. Well – it's odd. I think it's happened before. Can you look into it and get back to me? It's only because—'

He turned again to walk back towards the café, nodding once more at Olga as they passed, and the rest of his conversation was lost to her. Olga grimaced again, for in spite of her immensely frustrating day she could hardly help finding Rodion's words interesting – what show? What was odd? And what had happened before? – and yet she could hardly follow him back to Café Astana to hear more. Maybe Odrosov would overhear something, she thought, while hovering around the bar; she could ask him tomorrow. The man might have been talking about the Murder Express, she realised – that was a show, of a sort. Maybe this Rodion Rultava was some kind of theatrical critic, and thought they had stolen their script, or their poster, from some other troupe, just as Inessa Ignatyev had stolen the idea for *Find Your Rail Self* from Olga. But Rultava had gone, and she would never know.

Reluctantly she turned and forced her feet onwards, but then she stopped as something flashed past the corner of her eye. She turned quickly, a swivel of the hips, and started as she saw a man walking quickly along the opposite side of the road, ducking his head under the low-hanging eaves punctuated by broken fragments of old guttering. At least, she thought it was a man, judging by the cut of his coat, though his head and face were hidden from view by a substantial scarf and fur hat, and there was a certain sinuosity of movement in his gait that seemed to confuse her eye. Glancing across to where the man had sprung from, Olga saw a glowing red light on the ground: a discarded cigarette. So he had been – what? Standing there behind an old water butt or makeshift bulwark? A hen-pecked husband sneaking a forbidden smoke, perhaps? Or someone waiting for interesting conversations to overhear?

She watched as he looked quickly behind him and jumped across the road in two quick steps, before disappearing around the corner. Olga couldn't tell if he'd gone into Café Astana or not, but she thought not. Maybe he, too, had found the conversation interesting, and had intended to follow the other man into the café, before changing his mind when Olga appeared on the scene – or perhaps he'd just been out for a smoke.

Olga shrugged again and turned to head for home. Whatever was happening, she told herself firmly, it was no concern of hers. She'd had enough goings-on for one day, and besides, Vassily was more than capable of keeping an eye on things around the village. Vassily and Rozalina, that is. Vassily, and Rozalina, and Kliment, but not Olga Pushkin. Her home was not the police station but the house she shared with Anna and Pasha and the boys.

She pushed open the gate and walked up the narrow path that led to the front door. But then she stopped and gazed up at the house she had bought for Anna and Pasha and the boys, thinking of Inessa Ignatyev and Boris Andreyev and little drones operated by spotty teenagers in Russian Railways uniforms.

Her home, yes, her home – but for how long?

2

Early Departure

'Oh, Olga,' said Anna Kabalevsky the next morning, her eyes glowing. 'It must have been the actors you saw!'

'From TV?' said Boris, Anna's eldest. 'There are people from TV here in Roslazny?'

'No – just from the train that's coming,' began Olga, but Anna cut in.

'Boris is right!' she cried, smiling fondly down at him. 'Several of the troupe have been in soaps and commercials and gameshows and – oh, lots of things! Look.'

She dug in her handbag and pulled out a crumpled flyer, before showing it to Olga in triumph. 'See – there's Sonia Alikovsky, from *Dni Nashikh Zhizhney*, you remember? She played Tania Golubev for years! And there's Larissa Lazarov, who used to be on that gameshow – oh, I forget the name, but she used to hold up those number placards. Red hair, tall – oh, you remember her! And there's Panteleimon Pomelov, who was on the drama channel for ages playing that tsar – Peter the Great, I think. And Rodion Rultava, from *Domoy i v' Put* – he's so handsome, Olga. Aren't we lucky to have them in town?'

Anna continued waxing lyrical about the troupe, which also included the director and playwright Ilya Putyatin – 'The same name as my own little Ilya! Could it be a sign?' – and his actor wife Agapa, who had once had a regular slot on the national weather channel, among other things. Olga smiled at her friend, and raised her eyebrows at the right moments, and nodded as enthusiastically as she could – but she couldn't help thinking of Rodion Rultava and what he had thought was odd about the show, and what had happened before. He hadn't been a critic, then, but an actor, on the inside of the troupe. So what was he worried about?

It was hard to concentrate on this, however, because Anna and the boys kept rattling on so excitedly about the stars who were coming to town, or rather to the village. For Olga's part, though, she couldn't help but think that these actors all seemed a little past it. None of them had done anything on television for years, and there was a fixity to some of their smiles in the publicity shots that spoke to Olga of faint desperation – a desperation sufficient to take on roles in an obscure murder mystery train touring the provinces at the start of winter. But Anna was so excited, so transparently elevated by this tangential dose of fame, that Olga didn't have the heart to contradict her.

Anna had enough to deal with, after all, with her three boys to look after and no job on the horizon, forcing her to rely on handouts from Olga to survive. Her livelihood had disappeared earlier that year together with her husband Bogdan, who had secretly re-mortgaged the hostel they ran together while simultaneously piling up debts so large, and from such dubious sources, that he soon felt obliged to flee the region altogether – leaving Anna quite literally holding the baby. No: if the train's visit to Roslazny was enough to make Anna just a little happier, then Olga was all for it.

'Well, it sounds great to me,' put in Pasha, poking his head through the window that led to the kitchen. 'The boys and I can't wait for the first performance – right, Boris?'

'Oh, Pasha,' said Anna, frowning at him with all the vigour of a parent who had hoped a difficult topic would not arise. 'I'm not sure if the boys can come. It sounds quite an adult play. You know, with people being' – she dropped her voice to a stage whisper – '*murdered*.'

Olga smiled at the inevitable chorus of dismay that arose from Anna's boys, who now jumped to their feet in unison to petition their mother so that they could attend after all. She shook her head at Pasha, who smiled and shrugged before ducking back into the kitchen to continue preparing the boys' breakfast. Pasha was a different breed from Kirillov, thought Olga, as her brother began singing old Red Army songs in his somewhat tuneless tenor. There weren't many ex-army men who would voluntarily surrender their freedom to help bring up three small boys, but that was Pasha all over. He, too, had lost his livelihood, having been discharged in disgrace when his superior learned his true nature; he, too, had to rely on handouts from Olga, repaying his end of the bargain with endless childcare, housework and maintenance, supplemented by the occasional impersonation of Olga when it was necessary for her to be away from her rail-side hut unobserved.

A knock came at the door, prompting a temporary interruption of the debate between Anna and the boys.

'I'll get it,' said Olga, prompting the debate to resume. She got up, walked to the door and opened it to behold Fyodor

Katin. The villagers called him *Mechtatel*, the Dreamer, on account of his endless schemes for the reform of Russia – schemes that had yet to progress much beyond the composition of large unpublished manifestos and little-read blogs on his personal website, Dead Square, in which he called (among other things) for the restoration of the tsars and reparations for Communist crimes committed by the Bolsheviks against Russia and the world.

Today, however, he had rather more local plans in mind, centred upon the gift of a basket of eggs from the Katin henhouse.

'It's not much,' he said, stepping in at Olga's invitation and stopping dead as his glasses steamed over. 'Er – hang on.' He plucked the spectacles off and began wiping them on his scarf, which smeared the moisture around until he had made matters worse than they were to begin with. 'Thanks,' he said, as Olga came to the rescue with some tissue, then beamed at the room and its occupants as his vision was restored.

'Good morning, Anna,' he said shyly, 'boys – Pasha. I've got some eggs.'

'An egg a day keeps the doctor away, is that it, Fyodor?' called Pasha, grinning.

'I – I don't know what you mean,' said Fyodor, cheeks burning crimson.

'He means Dr Vinozev,' cried Boris.

'It's *Zinovev*,' said Anna, shushing Boris and casting an anxious glance at Fyodor. Dr Zinovev had attended to Anna's children for years, Olga knew, offering free clinics at the community hospital in Tayga, but she suspected that his interest in the Kabalevsky family ranged somewhat beyond the professional sphere. It would be hard for Fyodor to compete with a qualified doctor, thought Olga, especially when a doctor would be so handy a person to have around a house with three small children. Her eyes softened as she looked at Fyodor, who was gazing at the carpet through his moisture-smeared glasses, scarf wrapped untidily around his neck and dangling over his ill-fitting patchwork coat. There was no doubt where her sympathies lay, but equally there was no doubt that blogs and pamphlets were a poor match for paediatric expertise on tap.

'Those look like good eggs, Fyodor,' she said softly, taking the basket from his hands.

'Oh, yes,' he said, 'the best! I thought that A– I thought you could do with them. And I also – well, I also thought—'

'Spit it out, *chelovek*,' said Pasha, merrily, leaning on the side of the counter with a cigarette on his lips. 'What did you think?'

'Well, I wondered if you . . .' Fyodor turned to Anna. 'I wondered if you were going to the show later. The train on the play. I mean, the play on the train. I thought I might go, and, well, you're probably busy, but—'

'No, we're going,' said Anna, smiling at him, then down at Boris, Gyorgy and Ilya. 'I suppose you want to come too?'

The boys shrieked in pleasure and danced around their mother, while Fyodor grinned in delight. He stepped forward and picked an egg out of the basket, tossing it in the air and catching it again – but his fingers slipped as he did so, and the egg fell from his grasp and cracked upon the hard wooden floor.

Olga walked up to her little rail-side hut, opened the door and popped her head inside to check that all was well. The iron stove had gone out overnight, so she gathered some wood from the store outside and bundled some paraffin-soaked rags on top to get it going again.

'There you are, Dmitri-*dimi-detka*,' she crooned, as her white-breasted hedgehog poked his nose out from the pile of old teacloths that served as his bedding. 'I'm sorry to wake you, but it's getting cold and I need to light the fire.'

But Dmitri only snuffled in response, before burying himself deep in his teacloths again.

'Sensible boy,' muttered Olga. 'That's what I'd do myself, given half a chance.'

She lit the stove, then stood up and looked around the hut, taking in the low, sloping roof-beams, the fractured white paint, the bleached photographs pinned on the walls, and the rather dilapidated bookshelf that still held the classics her mother had bought for her on a visit to Tomsk State University, long ago. And the smell . . . She realised it wouldn't exactly qualify for bottling as perfume, but for her it was a blend of many familiar things: heat and fumes from the stove, the scent of tea from the samovar and paraffin from the rags, a hint of mouldy paper and damp wood, and threaded through it all the reassuring scent of diesel oil from the tracks outside.

She hadn't meant to stay long in the hut – indeed she couldn't stay long, for she was due to welcome the train to the siding in less than ten minutes – but now that she had stepped in she found it hard to tear herself away. So much had happened there, from the writing of her masterpiece to the discovery of that poor tourist's body by the tracks, and so much had changed since she had first walked into the hut with its faded paintwork and peeling Russian Railways logo . . . So much had changed, and Vassily above all: first he had gone behind her back with Nevena Komarov, albeit with the best of intentions, and now he had vanished from her life altogether, withdrawing into domestic bliss with Rozalina and Kliment. Yes, she had lost Vassily, and with this new book from Inessa Ignatyev she had probably lost her bestseller – and now she might lose her job and the hut, too, if Ekaterina's words were true. And then she would have lost everything.

Dmitri snuffled again under his teacloths, and Olga smiled despite herself. 'Well, almost everything,' she said, bending and gently stroking his head. 'As long as I have you, and Pasha, and Anna and the boys, I'll survive, won't I? I'll survive, little Dimi, little *detka*.'

She closed the door with a sigh and set off down the track towards the siding, thinking how much she would give to go back to the year before. Then perhaps she could have done something to prevent what had happened since, or cast some spell to keep things as they were.

The track unfolded by her feet as it always did, a sight Olga had seen so often that she knew the individual sleepers and even many of the fixings that kept the shimmering metal rails in place: there was one she'd had to hammer into place in the coldest winter she could remember, and another she'd had to coax to the side after a thermite welding repair following a shunter derailment. The tracks changed over time, but not really: it was as if they were a face known of old, which matured as it aged, and whose wrinkles did not change the underlying continuity.

Some things, she had to admit, had stayed the same in Roslazny, even if – unlike the well-worn tracks – they were rather undesirable in themselves. Roslazny was still plagued with petty wrongdoing, for example, keeping Vassily Marushkin busy on the trail of numerous crimes with no obvious suspects – just as he had been earlier in the year, when a devious and skilful operator had undertaken to frame Polina Klemovsky, Olga's proposed replacement during her aborted trip to Mongolia. (Olga still wondered from time to time what might come of the threats Polina had made upon her departure – or, rather, tried not to wonder: nothing good could ever come from the life and work of Polina Klemovsky, clog-wearer, hedgehog-kicker and bureaucratic rule enforcer *par excellence.*)

Her father Mikhail was still up to no good, for another thing, in conjunction with his long-standing cronies, Vladimir Solotov and Zia Kuznetsov, Olga's aunt. They had purchased the Kabalevsky Hostel from the bailiffs not long ago, and were now busily setting it up as a rival to Odrosov's Café Astana. Since Roslazny barely had the populace to support one restaurant, this raised the unpleasant possibility of Mikhail Pushkin & Co running Odrosov out of business and presiding over the village's sole watering hole. The Red Star, as they called it, had already cornered the catering for the Murder Express performances, cutting out Odrosov with bargain-basement pricing and a shrewd exclusivity clause.

She could see them now, in fact, setting up a stall with – predictably enough – a red star on top, like the stars the Soviets used to fix on the smokebox doors of old steam engines. Mikhail had placed it near the tiered seating that the Tayga workmen had put up the week before in preparation for the Murder Express, complete with roofs and heaters to protect the audience from the elements. As if sensing Olga's gaze, Mikhail caught her eye, quickly looked away and barked an order at Zia. It was lucky, thought Olga, that the stall was on the far side of the seating. Otherwise, she might have had to talk to them.

She reached the buffers she'd set up with the help of the mobile track-maintenance crew and looked at her phone for the time. 09:59, she read, and the train was due at ten – they'd be late, then, as there was no sign of it yet, but Olga didn't really mind. She was just glad she had arrived before the Murder Express, for there was no more glorious sight for an engineer than a P36 steam locomotive seen from the smokebox end. Olga had no illusions about the past, which (as her mother Tatiana had told her) was drenched in oceans of blood – but one thing at least had been better then: the engines. What could be more evocative, more romantic than a locomotive sweeping along snow-bound tracks at full steam, wreathed in clouds of white and grey, pistons thrashing and connecting-rods moving faster than the eye could follow? And the carriages coming behind, decked out in dashing red or gentle blue and punctuated with glowing windows offering snapshots of events within, a parade of fleeting dioramas portraying romance, small disagreements, or high affairs of state. Revealingly, she always thought, her father Mikhail had never cared for steam engines, despite half a lifetime spent working – or pretending to – for Russian Railways. 'Waste of time,' he'd said to her whenever they saw one on the tracks. 'Too slow, too expensive, too bloody noisy.' But Olga had never listened. For her, the old steam engines were the epitome of life on the lines, the true expression of the spirit of the railways.

Maybe that's where my next job will come from, she said to herself. I could move to St Petersburg, work on the old engines at Moskowsky or Vitebsky . . . There could be worse fates, she thought, her eyes crinkling into a smile as she heard the unmistakable sound of an approaching locomotive under load. Yes, there would be worse things than looking after tamed monsters like this.

The P36, vivid in its green livery, rounded the corner and passed over the old points that connected the siding to the main line, moving slowly now, yet with an appearance of immense weight and momentum that somehow eclipsed the newer, more powerful diesel units that Olga was used to. The locomotives, Olga knew, were nicknamed 'the Generals' because of the red stripe that ran along their flanks, but it would have been a good epithet in any case. She couldn't imagine anything more commanding.

The engine was close enough now for Olga to breathe in the intoxicating mix of hot metal, protesting brake drums, coal fire, hot vapour and oil, and as the P36 shuddered to a stop just short of the buffers she found herself bathed in vast arabesques of white steam that encircled her like a dancer's dress.

Stepping to the side of the track, she saw the tender behind the engine, and behind that two 1950s coaches in their original dark red paint. She'd heard at Tayga that the first carriage had been specially adapted for the murder mystery performance, and looking closely she could see the newly cut grooves along the carriage, indicating where the wooden side-wall could be raised to reveal the interior to the audience across the siding. The second carriage, Olga knew, had been repurposed as a dressing room for the actors, with most of the seats cleared out and replaced by a series of compartments, in addition to a dressing area with screens, tiny desks and mirrors. Looking closely, she could see signs of life at the edges of windows – but before she could make out any details, the engine crew jumped to the ground in front of her and blocked her view.

'Pushkin? Olga Pushkin?' said one, looking at a clipboard attached to his boiler suit with a lanyard.

'Course it's her, Vad,' said a second, rolling his eyes.

'Step aside, both of you,' said a third, pushing them out of the way and stepping forward. 'Lev Myatlev,' he said. 'Engineer for twenty years, trainee for five, teenager for eight, infant for ten, and this here is Vadim Lilov, our fireman –'

The man with the clipboard nodded brusquely at her.

'– and Simeon Zarubin, our driver.'

Simeon nodded at her with an air of world-weariness, and jerked his thumb over his shoulder. 'All set up for the performance, then?'

'All ready,' said Olga. 'Seats in place, half the village desperate to come – we don't get much entertainment round here, you know.'

'Not what I've heard,' said Lev, raising a conspiratorial eyebrow. 'Serial killers, dodgy policemen, derailments and deaths to follow . . . They say Roslazny's the most dangerous village in Siberia.'

'Probably a load of made-up rubbish to attract crime tourists,' said Vadim, pursing his lips. 'I've seen that before. Invent a heap of so-called murders, weave some story around it, and watch the rubberneckers flood in.'

'Speaking of which, we'd better get the show on the road, hadn't we?' said Vadim. 'That carriage won't open itself up, you know.'

Simeon sighed. 'Suppose so,' he said, reluctantly. 'Can't understand why anyone would plan an open-air play in November.'

'Weather's mild,' said Lev, jerking his head upwards.

'Lucky, though. Could easily have been snow, this time of year,' replied Simeon.

Olga looked around her, taking in the drab November skyline of bare trees and a carpet underfoot of mud and dead leaves. Simeon was right – the usual snow and ice would have made the play much harder to stage – but she wished there had been snow, all the same. It had a way of calming the senses, of casting a chill blanket of enforced restfulness over the busiest, most frenetic of scenes. Like all Siberians, Olga had grown up with snow, had gone to school in snow, had played and laughed and wept in snow, a constant companion for each six-month that passed. The snow had already come earlier that year, in autumn, but the warm spell that followed seemed to have banished it for ever, as if solving some equation that balanced the allocation of cold and heat to the air above Roslazny. Now she yearned for the snow's return, like a fish longing for water, as if its flakes tumbling gently from a gunmetal sky could heal the rifts in her soul. Maybe when she was surrounded once more by its pristine folds she could accept the sorrows of this tumultuous year, and begin to plan a different future, a different life. Maybe then. Maybe.

Mid-afternoon arrived without the longed-for snow, yielding instead a crop of colourfully dressed villagers and even one or two younger residents in their Mishka Festival bear costumes. (The Festival had been cancelled that year, since the village had consumed most of the allotted sweetmeats during the unexpected and prolonged snow-enforced lockdown the month before; but the Roslazny children had decided to regard it as a movable feast.)

Olga stood in her place by the buffers, in obedience to her standing orders to render any assistance necessary to the train crew prior to the performance. On the explicit orders of the troupe director, Lev and his colleagues had kept up steam on the P36, so that the locomotive continued to weave fragrant threads around the siding and its steadily growing population of eager theatregoers. They had begun flocking in as soon as the gate was opened, picking their way over the muddy ground and skirting the remnants of old equipment that protruded here and there from the straggling, half-trimmed bushes that ran along the track. Most of the village was there, as far as she could see, with a healthy sprinkling of outsiders from Tayga and beyond.

The enthusiasm was understandable, thought Olga, as she watched Nikolai Popov, butcher and provider of unsolicited driving advice, helping his wife Nadya into her seat on the top tier, both crammed into outfits that plainly hadn't seen the light of day since the consumption of several thousand hearty dinners. There hadn't been a play staged in Roslazny for years, after all – not since the days of the *sozhkhov*, the state farm that had once supplied the lion's share of the village's livelihoods, unless one counted the adult videos Bogdan Kabalevsky had begun to film in the old church hall earlier that year. Olga could still remember the last years of the state farm, when the villagers had stretched the Kremlin's meagre allowance to stage discos and movie nights and even the occasional play, performances of Soviet classics put on by wandering companies like the Murder Express, though with far smaller budgets. But then the allowances shrank and finally dried up altogether, leaving the villagers to fend for themselves in terms of entertainment, just as with everything else. They had privatised enjoyment, as Fyodor Katin had once put it, confining young and old alike to their homes and the flickering, inconstant glare of cheap televisions.

There was Fyodor now, tripping over his scarf as he tried to help Anna Kabalevsky and her boys to their seats on the second row, with Olga's brother Pasha coming behind in support. Like the Popovs, Fyodor Katin had also made something of a sartorial effort, borrowing what looked like his father's overcoat – Gospodin Katin had once cut rather a figure in Tomsk society – and brushing his lank hair into an unusual semblance of order: no doubt he was concerned to compete with the rather more eligible Dr Zinovev, who was sitting in a prominent position on the front row. Anna, meanwhile, had put on the dress she usually kept for Easter, and had squeezed Boris into the outfit she'd sewn for his birthday the year before.

Indeed, most of the villagers were decked out in seldom-seen finery, elevating the old familiar faces from the drudgery of the day-to-day and casting them in a different light. There was Nonna the hotel-maid, tightly encased in what looked like a cocktail dress under her fur coat, and next to her Svetlana, Igor Odrosov's daughter, who had dropped her usual outfit of leather minidress and fishnets for something resembling an evening skirt. And there – though Olga could hardly bring herself to look – there was Vassily Marushkin, looking uncomfortable as he always did in civilian clothes, and beside him Rozalina in tight leopard-print and faux fur, and Kliment in what looked like his school uniform. He was a little peaky, thought Olga. No doubt Rozalina wasn't feeding him properly. Boys like him needed good Russian food, not some rubbish bought from a fast-food outlet in Tayga.

Not all the guests were as welcome to Olga's eyes: she groaned as she saw Boris Andreyev taking his seat, pointedly scruffy as usual in his comrade's uniform of fur-lined greatcoat and Ushanka hat. He seemed to be accompanied by an assortment of bigwigs, a short row of men in similar suits, and at the end was Captain Zemsky, the mercurial head of police at Tayga, so that both Olga and Vassily's superiors were in attendance. (It's about all we have in common, these days, thought Olga, rather sadly.)

There was no Ekaterina Chezhekhov, or – to Olga's relief – Slava Kirillov; but sitting next to Boris was Koptev Alexeyev, the mechanic, in a brown suit Olga had last seen him wear to a funeral, and behind him was Igor Odrosov, who was smart in a white shirt and leather jacket – though he rather spoiled the impression by casting constant angry glances at the Red Star food stall to his left, where Mikhail, Olga's Aunt Zia, and old man Solotov were already doing a brisk trade selling hot cider, sweet dough balls, and *chebureki* made with indeterminate meats.

The people-watching was probably better than the play, thought Olga, realising in the same instant how much she'd needed a distraction from her churning thoughts and stomach-sapping anxieties. So much had happened to her yet again – why did everything have to happen so much? The disastrous visit to Kirillov, surrendering her secrets to a good-for-nothing thief; the new book by Inessa Ignatyev, another thief; and a third thief, Boris Andreyev, who wanted to steal Olga's entire livelihood – and all this on top of Vassily and the unexpected return of his wife Rozalina. Yes, distractions were imperative, with all that going on.

It reminded her of a life lesson from her book:

> *Life Lesson No. 86: Tunnel vision is to be avoided. Sometimes, when engine drivers work for a long time on a particular day, they stop looking at the world around them, and focus too much on the tracks ahead of them, ignoring everything else. That can be described as tunnel vision, especially when the trains are actually going through tunnels. But this is dangerous, for drivers who only look at the tracks don't see threats from the outside, like cars veering towards the line or teenagers out to cause mischief. It's good to be a little distracted from time to time. Being distracted could save your life.*

That was a particularly good one, she thought, expressing exactly what she meant with the minimum of words – though of course all of them were good, or they wouldn't have been included.

But then she smiled wistfully. It didn't really matter what she'd written any more, did it, now that a well-known author had got there first? Ekaterina had said she should call her editor to discuss the new book, and Pasha and Anna agreed, adding that she should try to find out how on earth Ignatyev had found out about the idea in the first place – but Olga didn't really see the point. For one thing, Maxim Gusev, her editor, was exceedingly hard to get hold of, preferring, it seemed, to communicate via telepathic impulses than via phone, letter or email. And even when Olga did manage to get through to him, he spoke only in allusive, elliptical phrases that left her wondering what he had really meant to say in the first place. And she felt he would be more than unusually dismissive about the Inessa Ignatyev case, brushing off the setback with one of his obscure quotations from eighteenth-century Russian literature – the century that nobody remembered – and bundling her off the phone before she'd had time to ask any difficult questions.

She was gazing at the ground again, she realised, and thinking how nice it would be to live on a smaller scale – to be one of the spiders or ants who inhabited the miniature worlds her mother had revealed to her, and to have nothing to worry about bar the source of their next meal. The source of *my* next meal might not be so easy, she said to herself, if Boris has his way . . .

'Pushkin,' cried a voice. 'Pushkin!'

Olga jumped guiltily, suddenly aware that she had been asked to stand there for a reason, and not just to think philosophical thoughts.

'What is it, Lev?' she said, addressing Lev Myatlev, the guard for the P36.

'It's time,' said Lev, nodding over his shoulder. 'We're going to stop letting off steam, so you'd better step back from the buffers. Don't want to get in the way of the thespians, do we – though did I ever tell you I used to do amateur dramatics? Proper Yul Brynner, I was. Once I led a performance of *Uncle Vanya* . . . You never saw a better Professor Serebryakov! I even improvised some of my lines . . .'

Lev carried on talking as he and Olga retreated from the track, the moving wall of steam behind them thinning and dissipating as Simeon and Vadim reduced pressure and damped down the fire at the heart of the great P36. And then the three-tiered audience gasped in surprise, a collective exclamation that brought even Lev's interminable recollections to an end – for the clearing air had opened the stage to view, the specially adapted first carriage with its movable side raised to reveal the scene and players within.

'The tsarina is unwell!' cried a voice. Olga moved swiftly to a position beside the seating enclosure, and perched on a rusting bogie where she could see the stage. The speaker was a man in his early forties, of average height but muscular, with a flowing beard and shoulder-length hair, and dressed in a strange kind of clerical habit or robe.

'Yes, Tsarina Alexandra is sick, and the royal family have found no doctor to heal her,' said the man, pacing up and down the stage. 'So, of course, they turned to a higher authority,' he went on, crossing himself. Olga glanced at Anna Kabalevsky, and smiled as she saw her nodding approvingly – but then Anna's face turned from agreement to disapproval, for the man went on: 'I mean myself, of course! Who else could save her from her illness, and preserve the august reign of her husband, Tsar Nicholas the Second? Who else could keep the royal train moving, and get the family to Tomsk? Why, none other than me, of course – the divinely inspired lover of women and their souls, your humble servant Rasputin!'

The crowd laughed, and several applauded. 'Rasputin' bowed deeply, and then – to another gasp from the audience – he somersaulted to the ground and ran to the end of the train, disappearing behind it just as a lady appeared on the stage and gave a loud cry.

'The tsarina is sick!' she wailed. 'I fear for her survival – yes, I, Maria Nikolaevna, the finest nurse of my time. And if she dies, what will become of the tsar, the Little Father of all the Russians? What will become of our great Empire? And what will become of *me*?

'Oh,' she went on, throwing herself into a chair with heaving breasts, 'it is all too much – yes, too much by far!'

She was tall and fairly young, this nurse, with a mane of glossy hair, and dressed in a nurse's uniform of long skirt, ankle boots and a trim, white-edged cardigan. The costume was perfectly done, but Olga couldn't help feeling a slight sense of incredulity. Were they really expected to believe that this elegant creature would have been content to wait upon the imagined maladies of a bunch of pampered hypochondriacs? It was a performance, of course – Olga knew that – and actors should really be allowed to play whomever they liked, but surely it was worth at least trying to match persons with *dramatis personae*.

Olga frowned. It seemed rather unfair that washed-up TV personalities like this woman could take all the roles in drama when their on-screen work dried up. She was sure there must be worthy actors in the provinces – apart perhaps from Lev, who thought himself qualified to make up lines on Chekhov's behalf – actors who deserved a shot at bigger roles than playing the clown at birthday parties, or Ded Moroz at Christmastime. Yes, it wasn't fair at all, thought Olga, with all the righteous indignation of an author supplanted at the last minute by a better-known competitor.

Then she frowned again, this time from irritation at herself – for despite her best intentions, she found herself curious as to the nurse's real identity. She leaned over the edge of the seating and poked Koptev Alexeyev's elbow, gesturing at the shiny programme he'd bought at the ticket-booth, and smiling as he willingly passed it into her eager hands. She flipped past the introduction, the synopsis, the advertisements and the credits, and went straight to the biographies and head-shots at the end. And there she was, Nurse Maria Nikolaevna – Larissa Lazarov! A former gameshow assistant, as Anna had said, which helped to explain the air of glamour and sophistication, the air of moving in circles far removed from the reek of morphine and chloroform and formaldehyde.

The programme had all the other actors' biographies too, and when Nurse Maria turned to the next stage entrant for comfort, Olga recognised Rodion Rultava, the man she'd heard saying intriguing things on the phone outside Café Astana the night before. He was good-looking, as Anna had said with a smile, but there was also something slightly off-putting about his eyes, which gave him a slightly hooded, even menacing demeanour that can't have helped – thought Olga – with the longevity of his career in light-hearted soaps.

He was a good actor, though. Olga had to give him that. His character, Colonel Glazunov, displayed just the right tone of impatience when Nurse Maria had tried to throw herself into his arms: he was a military man, after all, and a man of ambition, who would be far more interested in carrying out his orders to the letter than he would in some romantic dalliance with a family servant. Olga nodded admiringly as he brusquely dismissed Maria's entreaties and briskly extracted from her all the relevant details: Tsarina Alexandra was sick; her case was despaired of by the local doctor (here Olga saw Anna flick a rapid glance towards Dr Zinovev in his front-row seat); the tsarina had called for Rasputin, but he had left the party to visit a local monastery, the Aleksiyevskiy Monastery of the Mother of God, to visit an old superior.

'No matter,' said Rodion Rultava briskly, still playing the bluff army colonel to perfection. 'I'll have the guard stop the train at the next station – I will alight and find a horse, or two if I take that good-for-nothing manservant of mine. Then Rasputin had better put down his bottle, and step away from the local nuns' – the audience tittered again – 'for he'll be sitting on the back of my horse within ten minutes of my arrival, or my name's not Grischa Alexeivich Glazunov!'

Some of the audience cheered and clapped as Rodion set off for the door that led towards the second carriage, and laughed as he staggered and half tripped on a carpet, adding (thought Olga) a clever note of slapstick to the proceedings. He left Nurse Maria weeping on the chaise-longue in despair, though she soon pulled herself together when a bell rang on the side of the compartment. The audience murmured in surprise as the carriage side descended briefly and then, after a certain amount of muffled clattering and whispered instructions, rose again to reveal a different scene within: the tsarina's sleeping coach, voluminously draped in deep purple velvet and thickly populated with new cast members, who were variously positioned around Alexandra Romanov's sick-bed, silently gesturing at each other or scanning through what looked like medical textbooks.

Olga read furiously through the biographies and tried to match the posed black-and-white headshots with the richly costumed actors arrayed before her. There was the tsar, of course, played (she read) by Ilya Putyatin, the celebrated thespian with past triumphs in St Petersburg, Moscow and Paris, now got up in the requisite army uniform, thick moustache and beard – though he was, if truth be told, a little too jowly to play the slender Nicholas with real conviction. Then there was his wife, Alexandra Feodorovna, propped up on her bed and facing the audience to display her enviable figure in a rather tight nightdress, and played by Ilya's real-life spouse, Agapa Putyatin, who (as Anna had related) had once anchored a national weather programme, as well as playing leading roles in several landmark drama festivals and other events.

Rodion Rultava had departed the scene, of course, on the trail of Rasputin – played, Olga now learned, by the fantastically named Panteleimon Pomelov, who (as Anna had already told her) had once starred in a Russia-K TV series about Peter the Great – but Nurse Maria was still in attendance, dabbing a damp cloth on the tsarina's fevered brow. Also present were Sonia Alikovsky, a former soap actress who now played the tsarina's lady-in-waiting, Sophie Buxhoeveden, with a sarcastic, waspish tone that made Olga think she would have preferred a more prestigious role. The tsar marched up and down at the front of the stage, barking orders at all of the household and making no secret of his irritation and anger – attributed by the nurse, in the following scene set in the train's galley, to his anxiety about his wife, Alexandra Feodorovna. But the next scene, featuring Tsar Nicholas alone with Sophie Buxhoeveden in her bedchamber, presented a different – and rather less admirable – alternative.

Olga smiled to herself as scene followed scene and revelation followed revelation. It was all very well done, she thought, all very professional and carefully constructed, laid out so that each scene led naturally to the next, with just enough cliff-hangers and unresolved questions to keep the audience guessing without putting them off with too much complexity. Yes, it was impressive in its way, thought Olga. Maybe this is the kind of thing I could learn how to do, if I ever get to Tomsk State University, she reflected – how to put stories together, how to entice readers and make sure they keep turning the pages in eagerness to find out what happens next . . . She had already written one book, of course, and had a sequel in mind, but what she really longed to do was to write novels – novels of the kind her mother Tatiana had loved, sweeping epics of Russian literature with every shade of colour, bursting with beauty and humanity and lessons that went far beyond the life learnings of a trackside engineer (second class) at the Roslazny outpost.

She started from her reverie as the crowd erupted into a roar of approval, for here was Rasputin, or rather Panteleimon Pomelov, returned to the scene of action by Colonel Glazunov, who was visibly sweating as if he'd just dismounted after a thundering ride from Tomsk. Again Olga admired Rodion Rultava's commitment to his craft, and while the crowd were clearly enthralled by Rasputin's antics – he had just caught sight of Nurse Maria, and instantly set about establishing a romantic attachment – Olga's eyes followed instead the hirsute cavalry-man who had been charged with Rasputin's retrieval.

Throughout the scenes that followed, featuring rumours of an army mutiny in the east alongside Rasputin's increasingly outlandish schemes to cure the tsarina while also having his way with Nurse Maria, Olga was particularly intrigued by Colonel Glazunov and his evident discomfort with proceedings.

She knew, of course, that some actors liked to dive so deep into their characters that they almost became the people they portrayed, but Rodion seemed to be taking this to an almost incredible extent. Agapa Putyatin's thin-lipped portrayal of Tsarina Alexandra was impressive enough, and Panteleimon Pomelov's Rasputin was certainly a thing of beauty – but they both paled, in Olga's view, next to the red-faced Colonel Glazunov. He dominated every scene with his glowering, close-eyed presence – haunted, it seemed, with some terrible secret, robbing his lithe figure of energy and dogging even his faltering steps from stage to stage.

Olga jumped as Vadim Lilov, the crew fireman, hissed at her. 'Pushkin,' he whispered, but still loudly enough for a couple of the onstage servants to glance at him. 'It's nearly intermission – can you get back to the buffers in case we need to shift the train?'

Olga sighed, and privately rolled her eyes as Vadim moved away. Why on earth could they possibly need to move the train? There was no conceivable reason – but Olga knew that most crews had a Vadim Lilov, the jobsworth to counterbalance the easy-going Simeon Zarubin or the loquacious Lev Myatlev. It wasn't always a bad thing: you needed to have people with eyes on the details when you were operating a five-hundred-ton piece of machinery. But the problem with people like Vadim was that they couldn't switch it off. They would be just as annoying at home as they were at work, thought Olga, as she reluctantly got up off her makeshift seat and began to make her way towards the buffers.

It was especially annoying because the play had really begun to accelerate, hurrying towards the looming intermission at breakneck speed. A party of rebels had blocked the tracks ahead, the audience learned, forcing the train to a sudden imaginary stop while Colonel Glazunov scouted ahead – and when he returned a little later, it was to a scandalous tryst between Rasputin and Nurse Marie.

'What the devil is going on here?' cried Glazunov, or rather Rodion Rultava, sweating again, and staggering slightly as he flung open the door to the nurse's bedchamber. 'Here I am – looking for the – for the—'

'*For the tsarina*,' hissed a voice just beyond the door to the second carriage. By now, Olga was almost at her station by the buffers, and from her perspective – at a much sharper angle than most of the audience – she could see a bespectacled man beyond the door, holding what looked like a script and gesturing at Rodion. '*For the tsarina*,' he whispered again, louder this time, prompting some of the less cultured members of the audience to elbow each other and start pointing at the former star of *Domoy i v' Put,* speculating, perhaps, that he might have had a little too much Dutch courage before the play.

And indeed, thought Olga, he didn't look very well. Was it just particularly good method acting, or could she see a tinge of green beneath the sheen of perspiration that covered his face?

She was momentarily distracted by the entrance of Tsarina Alexandra, who swept into the room on the arm of her lady-in-waiting, Sophie Buxhoeveden, with all the convincing fury of a woman who has found her lover in the arms of another.

'Rasputin,' she cried, 'what is this? I find my nurse debauched, and my hospitality violated, my morals outraged, as I lie on my very sickbed! What do you say, Glazunov? Oughtn't he to be horsewhipped and kicked into the River Tom?'

Glazunov – Rodion Rultava – uttered a hoarse laugh, and even went so far as to slap his thigh, rather unsteadily. This was part of the plan, judging by the satisfied look of the bespectacled man through the door, whose face Olga could still see from her position by the buffers. But then Rodion seemed to go beyond the script: he staggered, swayed, and threw his arms about his stomach, before falling to his knees and vomiting copiously across the stage. His mouth gaped open, then shut, and open again, but wordless the whole time, and he waved his arms around him as if he were grappling with some invisible spider's web. Then, as the audience gasped in horror, he jerked his back ramrod straight, inhaled a terrible, rattling breath, and cried aloud: 'Agapa! Agapa!'

Agapa Putyatin, playing the tsarina, clapped a hand to her chest, then ran to Rodion and embraced him. But it was too late: he fell forward in utter stillness, clattering upon the hard wooden floor like an iron poker upon the hearth.

3

Post Mortem

'Stand aside,' cried a voice, reedy yet authoritative.

Olga watched as Dr Zinovev vaulted over the railing in front of his seat and ran up to the carriage. He put his hands on the side and pulled himself up, like a man getting out of a pool, then rushed to Rodion Rultava and knelt next to him on the wooden boards. After a moment, Zinovev called for help to turn Rodion on his side.

As the other actors ran to his aid, Olga couldn't help thinking of Fyodor Katin, who had finally secured his long-desired date with Anna Kabalevsky only to be quite literally upstaged by his rival from Tayga's community hospital. It was bad luck to be competing against a doctor, she thought, for surely there weren't many situations that would require Fyodor's presence so urgently. A last-minute debate on the merits of Alexander the Second's reforms, perhaps, or an unfinished manifesto on anarchism that was due at the printer's yesterday . . . She smiled as she imagined Fyodor running into a café or meeting-room, scarf flying and spectacles flashing, whipping his ever-ready pen out of his pocket to get to work.

But then she shook her head impatiently: a man was sick, possibly seriously ill, and here she was, musing on the romantic challenges of the village dreamer. It was her job, after all, to look after the train and its occupants while it was in Roslazny, or in a nearby siding, and really she'd been lucky, notwithstanding Fyodor's feelings, that Dr Zinovev had been in the audience. Olga watched the doctor at work, opening Rodion's collar and reaching inside towards his chest, his long, slender hands confident and assured, his face as alert and focused as ever – though wasn't he looking rather tired? Olga didn't remember seeing such heavy bags under his eyes before, or such a sallow tint to his skin. They must be overworking him at that hospital, she thought. It was underfunded and oversubscribed at the best of times, and worse still in the winter months.

At least Rodion Rultava was likely to be an easier case: probably he had drunk too much before the show and simply needed a few pints of water and a long lie-down before the evening performance. He wouldn't be the first actor, surely, who had overdone it before a premiere; and it would do the doctor good, thought Olga, to have such a high-profile and manageable case.

But Dr Zinovev's next words dispelled this comfortable illusion for ever.

'Poison,' he cried, looking over his shoulder at the actors, then out at the audience across the siding. 'I think he's taken poison of some kind, and now he's – he's – now this man is dead!'

Looking back later, Olga wondered if she had been suffering from some kind of shock. Another death in Roslazny! How many had there been that year? Olga could hardly keep up. It had all begun with the American tourist, and then the policemen, and the crew member . . . But there'd also been the business with Nevena Komarov in the autumn, when yet more crosses had been raised in the Roslazny churchyard. And now there was Rodion Rultava to join them, the actor with the hooded eyes and the failed career in soap-opera television . . . Colonel Glazunov had been his last role, and perhaps his greatest – for how could any actor have bettered his portrayal of the impatient army man with a leaning towards clumsy slapstick?

And yet – was all that really acting? Olga's eyes narrowed as her gaze turned inward, scanning her memories of Rodion's final minutes. He'd sweated, as if having ridden far and fast; he'd tripped, as if in a droll aside to the audience; he'd laughed hoarsely and staggered about the makeshift stage like a man overcome, until indeed he was overcome by whatever had killed him. But none of that had been acting, realised Olga. No: he'd been desperately unwell, and had fought it like a true professional, until he could resist it no longer. And then he had died in full view of sixty people – more than sixty people, in fact, if one counted the children in the audience, and Mikhail and company at the Red Star stall, and of course Olga and the train crew.

That came to seventy or so, thought Olga, or maybe seventy-one – for now yet another person emerged, pushing open the door that led to the second carriage, where the troupe had established their dressing rooms and staging areas. He must be the bespectacled man whose face she had glimpsed during the performance: a man of medium height and indeterminate age, with thinning hair and thick, black-framed glasses through which he peered myopically around him, looking – to Olga's eyes – very like a mole that had been thoughtlessly stranded above ground. In one hand he carried a clipboard to which several well-worn sheets of paper were attached, but he dropped this when he saw Rodion lying still on the stage, and ran to his body as if he could render some assistance beyond the reach of mortal hands.

'Oh, calm down, Yegor,' said Tsarina Alexandra – or, rather, the director's wife Agapa Putyatin, said Olga to herself, covertly glancing down at the programme in her hand to remind her of the relevant name.

She looked in vain through the glossy brochure for a Yegor, though, for he wasn't listed in the actors' biographies. Then again, that wasn't surprising if his only role was to issue hissed reminders to faltering actors. But the clipboard didn't look like a script. Perhaps he also played the role of an administrative assistant, she thought, or a secretary of some kind – an impression reinforced by Agapa's disdainful follow-on remarks, in which she told Yegor to pull himself together and get some vodka for her colleagues on stage, and for the good doctor, too, of course.

'He looks like he could use a drink,' she said, truthfully enough – for Dr Zinovev had buried his head in his hands as if in despair at his failure to save Rodion from his untimely death. 'Hurry up, Yegor – there's a bottle in the drawer under the desk in my compartment. Come on, man, for God's sake!'

Yegor scurried off obediently, looking more like a mole than ever, while Agapa turned to her colleagues, her arms opened wide in sympathy. They had gathered around Rodion's body, Olga saw, with some – like Panteleimon Pomelov and Larissa Lazarov – openly weeping while others, like the troupe's director and Agapa's husband Ilya Putyatin, merely stood and gazed downwards at the mortal remains of the man who had played Colonel Grischa Alexeivich Glazunov. Agapa herself was standing at the back of the carriage and speaking on the phone – calling the police, maybe, not realising that half the Tayga force were already in attendance, if yet to be galvanised into action.

Suddenly Anna's son Boris called out – Olga had heard him crying and screaming in so many fights with his siblings that she could have identified him in a crowd of thousands – and she stirred, realising she'd been so focused on the few souls in front of her that she'd forgotten the existence of all the others behind her. And yet, she thought, as she turned to look at the rows of faces, perhaps that wasn't so stupid of her after all – for they were sitting in stony, white-faced silence, as if stunned into immobility by a real murder taking place within the disarming setting of a murder mystery.

But then Nikolai Popov turned to his wife Nadya – and, of course, it *would* be him to speak first, thought Olga – which prompted Koptev Alexeyev to swivel backwards and call something across to Svetlana Odrosov, and so on until the whole stand was alive with chattering heads, gesturing hands and raised eyebrows. Olga was glad, in a way: it would help Anna to distract her boys from what had happened, or to explain it in some unthreatening way. Or so she hoped, anyway. Maybe Pasha could help. He'd seen enough death to last him a lifetime, in the army, and that was before everything that had happened since. Thank God he'd left it already. Thank God.

Olga stood by her allotted position next to the buffers, feeling somehow that she owed it to the dead man to do her duty, so she heard little of the conversations taking place across the siding. But occasional words floated across to her like bursts of radio static, rising above the hubbub with a piercing and inexplicable clarity.

'We're cursed,' said Nadya Popov. 'So many deaths . . .'

'It's a judgement,' said Anna Kabalevsky, glancing at Fyodor Katin next to her, and blessing herself as if she were being punished for associating with a known agnostic and self-declared intellectual.

'It'll be good for business, mark my words,' boomed Olga's father Mikhail in his foghorn voice, leaning out of the Red Star food-stall and gazing greedily at the crowd, while old man Solotov and Aunt Zia nodded in agreement.

Olga tutted. She didn't see how another murder in Roslazny could possibly be good for business – wouldn't people stay away, for fear of being bumped off themselves? – but even if he were right, what a thing to say at such a moment!

She tutted again, and this time shook her head for good measure. The worst thing about her father was not that he was so awful, but that so many people in Russia were just like him. How had it come to this? she asked herself. How had kindness and decency and restraint been allowed to leach away so completely, until only a hard, astringent residue remained in the shape of people like him, Slava Kirillov and old man Solotov?

But now another voice penetrated her consciousness, distantly at first over the hubbub and the whirling maelstrom of Olga's thoughts, but then more sharply, arrestingly even, and with an air of command that finally drew Olga's eyes front and centre. And there they beheld Vassily Kirillovich Marushkin, tall and commanding even in his off-duty civvies, an ill-fitting cagoule with a hole in the collar and a thick grey jumper with an odd, bumpy texture that reminded Olga of her hearthrug at home.

Olga cursed her father, beneath her breath, for his unpleasant words had distracted her from her duties, giving Vassily an opportunity to catch her off guard.

And now here he was, standing in front of her: standing, and breathing, and watching her with his dark bottomless eyes, and waiting for her to respond.

'Oh, er, yes, Vassily,' she said at last, 'were you calling for me? Sorry – I was miles away. What is it?'

Caught off guard, she had spoken in her old, familiar manner rather than the more cautious tone she had adopted of late, and in response he smiled for an instant, as if they were sitting together by the fire in the Roslazny police station before Rozalina had appeared like a magician's assistant, or as if they were walking down the path that led to Olga's rail-side hut for the thousandth time. But then his gaze went cold again, and he tilted his head, glancing over his shoulder towards Rozalina and Kliment, before turning to look straight at her once more.

'Yes, I was calling for you,' he said, quite coolly. 'You're in charge of the train, aren't you, Olga? Well, I need you to set up a cordon around the carriage – carriages – engine – the whole damn thing, front and back, this side and that.'

'A cordon?'

'It's a crime scene, Olga,' said Vassily, patiently, 'unless you think the man poisoned himself . . . So we've got to stop the likes of him' – pointing to Popov the butcher, who had left the seating and was edging closer to the train for a look at Rodion's body – 'and her' – gesturing at Svetlana Odrosov, Igor Odrosov's daughter and de facto second in command at Café Astana, now also sidling away from the tiered stand – 'getting too close to the action. I've told them all to stay put, until we can get statements from everybody. Kliment will keep an eye on them all for now.'

Looking beyond Vassily, Olga could see Vassily's son standing near the Red Star stall and writing something in a little book – the names of the audience members, Olga supposed, or as many as he knew, anyway. The ghost of a smile flitted over her face as she gazed at Kliment's tall, bowl-headed figure: she loved him as if he was her own son, the son she had never had and perhaps now never would. But Vassily was still talking.

'I'll get my gear later, but in the meantime can you find a piece of rope somewhere, and some old buffers or signals or whatever you train people have lying around, and rig something up?'

Olga laughed despite herself. 'Buffers? Signals? You do realise they weigh a good few tons apiece? You policemen . . . But yes,' she continued more seriously, 'I'm sure I can find something around here. Russian Railways never really retire sidings, you know – they just abandon them.'

But he didn't smile. He merely nodded at her, quite curtly, and moved away towards the carriage, where the actors had mostly retreated from Rodion's body to stand in small groups by the tsarina's bed or further to the left, by the door to the second carriage.

Olga sighed, then turned to the bushes beyond the temporary buffers, where she thought she remembered seeing some old metal rods that could probably be pressed into service for an improvised cordon – but she'd only gone a few yards when a second peremptory voice interrupted her progress.

'Pushkin!' called Boris Andreyev, the foreman at Tayga, advancing on her with a barely concealed rage that made Vassily's slight coldness feel like a mild summer breeze. 'Pushkin!'

'I heard you the first time,' muttered Olga.

'Oh, you did, did you? Well, I'm glad something works, on that thick head of yours,' he said, and to Olga's astonishment he lifted a sausage-fingered hand and actually tapped the side of her Ushanka hat. 'I'm glad, for your sake. Soon you'll need all your wits about you, eh? To get another job, maybe?'

'Don't be ridiculous, Andreyev,' said yet another voice – another male voice, to be precise – which on closer inspection belonged to Vassily's superior, Captain Zemsky, who had marched up to the tracks on Boris Andreyev's heels.

'Don't be ridiculous,' he said again, but softening his words this time by dropping a weighty hand on Andreyev's shoulder. 'We can't get rid of Pushkin! Don't you remember what she did in the Petrovich case? She's got more gumption than half the coppers in Tayga! An FSB agent of my acquaintance – you'd remember him by his disguise – told me once that he'd sign her up in a heartbeat, if she wasn't so principled.'

'He said that?' said Olga, incredulously, bringing the agent in question to mind, and feeling somewhat astonished that he'd even remembered her existence.

'And she knows about railways, too,' went on Zemsky, ignoring Olga's question, 'and probably far better than you do by now, Andreyev, eh? Stuck in that office of yours all day? And I have a feeling,' he continued, smoothing the ends of his moustache with yellow-stained fingertips, 'that an inside track – ha, did you get that, Andreyev? – an inside track on day-to-day operations might become important by the end of this inquiry. So I'll need you to make it happen, eh, Andreyev? Otherwise, who knows, we might have some, shall we say, *informational* leakage about a certain – ah – internship scheme targeting attractive young ladies?'

Andreyev quite literally bristled, indignantly pushing out his own generously hirsute moustache, and opening his lips to respond – but Zemsky shouted over him: 'Marushkin – hey, Marushkin!' he called down the track, to where Vassily was talking to Yegor and Agapa Putyatin. 'Marushkin – come down here a second. I want you to talk to Pushkin.'

Olga put a hand to her forehead, feeling as if she were in some kind of surreal play-within-a-play, in which the vast P36 locomotive and its carriages served as the backdrop for a side-plot in which a hard-working woman had to endure a maddening set of lectures from men in positions of power. But at least Zemsky appeared to be on her side, which was something. In fact, if he could help her keep her job, it would be everything.

Zemsky looked, Olga had always thought, a little like a caricature of a man in his position, with a sharp face like the edge of a snowplough punctuated by a military moustache, and fitted with a pair of pale blue eyes, whose piercing gaze had forced innumerable confessions by willpower alone. Vassily, she knew, always dreaded meeting him, since Zemsky was liable at any moment to invent new and undesirable tasks for his subordinates, but she had never expected to be directly affected by this unpleasant habit. And yet here was Zemsky, forcing Olga and Vassily together again despite all possible awkwardness.

'At last, Marushkin,' cried Zemsky, as Vassily approached. 'What took you so long? You'd almost think you were investigating a murder!'

Vassily frowned slightly and glanced up at the actors near Rodion's body, but didn't seek to challenge his superior over his ill-timed levity. In any case it wasn't possible to get a word in edgeways, for Zemsky was still talking. 'Listen, Marushkin, I want you and Pushkin here to work together on the case, understand? We've got to make the most of what we've got in front of us – and Pushkin's a jewel without price, eh, Marushkin?'

Vassily looked at Olga, and Olga, for her part, looked back at Vassily, and then at the ground.

'Well?' cried Zemsky, after a moment.

'Well – well, yes, sir,' said Vassily at last, glancing at Zemsky and back at Olga again. 'Whatever you say.'

Olga forced a smile and muttered some suitable words of agreement.

'Great,' said Zemsky, a little sarcastically. 'You can make a start by getting statements from the luvvies. I've called Davidov down at the station – he'll be here shortly to corral the punters. All settled, then, Marushkin? Let's divide and conquer, *da*?'

Vassily nodded and flashed a quick salute, albeit rather a half-hearted one, while Olga looked back at the ground beneath her cold-weather boots.

Damn Zemsky, she thought. Vassily was right: he was too unpredictable by half. Zemsky was only a captain of police in an obscure town in western Siberia, but he still had the power to order them all around – even Boris Andreyev, on whom Zemsky clearly had some juicy *kompromat* – as if they were serfs on some tsarist estate. His was the boot that could stamp all over the ants on their little patch of ground, and the fact that somebody else had already killed off one of the insects would only extend and deepen his carte blanche. It was his job, after all, to be the long arm of the Kremlin. What was it people said? All was fair in love and war; but love had left Russia like an abandoned siding, leaving only rusting remnants behind.

Zemsky was as good as his word: within ten minutes of speaking to Vassily and Olga, Junior Sergeant Timofei Davidov arrived at the siding in haste.

'Sir,' he said to Zemsky, rather breathlessly: like Nikolai Popov, Davidov liked his dinners on the hearty side, and though he was only thirty-one it had already begun to show on his physique. 'What's all this, then?' he added, jerking a thumb over his shoulder at the carriage.

Then he leaned forward with a familiar air. 'Another *'svoloch* got himself knocked off in Roslazny, eh?'

'Language, Timofei,' said Zemsky. 'But, yes, you're right – that's exactly what's happened. One of the actors.'

'Guessed that,' said Davidov, with a wink, tapping his nose. 'On the stage, and all that. So when do we start solving the case?'

'You don't start solving anything, Davidov,' put in Vassily, who – Olga knew – always found Davidov's chattiness irritating. 'You're here for glorified crowd control. Just make sure nobody leaves – my son can give you a hand – and get them lined up for initial statements.'

Davidov sighed. 'That lot?' he said. 'A bunch of grocers, housemaids and mechanics – it's hardly the *Solntsevskaya Bratva*, is it?'

'Oh, well, perhaps you'd like to do something less boring, Timofei?' asked Zemsky. 'Spot of early lunch back at HQ, maybe, or target practice in the armoury?

'Snap out of it!' he barked suddenly, wiping the pleasant look of anticipation from Davidov's face: clearly Zemsky had also tired of his casual approach. 'Get over there and take those statements before I get you transferred up to Yakutia. You know how cold it gets there in winter? Cold enough to freeze your *yaichki* off in two seconds – if you had any, that is. Get on with it!

'Now, Marushkin,' he went on, as a chastened Davidov scurried off to do Zemsky's bidding, 'let's get up in that carriage and see what's what. You come, too, Pushkin – give us the Russian Railways perspective on all this. Though if you're anything like the trains, you'll do it late and at three times the price, eh? Eh?'

Olga was spared from replying to this by Zemsky's phone, which suddenly rang with a deafening Mexican ringtone that made them all jump.

'What?' he barked down the line. 'No, I can't do it now . . . What? Nazarov himself? What's it got to do with him? . . . Oh, for God's sake . . . I don't know why I bother,' he went on, ending the call and turning to Vassily and Olga. 'Nobody can do anything unless I'm there to watch over them – and now I've got to go to Kemerovo because the mayor's got his *trusiki* in a twist. Look, Marushkin, you can handle this, can't you? Because I don't want any more disasters in Roslazny. We've had enough for one year. We've had enough for a lifetime, in fact, and it all began when you arrived back here, didn't it? Something to think about, Marushkin. Something to think about . . .'

Zemsky's voice tailed off as he walked away, still wagging his finger in the air, then gesturing to his driver to finish his cigarette and get moving. Olga had no sooner puffed her cheeks and breathed out – her standard reaction to Zemsky's departure – than Boris Andreyev thrust himself back into her personal space.

'Now listen here, Pushkin,' he hissed, through gritted teeth. 'You may have swerved going to Mongolia, and you might have somehow got that glorified traffic-director on your side, but that won't save you. I've got your number – oh, yes, I've got my plans for you, and they don't involve long-term employment at Russian Railways!' He turned on his heel and stalked away, shaking his head and muttering as he went, and barking at his driver, in turn, to pull his thumb out of his *zhopa* and get the car turned round, leaving Olga and Vassily staring after him in mutual distaste.

Again Olga had the sense of appearing in a play, or a sideshow staged as part of a play, with a series of dramatic departures arranged to follow the equally dramatic arrivals, and with a large audience ideally placed to enjoy all the events as they unfolded. After the first shock of Rodion's death, they hadn't seemed particularly discomfited, she thought. Indeed, they seemed quite content to follow Junior Sergeant Davidov's shouted instructions and stay in their seats, the people nearest Mikhail Pushkin's Red Star stall taking orders and cash from others in the audience, then passing up *pelmeni*, *pirozkhi*, and little plastic cups of vodka to whoever had ordered them.

Some were quiet, pensive even, but most had begun chatting with their temporary neighbours, leading to a growing hum of conversation and laughter. Meanwhile, Rodion's body lay where it had fallen, covered now with a thick velvet drape that someone had taken from the far side of the carriage.

We've become too used to death, thought Olga, and not just here in Roslazny. But death is always a tragedy, she said to herself. If even death has lost its sting, what comes next?

At least some of the actors had the decency to appear genuinely dismayed, she thought, as she followed Vassily's gentle invitation and beckoning arm, and climbed the steps to the carriage. Larissa Lazarov, still encased in her nurse's costume, was sitting on the tsarina's bed with tears running freely down her cheeks, while Panteleimon Pomelov had put his arm around her shoulders, as if he was still in character, Rasputin angling for an entrée. Agapa and Ilya Putyatin stood at the far end of the bed, by the headboard, and were talking quietly together – discussing, no doubt, what to do now that one of their leading men had expired while treading the boards. Then there was Yegor the secretary, or dramatic assistant, or whatever he was, standing next to Sonia Alikovsky, who had played the tsarina's German companion, Sophie Buxhoeveden, with a cold disregard that said more, Olga thought, for Sonia's opinion of the play than for Sophie's attitudes to Ilya Putyatin's Tsar Nicholas. Yegor was standing so that he faced Sonia, but Sonia had turned away, giving Olga the distinct impression of an approach rebuffed.

'Where's the crew?' said Vassily.

The actors shrugged, but Yegor stepped forward. 'They're just seeing to the engine – sir? Captain?'

'Just Sergeant,' said Vassily. 'Senior Sergeant Vassily Marushkin, if you want to know. And this is my – my associate, Olga Pushkin, who's helping with the railway angle. Listen – er – what's your name?'

'Yegor,' he replied. 'Yegor Shulgin.'

'Well, Gospodin Shulgin, can you please jump down and ask the crew to come in as soon as they can? *Spasiba*,' said Vassily, as Yegor nodded and bustled off to the steps. Vassily watched him go, then glanced over at the audience opposite, still watching them all as if they were acting out the next part of the play.

'Can we close this?' he said, gesturing at the open side of the train. 'For a little privacy? It's getting cold, too,' he added, pointing up at the darkening sky. 'Whose idea was it to organise an open-air play at this time of year?'

'It was mine, Sergeant,' said Agapa Putyatin, advancing towards Vassily and offering her hand – a slight transgression of normal etiquette that was meant, thought Olga, to show them all that she meant business. 'Mine, and my husband's. We run this little production together, don't we, Ilya, *dorogoy*? As for the timing: what could be better for a play set in winter than wintry weather?'

'I'm not sure the audience would have seen it that way, if it had happened to snow,' said Vassily.

'I wish it would,' muttered Olga. 'Oh – nothing,' she said, in response to Vassily's enquiring look.

'I disagree, Sergeant,' said Ilya Putyatin, stepping forward and shaking Vassily's hand in turn. 'The audience are amply provided for, should the weather turn inclement. Witness the well-constructed seating, fitted with protective roofing and portable heaters! Could anything be more commodious, more fitting, and yet also prudent? Prudence is the Russian virtue, you know.'

Vassily glanced downwards, and Olga knew, from the twitch at the corner of his lips, that he was struggling not to laugh at Ilya's rather theatrical manner of speech – not to mention his accidental allusion to a favourite saying of Olga's father Mikhail, who lauded prudence in theory as much as he neglected it in practice. Vassily did not, however, look across at Olga, but only at Ilya Putyatin as he replied: 'Prudence? Russia? Once, maybe, but a very long time ago. Anyway, like I said, can we get the side of this carriage down? I want to talk to everybody.'

'I'll do it,' said Panteleimon Pomelov, getting up from his position next to Larissa on the tsarina's bed and walking to a spot near the steps, at the end of the carriage, where a thick red rope had been wound around a brass cleat. The troupe's Rasputin bent lithely to the floor and unwound the rope, then jumped to his feet once more, rope in hand, and began lowering the carriage side back to its normal position.

Vassily rushed to help, as if afraid that the slender Panteleimon might be overwhelmed by the displaced wooden wall as it fell downwards, but he only laughed and handed Vassily the rope.

'It's counterweighted,' he said. 'A child could do it.'

Olga watched, impressed, as the wall slid back into place with a well-oiled click. The troupe clearly had plenty of money behind them, she thought, to organise things so well – but then again, the ticket prices were fairly steep. If you charged a sufficient number of people five hundred roubles over a week of several performances a day, and put that together with the glossy adverts in the brochure and on the back of the tickets, you'd soon collect a pretty pile of cash – enough to fund specially adapted carriages, a steam engine and crew, and costumes to conjure the last days of the tsars with all their forgotten magic, not to mention the bribes required to get an old siding cleared by Russian Railways.

Olga glanced at Agapa and Ilya and wondered who was the real engine of the operation. Ilya was listed as the director in the programme, and was undoubtedly a clever man – a brilliant man, even, with an air of a Pushkin or a Goethe or some other great man of literature, and with a list of past dramatic successes that would be the envy of any director worth his salt. They must have run dry at last, though, to prompt his move into peripatetic theatre, and it was probably Agapa, thought Olga, who was really at the helm. She stood thin and tall, somehow dominating the scene despite her flimsy tsarina's nightdress, offset only by a woollen scarf around her neck and evening slippers on her feet. Olga could imagine her uttering persuasive words and forceful sentences, exerting a continuous, a subtle, and in the end an overpowering influence on whomever she needed to perform a service for her, whether it was her husband, the renowned director and actor, or some unknown member of Russian Railways' purchasing and procurement department.

But the humdrum world of Olga's day-to-day employment seemed far away from her now. The closing of the carriage side had cut her off from her workaday existence in the house and the hut and the depot at Tayga, transporting her back to a candlelit realm of tsars and emperors, boyars and princesses – a place where others were subjects, not citizens, and where people eschewed sandals and sweatpants for dashing cavalry uniforms and dresses cut from glittering fabrics. If she half closed her eyes and ignored Vassily standing next to her typing something into his phone, she could imagine herself standing in the royal train itself, next to the Romanovs and the mad monk, half charlatan and half genius, who had propelled them to their doom. Compared to the drab surroundings of her everyday life, the richly appointed period carriage seemed a fairy palace of enchanted beauty.

But who would she have been, had she lived then? She could have been a Lichnovsky, perhaps, if she'd had the luck to be in her mother's line – a line of counts and countesses with a St Petersburg townhouse and the country lodge at Astrazov, near Tomsk, where her mother had spent her childhood. But what if she ended up a Pushkin instead, part of a long line of glum servants, resentful labourers and work-shy layabouts? And what would happen to Pasha, if he had lived then? The past was not kind to those who – like Pasha, or Olga's schoolfriend Sasha Tsaritsyn – ended up loving the 'wrong' kinds of people. And what of Vassily's son, Kliment? Olga would never have been able to track him down in times gone by; and neither would Anna's children, who were always sick, have survived the hard winters of the tsarist days.

There was much to be said for the past, but there was also much to be said for the present. It was a shame they couldn't be merged, thought Olga, somehow preserving what was good from both while jettisoning the bad. Russia had had a conscience in the old days, Anna always said, whatever else was worse – something to steer by, even for those who did not believe.

Olga jumped as Simeon Zarubin, the engine driver, opened the door at the end of the carriage and stepped in, accompanied by Vadim Lilov, the fireman, and Lev Myatlev, engineer, followed by Yegor Shulgin, who tripped over the wooden strip across the threshold.

'Where d'you want us, boss?' said Simeon to Vassily, recognising, thought Olga, the natural authority that Vassily somehow exuded, despite his civilian clothing and slightly rustic exterior.

'Oh – just here's fine, by the bed,' said Vassily. 'I wanted everyone in one place so we can get the ball rolling.'

'What ball?' said Vadim, in his pedantic way. 'And rolling on what?'

Vassily sighed, and passed a hand over his face. He looked tired, Olga noticed, and drawn – rather like Dr Zinovev, another good man who worked too hard.

'Didn't you hear?' he said wearily. 'This man' – nodding at Rodion's body – 'was murdered. Poison, the doctor thinks – and until we get to the bottom of it everyone here is a suspect.'

'Us?' said Lev Myatlev, indignantly. 'Well, that's not fair – we've been killing ourselves on that bloody engine all day! How could we have done anything? What about all that lot out there – the crowd? Hundreds of 'em—'

'More like seventy or eighty,' put in Vadim.

'Well, whatever—' began Lev, but Vassily interrupted him.

'We're dealing with all that,' he said. 'Now listen: I was just introducing myself to the ladies and gentlemen here. I'm Senior Sergeant Vassily Marushkin, leading the investigation, and this is Olga Pushkin, track engineer, second class, who's advising on the case from the railway angle.'

The crew perked up at this, looking at Olga with interest – but just as Lev opened his mouth to discuss further, Vassily cut in again.

'Listen: we're going back to Tayga in a minute—'

'What?' said Agapa.

'What about Act Two, dear Inspector?' said Ilya.

'It's just Sergeant. And you aren't seriously proposing to carry on with the play after one of your actors has died?'

'Ah, well, we have understudies, you see,' began Ilya, 'and – and – well, no, Inspector, I suppose that would be inappropriate in the – ahem – in the circumstances.'

'We can't go anywhere yet,' said Vadim. 'We can't leave the engine till the steam's down, and that's a couple of hours from now at least. That's the law.'

Vassily glanced at Olga, who nodded in confirmation, then looked rapidly away again. It was going to be hard to work together, she thought, if he kept on like this.

'Fine,' he said. 'We'll catch up with you later. But in the meantime I want a list of everyone here, phone numbers, home addresses, the lot. Are you all staying in Tayga? At the Tayga Hotel, I suppose?' he went on, as some of the actors nodded. 'All right – we'll go there in the first instance – that'll be a bit easier than the police station, when there's so many of you. Actually, let me just get clear who's here. Why don't you – oh, thanks, Olga,' he said, as she poked him in the arm with her programme, opened at the page with the actors' biographies.

'So let's see who've got. Agapa, Ilya – both Putyatin? And then there's Larissa Lazarov, playing the nurse, and Sonia Alikovsky. And, last, Panteleimon Pomelov, is it? Rasputin. And for the crew, it's' – consulting a scribbled note plucked from a pocket – 'Simeon, Vadim, and Lev, is that right?

'Good,' he went on, stuffing the paper back into his pocket, and tucking the programme under his arm. 'Now, here's how we're going to do this.'

As Vassily began outlining the logistics for moving the party to Tayga, Olga allowed her attention to wander a little. It was a shame, she thought, to be exchanging the cosy warmth of the dimly lit carriage for the garish interior of the Tayga Hotel, which had been a little too redecorated the year before with a job-lot of pink and green wallpaper. And she supposed, too, that the awkwardness between her and Vassily, temporarily displaced by the shock of Rodion's death followed immediately by Zemsky's unexpected request for them to work together, would only grow over time.

The sense of loss continued as she stepped down onto the trackside aggregate a few minutes later, as if she were awakening from a beautiful dream, and leaving a hard-won temporary reprieve from a treadmill of day-to-day drudgery. She watched as Vassily called Timofei Davidov over to help with arrangements for transporting the troupe back to the Tayga Hotel hours earlier than planned, leaving Kliment in charge of taking statements from the audience. It looked like quite a few had already finished, judging by the growing crowd around the Red Star stall: Olga could see Igor Odrosov practically grinding his teeth at the sudden emergence of an unexpected rival to Café Astana's long monopoly. She saw Anna Kabalevsky, too, and her son Boris, standing next to Fyodor Katin in the queue for what remained of Mikhail Pushkin's greasy comestibles. But where was Pasha? She scanned the crowd, looking beyond the milling group of actors and policemen, and wondering if he'd already taken Anna's younger boys home.

But then she heard a voice hissing at her from behind, beyond the buffers where she had been stationed.

'Olga,' said Pasha, beckoning her to him. 'Come over here!'

'What is it, Pasha?' she said, frowning at him, and darting a glance over her shoulder to where Vassily and Davidov were still deep in logistical conversation. 'And what are you doing out here with Ilya and Gyorgy?' she added, as she walked rapidly behind the buffers and saw Anna's younger sons hand-in-hand with her brother.

'Ilya needed the toilet, and then Gyorgy decided he did, too,' said Pasha. 'Better for them to go for a walk, anyway, than to sit looking at – at that,' he went on, nodding at the carriage where Rodion now lay in solitary stillness. 'But never mind that. I heard something I thought – well, something I thought you might want to know about.'

'What did you hear?'

Pasha paused, as if he were uncomfortable with the subject matter. 'Well – it was Rozalina, you see,' he went on.

'Rozzalla!' shouted Gyorgy, who had taken to parroting everything that anyone said.

'Sh-sh!' said Pasha and Olga together, looking around to see who was listening – but thankfully nobody was in view.

Reassured, Pasha continued: 'I heard her making a call, from behind the stand – which was annoying, because I was trying to find somewhere secret for Ilya to – you know. That's why I went across the tracks. But anyway – I don't know who she was talking to, but she was telling them about that poor actor' – Pasha glanced at the boys staring up at him, wide-eyed, and dropped his voice to a whisper – 'dying on stage like that. And then she said—'

'Yes?' said Olga.

'She said, "What about me?" Then the other person seemed to get angry, or impatient. Rozalina got a bit short with her, anyway, and when she spoke again she took ages over each word. She said: "*Is – this – safe*?"'

Good question, thought Olga. A very good question indeed.

4

Welcome to the Hotel Tayga

Olga sat next to Vassily in his Volvo 240 and watched him drive, his browned farmer's hands assured on the wheel and gearstick as he navigated the narrow road to Tayga in the falling twilight. She stared at his movements and out of the windscreen with an almost painful intensity, as if by doing so she could avoid talking to him for the entire journey. Was that really possible, she wondered. Could you really sit next to somebody for a ten-minute stretch, coat-sleeves rustling together as if sharing their own whispered conversation, and refrain from uttering a single word – especially if that somebody had until recently been a close personal friend and ally, with strong indications of something more coming down the tracks?

Perhaps it would have been easier to talk, at least to attempt to pick up the broken threads of their relationship, if Rozalina hadn't given them such a cold send-off. After sending Pasha back to Anna with the boys, Olga had seen Rozalina walking up to Vassily with an enquiring look on her face, accompanied by frequent glances towards Olga. Then she had almost literally buttonholed him, grabbing his lapels and engaging him in what looked like an intense and earnest exchange. Olga was too far away to hear what was said, but she thought she could guess.

Vassily, how can you go off with that Olga woman? ran the hypothetical words. *You remember I've asked you never to be alone with her, or any other lady? Not that I'm worried about that old maid.*

(Old maid! scoffed Olga, indignantly, until she remembered that Rozalina hadn't actually said those words. She could just imagine her describing Olga in that way, though: a sad old maid who worked down by the tracks, doing men's work, and in men's clothes, too.)

Rozalina, be reasonable, replied the fictional Vassily Marushkin. *I'm just following orders.*

That's no excuse! You should have got different orders, said Rozalina, before turning on her sky-high heel and stalking away, her blonde ponytail wagging from side to side, like a reproachful finger wagging in someone's face.

Of course, Olga didn't know what had really been said, but she did know Rozalina was very strict about Vassily and other women. Only a couple of weeks ago, Svetlana Odrosov had told her that Rozalina had told him off in the harshest terms for chatting to Svetlana for a few minutes while ordering a plate of fish and dumplings – 'As if I'd be interested,' Svetlana had said, 'in some worn-out public servant. Ha! I've got bigger plans than that, Olga, believe me.'

Olga had frowned with indignation then, too, but that time on Vassily's behalf. He wasn't ancient at all – he wasn't even forty! Admittedly, his face was quite weather-beaten, but who didn't look like that after a good few winters – or, rather, a bad few winters – spent chasing criminals in all conditions?

She glanced sideways at him, at his tousled black hair sticking up in all directions as usual, and his strong forehead butting over his deep, dark-hued eyes, and thought how lucky Svetlana would be – how lucky any woman would be – to have a man like Vassily to look after them. Perhaps Rozalina was only being sensible, she thought, in trying to make sure she kept Vassily for herself now that she'd popped so disastrously out of the woodwork, and at the worst possible time. Was that what she'd meant, on the phone call Pasha had overheard? Is this safe – *is my relationship safe*? Maybe she'd already seen Olga standing close to Vassily outside, and following him into the carriage, and wondered if there was something afoot that was worse than murder. They'd hardly hit it off, after all, she and Rozalina – and perhaps that was to be expected, given Olga's close connections with Vassily ever since his arrival back in February. It was only natural that Rozalina should be cautious about a close female friend of her husband, especially one who had fought with him through danger and death on more than one occasion.

From the corner of her eye she saw Vassily glance at her in his turn. How did he feel about all this? He had won back his lost wife, yes, but at a cost. Maybe he didn't think it was much of a cost, of course – but it was a cost, nonetheless, to lose a friendship. Everything came with a cost, she pondered. If you didn't think that, you just didn't know what you'd paid yet.

But Vassily was an old hand, she thought, as he turned onto the bridge over the railway line and bumped onto the road that led through Tayga's uninspiring suburbs, switching on his headlights as he went. He had worked inner-city crime, had faced down cartels and kingpins, had robbed military archives during the long, lonely years he'd spent on the trail of Rozalina and Kliment . . . Of all people, Vassily knew what things cost. He had seen the price tag for Rozalina's return, thought Olga, and had decided to pay it. It was just her bad luck that she was the item on sale.

'Thoughts?' said Vassily, suddenly.

Olga started. Sunk deep in morose reflection, and staring with unseeing eyes at the smallholdings and breezeblock buildings as they passed by, she had almost forgotten that conversation was still a possibility.

'On what?' she blurted out.

'The murder?' said Vassily, with a smile. 'Unless you want to talk about the weather.'

'Well – we're nearly there.'

'Better be quick, then.'

Olga raised her eyebrows. 'Solve the case in two minutes? That's your department! Remember what Zemsky said: I'm only here for the railway advice.'

'So what would a railwayman – sorry, railway*woman* – say about the case?' he asked, turning off Oktyabr'skaya and onto Kirova Prospekt, the road that led to the station and the nearby Tayga Hotel.

'Er – well,' said Olga, trying to think, 'I suppose – it was a very public way to do it, wasn't it? During a play on a special train, an old carriage with a movable side, and with steam wafting around the place from the P36 . . . I mean, if you wanted to kill somebody on the railways, this was probably the highest-profile way to do it.'

Vassily grinned. 'My view exactly. Somebody wanted to make a splash! That suggests an actor, doesn't it? A personality with a touch of drama? And, of course, who else would know someone like Rodion Rultava, in a place like this?'

He waved his hand vaguely out of the window as they drove past the Tayga vaping emporium, next door to the betting shop and the cut-price carpet centre, each place displaying their latest offers in dimly lit windows.

'You sound like Polina Klemovsky,' muttered Olga, making Vassily laugh, and smiling in her turn. Anyone less like the fiercely bespectacled and ruthlessly ambitious Polina than Vassily Marushkin would be hard to imagine, not least because of her open contempt for Roslazny, its surroundings, and its inhabitants in general.

'That's true,' he admitted, turning down the road that led to the railway station. 'But it doesn't mean I'm wrong, either. I think the answer lies in here,' he went on, inclining his head towards the hotel as they drew up outside, 'and not out there.'

Olga nodded, but slowly: it was hard to disagree with Vassily's reasoning, but then again it was strange to think that the case could be solved from such an uninspiring location. Perhaps it was the unfortunate contrast between the railway station's grand, Alexandrine green-and-white façade and the rather undistinguished building occupied by the guesthouse, or maybe it was the slightly disappointing realisation that even glamorous actors had sometimes to lodge in humdrum surroundings – or possibly it was reluctance to believe that a troupe could turn on each other in such, well, dramatic fashion, and in the very first performance, too. But whatever the cause, Olga found it difficult to imagine anything mysterious or significant happening inside the Tayga Hotel, which Ekaterina Chezhekhov had often used for romantic assignations with gentlemen from other *oblasti*, and which served, from time to time, as the drop-off point for shipments of ill-defined meats destined for Popov the butcher and, in due course, Café Astana and elsewhere.

In the event, however, Olga was quickly proved wrong. Dr Zinovev met them at the hotel entrance, with one of the junior Tayga policemen by his side, a *ryadovoy politsii* named Fedot Obolensky. Both Zinovev and the police private wore latex gloves, and Zinovev held something in his right hand – a plastic carrier bag with what looked like a bottle of some kind inside, though it was hard to see in the faint glare of yellow streetlights.

'It's here,' he said, speaking nervously and quickly, and looking, thought Olga, more worn-down and harassed than ever, as if he didn't even have the energy to meet her eyes. 'I don't know how I didn't see it before. The symptoms all fit . . . It's quite clear, really, once you know. But it must have been done cleverly – assuming it was done by someone other than Rodion, of course, but who would choose to kill themselves like that? No, no, it had to be murder. It's obvious, quite obvious—'

'What's obvious?' cut in Vassily. 'What did you find?'

'Antifreeze, Senior Sergeant Marushkin,' cried Zinovev, holding up the carrier bag. 'The killer used antifreeze!'

Once Vassily had ushered Zinovev away from the hotel entrance, sitting him in the passenger seat of the Volvo and feeding him cigarettes and coffee, from Vassily's flask, he gave them a more detailed account of what had happened.

'I came on here and met Obolensky, like you suggested,' he said, glancing up past his long nose first at Vassily and then at Olga, leaning on the open car door, before looking quickly away again. 'It didn't take us long to search the rooms – you know what it's like inside, hardly the Hotel Metropole in Moscow . . . I never thought we'd find a trace of poison, because what kind of murderer would leave that lying around? But there it was, sitting in Rultava's rooms, bold as brass inside the nightstand, as if he'd been sipping it before turning in each night. A bottle of antifreeze, just like you'd buy from Alexeyev's garage.'

He reached down and took it out of the bag. 'See? About half full still. But that fits, too – you don't need a lot to kill a man.'

'And that goes with the symptoms, you mentioned?' said Vassily. 'The way Rodion Rultava died?'

'Yes, yes, I think it could,' said Zinovev, returning the bottle inside the bag and leaning back in the seat. He closed his eyes and took another drag on his cigarette, coughing as the thick Belamorkanal smoke flooded into his lungs. 'These are a bit strong, aren't they, Vassily? Anyway, yes, if you think about how Rultava died, it fits quite well. Remember his behaviour before he died – the sweating, the erratic movements, the stumbling . . . And then the final onset of terminal symptoms, the growing morbidity and cardiac failure – quite consistent with the ingestion of antifreeze. A significant amount, too – probably fifty mills, or more. Maybe up to a fifth of the bottle. I'd have to confirm it with the lab, of course, after the post-mortem.'

'Well, assuming it wasn't suicide—' began Olga.

'We found no note either on the body or in his room,' put in the doctor.

'Assuming it wasn't suicide,' Olga went on, a little more firmly, 'how did the murderer get him to drink the antifreeze? I don't remember him drinking anything on stage.'

'He wasn't on stage the whole time, though,' said Vassily. 'He could have taken a drink of something between scenes.'

'Maybe, though surely he'd notice the taste,' began Olga – but Dr Zinovev waved an impatient cigarette, showering them both with ash.

'No, no,' he said. 'You don't understand. Ethylenes like antifreeze take hours to work – up to a day, even, with slow change as the chemicals take hold in the body, followed by a period of rapid deterioration and death.'

'Slowly, then suddenly,' murmured Olga.

'Exactly,' said the doctor.

'So – what sort of timeframe are we talking about?' said Vassily.

'Hard to say exactly – but sufficient to cause death like that, in a man his size? Let me think: probably a day. No – a bit less.'

'And he died at about four this afternoon,' said Olga. 'So maybe—'

'Maybe it was dinner last night,' said Vassily, nodding, and flashing a smile at Olga, as if he'd forgotten their habit of finishing each other's sentences.

'There'd certainly be more chance of disguising the taste in a big plate of food,' said Zinovev, taking another – but more cautious – drag at his borrowed Belamorkanal. 'You know, I could get used to these. Take the edge off.'

'Things getting stressful at the hospital, are they, Doc?' said Vassily.

Zinovev looked up at him with tired eyes. 'What's changed?' he said. 'We've always been understaffed, underpaid and oversubscribed, and these recent budget cuts haven't helped. The clinics are really struggling to stay open, and I must admit that recently— Oh, here they are now,' he went on, standing up beside the Volvo and looking over the roof at a couple of taxis pulling up to the hotel.

They watched as the vehicles came to a halt, and the first passenger got out of one – Yegor Shulgin, thought Olga, judging by his glasses and the rather shapeless cut of his coat. More actors followed, until the cabs had given forth a steady flow of thespians with smartly cut overcoats and fur-lined jackets that put Yegor's outfit to shame. There was Agapa Putyatin, elegant somehow despite having merely thrown an ankle-length sheepskin coat over her tsarina nightgown, and beside her Ilya, her husband, statesmanlike in his Nicholas the Second regalia. Behind them came the others, who had arrived in the second taxi: no Rodion Rultava, whose body (Olga learned later) had been brought to Tayga in a hospital ambulance sent by Zinovev, but Larissa Lazarov, Sonia Alikovsky and Panteleimon Pomelov, who emerged wearing a long astrakhan coat over his clerical costume. (How much more understandable the madness about Rasputin would have been, thought Olga in passing, if he had really looked like Pomelov instead of a bedraggled has-been who'd been dragged twice through a hedge backwards.) Alone among the troupe, Larissa Lazarov seemed to have forgotten about her coat: she stepped slowly out of the taxi in nothing more than her nurse's costume, whereas Sonia Alikovsky, the last person to alight, was draped from head to foot in lavish furs both grey and light brown, above a pair of patent leather boots with wicked-looking heels.

Judging suspiciousness by outfits alone, Sonia Alikovsky would probably pip the others to the top spot. Glamour, thought Olga, could so easily seem callous. But, then, wasn't that just how a killer would think, too, therefore dressing down accordingly to avoid guilty appearances? By that principle, she supposed that Larissa Lazarov would come top of the list, having made no effort at all to don suitable attire for a November evening in western Siberia. She'd been weeping, too, hadn't she, when Rodion died – so could these things all form part of a master plan, a devious and dastardly scheme to ensure she flew beneath the radar of the Tayga and Roslazny policemen?

Olga wondered in passing what people would think of her, judging by her outfits. Not much, according to her father Mikhail, and – more recently – Slava Sergeivich Kirillov, certified therapist and acclaimed conciliator, mediator and part-time security consultant. She looked fairly anonymous, she guessed – a somewhat nondescript railwaywoman, or even (in unfavourable lights) a railwayman – a wholly undistinguished trackside engineer whose only achievement, a self-help book for women who struggled with the day-to-day, had now been gazumped by a minor celebrity with a leaning towards literary theft . . . In her waterproof trousers, fleecy top and high-vis jacket, Olga was neither suspiciously glamorous nor suspiciously bedraggled, and perhaps that was the most suspicious thing of all. Olga had found herself imprisoned once already that year: she hoped it would not happen again.

'Surprised you didn't get Davidov to escort them, Vassily,' said Dr Zinovev, cutting across her thoughts.

Vassily puffed out his lips. 'That *durak*? Not sure he'd have made any difference if they'd decided to take off! But that didn't seem likely, unless—'

'Unless they were all in it together,' said Olga.

Vassily nodded, and again flashed a quick smile at her.

'Can you stay, Yury?' he said to the doctor. 'I want to speak to them all one by one, or in small groups, anyway – maybe find out what happened yesterday, at dinner in particular. The medical perspective might be useful.'

'For another of these cigarettes, Vassily, I'd do anything,' said the doctor, inhaling luxuriously once more.

'You don't mind doing us together, do you?' said Agapa Putyatin, smoothing her skirt with elegant hands and perching on the edge of a chair in the hotel dining room. It was a medium-sized place filled with five round tables, each hosting four or five chairs, and with a small hot-plate and serving table below the net-curtained window that looked out onto the road that led to the station.

'Come on, Ilya,' she said to her husband, patting the chair next to her, and pulling him down gently by the sleeve. 'I just thought it would be quicker. We think the same about most things, don't we, *dorogoy*?'

'What? Oh, yes, yes – assuredly, yes. Most certainly, Inspector – most certainly,' said Ilya, smoothing the hair that surrounded his large forehead like a halo.

'It's just Sergeant,' said Vassily. 'I have mentioned it before . . . Anyway, we can start like this, yes, though I may need to speak to you separately later. You remember Dr Zinovev, and Olga Pushkin, from Russian Railways? They're kindly assisting with this early stage of the investigation.'

Agapa nodded at them both, bestowing a smile on Zinovev for good measure. 'Of course,' she said. 'Who could forget the good doctor who rendered us such speedy assistance?'

Olga rolled her eyes a little: Agapa was clearly the kind of woman who preferred men to her own kind, but her husband, Ilya, seemed not to notice. Or perhaps he was used to it, and his studious downward gaze a coping mechanism of sorts, the result of long practice.

At that moment Zinovev's hand shot to his pocket. He whipped out his phone and clapped it to his ear. 'Yes – yes – no,' he said, in tones of muffled urgency. 'Have you put her on diazepam yet? . . . Better do it now. I'll be right there . . . No – I'm just around the corner. Five minutes,' he added, and mouthing, 'Sorry,' to Vassily, he marched out of the room, leaving Agapa gazing after him with a smile on her lips.

'Like I said,' she continued, 'a good doctor.'

Vassily ignored this and got straight down to business. 'Can you tell us what happened yesterday evening?' he said. 'Did you all have dinner together, for instance?'

'Yes – yes, we did,' said Agapa. 'Or, rather, they did: I had to go out to see a friend at the station.'

'This friend could vouch for that, I suppose?' said Vassily.

'Oh, yes – take my phone and call her if you like. Mara Pavlov's her name. We used to be at the Mariinsky together, years ago. She was passing through on the way to Yekaterinburg

– a Chekhov festival – and we had something in the station café. I think the others ate together in here, didn't you, Ilya dear?'

'Why, yes, dear,' said Ilya. 'My wife is quite correct, Insp– Sergeant, I mean. We ordered some food from a nearby establishment – a Japanese place of some sort.'

'The Rising Sun?' said Olga, with a private shudder.

'That could very well be the case,' said Ilya. 'I never remember those sorts of things. But the odd thing was, the food was some sort of goulash. Isn't that a Hungarian dish? I can't imagine why they would serve that in a Japanese restaurant.'

'Restaurant is a generous word,' said Vassily. 'And they serve all sorts in there, mostly depending on what Aleksei Ivanov's got in the freezer. That's quite common, round here,' he added, shooting a wry look at Olga. 'Anyway, everyone had the same thing, did they? Goulash?' said Vassily, scribbling in his notebook. 'Who placed the order?'

'Probably Yegor,' said Agapa. 'He does that kind of thing for us. It's so convenient to have somebody who's good at that sort of job, don't you think? I don't know what we'd do without him, Sergeant.'

'He's been with you a while, then, has he?'

'Well, a little while, yes,' said Agapa, crossing her legs. 'Longer than the others, anyway – this is the first time we've assembled this particular cast.'

'I see,' said Vassily. Then he turned to Ilya. 'So, you ate goulash – and you all ate in here, together.'

Ilya nodded. 'Agapa didn't miss much, I'm afraid – I'm not terribly familiar with how goulash is meant to taste, but I must confess I found it disappointing.'

Olga shifted in her seat.

'Can you remember if anyone left the room at any point, or arrived later than the rest?' he asked.

Ilya narrowed his eyes. 'Oh, I'm useless at this sort of thing. I'm better at writing directions for plays than I am at observing real life. Did you know I once won a Golden Mask in Moscow? Ah, yes, now that was a splendid year. Thoroughly splendid. We were luckier, in those days. Things didn't sink so easily.'

'Ilya, my dear,' said Agapa, 'the captain and his associates don't need to know about your past triumphs and disasters! They just want to find out what happened last night. They don't need to know about anything else – you understand?'

'Oh, I know, I know – but it's so hard to remember, isn't it?'

'I'm sorry,' said Agapa to the others, spreading her hands wide. 'You see before you the artistic temperament, *par excellence*. Ilya is a director, an actor, a playwright, an impresario – yes, he is all these things. But a detective? A mere observer of the detritus of everyday life? I fear not, Inspector. Forgive me: Sergeant.'

Vassily changed tack. 'Rodion called your name aloud just before he died,' he said to Agapa. 'Why might that have been, do you think?'

Agapa smiled. 'Well, he was standing next to me at the time,' she said.

'But there were others on stage,' put in Olga. 'Others closer to him in – well, in age, if you don't mind my saying so.'

Agapa's smile became rather forced. 'That is true, dear,' she said, in a voice of cold crystal. 'But no others of my experience or – or *stature* were there, if you don't mind *my* saying so. I have – well, I *had* – taken poor Rodion rather under my wing. It would be entirely natural for him to think of me, his mentor, his guide, in his dying moments.'

Ilya nodded. 'My dear wife is correct, Inspector,' he said again. 'That is how I would write it, if I were composing a drama – the end of the first act, you might say. It all fits together quite nicely. And *fitting together*,' he went on, his eyes kindling into life, 'is the aim of all our art.'

'The aim of all our art,' repeated Agapa, glaring at Vassily with something that looked, thought Olga, rather like an air of triumph.

'We locked our hotel rooms from the inside when we went to bed,' said Yegor Shulgin. 'We all did, on advice of the management. They said they'd had enough problems for one year.'

Yegor was sitting forward in his chair, a little awkwardly – but, then, he was the kind of person who did everything a little awkwardly, thought Olga.

'So you're saying Rodion probably did that, too?' said Vassily. 'His room was probably locked from the inside overnight?'

'I've no reason to think otherwise,' said Yegor.

'Let me just get the timeline straight, then,' said Vassily, flipping open his little notebook and running his pencil down his notes. 'You got back here after the rehearsal at—'

'At the community centre,' said Yegor, as Vassily paused. 'It's just round the corner, on—'

'Yes, thank you, I know where it is,' said Vassily. 'So you got back here around six, and ordered in some food at around seven – and it arrived at about eight?'

'That's right,' replied Yegor. 'Though Dama Putyatin left us before then, to go and meet her friend.'

'You're close to her, are you?' put in Dr Zinovev, who had rejoined them after his quickfire visit to the Tayga Hospital and what he described as a challenging case of schizophrenia. 'Worked together a long time?'

'Well – no,' admitted Yegor. 'This is only the second time we've been together. As for the first time, let's just say it was – well, you could say I enjoyed being colleagues.'

'But you aren't really colleagues, are you?' said Vassily. 'I mean, Dama Putyatin, and her husband I suppose, are the ones who call the shots, as well as playing major roles – and the rest of them are actors, too, Larissa and Panteleimon and the rest. Whereas you're a – a—'

'An executive associate,' said Yegor, describing his somewhat vague job title with the kind of pomposity Olga might have expected of a senator or a prime minister. 'And, yes, I would say we are colleagues. The plays wouldn't get far without me, believe me.'

'You never wanted to be an actor, then?' said Vassily. 'No desire to tread the boards yourself?'

Yegor blinked behind his glasses, his eyes sharp and clear and glowing with a luminous shade of russet, like oak leaves in autumn sunlight. 'My mother – my mother told me I could be a great actor if I wanted,' he said primly, 'but I decided my talents lay in another direction. Had to, in a way – hard to be a leading man with inch-thick glasses, isn't it?'

Then he shrugged. 'Besides, bills don't pay themselves, do they? Better a bird in the bush than two in the hand.'

Olga frowned and opened her lips to speak, but Vassily beat her to it. 'What about after dinner? Did you all stay for a drink, or maybe go out somewhere together?'

Yegor smiled. 'You haven't done much acting, have you, Sergeant? The last day of rehearsals is always the most exhausting – the performances themselves are child's play compared to that! All of us were completely worn out, and went straight to bed after dinner. Probably around – oh, I don't know – half eight or nine, maybe?'

'And behind locked doors, too,' said Dr Zinovev, drily. Olga thought she knew what he was thinking: an early night in the hotel, with everyone's room inaccessible to a would-be murderer, meant that the window of opportunity for administering Rodion's poison was shrinking rapidly.

'What was the food like?' said Olga. She knew well enough, of course, having eaten at the Rising Sun earlier that very day, but she wanted to hear Yegor's take.

He grimaced. 'Maybe I shouldn't say too much,' he said. 'You're all from round here, I suppose – I don't want to tread on any toes.'

'This is a murder investigation,' said Vassily, with all the forbidding gravity he could muster on occasion. 'Please feel free to speak your mind.'

Yegor cleared his throat. 'Well, in that case,' he said, shifting uneasily on the edge of his chair, 'perhaps I'd better admit that it tasted pretty awful. I only managed a few mouthfuls before I gave up and took some biscuits from the glass jar in the dining room. I think the others felt the same. There was plenty of goulash left at the end, anyway.'

'Did you see Rodion Rultava eating much?' said Zinovev.

Yegor frowned. 'Well, it's hard to say, isn't it? There were quite a few of us round the table, vodka being poured, lively conversation – I can't say I was really watching him. It's a shame it's not the other way round, from that point of view.'

'What do you mean?' said Vassily.

'Well, he never missed a thing,' said Yegor. 'If you so much as dropped a pin from the needle-box, there he'd be with the shiny thing in his hand, pressing it into your own . . . He kept reminding us of things we'd said the day before yesterday, or a line one of the actors had delivered on a TV show way back when. It was irritating, in a way, because if you said you'd do something he'd hold you to it. Yes, you couldn't get anything past Rodion.'

Someone had, thought Olga – but Vassily was speaking again.

'And was he particularly close to Agapa?' he asked, quite casually.

'To *Agapa*?' said Yegor, his eyes wide in astonishment. 'No, I shouldn't say so. No, I wouldn't say so at all. I myself am far closer to her – or so I like to think at least. But either way I'm sure Rodion would never have said that he was close to her. He noticed everything, like I said – friendly looks and unfriendly, things done in passing and in secret.'

Olga threw Vassily a weighted look. Noticing everything, and remembering everything, could be useful attributes in many parts of the world. But in Russia it might – it just might – get you killed.

Vassily returned her look with interest, thinking along similar lines, and also wondering why, if Rodion had not been particularly attached to Agapa Putyatin, he had called her name aloud in his dying moments.

'Oh, Rodion could never have killed himself,' said Larissa Lazarov, eyes wide and staring. 'Not in a million years!'

'Now why do you say that?' said Dr Zinovev, in much the same tone, Olga imagined, as if he were talking to a distressed patient.

'Well, he was much too full of life,' said Larissa. 'Much too – much too— oh, I'm sorry,' she said, her voice breaking.

Vassily stepped forward, plucked a paper napkin from the cracked plastic holder on the sideboard, and offered it to her.

'Thank you,' she said, as she dabbed a tear from her eye – a real tear, thought Olga, not the imaginary kind that she'd seen Svetlana Odrosov and others shed by the hypothetical bucketful.

'And I'm sorry,' continued Larissa, more composed now, and sipping the glass of water that Zinovev had poured for her. 'It's just – Rodion and I were close. Oh, no! Not like that – only as friends. But he told me things, and I told him things.'

'What kind of things?' said Olga, trying to copy Vassily's seemingly casual style.

'Little things, mostly!' said Larissa, with the beginnings of a smile. 'We'd laugh at Ilya's pompous sayings, or Pan's antics – Panteleimon, I mean, but we all call him Pan. He's not to be trusted,' she added, looking straight at Olga. 'Not with ladies! But his heart's in the right place. Mostly.'

'Little things, mostly,' said Vassily, smiling along with her. 'But some big things, too?'

Larissa's smile faded, a change like the sun moving behind the clouds, and Olga could see how actors were born rather than made – a certain exaggeration of emotion, a preternatural expressiveness denied to ordinary mortals, lending drama to the most ordinary of circumstances.

'Well,' said Larissa, sitting forward in her chair, and brushing back her glossy red hair from her face, 'yes, maybe – I'm not sure. Rodion is – was – such fun, and was always making everything into a joke. He's so clever, too! I mean, he was – he could tell you where you'd been just by what kind of mud you had on your shoes, or by the stub of a ticket poking out of your handbag. Nothing got by him – nothing at all!'

'Yegor Shulgin said the same thing,' murmured Vassily, but this led only to a stern protest.

'Oh, what does Yegor know?' cried Larissa, jumping to her feet and pacing up and down. 'He's just a lackey – an assistant! No, no,' she said, stooping to Vassily and placing her hands on his shoulders, 'it took an artist to appreciate what Rodion could do – an actor, you understand, a fellow traveller! He could have been a great playwright, with all the things he observed, all the things he knew. And he would have been, perhaps, if he'd been spared – if only he hadn't noticed all those hints and clues and pointers along the way.'

'Hints?' said the doctor.

'Clues?' said Vassily.

'Pointers?' said Olga, after a moment, more from a feeling of obligation than a desire to speak.

'Well, yes,' said Larissa. 'I— What's that?'

They all turned to the window, following her staring eyes and outstretched arm.

'It's only a steam engine,' said Vassily, after a minute.

'We told the crew to bring the train back to Tayga and join us here,' explained Olga. 'Easier than keeping the crime scene safe in Roslazny.'

'I can imagine,' muttered Larissa. 'Anything can happen

there, it seems. Even murder . . . And all Rodion did was to see too much!'

'But what did he see?' urged Vassily. 'What kind of thing?'

'Oh, I don't know,' said Larissa, in a sing-song tone, dropping back into her chair with a rustle of extravagant skirts. 'He didn't tell me – just said he'd seen things. Unusual things. And he'd written them down in some notebook – a little black one, he said. I know the one he meant – he often had it with him.'

Dr Zinovev looked sideways at Vassily, who shook his head in mute negation. The book hadn't turned up in the initial search of the hotel, Olga divined – of course it hadn't, or Vassily wouldn't be questioning Larissa so firmly.

'Dangerous things?' prompted Vassily. 'Odd words for a man who dressed like Rodion.'

'How do you know how he dressed?' said Larissa, quite sharply. 'Oh, but the others must have told you – like an off-duty soldier, I suppose they said. That's true enough, but, oh, Sergeant, really he was nothing like one of those horrible army men – nothing at all! He was the sweetest man, and though he noticed so many things he never used them maliciously, as most people would. And suicide? Never, never – he believed in living life to the fullest margin, only in a quieter way than some. We stayed up drinking last night, while he went to bed – he was tired, he said, and wanted to give people the best possible value for money on the first performance. That's what he was like. That's what— Oh, I can't believe he's gone!'

Larissa subsided into sobbing, and after a moment Dr Zinovev got up and placed a hand on her heaving shoulder. There was no doubting, it seemed, the depth of her grief for her colleague. But grief did not necessarily mean innocence. Some people, thought Olga, asked for permission, but others preferred to wait for forgiveness.

'Is this going to take long, Sergeant?' said Sonia Alikovsky, sitting back in a chair and crossing her legs, encased in sleek leather trousers to match her high-heeled ankle boots. 'It's just that we haven't eaten anything since lunch, and it is getting rather late. Not that we want a repeat of yesterday's offering – that was the worst goulash I've ever tasted.'

Next to her sat Panteleimon Pomelov, who had suggested joining Sonia to accelerate the process. He patted her arm reassuringly.

'Oh, I'm sure Vassily and Olga and – and – I'm sorry, Dr Zinovev, but I didn't catch your first names?'

'Yury Sergeiivich,' said Zinovev, nodding curtly.

'I'm sure that Vassily and Olga and Yury won't keep us any longer than necessary,' he said, with an expansive smile. 'Even policemen have to eat, am I right, Vassily?'

'I'd prefer Senior Sergeant Marushkin for now, Gospodin Pomelov,' said Vassily, his face stern and forbidding.

'Right, right, gotcha,' said Panteleimon, pointing a finger at him. 'Keep things above board. Good plan. And then grab a vodka or two after hours, *da*?'

'Never mind all that now, Pan,' said Sonia, lighting a cigarette. 'Can we please just get on? What's to say, anyway? Rodion's dead. We're all very sorry about it, but there it is.'

'There's still quite a lot to be said,' replied Vassily, articulating each word very clearly. 'We're trying to establish everyone's movements last night, and especially during dinner and afterwards.'

'Well, we're not going to tell you anything different from the others, are we?' said Sonia. 'We ordered in for dinner, it was terrible, we hardly ate it – I think the manager's dog got most of that damned goulash. Then Rodion and a couple of others went off for an early night.'

'Which others?' put in Olga.

'Oh, well – I'm not sure, exactly,' said Sonia.

'Agapa, maybe?' said Panteleimon.

'No, darling – she wasn't there at all, remember? She was off seeing some friend of hers,' said Sonia. 'I'm glad she got away. She spends too much time around this lot,' she went on, throwing a sideways glance at the troupe's Rasputin.

'And why shouldn't she spend time around us?' said Panteleimon, a touch indignantly. 'She loves her actors, you know, Vas– I mean, *Sergeant* . . . She treats us like colleagues instead of employees – always asking about our families, our childhoods, our homes . . . making us feel valued.'

'She doesn't make *me* feel very valued,' said Sonia, crossing her legs the other way. 'I practically had to beg her to let me play Sophie. She wanted to cast me as an old maid, you know, the tsarina's mother – and she was already dead by 1878!'

'You could have played her as a corpse, Sonia,' grinned Panteleimon, elbowing her playfully. 'That'd suit your acting style!'

She laughed quickly, a bark of mirthless glee. 'Better than hamming it up in every scene, like you do . . . Maybe Rodion found out his character had died, too. Committing to the role.'

'For once in his life,' chuckled Panteleimon.

The actors were sitting with their backs to the windows that ran along the breadth of the dining room. Evening was now falling fast upon them, offset only by the dim streetlamps along Privokzal'naya Ulitsa and the fitful glare they shed upon the dirty panes of the Tayga Hotel. Vassily had not yet switched on the lights inside the dining room, and the actors were falling fast into darkness, silhouetted against the in-flowing yellow glow like cardboard cut-outs. Olga looked at their faces, their eyes fading from bright perceptible orbs to shadowed unknowable pools, and shuddered. One of them had taken a life that very day – or if not them, then surely one of their colleagues and bedfellows. Their light-heartedness might just be a reaction, a form of shock, but nevertheless it was jarring, in the circumstances – shocking even, or rather obscene: a lurid and wilful contradiction of morality.

That's showbusiness, some would say, thought Olga. If it was, she wanted no part of it. *Just as well*, a snide voice said in her mind. *Your books will never make it onto the screen anyway – though Inessa Ignatyev's might . . .*

'Can I remind you that a man has died?' said Vassily, cutting across her thoughts and almost making her jump.

'Of course, Sergeant,' said Sonia, re-crossing her legs a third time. 'You must forgive us – we're all a little on edge, and this is how we relax. Actors are like doctors. We see all human nature and re-present it to our audiences – so.' She bowed, sweeping low in her chair with arms extended. 'You mustn't blame us if we become like the good Yury Sergeiivich here – a little desensitised. It is just our way of coping, *da*, Pan?'

'Oh, yes, that's right, indeed,' said Panteleimon, nodding so that his long hair bobbed up and down. 'Though some of us cope better than others.'

'Look at poor Larissa,' nodded Sonia.

'Oh, I try,' said Panteleimon, grinning widely. 'I do try.'

'Train crew's here, boss,' said Junior Sergeant Timofei Davidov, poking his head around the door and only subsequently remembering to knock on it.

'About time,' said Vassily. 'Bring them in, then.'

'Oh – and the captain's back, too,' said Davidov.

'Zemsky's here?' said Vassily – but Davidov had already gone, in obedience to the unwritten Tayga rule of avoiding in-person encounters with the captain at all costs.

'Yes, I'm here, Marushkin,' said Zemsky, barging through the door and reluctantly holding it open for the train crew, who came into the room with coal-stained overalls and a faint aroma of hot metal.

'Davidov's brought me up to date on the case – I hear the thespians didn't volunteer anything useful . . . Look, I've wasted enough time today already, so I'm going to do this the fast way,' continued the captain. 'Right, you three,' he went on, turning to the crew. 'Remind me of your names, first of all. Engineer Lev Myatlev, right – you? Vadim Lilov? Fireman? And what about you?'

'Simeon Zarubin, driver, Your Honour.'

'Ha!' cried Zemsky. 'Don't call me honourable till you know I am. Anyway, where were you last night – all you three? From around six onwards?'

'With the engine at Roslazny,' they replied in unison, and then, as if to dispel any illusion of a prepared story, they launched into an elaborate trio describing – in great and perhaps even excessive detail – the steps required to prepare a steam locomotive and accompanying carriages for the safe delivery of a murder mystery play over several days.

'Safe?' cried Zemsky. 'Didn't seem too safe to me!'

'That wasn't anything to do with us,' protested Lev, and after a brief round of further questioning, Zemsky appeared to accept that there was nothing to be gained from further interrogation. The crew, it emerged, had been working on the engine at Tayga depot in plain sight of the other railwaymen until nearly midnight, after the end of the window that Zinovev had estimated for Rodion's poisoning.

Zemsky dismissed the crew quite brusquely, but stopped them as they began to file out of the door.

'Don't go too far,' he said. 'I've a feeling the play will be on again before long.'

'Sir?' said Vassily, as the door closed behind Lev, Vadim and Simeon.

'This is Russia, Marushkin! Do you really think the expiry of a single luvvie is enough to put the spokes in something Arkady Nazarov has personally approved? The Mayor of Kemerovo? No, no – it'll be on again by tomorrow, or the day after, at the latest.'

'But, sir, the case,' began Vassily, as Dr Zinovev also jumped up in protest.

'It'll be an accidental verdict, Marushkin – something of that sort. Or suicide.'

'We're pretty certain it wasn't suicide, sir,' began Vassily again, but again Zemsky interrupted him.

'Of course it wasn't suicide, but we haven't got any proof,

have we? Unless our resident railway expert's got anything to add?'

Olga sat up as the men all turned to look at her. 'Oh, no – no, I don't think so, not from the Russian Railways perspective in particular,' she stammered. 'But I do agree with Vassily that—'

'Good, that's all settled, then,' boomed Zemsky. 'Now, who does a man have to kill to get a glass of vodka around here?'

'You could start with Nazarov,' muttered Vassily.

5
Too Many Cooks

The following day did nothing to dispel Vassily's dissatisfaction with events, bringing as it did an official proclamation from Tayga headquarters that Rodion Rultava had perished from death by misadventure.

'Death by misadventure!' he cried to Kliment, reading the flimsy communiqué that Timofei Davidov had personally delivered to the Roslazny police station. 'As if Rodion had been taking antifreeze for fun, and accidentally drank a little too much . . .'

'But, Papa,' said Kliment, slowly, looking up at him from his seat by the hearth, 'we couldn't prove it was anything else.'

'Well, no,' said Vassily, plumping down on the seat next to him. 'Of course we couldn't, in half a day. We'd barely started the interviews when Zemsky barged in and shut us down. And now he says' – waving the communiqué – 'that the Murder Express performances will start again tomorrow. Tomorrow! What is Zemsky thinking? He's far too much in Arkady Nazarov's pocket. And God knows whose pocket *he*'s in . . .'

'What do you mean, in his pocket, Papa?'

Vassily looked at Kliment's round face and remembered how young he still was. How could a boy of fifteen even begin to understand the wheels within wheels of corruption that Russia had developed in place of a functioning state? No, Kliment had remained an innocent soul – somewhat miraculously given the horrors of his childhood – and Vassily could no more imagine him grasping the motivations of a Zemsky or a Nazarov than he could see him engaging in nefarious purposes of his own. 'Never mind,' he said, his eyes crinkling into a smile. 'I just meant that you can't always trust people to do the right thing.'

'But sometimes people do bad things for good reasons, don't they, Papa? Or – or for people they love? Isn't that a good enough reason to do something – if you love someone?'

Vassily blinked. He hadn't expected a simple moaning session to evolve into a far-reaching philosophical discussion of motivations and vested interests.

'Er, well – yes, I suppose it might be,' he said. Then he went on in a brisker, more no-nonsense tone of voice: 'Where's your mother? You look like you could do with a bit of feeding up!'

'She's still in bed, Papa,' replied Kliment, gazing at Vassily with his large, watchful eyes. 'She said she was tired from yesterday, and wanted to rest.'

Vassily nodded slowly. That was understandable, of course, but it was after ten in the morning – hadn't she rested enough? There was Kliment to care for, after all. Kliment still hadn't had any breakfast, and was looking, thought Vassily, increasingly thin from day to day. He hoped he wasn't going to start refusing to eat, as he'd heard teenagers did sometimes. Surely Rozalina wouldn't want anything like that to happen – would she?

Vassily had got used to looking after Kliment that year, of course, but part of him had hoped for a little assistance on that front, now Rozalina had come back to them. But *had* she really come back? That was the question, Vassily told himself, as he looked down at his boots, resting squarely on the rough wooden floor. Could anyone really come back and be the same as they were before, when the thing they'd been through since was so terrible? Tricked into deceiving Vassily, then swept away from him and the home they shared together, subjected to beatings and starvation, and then – worse still – separated from Kliment, too . . .

Vassily shook his head. Heaven alone knew how she'd borne it. It had been hard enough for him, during the long years of searching – but at least he'd never suspected that Rozalina and Kliment had been separated. He would have gone mad, he was sure, if he'd been in her shoes, knowing with certainty that their son was wholly alone in a world so filled with evil. It was a miracle that she was still sane, still operating – still capable of living a life, and laughing, and lying in bed in comfort.

And yet . . . And yet . . .

Her eyes were different, thought Vassily, with a sudden rush of insight. Her face had changed, of course: he knew that the *ublyudki* on those farms had beaten her, but despite that she was still recognisably similar to the fresh young girl who beamed from the faded photographs in Vassily's box of keepsakes. But her eyes – her eyes were different. They had lost their colour, somehow, become bleached or faded in the withering light on those empty, windswept farm-plains. Their warmth had seeped away, leaving only a cold residue – cold, and hard, and unforgiving, his heart told him (without quite being asked).

Yes: her eyes had changed, and if those precious things, those windows to her soul, had been transformed, what else might he find altered within?

'There's Sputnik, Papa,' said Kliment, suddenly, making Vassily jump. Kliment was pointing across the room to the corridor that led to the cells, from which now emerged Rozalina's chihuahua, squeaky toy between his teeth and miniature tail wagging buoyantly behind him.

Vassily jumped up. 'Where's Rasputin? Did you put him back in his cage?'

'Not yet, Papa,' said Kliment, looking around for Vassily's beloved ferret. 'I – I was busy doing something else. But it's fine – I'm sure Sputnik won't hurt him!'

'Not hurt him?' cried Vassily. 'Dogs don't like ferrets, remember, Kliment? It'd only take one nip of that monster's teeth and my poor Rasputin would go the way of the feral cat Sputnik brought here last week.'

Vassily explored the police station's cramped rooms until he found Rasputin sleeping beside the radiator in the back office – a favourite spot of his in winter.

'There you are, my beautiful boy – there you are,' crooned Vassily, to his rather dishevelled golden ferret, whose loveliness existed in Vassily's eyes alone. 'Let's get you safely back into the cage before that nasty little dog gets at you again. Let's get you into the cage.'

He found the cage – a heavy-duty affair liberated by Vassily's father from the ruins of the *sozhkhov* poultry department years before – and dragged the hatch open, dropping Rasputin inside with a couple of mice provided by Popov earlier in the week.

He sighed then, before heading to the kitchen to make something for Kliment's breakfast. Sputnik was undoubtedly annoying, and was certainly not to be trusted around precious pets like Rasputin, but the real problem was his owner, who seemed to think that Sputnik's livelihood and entertainment were now Vassily's responsibilities along with everything else. Of course, he reminded himself yet again, she had had – like Kliment – a traumatic time of it, having been (again like Kliment) plucked away from her everyday life and trafficked to other regions for back-breaking labour. All the same, though, she was here now. Couldn't she try to enjoy life in Roslazny a little more, rather than spending day after day staying late in bed?

And there was, too, a lingering sense of disconnection beyond the coldness of her eyes, a reluctance to pick up the threads of their old lives together that made conversations and mealtimes – let alone any approach to intimacy – hard to navigate. He and Rozalina had had the fairytale rendezvous, Vassily often thought, the almost unbelievable rediscovery of each other that would crown the finale to any romantic movie – but the movies didn't often cover what happened next. And that, Vassily had discovered, was when the work was really done.

Work was also being done elsewhere in the village that day. At Café Astana, for instance, the locals had set themselves to extracting every last drop of available information from those actors who had ventured to Roslazny for lunch on their day off.

'So you're not an actor yourself, then?' said Nikolai Popov to Yegor Shulgin, who was in the act of taking his first ever sip of Café Astana's proprietary vodka, Igor Odrosov's Rocket Fuel.

The resulting coughing fit took some time to subside, but eventually Yegor found himself able to speak once more, and with tears streaming down his cheeks he responded at last. 'No – no, I'm not,' he said, spluttering again. 'Does it always make you cough like this?'

'Only when you haven't had enough already,' said Igor, from behind the bar, grinning round at the locals and pouring Yegor a second tot.

'Pour one for me while you're at it,' said Panteleimon Pomelov, grabbing a stool and sitting on it in a single lithe movement.

'And me,' said Larissa Lazarov, standing beside him in an outfit of startling green. 'And – and one for Rodion, too.'

Igor looked at Larissa, her eyes shimmering with the gleam of unshed tears, then nodded and poured an extra glass for the absent man, as custom dictated. He reached to a counter behind him and placed a small piece of dark bread over the glass, signifying the one who would not come to drink again.

'To Rodion!' cried Panteleimon, glancing sideways at Larissa.

'To Rodion,' said Yegor, with several of the regulars who had half got to their feet from respect. Larissa, however, did not speak, but instead began to sing, a soft, sad melody.

Popov reached for Igor's hand, and nodded up at the television, still blaring the day's football results. Igor pressed a button on the remote, and silence fell in the café – silence, apart from Larissa's singing, with which Yegor soon joined, then Panteleimon, and several of the others, too.

Ne slyshny v sadu dazhe shorokhi,
Vsyo zdes' zamerlo do utra.

Whispers aren't heard in the garden,
Everything has died till morning.
If you only knew how dear to me
Are these Moscow nights.

The river moves, unmoving,
All in silver moonlight.
A song is heard, yet unheard,
In these silent nights.

Why do you, dear, look askance,
With your head lowered so?
It is hard to express, and hard to hold back,
Everything that my heart holds.

But the dawn's becoming ever brighter.
So please, just be good.
Don't you, too, forget
These summer, Moscow nights.

'She knew him well, then – his sweetheart, maybe?' muttered Popov to Yegor as they finished the song's haunting melody, almost sweet in its sadness. He nodded at Larissa, tears now streaming openly down her cheeks.

But Yegor shook his head in response. 'Not really,' he said. 'She only met him for the first time a couple of weeks ago. None of us had worked together before – except me and the Putyatins, of course,' he added.

'The Putyatins – that's the boss, is it, and the wife?' put in Koptev Alexeyev, the mechanic, face still streaked with oil from a particularly challenging engine replacement.

'What – them over there, in the corner?' said Popov, following the direction of Yegor's nod to where Ilya and Agapa Putyatin sat nursing a bottle of tonic wine. 'The tsar and the tsarina? Well! You move in high circles, my friend!'

'Not really,' said Yegor, shaking his head. 'I'm only their executive assistant, though I do help with cues and lines and other things. You could say I'm the swan's legs. I do the hard work below the surface,' he elaborated, seeing looks of blank incomprehension around him, 'while others take the lion's share of the glory.'

'What is it, Fyodor?' said Popov to Fyodor Katin, the Dreamer, who had scoffed aloud from his perch on the stool beyond Alexeyev.

'Oh, nothing,' he said airily, plucking a rather dog-eared tissue from his voluminous pocket and wiping his glasses – though it looked to Popov as if he were just smearing the dirt around and around. 'It's just that I might have expected a theatrical person – even someone who is an executive assistant rather than an actor – to avoid mixed metaphors in their speech.'

'Take no notice of him,' said Alexeyev to Yegor, elbowing him for good measure. 'He's just in a bad mood cos of Anna Kabalevsky.'

'Took the wind out of your sales when that army man died on stage, eh, Fyodor?' said Popov, winking at Fyodor. 'Then that doctor, what's his name – Vinozev? – put you in the shade, and no mistake.'

'Quiet, lads – quiet,' urged Igor Odrosov, hearing their conversation and jerking his head at Larissa Lazarov, now resting her head on Panteleimon's shoulder and gazing with unseeing eyes at the beer-stained counter. 'And there's this gentleman here, too, who's friends with the dead man – Segor, was it?'

'Yegor,' he corrected. 'Yegor Konstantinovich Shulgin.'

'Ah, yes,' said Odrosov. 'I knew there was an *s* in there somewhere . . . Anyway, *Yegor*, I apologise for my customers! They haven't all got the manners you'd hope for, even if we are stuck in the arse-end of nowhere. But we aren't all *pridurok*i and *debily* out here, you know!'

'You're on good form today, Igor,' said Fyodor. 'Better than I expected, anyway. Aren't you worried about the Red Star? About Mikhail Pushkin and company? I see a few regulars missing tonight – down at his food stall, no doubt.'

After the lucrative – if lethal – premiere performance of the Murder Express, Mikhail Pushkin and Vladimir Solotov had moved the stall to a new location just outside the churchyard, where it had reopened earlier that day. A few weeks ago, or even a few days, the advent of such an energetic competitor would have thrown Igor Odrosov into despair. But now he seemed surprisingly unconcerned.

'Well, you see,' he said, throwing his tea-towel over his shoulder and leaning an elbow conspiratorially on the counter, 'you could say I had a bit of good news today. News that might just change things around here!'

'Is it the Department of Environmental Health at last, Igor?' said Popov. 'Have they finally thrown out your case?'

'No, no,' said Odrosov, making a shushing sound with his

lips and glancing at Yegor. 'That's all in hand, Nikolai – all in hand! What's a few cases of listeria between friends? Besides, I've got bigger fish to fry these days. I got a phone call earlier from a distillery down in Omsk, see. They've heard about my vodka, they said – can you believe it, from all the way down there? They want to make my Rocket Fuel on an industrial scale, and sell it for me, too.'

'Almost sounds too good to be true, Igor,' said Fyodor Katin.

'I know, I know,' laughed Odrosov. 'I thought that myself, but they sent through a heap of brochures and franchise pricing offers and distribution lists afterwards. So it must be above board.

'Yes, yes,' he went on, holding up a little glass of vodka and swirling the blue-tinged liquid around in the light, 'soon you'll see big changes around here, and the Red Star' – he lingered with disgust on both words, *Krasnaya Zvezda* – 'will just be a disappearing dot on the far horizon. Ah, Vassily,' he went on, as the door opened and Vassily appeared. 'Come and hear about the good news!'

'What good news?' muttered Vassily, walking to the bar in a bad-tempered shuffle. He had the good grace to smile and nod when Odrosov told him about the proposed franchise, and even to ask a couple of questions, but it was obvious – to Fyodor Katin, anyway – that his mind was far from the world of the Spirit.

'What ails, Vassily?' said Fyodor, grabbing the bottle from behind the counter and pouring him a tot.

'Thanks, Fyodor,' he said wearily, passing a hand over his unshaven face. Then he glanced sideways at Yegor and the others, and beckoned Fyodor away to a side table. 'Don't you think it's a bit strange, these actors coming here and partying when their colleague's just been murdered?'

'I thought it was an accident, or something like that?'

'Don't believe everything you think, Fyodor. That man was murdered, I'm sure of it. And now the troupe decanting here *en masse*, as if Roslazny had nothing to do with it all . . .'

'I wouldn't say that, exactly. Larissa Lazarov is clearly upset – Panteleimon is comforting her now – and the Putyatins have been talking in sombre solitude ever since they got here.'

'You've learned their names already,' observed Vassily.

'What can I say?' said Fyodor, modestly looking at his nails. 'I'm a scholar, *nyet*? I remember things.'

'Well, what about the woman who plays the companion – do you remember her name? Sonia something?'

'Sonia Alikovsky,' said Fyodor, triumphantly.

'Ssh!' said Vassily, urging him to silence with a fierce gesture. 'No need to tell everyone what we're talking about!' he went on. 'Anyway, where's she got to? And what about the train crew?'

'The crew are still in Tayga, working on the engine,' said Fyodor. 'A leaky pipe, I heard, that they have to fix before tomorrow. I think it was on their recommendation that the actors came out this way, though – that's what Yegor said, anyway.'

'Just Yegor, now, is it? First-name terms?'

Fyodor shrugged. 'He's the only one who's made an effort to talk to us – maybe because he's not an actor. They keep to themselves, I find. Look at that Sonia Alikovsky, to answer your question from earlier – Yegor told me she's at a beauty salon somewhere, having her nails done.'

'Her *nails*?' said Vassily, shaking his head. 'Nails, at a time like this . . . Well, I haven't given up on the case, believe me. The lot of them are still here for a few more days – that might just give me enough time to find the killer.'

'Just you, Vassily Marushkin?' came a voice from behind his ear.

'Olga!' he said, almost crossly. 'You made me jump!'

'That was the idea,' she said, winking at Fyodor, and turning back to close the door behind her. 'Just keeping our resident policeman on his toes. And don't forget that Zemsky ordered me to assist with the investigation on Russian Railways' behalf. I'm just following orders.'

'So was Svetlana Odrosov when she made these *pirogi*,' muttered Fyodor, turning one of the Café Astana pastries over in its pool of grease.

'Don't you think we should discuss the case a little further, Vassily?' went on Olga. 'Now that we've slept on it, we can make a fresh start. I've got to keep Boris Andreyev happy, after all.'

Vassily looked up at her, standing over him and smiling despite the mention of her much-disliked superior, who – as all the village now knew – was threatening to kick Olga out of her beloved rail-side hut and expel her from the railways altogether.

'You're right, Olga Pushkin,' he said, getting to his feet. 'Let's go to the station – you can keep an eye on things here, Fyodor?'

Fyodor gave a mini-salute, then tutted and shook his head. 'Never thought I'd be supporting an agent of the state,' he muttered.

'How about supporting a friend?'

'That I can do,' he said. 'That I can do.'

'Rozalina – Rozalina, you remember Olga Pushkin? From the railway?' said Vassily, a touch nervously, as he knocked on the door that led to the cells. The Marushkins slept there when there were no criminals to accommodate, since the cells had the best insulation and heating of any room in the warren-like station – as Olga well knew. She had been incarcerated there earlier in the year, as part of a disastrous investigation, during an intense cold snap that swept a deep covering of snow over Roslazny and its surrounds. Now the pure white blanket had been replaced by endless mud, and glittering ice-crystals with numberless droplets on bough and bush and brick, and air so damp that water seemed to trickle directly onto hair and neck.

'What – what?' came Rozalina's voice, cross and sleepy, as if Vassily had torn her unreasonably from her midnight sleep, instead of carefully entreating her attention at two in the afternoon. But then again, it wasn't really all that unreasonable, Olga forced herself to admit, for someone who had until recently been labouring in forced servitude to relax a little, now and again.

'It's Olga, *dragotsennyy,*' went on Vassily, glancing backwards at Olga with an apologetic expression, and continuing into the cells and half closing the door behind him. Olga could hear a murmured discussion beyond: it sounded like Vassily was persuading and Rozalina resisting, and again Olga could hardly blame her for wanting to enjoy a little peace and quiet. She hadn't wanted Vassily to disturb his wife, but he had insisted.

'She'd love to see you again, Olga, I'm sure,' he'd said earlier, a little unconvincingly, as they'd tramped through the mud together on the short walk from Café Astana. 'I know you two haven't had the chance to see much of each other, so far,' he'd continued, 'but now that she's been here a while . . .'

He'd tailed off, leaving the obvious unsaid: that Rozalina had quite clearly, if not quite verbally, indicated that other ladies of marriageable age were not welcome at the Roslazny police station. Wisdom, thought Olga, would be to leave Rozalina well alone until she herself desired things to change; attempting to hasten her decision would only court disaster. And she knew, too, that Vassily, though often surpassingly shrewd when it came to police business, could be surprisingly dim when it came to matters of a personal kind. But it no longer fell to her, she reminded herself, to be a guide to him in this or indeed any other area of life. That was Rozalina's role, now – his *dragotsennyy*, his precious. Even her name, Olga realised for the first time, sounded fitted for the job. Rozalina – Roslazny. Rozalina – Roslazny. Where did Olga's name sound like? Omsk? Orsk? Orel and Grozny combined? It didn't have quite the same ring to it.

'Devushka Pushkin,' said a female voice, a voice as deep and rich as an actor's, and accompanied by the thin yapping of a lapdog.

'Dama Marushkin,' replied Olga, politely, looking up at the woman who now passed through the corridor that led to the cells and stood before her, a little taller than Olga and more elaborately dressed – she wore a leopard-print dressing-gown over a satin trouser-suit – but with hair in a similar shade of blonde, tumbling to her shoulders and almost serving as a blanket for Sputnik, who rested in her arms. It was a shame, thought Olga, rather cattily, that she'd chosen a dog of that particular shade of orange-brown: it clashed with her hair.

'Vassily tells me you're working together,' went on Rozalina, leaning against the door frame and caressing Sputnik's ears, 'though I can't imagine why . . . You work on the railways, don't you?'

'Well, yes,' said Olga, 'but we've worked together before, you know. Vassily's found the engineer's perspective useful, from time to time.'

'An engineer's perspective? And what is that? The view from the tracks – from the ground they run over?'

'I suppose so,' said Olga, feeling the blood rush into her cheeks, and wishing she could prevent it. 'But you can see a lot from the ground – and *on* the ground – if you look long enough.'

'So,' boomed Vassily – rather louder, thought Olga, than he had intended, and at any rate making both women jump, then turn to stare at him.

'So,' he said again, in a more moderate tone, this time reinforcing the heartiness by rubbing his hands together. 'How about some vodka and gherkins, *da*? I pickled them myself – borage and coriander. Then we can get started on that case, Olga, in the back office – and perhaps you could join us, if you like, Rozalina?'

'Oh, no, Mama,' said Kliment, who had come into the reception area from the other direction. 'You promised you'd help me with my homework – remember? The – er – the maths project? Sorry, Olga,' he added, sending her an apologetic look, and little realising, perhaps, how relieved she was at this unexpected intervention.

'Not at all, Kliment – not at all!' said Olga. 'Of course your mother must help you. There's nothing more important than education. How else will you grow up and pay your own way?'

Kliment nodded, before darting a glance at Rozalina, who laughed and ran a hand over Kliment's bowled head. 'There are many ways to make money, *nyet*, Kliment?' she said. 'Ways that pay more than a senior sergeant's salary, anyway. But of course I will help you – if I can. I was always better at spending money than counting it, just as Vassily was always better at complaining about criminals than catching them! He still hasn't caught the desperado behind all these little thefts in the village, you know.'

She chuckled, and left them then, bidding Kliment lead the way to the store-cupboard where Vassily had made him a desk, and leaving her discouraging words behind her, like a bad smell. Kliment sent Olga another look of tacit contrition, reminding Olga of how thin he had become, and worse still, how obviously unsettled he was – unhappy, even.

Still, it can't have been easy for Kliment to welcome a long-lost mother back into his life, as she said to Vassily while following him into the back office. 'There must be many things he's misremembered, or got wrong, somehow,' she said, sinking into one of the dilapidated armchairs that surrounded a heavy wooden desk. 'Or maybe he expected too much. Maybe he thought his mother would return just as he remembers her from his childhood, from before they were split up – but of course she's been through so much since then.'

'I know, I know,' said Vassily, sitting beside her, and once again passing a hand wearily over his face. 'But it isn't much fun living with a closed book.'

'She doesn't talk about it?' said Olga, and then, in response to Vassily's wagging finger of negation, 'Well, I suppose it must be very difficult to go back, even in memory. The things she must have seen . . .'

'Yes, yes – but I can't help her unless she speaks up, can I? I can't help her, if she just lies in bed in the cells all day, ordering

Kliment to fetch her this and buy her that! I can't help her if – if—'

He sighed, and sank deeper into the creaking embrace of his ancient chair. 'Oh, I'm sorry, Olga,' he said, looking across at her. 'I shouldn't be offloading all this onto you. It's just – I'm worried about Kliment. He's not doing all that well at school, and I'm not sure . . . well, I'm just not sure how good Rozalina is at helping him. But *I* can't do it – I'm out all the time, scouring the village and the outskirts to try to pin down whoever's carrying out all those stupid little crimes . . . And now there's this murder, too – I don't have enough hours in the day, Olga – I just don't!'

She gazed into his eyes, looking straight at him for the first time in as long as she could remember, and saw for the first time how red-rimmed and hot they were, as if they were the doorway to some simmering furnace within. His cheeks were unshaven, too, and his hair even more tousled than usual, while his clothes, she noticed, were stained and crumpled. Anger rose within her, that this man – this good man, who worked too hard – should find himself so ill-supported at home.

But it wouldn't help Vassily, she knew, to turn him against his own wife. And anger, she told herself, was best channelled towards some productive end. Perhaps if she could help Vassily solve the murder, he might feel better about everything else. At least, it was worth a try.

'I know, Vassily – I know,' she said. 'I've felt like that myself, at times, with the house to maintain, and the hut, and Dmitri – not to mention writing, too!'

'Oh, yes,' he said, sitting up a little, and looking at her with a less anguished expression. 'Did I hear something about another writer publishing a book like yours – a book about the railway?'

Olga grimaced. 'Yes, you did,' she said. 'I'm still trying to get to the bottom of it – can't get hold of my editor. I might need you to come to Novosibirsk with me one day, Vassily, and put the fear of God into him.'

Vassily laughed, a brief return of the old, familiar merriness in his eyes. 'If we can solve this case, I'll go wherever you like!'

'Then let's get on and solve it,' said Olga, jumping up from her chair and striding to the blackboard on the opposite wall, where Vassily always wrote his latest ideas for whatever case he was handling.

'Who's our lead suspect?' she said.

'Try suspects, plural,' said Vassily, getting to his feet somewhat reluctantly, and walking over to the blackboard in turn. 'We've got six, you could say – all the actors in the troupe. Seven, actually, if we include Yegor. And ten, if you want to count the train crew as well, though they'd only met— '

'But they'd only met the actors the week before,' said Olga, smiling at Vassily: their old habit was still going strong. 'But we can include them for now, anyway – just to be sure. Ten suspects, then, and none of them with a motive we know of.'

'And the train crew also lack means,' pointed out Vassily. 'They weren't at the dinner when the goulash was poisoned. Assuming – of course – that that's when it happened.'

'When else could it have been? Everyone's doors were locked – from the inside!'

'So they said.'

'You mean – someone could have let the poisoner in?'

'Why not? They were all working together in the play, so it wasn't as if they didn't know each other's voices. A quick look left and right to see if anyone was coming, a rapid knock on the door, an urgent question about costumes for the following day – wouldn't you open the door? Then pop in,' went on Vassily, 'start a conversation, suggest another nip of vodka, add a little something extra to Rodion's glass . . . Then take your leave a few minutes later with the door locked behind you, look left and right again, and slip back to your room, with nobody the wiser.'

'But what about the taste?'

'Maybe Rodion would just think he was still recovering from dinner.'

'No, no,' said Olga, getting to her feet and pacing up and down. 'How much did Zinovev said he'd had – fifty millilitres? I doubt you could smuggle that down someone's throat in a few tots of vodka.'

Vassily nodded. 'I agree, actually,' he said, digging in first one pocket and then the other for his cigarettes. 'So that brings us back to dinner. But we don't have much to go on there.'

'No fingerprints on the bottle, I suppose?' said Olga. 'The antifreeze, I mean.'

'Only partials – nothing conclusive. And the lab boffins said they didn't think anyone could have drunk from the bottle, anyway, given the angles involved.'

Olga picked up a piece of chalk and wrote all ten names across the top of the board. Then she paused, and turned to Vassily. 'The blackboard was already blank,' she said, with the air of one realising something she should have noticed all along. 'Why?'

He shrugged. 'I haven't got any leads,' he said, breathing out a maze of white smoke. 'Either some master criminal's given up jewel heists in St Petersburg and has come here to torment me with petty crime, or I've lost whatever skill as a detective I once possessed.'

'You know, Vassily, sometimes on the railways you've got to fix one thing before you can fix another. No point fixing the signals till the track's sorted out – so maybe if you solve the murder you'll solve the thefts, too.'

He smiled a sad smile. 'If I could stop people murdering, they could steal all they liked.'

'That's the right way round,' she said. 'But stealing can lead to murder, don't forget. Anyway – listen. Let's put a tick under each name that was at the dinner. That's all of the troupe, except Agapa Putyatin. And none of the crew. And excluding Rodion, of course, assuming he didn't poison his own dinner. That leaves five.'

'Larissa Lazarov, Ilya Putyatin, Sonia Alikovsky, Panteleimon Pomelov, and Yegor Shulgin,' said Vassily, getting up and standing beside her. 'So one of them would have needed to get some antifreeze, put it in the dinner, disguise the taste somehow and wipe the bottle down, put the bottle into Rodion's room, and get him to close and lock the door behind them . . . Unless the bottle was already there when he went to sleep, of course – that would make it easier.'

'Excellent, Vassily!' said Olga, smiling. 'Looks like we need another round of interviews.'

'Ye-es,' said Vassily, slowly, his eyes turned inward. 'And I wonder if Odrosov might know what kind of thing you could use to disguise the taste of chemicals – what kind of flavouring, or maybe a bitter herb of some sort. Or we could ask Popov, or even—'

'Or even my father Mikhail?' said Olga, laughing as she completed Vassily's sentence. 'I know he's set up a restaurant, Vassily, but you'd be more likely to get spiritual advice from Svetlana Odrosov than culinary expertise from him and his cronies. In fact, if you want to solve a crime, just keep an eye on their food hygiene – or the hospital beds at Tayga! But we're getting off track. The important thing is that one of our suspects *does* know about food – enough to doctor food for six, and kill only one. And we need to find out who.'

Vassily nodded. 'And we could widen the net further,' he said. 'Go door to door in Tayga, check out all the shops and restaurants and see if anyone was asking about food colourings or flavourings and suchlike. This could have been a long-planned enterprise, in which case the murderer would have come to Tayga with everything prepared and already in hand. But it might have been a last-minute idea – and in *that* case we might still be able to pick up the trail.'

'Shame the hotel puts their bins out on Tuesdays,' said Vassily. 'I'd give a million roubles to get those dinners analysed.'

'A million roubles, Vassily – pretty steep! I'm not sure what Rozalina would have to say about that.'

He smiled, but a little sadly, and lit another cigarette.

'I've no idea,' he said. 'I have simply no idea.'

She and Vassily agreed to get together in Tayga the following morning, some hours before the Murder Express renewed its performances, to ask a few searching questions of the actors and the train crew. Then Olga took her leave, walking past Kliment and Rozalina at work on the main reception desk, Kliment bending his round head over pages full of scribbled writing, while Rozalina filed her nails and gazed out of the window.

Rozalina looked up and flashed a smile at Olga as she came down the corridor that led to the back office.

'Thank you for coming, Devushka Pushkin! I hope you can help my husband with his inquiry – though why Captain Zemsky thought he'd need a trackside engineer on the case, I really can't guess.'

Olga smiled back at her, taking care to preserve her friendly expression, and wondered for the hundredth time if Vassily might have been happier if Rozalina had stayed lost. She sympathised with her, of course – everyone did who looked at her, and saw how she'd been beaten by cruel hands. She was still recognisable as the Rozalina from Vassily's old photographs – just – though undeniably changed in some respects. But sympathy wasn't the same as liking, thought Olga, as she pushed her way past the front door, sticking on the floor as usual, and headed to work at her little rail-side hut. A murder might have taken place, but trains still had to run, and signals and points do their allotted work at the allotted time, or yet more lives might be lost.

But she thought again about sympathy and liking later that day when her shift was over and she walked down the narrow path that led to the house she shared with her brother Pasha and Anna Kabalevsky. No, sympathy wasn't liking, she reflected, any more than pity was the same as love. But the odd thing was that she both pitied Vassily and loved him: she pitied him for his obligations to Rozalina, and she loved him for things that were all his own.

She found Pasha, too, in reflective mood, sitting in the lounge and smoking, with a chair drawn up to the window that looked out over the little garden with its straggly border of bushes and stunted trees.

He smiled at her. 'There you are,' he said.

'Here, indeed, I am,' she said, pulling up a chair and peering out at the dim afternoon light. 'But Anna is not?'

'Gone to Nonna's with the kids,' said Pasha. 'She said she thought I'd had enough noise for one day, and wanted to give me a break.'

'That's Anna,' said Olga. 'A saint among us.'

'Yes,' said Pasha. 'Yes, she is. Only—'

'What is it, Pasha?'

'Oh, I miss them when they're gone,' he said. 'It's quiet, and – and there's too much time to think. This latest death . . . So much death – when will we stop, all of us? Isn't there enough misery in the world, with illness and poverty and bad luck, too?'

He turned to Olga, resting his hands on an uplifted knee.

'I was in Crimea, you remember, before I left the army. Before they threw me out, I mean. The fighting was over then, or so we thought, and I told myself it was all done, finished with – but if I was honest with myself, I knew you could still see the bullet-holes in the buildings, and the terror in the people's eyes . . . And now it has all started up again, a thousand times worse than before – no, a million times worse. And just like here, in our poor little Roslazny, each death is a layer cake – if you cut down deep enough you find the state at the bottom, a sick layer of rotten hypocrisy and evil. And who supports it all, who keeps it going with taxes and votes and quiet consent? We do, Olga! We do.'

He turned again towards the window, and knocked the ash off the tip of his cigarette. 'We do. It's us. We are the ones who have to change.'

Olga followed his gaze outside and saw Anna walking back with baby Ilya in her arms, and beside her Gyorgy and Boris, dragging their feet as usual, and making Anna stop and encourage them onwards with everlasting patience.

Then Olga glanced sideways at Pasha, who had begun to smile and wave at the boys despite his sadness, and her eyes unexpectedly filled with tears. How could there be such good people in the world, and at the same time such bad people? How could there be Pashas and Annas and Vassilys and Fyodors, and on the other hand so many cold-blooded exterminators of their fellow humans, in Roslazny or elsewhere? Where were all the good Russians, the ones who would rise up and topple those who oppressed them, near and afar? Where were they?

A soft snuffling sound distracted Olga's attention, and she looked down to the floor, where Dmitri, her white-breasted hedgehog, was nudging her foot with his nose. She had brought him back from the hut after rumours of a stray dog in the vicinity, and now he was hungry for his early-evening snack.

She put a hand on Pasha's arm and got up in search of mealworms. Yes, there were Dmitris in the world, for which she was thankful, but there were also Rasputins and Sputniks.

And perhaps it was quite simple, after all: being a good Russian was just protecting the hedgehogs from the dogs and the ferrets. In the end, that was the only work that really had to be done.

6
Second Act

'What d'you mean, relax?' said Olga, the following morning, in a tone that expressed the opposite mood. 'You can't just sit there and tell me nothing's wrong, when there's a woman out there making millions from my bloody idea!'

A muffled laugh came down the phone line. 'Millions? Steady on. New authors are lucky to get to half a million, these days. The industry's not what it was. Our costs—'

But Olga spoke over the patronising tones of Maxim Gusev, commissioning editor (fiction, non-fiction, and military) at Lyapunov Books in Novosibirsk. She was standing in her rail-side hut, over by the window where the reception was best, and if there was one place on earth where she felt capable of pushing back against know-it-all men, the hut was it.

'Look, there's only one thing I want to know,' she interjected. 'Did you tell anyone about my book? Because I don't see how Inessa Ignatyev managed to come up with *All on the Line* despite never having worked for Russian Railways, or how she managed to write it up and release it only months before my version.'

'Well, it's like you say, Olga,' replied Maxim. 'It's just your version, isn't it? We don't own ideas, do we? All we own is the way we express them. You had a good idea, and wrote it down – and very well, too, I might say. But then again, so did Inessa, and she's a bit better known than you, isn't she? That helps a lot, these days – the industry's not what it was.'

'So you've said,' replied Olga. 'But maybe it's people like you and Inessa that make it the way it is.'

She hung up and threw her phone onto the desk, where it clattered noisily and came to rest next to her copy of Inessa's book. Then Olga cursed: she hadn't meant to get so worked up, and maybe *All on the Line* wasn't Maxim's fault, after all – though she found it hard to believe that Inessa Ignatyev had just come up with the idea herself. She was a journalist, after all, and used to digging up secrets. She was based in Novosibirsk, too, and a brief internet search had failed to reveal any previous writing on railways – so why the sudden interest, if not prompted by a spot of literary inside trading?

It reminded Olga of one of her own Life Lessons, no. 49, in fact, which said—

But no. No, she didn't want to think of the Life Lessons just then, or anything to do with *Find Your Rail Self: 100 Life Lessons from the Trans-Siberian Railway*. It was too painful to think of – and, besides, she told herself, there were other and more pressing mysteries to solve than how some TV hack had stolen her ideas. Everyone in Roslazny and Tayga seemed very relaxed about the death of Rodion Rultava, for instance, having apparently settled on the view that Rodion had decided to kill himself for reasons unknown – but how could that possibly be true when the lab said he was unlikely to have drunk the antifreeze from the bottle himself? And how could it have been suicide in the absence of a note, or any other indication that he had been sufficiently distressed for such an act? Vassily had told Olga the day before that they'd checked his police history, bank accounts and phone contents, as well as his luggage, and nothing had raised any red flags. And what about the little black book he'd told Larissa about – the notebook in which he kept a record of things he'd seen with his shrewd eyes, but which had disappeared since his death? Wasn't that a strong sign of something untoward – something worse than suicide?

No, no: everyone else might be quite happy with the verdict that Captain Zemsky had passed down, but Olga was no more prepared to relax in this regard than she was about a literary rival stealing her crown before it had even been fitted to her head. Rodion Rultava's body had been laid in the Tayga morgue, but Olga was certain it wasn't resting easy. And if anyone could help Vassily solve the case and find the murderer, it was surely a Russian Railways veteran with fifteen years' active experience under her belt.

She picked up her phone, checked it was still working, put it into her pocket and walked towards the door. But then she turned, grabbed a pile of discarded papers from the box by the stove, and threw them over Inessa Ignatyev's book until it was buried in an avalanche of old schedules and Russian Railways memos.

It wasn't a long walk to the police station from Olga's hut, but she felt her footsteps dragging as she set out – probably just a delayed reaction to the murder of Rodion Rultava, she told herself, and certainly not any kind of reluctance to see Rozalina again, even in passing. Certainly not that.

She breasted the small incline that signalled the end of the forest that marched along the tracks, and turned north-west along the path that led to the Roslazny police station, taking the shortcut that skirted the remains of a dairy and ran through the edge of the Petrovs' long, narrow garden It all looked so dreary at this time of year, she thought – patches of stunted grass smeared with mud, and browned stalks of dead flowers nodding in the chill breeze by the rusting skeletons of fences and tractors and doors that led only to empty spaces. Give me the hot summer with its scented air and living dots of colour, she said to herself, as she tramped through the Petrovs' overgrown allotments, or – better still – the snow with its blessed anonymity. Then I could be anywhere – in the north where few people go, or in some kinder land far to the west where the only thing to fear in the ice is frostbite.

She paused and looked up, but there were no spiralling snowflakes to be seen, only a drab sky with a hint of rain tugging at the clouds' edges. She sighed and turned her eyes downwards again, but then she caught her breath and moved her head sharply aside. What was that she had seen, over to the left – by the path that snaked away from the Petrovs' and down towards Nikolai Popov's butcher's shop? Only a dart of movement, a sliver of black amid the duns and soiled greens of Siberian winter, but something undoubtedly alive, moving, *human* among the deserted outhouses and gaping ruins . . .

Calm down, Olga, she told herself. It was just Koptev Alexeyev, out for a bit of exercise – or Svetlana Odrosov off to Popov's to pick up some horsemeat, and in a hurry since she'd forgotten Igor wanted it for breakfast. But Alexeyev didn't exercise, said a quiet voice in her head, and neither did Svetlana hurry at any time or on any account, least of all her father's.

She resolved to put it out of her mind, to carry on to her appointment with Vassily Marushkin and to think no more of it. But that figure had been unsettlingly fast in its movements, somehow horribly *lithe*, and what were they looking for but a man – or a woman – who lived at ease in the shadows, and struck at will among the living until they were the dead?

'You saw – what?' said Vassily, when she got to the station and told him.

'Maybe she saw a ghost,' said Rozalina, who was sitting behind the reception desk, smiling softly up at him. 'Where's Kliment? Maybe he could tell us a tale of monsters under the bed!'

'It could be our killer, Vassily,' said Olga, pretending she hadn't heard. 'Or at least it could be the person who's doing all those things – you know, stealing stuff, and burning things down. Maybe you could ask the Petrovs if they saw anything round their way this morning – or Popov. Oh, and Alexeyev, too. I think it was a man – somebody quick, anyway, dressed in black, and who knows the shortcuts.'

'I will, Olga,' said Vassily, pulling on his coat. 'I will ask them – but not now. I told the actors we'd be there at eleven, which doesn't leave much time to do the rounds of food shops and cafés in Tayga. Rozalina, can you tell Kliment to tidy the papers in the back office? He left them in a terrible state.'

'Did he now?' said Rozalina, no longer smiling. 'Oh, I'll tell him, Vassily. I will!'

Tayga was a mid-sized town by Siberian standards, with twenty-five thousand souls, and shops and eating establishments to feed them. Vassily and Olga were hard-pressed, therefore, to cover all the relevant ground in time for their appointment with the actors of the Murder Express. At Olga's suggestion they focused on the ten or so places within a mile of the railway station and the Tayga Hotel, but even so the schedule was extremely tight, barely leaving them time to walk between the various cafés, shops and restaurants, find someone willing to talk to them at that time in the morning, and ask a few sharply focused questions regarding the troupe.

'We should have started this yesterday,' said Olga, puffing as Vassily hurried them along Kirova Prospekt towards the bakery on the corner of Chkalova. 'They might have guessed we'd focus on the nearest places, and gone farther afield.'

'I agree, but what could I do, Olga?' said Vassily. 'After you left, Koptev Alexeyev came to complain about yet another theft, so I had at least to inspect the scene quickly. Then there were things at home, issues and – and challenges,' he added vaguely. 'And you were at work yourself, don't forget,' he added, more vigorously. 'It just wasn't possible.'

'No,' said Olga, in a more emollient tone. 'I wasn't trying to blame you, Vassily. It's just – I'm just keen to find something to work with, that's all, and I'm afraid we won't.'

In the event, however, Olga's fears were unjustified, for they quickly uncovered important information relating not just to one but to two members of the troupe. The owner of a small grocery store on Maslova remembered selling a bottle of cider vinegar two days before to a woman matching the appearance of Agapa Putyatin, while the cashier at another place, a larger and more expensive shop selling fresher ingredients, talked of a lady who bought some household supplies on the same morning. She had kept her face covered with a black scarf, but she sounded, nonetheless, very much like Sonia Alikovsky.

'She had heels and leather trousers on,' said the woman. 'Leather! In this weather!'

'Yes, but what do you mean by household supplies?' said Vassily. 'Dishcloths, mops, soap – what?'

'How do I know?' said the cashier, an elderly lady with glasses that covered more than half the surface area of her face. 'Things like that, maybe. Yes – I think some soaps. Washing-up liquid, maybe, or detergent. Everyday things, like I said. Why?' she said, suddenly suspicious, and glancing around her as if spies might suddenly emerge from between the shelves. 'What does it matter if some woman buys stuff to keep her place running smoothly?'

'It matters if she's staying in a hotel,' said Olga, and adding in her mind, *And if she sounds like Sonia Alikovsky.* 'Besides, that's police business,' she went on, with a satisfied air, speaking before Vassily had a chance to. 'You can leave that to us!'

'Well said, Olga,' said Vassily, smiling at her as they left. 'Who knows? You might end up in the police yourself, one of these days.'

Olga sighed, her own smile fading away as she thought of Boris Andreyev and his schemes to replace her with a floating robot. 'I might have to,' she said. 'I might just have to.'

They heard the troupe before they saw them. No sooner had the squeaks and rattles of Vassily's geriatric Volvo died away than they heard raised voices floating out of open windows on the ground floor.

'Not there, Lev, for God's sake,' came a voice, as Olga got out of the car – Agapa Putyatin's voice, she thought, raised in irritation.

'Yes, do try to remember the instructions in the script, my dear fellow,' came a gentler voice – Ilya Putyatin's, thought Olga, picturing his serene countenance.

'I'm just trying to improvise a little,' came a testy voice in response – that of Lev Myatlev, presumably. 'Is that a crime?'

'Lev . . . isn't he the engineer from the train crew?' said Vassily to Olga, as they walked towards the main entrance to the sound of vigorous disagreements.

'They must have commandeered him to fill Rodion's shoes,' said Olga, pushing open the door. 'They haven't got much time, though – it's only five hours or so, isn't it, until the performance today?'

'Then they won't welcome us,' said Vassily, following her inside and blinking as his eyes adjusted to the gloom of the heavily curtained reception area.

'One of them won't,' muttered Olga, pausing at the breakfast-room door and running her hands up her arms.

'What is it, Olga?' said Vassily.

'I don't know,' she said. 'I was cold, all of a sudden – cold and shivery.'

'A draught, maybe?'

'I don't think so,' she said. 'Oh, Vassily, I'm afraid! Everyone's so eager to carry on as if nothing had happened, but isn't there a murderer – or murderers – in that room? There must be, surely, unless Rodion was killed by some expert assassin from outside.'

The shadowy figure she had seen in Roslazny leaped nimbly into her mind, as well as the person she had seen creeping down the path outside Café Astana when she'd heard Rodion speaking on the phone – but she pushed them out of her thoughts again and continued: 'What if they haven't finished?' she said to Vassily. 'What if they kill again?'

Vassily looked down at her, the urgency clear in her staring eyes, and nodded. 'You're right, Olga – you're right! But don't worry, I'm here. I'm on the case, as are you. Together we'll find him, or her, and put a stop to it all.'

'To it all? If only we could,' she replied.

Yegor Shulgin edged out of the breakfast room in response to their knock, and eased the door shut behind him.

He sucked the air through his teeth. 'It's a bit of a tricky one, to be honest,' he said, gazing earnestly at them through his thick glasses. 'We haven't got a lot of time.'

Vassily glanced at Olga.

'Oh, you haven't much time?' he said to Yegor, in the tone he sometimes used when Kliment hadn't got round to his homework. 'Well, let me tell you—'

'Listen, Yegor,' put in Olga. 'We want to find out what happened to Rodion, *da*? Surely that's something everyone wants to help with. We know there isn't much time – we just want to ask a few quick questions, that's all. You too, if that's all right – then people can get back to rehearsing. And – and not everyone's on stage at once, are they? Couldn't you send them out when they aren't needed for a few minutes?'

Yegor frowned, looking from Olga to Vassily, then back again. 'Well, I suppose that's true,' he said grudgingly. 'And of course we want to know what happened to Rodion. He was a real gent, you know. A rough diamond. No – a diamond in the rough, I mean. Look,' he went on, patting his pockets, and reaching first into one before quickly switching to the other. 'I've got the running order here,' he added, pulling out a crumpled piece of paper, 'so we can go by that. First we could do – we could do Ilya, Sonia and Pan together, and then Agapa and Larissa on their own.'

'Three of them at once?' said Vassily. 'I think we'd rather—'

But Olga interrupted him: 'That's fine, Yegor – bring the first group out. What?' she said to Vassily, shrugging. 'The others can check what she says.'

'What who says?' said Yegor, looking at her curiously.

'Never mind that,' she said. 'Just run along and bring the first three out!'

Vassily stared at her as Yegor frowned again, but turned nonetheless and went back into the breakfast room. 'Why don't I just let you run the whole thing?'

'I do wonder, sometimes,' said Olga. 'It would be much simpler.'

'That wasn't me,' said Sonia, quite firmly. 'It can't have been – can it, Pan? Ilya?'

Panteleimon chuckled. 'Afraid she's right, Vassily – I can

call you that, can't I? And Olga? But, yes, Sonia can't have been to the shops.'

'No, no, she couldn't possibly have obliged,' put in Ilya, his voice deep and resonant as if he were declaiming lines from Chekhov.

'Why not?' replied Vassily.

'She was with us,' said Panteleimon, winking and pointing a finger upwards, and prompting Olga's imagination to ascend from the frowsty hallway in which they stood to the equally frowsty guestrooms upstairs, where pink duvets and green pillowcases fought with an ochre-patterned wallpaper for the eye's horrified attention. Olga had visited the first floor once with Ekaterina Chezhekhov, who had arranged a rendezvous with a gentleman over the internet and wanted her support at their first meeting. Neither the room nor the gentleman had inspired much in the way of repeat business, nor benefited the hotel's reputation as a preferred location for romantic trysts, if romantic was the right word; and now Olga's mind boggled at the thought of what Sonia might have got up to with Panteleimon and the notably less virile, but still reasonably handsome, Ilya Putyatin.

Panteleimon, however, read her expression and hastened to disabuse her of any such lurid notions. 'No, no,' he laughed, 'nothing so shocking, I can assure you – it was just that I wanted help repairing my costume, and Sonia kindly agreed. But when we started picking a seam apart the whole thing had to be re-sewn . . . She was with us for hours – almost the whole morning before the play, and certainly during the time you mentioned.'

'We have to do these things ourselves, these days,' added Sonia, spreading a hand wide.

Olga sighed. Here was another dead end – though it was also a beginning: if Sonia hadn't bought the household supplies, which could very easily have included the bottle of antifreeze they'd found in Rodion's things, then who had? Someone disguised as Sonia, was the obvious answer – and who could pull that off? Any one of the actors, was the depressing reply. But at least it was something to think about.

'And you, Gospodin Putyatin?' said Vassily, after a moment, jotting notes in his little pad, then pointing the miniature pencil at Ilya. 'Why did you get involved in the costume repair?'

'Oh, well, I generally like to – to *oversee* these things, you understand,' said Ilya. 'It's my production, after all – well, mine and my wife's – and you have to stay on top of every little detail, or things get out of hand. Can you imagine a Rasputin with all his threads out of place, despite the tsarina and all the other women fussing over him? No, no, it wouldn't do at all – it wouldn't do.'

Vassily looked briefly at Olga, just a swivel of his eyes, but she could tell he was amused. They both knew a Rasputin, rather different in size and deportment, whose threads were never *in* place.

'Yes, we find Ilya's input just delightful.' Panteleimon grinned. 'So relaxing, so soothing, to have your every move inspected with a microscope, and fault still found with every little detail. I'm surprised he doesn't come to the bathroom with us, *nyet*, Sonia?'

Sonia flashed a smile at him, deliberately fake and fleeting, before pulling out a cigarette and lighting it in a rather hurried, irritated manner.

'You all smoke a lot, don't you?' observed Olga.

'So would you, if you lived our life, *dorogoya,*' said Sonia. 'So the hell would you.'

'You bought some apple cider vinegar in town on the morning of the first performance, we understand, Dama Putyatin,' said Vassily.

'How on earth did you know that?' breathed Agapa, with wide-open eyes.

'Never mind that,' said Olga, in what she hoped was a firm, business-like tone. She found Agapa's icy stare rather intimidating and was determined to hide it. 'Just answer the question, please.'

'Well,' she said, quite crossly, 'I suppose I'll have to, won't I, if it's a direct police order?'

'I'm afraid so, yes,' said Vassily, after a slight pause.

'Look,' she said, dropping her eyes, 'when you get older, your voice isn't . . . well, it isn't the same as it once was. And it's a bit of a strain projecting to a stand of seats like we've got in Roslazny – you don't get any help from the surrounds, you see, like you do in a proper auditorium. And so I – I—'

'You?' prompted Olga.

'Oh, I gargle it, if you must know,' she said, glaring at Olga as she burst out with a peal of unexpected laughter.

'Sorry, Dama Putyatin,' she said, quelled into unreasoning terror once more. 'Only – I didn't think you'd say that. But why would you gargle vinegar?'

'Apple cider vinegar,' corrected Agapa. 'There is a difference, you know. Oh, it's an old theatrical trick – I learned it from

Galina Belyayeva, back when I was an understudy at the Mayakovsky. But it wouldn't do for others to know about it,' she said, her voice suddenly switching from a tone of command to one of entreaty.

'You have to help me keep my secret, Inspector – from my husband, especially, but the others too,' she went on, looking at Vassily. 'I'm not as young as I once was,' she added, turning her head gently to the side in such a way that Olga felt herself responding with sympathy, though it was ridiculous: Agapa was far from being an old woman, and was really quite attractive, thought Olga, in a frosty kind of way. You had to watch yourself around these actors, said Olga to herself. They'd have your heart in a second, if you let them.

'Oh, yes, that's fine – fine,' said Vassily, looking, thought Olga, slightly abashed, as if he'd walked in on her getting changed. 'Fine.'

'What about the food?' said Olga, a trifle impatiently.

'Oh, yes,' said Vassily. 'Do you know who took the food inside when it arrived at the hotel from the restaurant the day before Rodion died – the takeaway from the Rising Sun?'

'I told you before, Inspector,' said Agapa Putyatin, to an audible sigh from Vassily, who didn't feel he could really tell her 'Sergeant' any more times. 'I wasn't there, remember? I was at the station.'

She stood before them, hands on hips, clearly impatient to get back to the rehearsal, whose noisy progress was clearly audible beyond the closed door that led to the breakfast room.

'We know that,' said Vassily, 'but we wondered if you'd *heard* anything from the others about the dinner – Yegor ordered it, we understand, but who suggested getting it from the Rising

Sun? Who received the food at the door, and who put it out on the table? Who threw it away, even – anything that might shed a bit of light on what happened.'

'I can't help, I'm afraid,' said Agapa, shaking her head irritably. She looked suddenly tired, Olga thought, and brittle somehow, as if one more setback for the troupe would finish her off.

'All I know is, the food was terrible,' Agapa continued. 'What a surprise, in this Godforsaken neck of the woods! No offence, but really . . . Why don't you speak to someone who was actually there? Now, can you excuse me, please? I've got a play to put together by lunchtime, and the rawest of raw material to work with.'

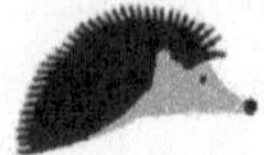

'She said *what*?' said Larissa Lazarov, eyes narrowing fiercely. 'That *suka*.'

'To be fair, Dama Putyatin didn't mention you specifically,' said Olga.

'Isn't one of the train crew filling in for Rodion Rultava?' said Vassily. 'Lev Myatlev? He's an engineer . . . Maybe that's what she meant.'

'What's being an engineer got to do with it?' asked Olga.

'Oh, nothing, nothing,' said Vassily, quickly. 'I just meant – well, since he's not used to acting . . .'

'Maybe,' replied Larissa, distracting Olga, to Vassily's relief. 'But she's been on my case since we got here. Agapa, I mean.'

'How so?' said Vassily, quite innocently.

'Oh, just digging around for this and that,' said Larissa,

glancing from Vassily to Olga and back again, as if she had said too much. 'Asking about my people, and suchlike – as if she were implying I didn't come from a good enough heritage to act in her troupe . . . But what's my family got to do with it? I don't want to talk to people about all that! I got into acting to get away from my past, not revel in it.'

'Anyway,' prompted Olga, after a moment's angry pause, 'Sergeant Marushkin here was asking about the food—'

'Oh, for God's sake,' snapped Larissa. 'I've told you everything already! Yegor ordered it from the Rising Sun – I can't remember why. Maybe Pan suggested it. He loves his food, you know,' she added, accompanied by a sideways glance between Vassily and Olga. 'So Yegor rang up and found out what they had available, and placed the order. Didn't take them long to get it out – I remember Sonia saying it was almost suspiciously quick, as if it had been heated up in a microwave. Who answered the door and took it in? Oh, I can't remember. Yegor, I suppose, as he ordered it. Yes, I think it was probably him. Or maybe it was Rodion. It could have been him . . . I can't remember, to be honest. Can I go now? Engineer or not, Lev Myatlev's a complete disaster as the colonel, and it's down to me to fix it. Oh, how I miss poor Rodion! That man knew how to act.'

'She said what?' said Yegor Shulgin, a few minutes later. 'No, no – it wasn't me who took the order in. I think it was Rodion, just from a glimpse I caught of the front door as I walked through the corridor . . . I did order it, yes, on Pan's suggestion – he'd walked past the place and thought it looked tolerable – but I was in the back room when it actually arrived, trying to get the maid to send an extra blanket up to my room.'

He took off his glasses and began to polish them on a corner of his shirt. What was it about him, wondered Olga, that reminded her so strongly of Fyodor Katin?

'I get cold in these winter nights, you see,' continued Yegor, and then Olga had it: it was the hint of fussiness, the faint impression that he could do with a strong injection of common sense from some external source. 'And by the time I'd sorted that out and got back into the breakfast room, everything was already arranged. Didn't the others tell you?'

They hadn't, of course, and Olga thought she knew why: Yegor was the kind of person whose presence – or absence – you wouldn't really notice. Since he had ordered the food, and was almost always around to take care of things for the troupe, everyone had assumed that he'd also taken in the food. But Yegor's assertion that he had been absent at the time of delivery, and that Rodion had probably been the one who took the food inside, had the ring of authenticity, to Olga's ears at least. That would have given Rodion, and probably him alone, the chance to put antifreeze into one of the dinners, and maybe something else into all the rest. But given the choice of all the dinners, Olga wondered, why would he poison his own?

'It must have been meant for someone else,' said Vassily, a little later, getting into the Volvo and closing his door with a solid thump. 'Someone bought the stuff dressed up as Sonia, right?

So maybe it was Rodion who bought it to poison some other member of the troupe.'

'Yes, but who? We can't exactly ask Rodion now,' replied Olga, closing her door in turn.

Vassily shook his head, then suddenly reached his left arm behind Olga's head. She almost gasped, then realised he was only turning to see where he was reversing to, rolling slowly, then quickly, back into the road that led to the station, before spinning the wheel and heading forwards, back to Roslazny, once more.

'We've been asking the wrong questions,' he said, as Olga tried to calm herself. 'We've been focusing too much on *how* Rodion was killed, and not thinking enough about *why* anybody was killed at all. Because if we think about *anybody*, of course we have to include Rodion. People make mistakes – and it's hard to imagine someone like him having a secret criminal past. But maybe he was willing to risk a criminal future to get rid of someone who'd threatened him, or blackmailed him . . . We've been asking the wrong questions!'

Vassily looked so annoyed with himself – so genuinely upset and angry – that Olga felt obliged to respond with encouraging words, though she privately agreed that they had made a poor start to the investigation.

'So – we regroup,' she said. 'Give them today to put their play on and recover themselves, and while they carouse' – Vassily laughed: 'Carouse?' he said, with a smile – 'while they *carouse*,' she said, more firmly, 'which is what actors do in the evenings, you and I will put our heads together and make a new plan of action. Well,' she went on, 'not put our heads together. I mean – you know what I mean. We'll work together, in the police station. Rozalina will be there,' she continued, feeling more and more uncomfortable and wishing she would stop talking, 'and Kliment, too, of course. It's a family home as well as a workplace, don't forget! And then – then,' she went on, feeling the blood rushing into her cheeks despite all her best intentions, 'we'll pay another visit tomorrow morning and find out what we can. After all,' she summed up, speaking with an almost desperate intent to avoid saying anything awkward, 'we make a pretty good team. Not that you need my help, of course, but—'

'Olga,' said Vassily, smiling across at her in that relaxed way he had, 'don't worry! Of course we can start again. There's plenty of time,' he went on, putting on his indicator and turning into the road that led to the village. 'The actors aren't going anywhere! The play's still got days and days to run. We've got all the time in the world.'

As it turned out, however, they didn't – not because the play came to an abrupt end, like last time, but because rather more decisive means came into force.

The play, in fact, was a great success, performed in front of a capacity audience who had been generously lubricated by a combination of Mikhail Pushkin and Vladimir Solotov's Red Star stall, on the right-hand side of the stand, and Igor Odrosov's newly established Rocket Fuel stall, on the left-hand side of the stand, thrown together on the strength of his upcoming vodka franchise, and doling out blue-tinged shots at the discount price of fifty roubles apiece. Many of the audience were repeat guests who had come, Olga guessed, to see if anything untoward might occur once more to amplify the entertainment on offer, but there were also several new faces from Tayga and beyond, attracted by word of mouth and discount tickets offered to friends of friends.

Among the familiars were Captain Zemsky, who nodded sharply at Vassily when he arrived with Rozalina and Kliment, and – less welcome still – Olga's superior Boris Andreyev, who insisted on Olga occupying her old place by the buffers despite her unofficial secondment to the police for the duration of the case.

'Just because there's an engineer in the play, don't go getting all hoity-toity,' he said to her, when she arrived. 'I used to act at school, you know. I should be up there myself,' he went on, jerking his fur Ushanka hat at the stage beyond Olga's head.

'It'd be pretty good comedy if you were,' muttered Olga, and then more loudly, in response to Andreyev's barked words of enquiry, 'Oh, nothing, sir – just saying it'd be good if you were. Yes, enjoy the show. I'll be here enjoying myself, as usual, at my station.'

Olga had spoken with mild sarcasm, as she often did to Andreyev, but somewhat to her surprise she found her words coming true. This was partly because of the weather: the sun came out unexpectedly just before the curtain rose, bathing the train and its audience in a serene and limpid light and reminding Olga how long its gentle rays had been smothered in damp and leaden skies. But it was also because of the play itself, which proceeded along its course with surprising ease given the events of two days before, and considering that the role of Colonel Glazunov was now being played by a suborned railway engineer. Lev Myatlev, in fact, acted his role with admirable competence, needing only four or five whispered prompts from Yegor Shulgin, whose bespectacled countenance Olga could see hovering behind the door that led to the second carriage.

Responding to the troupe's energetic performance, the crowd followed the drama with eager attention, often supplemented – thanks to the plentiful vodka – with a chorus of exclamations and laughter, and frequently punctuated with the sound of winter boots clumping up and down the steps to the outdoor lavatories that stood behind the seating like giant plastic dominoes. As the Murder Express wound on to its unlikely close – in which Colonel Glazunov banishes Rasputin to Tashkent, rallies the army to rout the Bolsheviks, and generally saves the empire of the tsars – the audience was roused to fervent applause and to a peal of cheers and shouts of 'Bravo, brava!' for each actor who appeared once more on stage and bowed deep down towards the polished wooden floor.

Swept along with the crowd despite her forced abstinence from Rocket Fuel, Olga had found it possible temporarily to forget the stalled investigation into Rodion's death – an investigation in which every new lead encountered an irrefutable contradiction in alibis and circumstances, and in which the most likely suspect had turned out to be Rodion Rultava himself, yet without any obvious motive or even basic logic to support this unsatisfactory conclusion. For if Rodion had wanted to kill himself, why not simply drink the antifreeze in his room? Then no disguise would have been necessary, no elaborate scheme to dress up as Sonia and buy some household supplies in some Tayga shop picked at random. And if, on the other hand, he *had* wanted to kill someone else, why do so in such an evidently unsafe manner that he might end up dead himself – as indeed he had?

These and other questions formed the basis of Olga's discussion with Vassily later that afternoon, taking place – as

Olga had foreseen – in the presence of Rozalina and Kliment at the police station.

'I loved the play, Olga, didn't you?' said Kliment, as they walked back together after the show, Captain Zemsky and Boris Andreyev having grudgingly released them from their immediate duties. 'It was good to – to forget about everything else for a while.'

'I did enjoy it, yes,' said Olga, 'though I didn't have as good a view as you! I was down by the buffers, don't forget.'

'Well, someone's got to do those kinds of jobs, I suppose,' said Rozalina.

'And we're lucky that she does,' added Vassily, quickly. 'Lucky, too, that Boris let you go, Olga! I thought he'd make you stay till they moved the train.'

As a result of Lev Myatlev joining the cast at short notice, several vital maintenance tasks had not yet been performed on the vast P36 steam engine – which meant the crew had to make plans to move the train back to Tayga later that day.

'It's a damn nuisance, Lev,' Simeon Zarubin had said to the engineer, as the troupe began packing things away after the last curtain-call. 'Ideas above your station, that's what it is, and only because you look more like the dead 'un than me and Vad do. Ha – did you hear that, Vad? Above your station?'

'You railway people all tell the same jokes,' said Vassily, when Olga related the conversation as they arrived at the police station. 'But, then, what do you expect? You can't steer a train, can you? Anyway – let's go through into the back office. Rozalina, or – or maybe, Kliment, could you get the samovar going? We'll have some tea – I could do with something other than vodka.'

'Odrosov's going to town on his new plans,' observed Olga.

'He's already taken out a loan from the bank in Tayga,' said Vassily, clearing a space for her to sit on the wooden bench that ran along the side wall of the office. 'Zemsky told me – he drinks with the manager. And I hear big renovations are planned for the café, too. And he hasn't seen a bean from the franchise people yet!'

'A tomtit in the hands . . .' she began, but Vassily finished, '. . . is better than a crane in the sky.'

'Well, we'll see what happens there,' said Olga, smiling at him. 'I hope it's all above board – not least because it will annoy my father to see Igor outstrip him in sales. Oh – thanks, Kliment,' she went on, as Vassily's son came into the room with two *podstakanniki* filled with tea, the hot amber liquid gleaming through the glass and sending fragrant eddies of steam into the air. 'Just the ticket,' she added, to a groan from Vassily.

'Please, no more puns,' he said. 'Let's get to the matter in hand, shall we? Time to update the board.'

He got up and went to the far wall, taking chalk in hand and adding what little new information they had to the chart Olga had already drawn, talking animatedly as they struggled to make sense of what they had seen and heard. Kliment was called to bring more tea as night began to fall, and as the light faded Vassily lit gas lanterns to supplement the meagre electric light bulb that hung disconsolately from the cracked ceiling, and set fire to the small pile of kindling and scrap paper that lay in the stove by the corner of the desk, sparks flying up the tubular chimney and out into the cold and starry night.

At one point, Olga set down her cup and smiled inwardly. This was one of the things she loved so much about Vassily – his enthusiasm for justice, for solving crimes, for doing the right thing, when so many others were content to take the easiest path, like a meandering flood finding a hill to trickle down. He looked at her then, his eyes kindling with the red of reflected firelight, and Olga's heart turned over.

Realising that he was waiting for her to answer him, but not having heard what he had said, she opened her lips to say something of a general nature – but at that instant a thunderous knocking came upon the front door, making them jump and, by the sound of a falling chair in the reception area, making Kliment jump too.

Vassily ran through and flung open the door. Vadim Lilov, the P36 fireman, was standing in front of him.

'Sergeant – Marushkin,' he panted, trying to catch his breath. 'You've got to – come back to – the tracks. We just moved the train and – and we ran someone over!'

'You – what?' cried Vassily, pulling Vadim into the station. Olga saw that his hands and chest were covered in the dark crimson of freshly shed blood.

'Yes, we – we ran over one of the – one of the actors,' went on Vadim, tears now coming to his eyes. 'One of the women. Oh, God – we killed her!'

'Who?' said Olga. 'Which actor was it?'

'Larissa,' moaned Vadim, burying his head in his hands, then lifting it up to glare at them with tortured eyes. 'We killed Larissa Lazarov!'

7
Locked Doors

'No, don't, Olga,' cried Vassily. 'Please – I don't want you to. Nobody should have to witness things like that.'

He flung out a strong arm to block her way, and she made as if to wrest it aside – but then she paused, heaved a deep sigh, and told herself that Vassily was right: that nothing good could come of rushing to the tracks where Larissa had breathed her last – that she could render no aid, but might herself be stricken with things she could never unsee. The night was heavy with fragrant wood-smoke from the nearby houses, and the zing of steam and hot metal from the P36 a few feet to her left, which was still hissing out hot white clouds like a sleeping dragon. But there was something else, too – a tang of salt, a loathsome slipperiness to the air that made her almost gag as she breathed it. It was blood, Olga realised – blood, and the mortal remains of Larissa Lazarov, split apart by a hundred tons of steel concentrated in the rim of a driving wheel and pressed upon the glittering metal rail with irresistible and fatal force until Larissa – until Larissa—

No, Olga thought, no. She would not sully that beautiful girl's memory by thinking of how she had died, or the overwhelming horror that must have swept over her in her last seconds or fragments of seconds, the sudden and appalling certainty that the gleaming engine they had all so admired would be the last thing her eyes ever saw.

Vassily stepped forward and quietly placed his padded police jacket around her. 'Where are the ropes we used to cordon off the train last time?' he said, speaking as softly as he could over the P36 and its sibilant murmurings. 'When Rodion died?'

Olga stirred, struggling to channel her thoughts away from the outlandish scenarios that ran through her mind in a vain attempt to piece together what might have caused such a horrendous accident – scenarios that kept returning, time and again, to the fact that the train crew must have got it wrong, Vadim and Lev and Simeon, catastrophically wrong, for a beautiful young woman to perish beneath their wheels.

'The ropes?' she said, her thoughts still distant. 'Ropes – oh, the cordon. Yes, they're still round here, I'm sure. Lev told me he'd tucked them away out of sight, before he joined the troupe – maybe behind the stand, near the toilets? I'll go and have a look.'

'No – I'll go,' said Vassily, looking closely at Olga and taking in her distracted gaze and pale cheeks. 'Why don't you sit down for a minute – catch your breath?'

'Oh, I'm fine, Vassily – really, I am,' she replied, but so half-heartedly that he didn't bother to argue, setting off into the night, torch in hand, already scanning the uneven ground ahead of his feet. As if sensing her eyes upon him, he half turned and gestured vigorously at the seats to his right, before moving on and disappearing into the darkness.

Olga sighed, but nonetheless followed her instructions

and went to the stand, sinking onto one of the hard wooden benches and lifting her head to take in the scene that lay before her, lit dimly and fitfully by the faint glow of the light bulbs strung along the top level. The P36 locomotive was to her right, a vast apparatus of rods and pipes and wheels bound together with rings of steel, and alive still with a fiery blaze at its heart: Olga could just see a red glint in the growing darkness, and imagined – no, almost felt in her fingertips and on the lids of her eyes – the fierce, scorching heat that flowed out of the open fire-door and into the cramped surrounds of the engine cab, where driver and fireman worked in tightly coiled routines of efficient, coal-stained movements. Or, at least, they did in normal circumstances, but these were far from normal circumstances, and Olga could see the shadowed outline of Simeon Zarubin, the driver, standing against the back of the cab and rocking from one foot to the other, then back again, and again, in an endless chain of movement, a silent expression of the agony that he must have been living through, the desperate beating-heart hollowness that follows terrible things.

Behind the engine was the tender, painted in identical green livery and bearing vast, all-but-untouched stores of coal and water; and still further to the left were the two period carriages that served as the dressing room and stage for the Murder Express. The carriages were quiet now and dead-looking, with the movable side returned to its normal position on the first carriage, and with no lights to be seen in either this or its rearwards counterpart. The actors weren't there, Vadim had told them – Vadim Lilov, that is, the crew fireman, who had run to fetch them from the Roslazny police station, and who was still there, as far as they knew, being attended to by Kliment and (no doubt reluctantly) by Rozalina also. He'd left Simeon in charge of the locomotive, Vadim had added, while he ran to get help.

'But it was an accident, really it was – we didn't know she was there. Oh, God – we didn't know she was there!'

Vassily had reassured Vadim that they believed him, and indeed it had been hard not to believe him, when in full sight of his tortured countenance – but now, back at the track, in the falling night and only yards from the ruined body of Larissa Lazarov, it was hard to know what to think. There was a killer among them, Olga reminded herself, assuming that Rodion Rultava hadn't after all committed suicide by mistake – and she kept thinking back to the shadowy figure she'd seen running through the outskirts of Roslazny like a wraith, and the unknown man walking past Café Astana. Had Larissa, too, met her end by an accident that was not, in the end, an accident at all? How could someone fall under the wheels of a steam engine, without some malicious hand applying fierce pressure at just the wrong moment?

There was no time to dwell on such speculations, however, for at that moment two different events occurred more or less simultaneously: Vassily returned from the darkness beyond the stand, holding a pile of wooden stakes and dragging a long loop of rope behind him, while at the same time a group of people came noisily down the path that led back to the village, half walking, half running, and conversing in loud tones of grief and disbelief.

'Larissa,' wailed one voice, which Olga knew but temporarily couldn't place, 'Larissa – no, it can't be true, not Larissa!'

The owner of the voice came around the corner, and Olga saw it was Yegor Shulgin – of course it had been his slightly anonymous tones, rather than one of the actors' distinctive voices, that she'd struggled to place – Yegor Shulgin, and beside him the remaining actors: Ilya and Agapa Putyatin, Sonia Alikovsky, and Panteleimon Pomelov, with Lev Myatlev, whose engineering background had apparently not precluded an invitation to join the troupe for drinks and dinner, such as it was, at Mikhail Pushkin's newly established Red Star restaurant. But their faces, pale and stretched, and framing wide, staring eyes already shot with despairing tears, showed that any thoughts of their evening's entertainment were far from their minds.

Vassily turned in surprise as they arrived at the tracks, and – dropping the cordon on the ground – advanced with arms outstretched to prevent any further movement.

'Stop here, please,' he said. 'We need to keep the scene untouched.'

'Don't say – don't tell us she was *murdered*,' breathed Agapa Putyatin, hands over her chest.

'*C-Calm* yourself, my dear,' said Ilya, placing a hand on her shoulder, though his voice quivered. 'Vadim – Vadim said nothing of that when he called you.'

'Oh, come on,' said Panteleimon loudly, angrily, even, though his eyes were full of sorrow. 'Rodion dies, then two days later Larissa goes, too, and you think it's a coincidence? Somebody's after us, and I want to find out who before any more people die. This is your job, Sergeant! How are you going to keep us safe?'

'An excellent question,' boomed another voice, but not one that belonged to any of the troupe or train crew. Olga could make no mistake about its owner, however, not this time, for it belonged to no other person than Captain Konstantin Zemsky, head of the Tayga police, who (Olga now saw) was accompanied once more by Junior Sergeant Timofei Davidov.

'An excellent question, indeed,' said Zemsky again. 'So tell us, Marushkin – how *are* you going to keep them safe?'

Vassily's response had been simple but effective: he had forestalled Zemsky's criticisms by taking the bold step of asking the troupe and train crew to get back onto the carriages, installing each person in their own separate compartment, and locking the doors behind them – for their own safety, he told them, while the events surrounding the death of Larissa Lazarov were investigated.

'Let them stew for a while,' Vassily said, stepping back down from the ladder. 'We'll speak to them all in a bit, but I'm not hurrying anything – I want to get to the bottom of what happened here, accident or otherwise.'

He glanced up at the P36, then turned quickly to Davidov, who was following him down the ladder. 'Davidov, go to the police station while I get this cordon up, would you, and get Vadim Lilov to join us? He can go onboard, too. Until we work out what's going on, I don't want him hanging around my son. Or – or my wife.'

Was it Olga's imagination or did Vassily hesitate a little over the last of his words, as if in some private doubt? But Vassily was still speaking, and Olga attempted to force all thoughts of his private life from her mind.

'And call someone from the depot at Tayga,' he said. 'Get someone out here to look after the engine while we interview everyone.'

Zemsky nodded at Vassily, seemingly impressed, as Davidov pulled out his torch and scurried off towards the village. Olga was impressed, too. Until Vassily had taken the drastic step of commandeering the Murder Express train as an impromptu police station, Captain Zemsky had had the strong air of a superior officer about to pull rank and take over the investigation. He'd even made a song and dance about how he'd heard about the death, via a phone call from Boris Andreyev (who'd heard it from Vadim Lilov), rather than via official police channels from Vassily. But now he seemed mollified, bending his head close to Vassily's and discussing the details of the case as if nothing had ever gone wrong between them.

Yes, decisive action was the key, thought Olga, and then a second thought came to mind, following the first like a tender or carriage: what similar action could she take to forestall the planned closure of her rail-side hut?

But then she tutted, reproaching herself and glad that Vassily couldn't read her thoughts. Larissa Lazarov had died – yet another death in Roslazny, and yet again by the tracks – and here was Olga, thinking selfish thoughts first about Vassily's wife and then her own career! No: there *were* things she could usefully do, but they were small, undramatic, hidden things – helpful things that nobody would hear about, but which would be useful things to accomplish, all the same – things for others instead of herself. Those were the things she should be thinking about.

'Vassily, let's get the train generator going,' she said, across his murmured conversation with Zemsky. 'It's cold enough now, and it's going to freeze overnight, they say, so they'll need heating. Then I'll go to the village and bring back some food for everyone – we can set up in the first carriage and interview people there.'

'Excellent work, Pushkin,' said Zemsky. 'Your father's set up a restaurant now, hasn't he? Is that where you're going?'

'Not exactly,' said Olga. 'I follow a different star.'

'Well, don't take too long tracking it down,' said Zemsky. 'I want progress tonight, Marushkin, d'you hear? Tonight! I've got something to look into in Suranovo' – a small town to the north-west of Tayga – 'and I've got to get to Kemerovo later, so I can't stay. But I'll be waiting for your call to update me later on. Doesn't matter how late it is, Marushkin,' he said, beginning to walk away, and raising his collar around his ears. 'I never sleep when there's murder to sniff out!'

'Bet you never thought you'd be dining on a royal train, Olga,' said Vassily, raising an imitation crystal goblet and inclining it towards her.

'Ha,' she said, looking around her and taking in the rich velvet furnishings, delicate gaslights arranged at regular intervals along the walls, and elegant little chairs and sofas upholstered in brocade. 'Maybe not,' she said, 'but it's hardly food fit for a tsar, is it?'

She took another mouthful of the Café Astana borscht, before grimacing and putting down her spoon. 'Obviously I'm on Igor's side, and not my father's,' she went on, 'but really, he's got to churn out better food than this if he wants to beat the Red Star.'

'He might still manage it,' said Vassily, through a mouthful of Stolichny rye bread. 'Igor should have plenty of money to work with, if he plays his cards right – and if the franchise pans out.'

'I'll believe that when I see it,' said Olga. 'It sounds like one of Bogdan Kabalevsky's schemes to me.'

Vassily flashed a wry smile at Olga's reference to Anna's husband, last seen fleeing the region after falling foul of some loan-sharks with interests in adult films, and with a long list of failed business endeavours to his discredit.

'Well, beggars can't be choosers, I suppose,' he said. 'We were lucky Odrosov had enough to feed the whole troupe. And speaking of which—'

'Yes, I know,' said Olga, finishing her glass of Rocket Fuel. 'We should start talking to them all again. But, Vassily, this is the third time we'll have interviewed them, and without much to show for it!'

'Don't I know it,' he muttered, taking a last bite of bread and dropping the rest on his plate without much regret. 'We're getting nowhere . . . You heard what Zemsky said. We've got to find a better way in somehow, or – or – well, I don't know what will happen. Worst case, someone else dies – but even if they don't, the Murder Express will almost certainly be shut down, and that'd spell disaster for you and me, via Boris Andreyev and Zemsky. The way this whole thing's been set up, it's got Arkady Nazarov all over it.'

'The Mayor of Kemerovo? Boris told me the same thing.'

'Mm – well, trust Boris to know! I wouldn't be surprised if he's in on the deal. It could even be a money-laundering operation – they love cash businesses, you know.'

Olga got up and walked over to the windows overlooking the stand.

'A new way in,' she murmured to herself. 'A new way in . . .'

'What's that?' said Vassily, getting up and joining her.

She continued to gaze out at the dimly lit stand for another moment. Then her expression cleared, and she turned to him.

'You said we need a new way in? Well, here we are!'

'Here we are – where?'

'The siding! Don't you see, Vassily?'

'I really don't.'

'Well, think about what happens when they make a new siding off the main line. They don't do it very often, these days, but they used to do it all the time. And the people who did it were blazing a trail – breaking new ground, you see?'

Vassily began to nod, out of politeness, but honesty won after all and he admitted frankly that, no, he didn't see at all.

'Those engineers were out of their comfort zone, Vassily! They were used to maintaining track, and suddenly they were laying it. They were used to working on the main line, but then they were out in the middle of nowhere. And anyone who lived in those areas could see them, and would know them for strangers.'

'All right,' said Vassily. 'I think I'm following you, so far – but what does that have to do with the Murder Express?'

'Well, look at this way – everyone on our suspect list has a clean record, *da*? No murders, or attempted suicides, or anything like that? Good. So they've all been like engineers working on the main line. But now one of them—'

'Or more,' muttered Vassily. 'We can't limit it to Rodion.'

'Now one or more of them has broken out and started laying

a new bit of track – a murderous line of work, with two deaths to their name and maybe more to come. But perhaps if we can think of them in that way – as someone new to the field, then—'

'Then we can get to grips with them,' said Vassily. 'Of course, Olga! You're right – we should be thinking of them as novices, not experienced killers. They're probably panicking at this very moment, worried in case they've made some major mistake, desperately trying to keep up the façade of normality, like—'

'Like a track crew deep in the back end of nowhere and terrified of the locals,' said Olga.

'This is very good,' said Vassily, pacing up and down the highly polished floor, and weaving around the little tables and planters that dotted the carriage. 'And maybe – maybe that means we need to let them be who they really are . . . We need to let them feel in the back end of nowhere – to feel terrified.'

He turned on his heel and pointed a finger at Olga. 'Yes, Olga! I see it now. I – we – have been asking them too many questions! We should let them speak more – give them enough rope to hang themselves with. I knew a police captain up in Novosibirsk who thought criminals hated silence more than anything – that they saw themselves mirrored in its emptiness and didn't like it . . .'

'So – we're on the look-out for nervous talkers,' said Olga. 'Good thing Fyodor Katin's not a suspect!'

'Ha,' said Vassily, breaking into a smile. 'Fyodor's only really nervous around Anna Kabalevsky. But no doubt you know more about that than I do?'

Olga smiled. 'We'll have to wait and see. Dr Zinovev's interested too. Who knows what will happen? Sometimes things seem about to go one way, and then they go another.'

Vassily looked at her for a long moment, then turned away. 'I know that,' he said. 'Oh, yes, I know that very well indeed.'

'I told you already,' said Simeon Zarubin. 'We had to move the loco, see,' he said, 'as time was running out to get to the workshop at Tayga. The locomotive, I mean – the P36. This old girl needs constant work done – don't you, you old *suka*?' he called, turning in the direction of the engine at the front of the royal carriage. 'Anyway, we'd got everything loaded up and tied down, so I tipped the wink to Vad and Lev and opened her up.'

'You mean – you started the engine?' said Olga.

'Not really. The steam's already up, see? You don't start an engine, you just take the brake off, bung her in gear and open the regulator. So that's what I did – only then I heard this terrible noise, as if we'd got a leak somewhere.'

'What kind of noise?' put in Vassily.

'Well, it was screaming, wasn't it? That Larissa woman,' said Simeon. 'Anyway, I didn't know that then, but I put the brake on anyway – it's safety procedure. Then I looked out and saw – and saw—'

'Here,' said Vassily, pushing a glass of vodka towards him. 'Take your time,' he added, imagining the horror of Larissa's gory death relived in Simeon's mind.

'Well – you know what I seen,' he continued, after a pause and a sip. 'Fair turned my stomach – but I can't see as how anyone can blame me. How did I know she'd be there? And even if I did, why the hell did she jump under the wheels like that? Suicide, is what it is – same as that actor chappie. What's his name? Rultava.'

'You can't blame yourself for it,' put in Olga, remembering him rocking from side to side in the cab as if replaying the disaster in his mind. But his answer surprised her.

'Oh, I don't! I'm more annoyed, if I'm honest – we get these people now and again, see. It's part of the job. And then I'm stuck freezing my balls off, pardon my French, hopping from foot to foot in the cab just to keep warm.

'It's these artistic types,' he continued, as Vassily and Olga glanced at each other. 'Can't take the pressure, see – not like us railway people, eh, Devushka Pushkin?'

'It's Dama,' she said, but Simeon didn't take any notice, continuing to expound the virtues of a railway life until Vassily interrupted.

'Yes, yes, it's the life of kings,' he said, quite sharply. 'But did you actually see Larissa down by the tracks – Larissa, or anyone else?'

'Apart from Vad and Lev, you mean? Not a soul.'

'Nobody?' said Olga. 'You didn't even see Larissa?'

'Nope,' said Simeon, his eyes darting between them. 'Look, am I under suspicion here, or something?'

Vassily didn't reply, merely gazing steadily at Simeon until the driver shifted in his chair, a slight Victorian affair, which creaked uncomfortably under his substantial weight. Simeon cleared his throat, looked again between Vassily and Olga, and began to sweat on his forehead.

'All right, all right,' he said at last, 'I'll tell you, though it's not worth the paper it isn't written on. I might – I *might* – have left the train for a minute or two. I needed to empty the old onboard steam valve, if you take my meaning, and I don't like doing it in the cab. You've got to put up with the smell then, don't you? And so what if I had a quick smoke while I was at it? Then I got back in and it was time to go.'

'So – what, you were out of the cab for five minutes or more? On which side?'

Simeon nodded towards the back wall. 'That side. Wasn't going to risk any busybodies coming to tidy up the seats, or something, and seeing the fire hose at work, was I?'

'Why didn't you just say so in the first place?' said Vassily.

'It's against regulations to leave the cab while steam's up,' said Olga, while Simeon nodded almost self-righteously, as if she had scored a point in his defence.

'That's why we've got Yefim Burtsov from the depot on the footplate now, to replace Lev while he's acting, or whatever he's doing,' said Simeon. 'Though between you and me, Yefim isn't the best at steam engines. Let's just hope he don't blow us up, eh!'

Vassily's eyes swung nervously towards the front of the train, but Olga carried on talking. 'All right, so you didn't see anything by the tracks. What about the others in the crew?'

'Well, Lev's no use – he was out with his fancy new friends. You could ask Vad. He was down the back end, beyond the last carriage. We think there's a brake leak, though I'm buggered if I can find it . . . But he's no use either, if I'm honest. He swallows every kind of conspiracy theory going. Did you know he's got a survival bunker packed full of tinned vegetables? I think he volunteers in some kind of neighbourhood watch scheme, too – so he's primed to see things when they aren't there, understand?'

'We'll be the judge of that,' said Vassily, his eyes swinging back towards the large figure of the driver. 'You can go back to your compartment for now.'

'Going to be more snacks, is there?' said Simeon, standing up to what sounded like a sigh of relief from his overloaded chair.

'We'll see,' said Vassily. 'I'm hoping this won't take all night.'

But it did take all night, or very nearly – so long, indeed, that Vassily ended up sending Junior Sergeant Davidov back to Café Astana for a second round of victuals, though as these were composed of Igor Odrosov's end-of-night cast-offs they were not very well received by the troupe.

'What's this rubbish? Prison food?' said the second-last of their interviewees, Agapa Putyatin, who joined them in the royal carriage at nearly ten o'clock. She looked exhausted, thought Olga, and was almost slumping rather than sitting in one of the high-backed chairs that lined the back wall. Her eyes were red-rimmed, and her make-up – usually thickly applied – seemed to have faded from her pale skin, as if worn thin by the events of the day.

'Never mind the Stroganoff,' said Vassily. 'We want to know what you heard about arrangements today.'

'Arrangements?'

'Yes, arrangements,' he replied tersely. 'How things got arranged.'

'What – with Larissa, do you mean? How should I know?'

'You tell us,' said Olga.

'I didn't know anything about it,' said Agapa. 'All I know is that she wasn't with us at the Red Star. She'd made some excuse – an urgent meeting, or something like that – but she didn't say anything to me.'

'Who did she say it to, then?' said Vassily.

'Search me,' she said, staring back at him with a firmness that impressed Olga, in the circumstances. Olga was tired enough herself, at the end of a long and traumatic day – but Agapa, who was considerably older, must be yet more exhausted. She was grieving a second colleague who had died unexpectedly, after all, and was possibly about to witness the disastrous end of her latest theatrical enterprise to boot . . . Olga would have forgiven her for crumpling into a heap and giving up. But that clearly wasn't the Putyatin way of doing things.

'Why don't you ask the others?' Agapa went on. 'I'm sure one of them will know. But wait – it's late. You already have, haven't you? And now you're checking to see if I say the same thing?'

Once more, Olga was impressed: there was shrewdness as well as strength behind Agapa's eyes. For, of course, that was precisely what they were doing. Quite early on they'd heard from Yegor Shulgin that Larissa had sent her apologies for the Red Star dinner, claiming she had to make some important phone calls. But Sonia Alikovsky, a couple of interviews later, had said she thought Larissa was going to meet Panteleimon Pomelov, the long-haired Rasputin impersonator. When pressed, though, she had struggled to substantiate her impression with anything concrete.

'I don't know why,' she'd said. 'Maybe something she'd mentioned.'

'I imagine so, yes,' Vassily had replied patiently, 'but can you remember what, precisely?'

Sonia had sighed. 'I'm sorry, no.' Then she'd become annoyed. 'Why should you think I would remember, anyway?'

'Well, because you work with words all the time, don't you? As an actor?'

Sonia had laughed then, flicking her hair over the shoulder of her blue leather jacket, leaning back in her chair, and crossing her long legs. '*Dorogoy, dorogoy*,' she said, in best theatrical tradition – darling, darling. 'Did you really think we know about words just because we learn them for a living? Have you ever seen an email written by an actor? Most of us can barely put one letter in front of another.

'Come to think of it, though,' she'd added, uncrossing her legs and sitting forward once more, 'Rodion was always writing things down. That little black book of his – did you ever find it? No? Pity. You should try harder – that would probably help find his murderer, I should think.'

'Thank you, Dama Alikovsky,' Vassily had said, with a somewhat forced smile. 'That's good advice. But for today we're focusing on the events that led up to Larissa's death.'

'Well, try talking to our esteemed director, then,' Sonia had responded. 'He had the hots for her, I'm sure of it. Did you see him down by the track? The way his upper lip was quivering, holding back tears? He put a brave face on it, but I'd say he's a strong candidate for another early departure – death by broken heart. Agapa's not as young as she used to be, you know, Inspector.'

'The *hots*?' cried Ilya Putyatin a few minutes later, his Olympian countenance unusually animated. 'Sonia said I *had the hots* for Larissa Lazarov? The slang these young people use . . . And Sonia an actor, too – what happened to enamoured, entranced, captivated, besotted, infatuated, smitten, head-over-heels, lovesick?'

'Well, our concern isn't so much with her language, as with—' began Olga, but Ilya cut in.

'No, no, I quite understand – that was in parenthesis. As to the rub, if I might borrow from the Bard, I can state quite unequivocally that I did not *have the hots* for Larissa. I am married to the theatre.'

'And to Agapa,' put in Olga.

'And, indeed, to Agapa,' carried on Ilya, 'but the point I am making is simply this: my concern with that poor young lady, now tragically departed from this vale of tears, was purely dramatic. She was contemplating leaving the stage for more – ahem – *humdrum* employment elsewhere, and I was concerned to change her mind. She had considered taking a job in some office somewhere – attached to a factory, I believe, of all places! – and this I simply could not countenance, however much they had offered her. Though now, of course, the matter is moot: Larissa has escaped indeed, though to happier climes than these – and a happier fate, one might say. After all, what is life away from the boards? A succession of drab and dreary meetings, deadlines, and the so-called "away days" . . . The home of the mediocre. Present company excepted, of course.'

'Thank you very much,' said Vassily, drily. 'But what about the events that led up to Larissa's death? Do you know why she was down by the tracks, for instance?'

'I've no idea, I'm afraid, Captain,' said Ilya. 'I thought I heard one of the crew say something about a meeting with Panteleimon – but then again, Yegor said she had intended to make some phone calls. Can't one check that kind of thing, these days? Look something up on the internet?'

Olga suppressed a smile, but Vassily replied quite seriously: 'We're looking into that, yes. But her phone was unfortunately destroyed by the incident, and as it was registered in another *oblast* there is a slight delay in finding out more.'

Ilya sat back and smiled at them as if he had won a point in a debate. 'Well, as I always say, technology has its limits. We were better off when it was pen and paper by candlelight, don't you agree, Corporal?'

'I suppose we've got some kind of a motive for Ilya,' said Olga, as Davidov escorted Ilya back to his compartment in the second carriage. 'He was desperate not to lose a valued member of his troupe, wasn't he, so he confronted her, and things got out of hand when she told him she was leaving anyway. He vowed that if the Murder Express couldn't have her, nobody could – so he made a second appointment to meet her, then pushed her under the wheels when the train moved.'

'Except that he was in the Red Star at the time,' pointed out Vassily.

'We don't even know that for sure,' replied Olga, with some justification – for Mikhail Pushkin and Vladimir Solotov were most unreliable witnesses. Vassily had sent Davidov to the Red Star earlier to check on the alibis provided by the troupe, but the picture he had returned with was a rather confused one. The troupe – and Lev Myatlev, the co-opted train engineer-turned-actor – had all been there, confirmed Pushkin and Solotov. But there was a lot going on, with impromptu performances of favourite scenes to the growing group of new clientele stolen from Café Astana by the Red Star Happy Hour (three vodkas and two *pelmeni* for a hundred roubles before seven o'clock), and they couldn't swear to everyone being there all the time. The troupe weren't much help on this point, either.

'Oh, it's impossible to say, Officers,' Yegor Shulgin had told them earlier on, fixing them earnestly with his deep spectacles. 'People were filtering in and out – going out to smoke, and paying calls on Mother Nature. The Red Star facilities became blocked quite early on, so it was really every man for himself. And woman, of course,' he added, nodding at Olga. 'But then again, maybe you're asking the wrong people. We theatrical types aren't exactly the steely-eyed amateur sleuths you're looking for! Maybe you should talk to Lev. He's an engineer, don't forget – not really an actor at all. It's probably much more his cup of vodka. Tea, I mean – tea.'

'He didn't seem too pleased about Lev, did he?' said Olga, as Davidov took Yegor away again. 'His joining the troupe, I mean.'

'Probably fancied himself the obvious choice of understudy, I suppose,' said Vassily. 'What was it his mother told him – d'you remember? That he could have been a great actor if he wanted?'

'Mm – yes,' said Olga. 'But he thought his talents lay elsewhere, or something. And the way things are going, you can hardly blame him.'

'True enough,' said Vassily. 'Life expectancy for actors isn't great, it seems. Ah, Gospodin Myatlev,' he went on, as Davidov led the engineer into the room. 'I need to ask you some questions about the Red Star.'

Somewhat to Olga's disappointment, however – she had rather liked Yegor's allusion to steely-eyed amateur sleuths – Lev Myatlev had no more insight to share on the topic than had Yegor.

'I'm sorry, sir,' he said to Vassily, 'but I've no idea what was going on. The vodka was flowing pretty freely, and I might have had a couple too many.'

(Judging by the haze of alcoholic spirit that still surrounded Lev's sharp-edged features, Olga thought it might have been more than a couple.)

'I even thought there were two Pans at one point,' Lev continued, shaking his head.

'Two what?' said Vassily.

'Two Pans. Y'know, Panteleimon. Panteleimon Pom-Pomelov,' he slurred. 'Our Rasputin? Long-haired bloke, bit of a ladies' man?'

'Got it,' said Vassily. 'But two of him?'

'Well, I wouldn't shw-swear to it,' said Lev. 'It was just for a moment. I looked up and saw him by the bar – well, what they're calling a bar – it's just a heap of packing cases nailed together. But then the door opened and in he came that way, too. I looked back to the bar and there he was, and then that Sonia walked up nexsht – er, next to me and distracted me. She's a slinky miss! Hard to concentrate on my lines when I can look at hers, and no mishtake.'

Olga cleared her throat, and Lev realised that he had forgotten himself to some extent. 'Anyway,' he went on, sitting up a little straighter, 'then I remembered about th'other Pan, and turned to the door – but he was gone. And then it was just the one again – but I saw him, plain as day, I swear, Officers!'

The hair rose on the back of Olga's neck. Lev Myatlev had undoubtedly had more vodka than was good for him, but in her experience people didn't see things when they drank. In fact, the opposite was true: too much alcohol only made things harder to see. Olga had always vowed that, when she finally became a great Russian novelist after studying literature at Tomsk State University, she would never use wine or beer as a lazy explanation for people seeing things that weren't there. And here was living proof that those slapdash writers were indeed wrong – for there was truth in Lev's (slightly blurry) eyes, that much was evident. Truth, and maybe also a touch of fear.

There was, however, also more than a tinge of green around his gills, and as he began to belch and massage his temples Vassily realised the end was near.

'Oh, take him out, Davidov, for God's sake,' he called, 'and stick him in the toilet compartment. Get him some water, too – and send in Pomelov, will you?'

In the pause before Davidov's return, Olga turned to look at Vassily.

'So: two Pans,' she said.

'You believed him, then? So did I – and it looks like we might be on to something at last. Someone's been playing an extra role on the side – impersonating Panteleimon, maybe, to lure Larissa to her death!'

'Yes, but who?'

Vassily shook his head. 'One of the men, I suppose. Yegor or Ilya?'

But Olga shook her head. 'They're all actors, Vassily – it could just as easily have been Sonia or Agapa. With enough stagecraft, anyone can play anyone.'

'Stagecraft,' muttered Vassily. 'Yes, yes – that's good. We should look into that. Maybe do another search of the hotel, see if anyone's got clothes they shouldn't have or—'

But Vassily's speculations were interrupted at this point by a loud knock on the door, followed by the equally loud voice of Junior Sergeant Timofei Davidov.

'Panteleimon Pomelov,' he announced, somewhat unnecessarily, while holding open the door and ushering him inside, before retreating into the second carriage once more.

'We hear Lev's been seeing double, Gospodin Pomelov,' said Vassily.

'What do you mean, Sergeant?' said Panteleimon, looking bewildered.

'Well, just what I said, Pan – can I call you Pan? Everyone else seems to, even engineers-turned-actors who only joined the troupe in the last couple of days.'

Panteleimon tilted his head sideways and narrowed his eyes, giving Olga the unmistakable impression of an Afghan hound with a keen interest in his dinner bowl. It must be the long hair, she thought – the hair, and the soulful eyes in which it would be all too easy to lose oneself. That, at least, he had in common with the real Rasputin, if the history books were anything to go by.

'Of course you can call me Pan,' he said, after a minute pause, 'but I still don't see what you mean about two of me – or should I say two of us?'

'Lev Myatlev said he saw you at the bar, or what passes for the bar, of the Red Star,' put in Olga, 'but then he saw you coming in the door at the same time.'

'So, naturally, we're curious as to what might be going on,' said Vassily.

'Two of me?' said Panteleimon. 'Two?'

The soulful eyes clouded, as if his gaze had turned inward, and his forehead furrowed in thought.

'Then there must – there must have been someone pretending to be me,' he said at last. 'But why – why would anyone do that?'

Vassily made to speak, but he paused when Olga coughed noisily, and then pursed her lips. Men, she thought – they never could seem to remember anything. Didn't Vassily see that this was a perfect opportunity to make the most of silence?

Panteleimon looked from Vassily to Olga, and back again. 'You know already, don't you? It's something to do with Larissa, isn't it? You think I was involved in her death! You think I was capable of hurting her even in the smallest degree, that pure, pure creature – that woman, unsullied somehow by the torrents of filth around us – that poor, poor girl, pushed under the wheels of the train she loved . . . Oh, yes, she loved railways, didn't you know? Said they were so romantic, and steam engines in particular. She wanted to meet someone in an old café by a train about to depart, and have to leave them for duty's sake, only for the man to jump on the train and abandon his whole life for her . . . That girl! So full of life and now dead – dead – dead . . .'

His eyes, already shimmering with unshed tears, now spilled over, and Olga felt her own eyes pricking unexpectedly in sympathy with Panteleimon. She knew actors couldn't be trusted, that they could turn emotions and their characteristic displays on and off at will – but surely, surely this display could not have been falsified or counterfeited. Pan had loved her, had perhaps imagined he would be the man to abandon his life for her, and dash onto a departing train in pursuit of doomed love.

'Oh, I know it isn't their fault,' he went on, wiping the tears from his cheeks. 'Ilya and Agapa, I mean. They didn't set up the Murder Express so that people would be murdered! But I can't help hating them, too. If it wasn't for them, if they hadn't organised this, then dear Rodion and Larissa, my Larissa, would still be among us.'

Shortly after this, Vassily again summoned Davidov and asked him to take Panteleimon back to his compartment. They hadn't managed to wring anything useful out of him regarding the potential identity of his impersonator. Nor – on his account – had he spoken to Larissa about a private meeting that day.

'So he claims, anyway,' summarised Vassily. 'Oh, Olga, we're back in the same hopeless situation as before: no clear motive for anyone, and equally solid – or equally weak – alibis all round.'

Olga nodded. 'Anyone could have slipped Larissa a note to arrange a meeting with Pan, or rather "Pan" – I'm guessing that's why she said something about it to Sonia. And then someone slipped out of the Red Star, flung on a disguise to create a superficial resemblance to Pan, just like someone did for Sonia back in Tayga, and then met Larissa to push her under the wheels before popping back to the bar and getting inside before anyone was any the wiser.'

Vassily frowned. 'But there's something I don't understand. Why come back into the Red Star still in disguise, so that Lev saw there were two Pans?'

Olga felt a shiver pass over her skin, for she thought there was only one explanation. 'Arrogance,' she said. 'Stone-cold conceit – a belief that they were too clever to be caught, despite the dangers of walking into a room that already contained the real Pan. Even in a tightly packed place – and you know how cramped the Red Star premises are – that was running a pretty high risk.'

Vassily raised his eyebrows, dark over his eyes in the dimly lit royal train, and puffed out a long breath. 'Maybe there's a weakness there,' he said. 'The arrogance, I mean. Pretty much the opposite of what we thought about a novice killer . . . So maybe we play on that, set some kind of trap, tempt them out of cover one more time . . .'

'Maybe. But what are we going to do in the meantime? How are we going to get them all back to the hotel?'

'Oh, they aren't going back to the hotel,' said Vassily.

'What? Where, then?'

'Right here,' he replied, a faint smile playing around his lips. 'We've got lockable doors, food, drink – a generator . . . And Davidov can watch over them,' he went on, as the junior sergeant came back into the room with a set of keys in his hand. 'That's what junior sergeants are for.'

'But, sir,' protested Davidov, 'I already told a girl I'd meet her at – but no, no, that's fine,' he added, taking in Vassily's fierce glare, 'I can give her a ring and cancel. Yes, yes, I'll do that now.'

Vassily nodded in satisfaction as Davidov scurried off, phone in hand. But Olga didn't feel quite so relaxed. The Murder Express, after all, was powered by steam – and hadn't they just tightened the lid?

8

Dmitri Intervenes

Olga slept poorly that night, tossing and turning in her little bedroom, on the garden side of the house she shared with Anna Kabalevsky and her brother Pasha. No matter how she tried to distract herself with calm thoughts of still seas or snowy log-cabins, her mind kept drifting back to the Murder Express and the actors locked into their old-fashioned compartments, with only Junior Sergeant Timofei Davidov to keep a doubtful watch through the night. Unless she and Vassily were much mistaken, at least one of the carriage's occupants was a murderer, and Olga kept thinking of ways in which a determined assassin might fight their way out of the ageing wood that constrained them to kill again, and again, and again . . . In the dark, uncertain hours, no scenario, no situation seemed too improbable – yet Olga didn't think she could bear it if one more person perished on the train, or anywhere else in Roslazny. For all that she'd spent much of her life wishing she was elsewhere, Roslazny would always be home – and who wants their home to become the playground of ruthless killers?

Olga lay on her side, hugging her hot-water bottle to her, and stared into the darkness through her open curtains, relieved only by a distant glow that spoke of Tayga's industrial outskirts to the south-east. She almost thought of getting up and walking to the siding herself – of checking with Davidov that all was well, and that all the actors (and Lev Myatlev) were still alive and intact. She even got up once, and reached for her puffed jacket and winter boots, before chiding herself for overreacting and forcing herself back into bed. But still it was difficult to lie still. It was very much like the nights when one of Anna's children had been ill, which meant it was only a matter of time before one of the others also became ill. When that happened – and it invariably happened in the early hours of the morning – it was all hands on deck, with no sleep for anyone. But at least then it had been got over with – at least then the worst had happened. She could hardly wish for the same for the Murder Express, though, since this would mean another death.

Even when morning finally limped into view, reluctantly stretching a grey-white canvas across Olga's windows, events conspired to delay the relief of her fears – for the promised breakfast materials at Café Astana, arranged by Vassily the night before to feed the troupe on board the Murder Express, had disastrously failed to materialise.

'But where is it, Igor – where's all the food?' said Olga, standing incredulous at the beer-stained bar at Café Astana.

'I told you, Olga – the delivery didn't arrive,' said Igor Odrosov, spreading his hands wide. 'What can I do, if the *priduroki* don't bring the stuff on time? My shelves are bare – I can't make breakfast out of thin air.'

Odrosov looked considerably less ebullient than he had when announcing his new vodka franchise to all and sundry, Olga noticed. His dislike of mornings was legendary, but even so he was far more bleary-eyed and miserable than usual at this time of day.

'Is everything all right, Igor?' she said. 'With – with the vodka deal, and everything?'

'Fine – fine,' he snapped. 'It's all fine. Going swimmingly! Couldn't be better. And now, if you'll excuse me, Olga, I've got a bar to clean up, and no sign of that daughter of mine. Svetlana?' he shouted, directing his voice towards the back of the bar, but with no answering echo. 'See yourself out, will you?' he added grumpily, before stalking off in search of Svetlana, who – if anything – hated mornings even more than her father did.

Olga sighed. She knew what this meant in terms of her next step, and immediately wished she had worn something less utilitarian, less commonplace and homespun – for she knew what her father Mikhail would say, when she went to find out if Roslazny's only other restaurant had breakfast supplies to spare. *Is that how you go around these days?* he'd sneer. *Looking like a male shot-putter at a gymnastics convention . . . No wonder Marushkin dumped you for his wife – must be the first time a man's done it that way round!* And so on, *ad nauseam*, digging ever deeper into his endless store of insults until she felt the blood rushing to her cheeks, displaying her chagrin to whatever audience Mikhail had mustered in his fledgling eatery.

But there was no alternative, Olga acknowledged, as she set off on the walk towards the Kabalevsky hostel or, as it now was, the Red Star. She was already running late, having agreed to meet Vassily back at the train at nine o'clock, so borrowing a car and dashing to Tayga was out of the question – and short of finding Nikolai Popov and seeing what outlandish meats the butcher had squirrelled away in his freezer, she had no choice but to patronise Roslazny's newest business at least once in her life.

That didn't make it any easier, though, when it came to walking up to the place and pushing through the door. Olga had been there many times before, when it had been a guesthouse run by Anna Kabalevsky and her now-estranged husband Bogdan, but in those days she had come as a welcome guest, a participant in joyful dinners or a helpful pair of hands with the children at difficult times. Now, as she came down the last few yards of the straggling, grassy pathway that led to the house, she eyed the familiar breezeblocks and crumbling facing with a sense of intense dislike. It was strange, she thought, how the very same things, the very same places, could take on such a different aspect with the passage of time, as if all houses, all places, were themselves only acting, assuming first one persona and then the next, playing roles in some great drama of which only a sliver was revealed to any one age.

Anna's bells chimed as she opened the door, the well-known, homely sound jarring sharply with the atmosphere she encountered within – for old man Solotov had taken the red-star theme and run a long way with it, plastering almost every available inch of wall with Soviet propaganda, posters of Russian heroes, and more recent materials advertising the virtues of Vladimir Putin and his cronies, all of them visible, if barely, through a thick fog of cigarette smoke and oily vapours from the kitchen beyond the reception area. The clientele, too, were not particularly to Olga's taste, representing an assortment of mostly rather undesirable characters from Roslazny, Tayga, Suranovo, and other villages in the area. Olga knew most of them, by face if not by name, from poker nights hosted by her father Mikhail in the days when they had lived together, and from the glances turned upon her now, she could tell that they recognised her also. Some of the men looked at her and turned away with disinterest, while others stared a little too long – but Olga was happy to ignore their leering. The main thing was that her father did not seem to be there, or Vladimir Solotov. Perhaps she could place an order with someone else, and beat her retreat before Mikhail or Vladimir turned up. Perhaps she could—

'Olga!' called a deep male voice. 'What the hell are you doing here?'

'Father,' she said, the word uttered almost as a sigh, 'I – I just need to buy some food.'

'Surprised to see you darkening my doorstep,' said Mikhail, advancing towards her in his usual outfit of sandals, sweatpants, and knitted jumper, this time paired with a camouflage T-shirt that showed through at the neckline. 'Then again, you've gone down a bit in the world recently, haven't you?'

'What do you mean?'

'Well . . .' he said, leaning on the counter and smiling at her – a maddening, superior kind of smile that already threatened to send the dreaded blood rushing to her cheeks. 'Well, you've been edged out of that police station, haven't you? Downgraded to a glorified office boy – or what is it they always say these days? A partner? A *colleague*?' He spoke the word as if it were an insult. 'And I hear your hut's on the rocks, too. What will you do then?'

Olga had been about to say, *Mind your own business*, but remembered in time that she still needed to buy breakfast for the troupe. 'I'm sure I'll find something,' she said, far more brightly than she felt. 'Now, do you have any *pelmeni* – or *pirogi*, perhaps? Or – or *syrniki*?' she said, after a minute pause, naming the cheese pancakes that her mother Tatiana used to make for her on Saturdays, long ago.

'I might do,' said Mikhail, giving no indication of remembering his dead wife or the sticky treats she had once prepared for their only daughter. 'Depends on the price, don't it?' he added, winking at her.

Of course it did, thought Olga, before entering upon exactly the kind of negotiation she'd anticipated, ending up by paying a small fortune for a couple of carrier bags of last night's *ponchiki* and a Thermos of weak coffee.

'Pleasure doing business with you, daughter,' said Mikhail, pocketing the wad of rouble notes and winking again, only this time directing it to one of his customers, a thick-set, greasy-haired man Olga thought she recognised from a barber's shop in Tayga. 'Same time again tomorrow? No, don't bother trying Café Astana first – they haven't got long left, or they won't, anyway, if I have anything to do with it! Don't forget to come here alone, though – we don't allow any *fruit* in here, do we, boys?'

Olga stared at him in disgust. How could a father speak about Pasha, about his own son, in that way? She knew that someone like Mikhail would never understand what it was like to grow up gay in Russia, and was harder still, to be a gay soldier in Putin's army. Mikhail should be on his knees giving thanks that Pasha had been discharged before the war, and hugging his beloved son to his chest with arms of steel. There were many parents who longed for nothing else and who would never have that joy again in all their long lives.

She walked out of the door with a shudder of revulsion, offset by a tinge of sorrow and even self-pity that she could have ended up with such a father – that he should have lived while her beloved mother had died. How different her life could have been, she thought, had the opposite occurred – how much gentler, and calmer, and more meaningful . . . Tatiana Pushkin would never have forced Olga to work for the railways just because her father had. Indeed, it was Tatiana who had given Olga the dream of studying literature at Tomsk State University, a dream inspired by repeated visits to the campus and its grand buildings, cafés and bookshops.

She started back towards the siding on the south-west of the village, where a faint wisp of dark smoke indicated the train's generator at work. It wasn't all that cold yet, by Siberian standards – three or four degrees, probably, she thought – but still you needed something to take the edge off the chilled air when you were confined indoors. No doubt the actors had badgered Davidov until he felt obliged to start things up again, emerging grumbling from his own compartment and pulling the generator's handle repeatedly until the ancient thing quaked into life, providing light and heat – and smoke. Then Davidov would retreat to his compartment, she imagined, seeking an extra half-hour's kip until breakfast arrived with Olga and Vassily.

Timofei Davidov wasn't a glowing advertisement for the police, thought Olga, though there were worse coppers around, as she knew from bitter experience.

And what about Kliment? Would he become a policeman, and if he did, would he be like Vassily, or Davidov? She rounded the last street corner in Roslazny and breasted the little incline that led to the tracks, wondering where Vassily had got to – they had arranged to meet at the train at nine, and it was already ten past – and wondering, too, if Vassily would force Kliment to follow in his footsteps, as her father Mikhail had done. Kliment helped him with tasks around the station between his schoolwork, Olga knew – or at least he had done when Olga used to visit. Now, in the age of Rozalina, she wasn't so sure. Vassily's lost wife seemed less interested in Kliment's future than she was in his present, and specifically his ability to make her life more comfortable by running errands and fetching blankets, cushions and drinks. But then Olga reproached herself, if somewhat half-heartedly. Rozalina had had a hard life, after all, and maybe she had earned a little comfort. Olga just hoped it didn't come too much at Kliment's expense.

She walked down the path that wound along the siding, like a muddy snake, the clear November air punctuated with occasional whiffs of acrid generator smoke, and the train sitting stark and tall on the tracks, a symphony of straight lines amid a tumble of amorphous branches and leaves. The P36 had steamed into the siding first, with Lev's replacement, Yefim Burtsov, standing by Simeon at the controls, so that first she saw the two carriages, but there in front was the vast machine, cold and sleeping now but still sleek and massy, conveying sheer power through its wheels and rods and high running plates. Olga shook her head, marvelling at the ability of these inanimate creations to stir her heart after all these years. Mikhail Pushkin might have forced her into a career, but at least he'd picked one with a kind of everyday beauty about it.

There wasn't much beauty about the men who now stepped down to the ground. There was Timofei Davidov, which was to be expected: he must have heard her boots crunching along the new-laid gravel in front of the seating stand, now looking rather sad and empty in the morning damp. But there was another man behind him, whose shape Olga did not immediately recognise, it being disguised by a vast overcoat with fur collars upturned against the early chill.

'Ah, Pushkin,' said the figure, turning to her as she approached, and she saw it was Captain Zemsky. 'You've brought breakfast, have you? Then who needs Marushkin?'

Vassily, however, arrived not long after Olga, sending gravel flying as he clattered along the path before skidding to a halt at the sight of Zemsky.

'Sir!' he said, breathlessly. 'What are you doing here?'

'What am I doing here? Excellent question, Marushkin, since if you'd been doing your job properly I could have been in Kemerovo today, glugging down vodka and heading to the baths at my club. Today's the day when all the colonels and majors and captains get together,' he added, by way of explanation, 'but I only show up to sign my name, then take off. I had it all planned – but then I get a call from Mayor Arkady Nazarov, don't I? And a very disgruntled mayor at that. He knows the Putyatins, Marushkin. Did you know that?'

'So – the siding,' muttered Olga.

'So – the siding,' agreed Zemsky. 'They'd never have got all this arranged without a push from higher up. And now that higher-up person is getting worried about how we're treating his fancy friends. God knows what they've got over him . . . But Pushkin gets it, Marushkin! Our little railway engineer here' – putting an arm around Olga's shoulders – 'gets it, so why can't you? We need to make progress, and fast.'

'But, sir,' began Vassily, 'I thought you were happy with the plan to—'

But Zemsky interrupted: 'Look, Marushkin, it's fine to lock a few thespians up for a night if you get results – we can always get that past the courts. But if it's day two and there's nothing to show for it, and if the actors start making trouble with the mayor in Kemerovo, we need to start moving a little faster, *nyet*? No substitute for dropping by in person, that's what I've found. So here I am, and we've already done more than a day's work, eh, Davidov? Why don't you tell Marushkin, and our little railway engineer, what we got up to this morning, eh?'

Davidov glanced nervously at Zemsky, and began to describe the interviews they had conducted first thing that morning – but it wasn't long before Zemsky took over.

'Always catch 'em off guard, Marushkin,' he said, with a chuckle, 'and that means first thing or last thing! They were fairly rubbing their eyes, *da*, Davidov? Bit of a waste of time, though, if I'm honest – the wardrobe inspection got us nowhere. They don't lock the cupboards,' he elaborated, 'so anyone could get at the costumes, wigs, make-up, all that jazz, whenever they damn well like. And that means all the lab stuff – DNA and fingerprints – is also useless . . . So if someone was pretending to be that long-haired feller – what's his name? Pantelov? – then we're none the wiser as to who it could be. And then there's the notebook . . .'

'Rodion's notebook?' put in Olga.

'That's the one. Well, we searched high and low, didn't we, Davidov? Went through all the compartments like a dose of salts – but never a sign of it. So, without that, and without anything concrete on the clothes set-up, we're in a bit of a hole.'

Vassily bit his lip, as if to stop himself speaking, and Olga could tell by his eyes what was going through his mind: *Yes, indeed – so how, exactly, have I not been doing my job properly?*

Aloud he merely said: 'So what do you suggest doing now, sir?'

Zemsky laughed again. 'The only thing we can do, Marushkin. Dive into the paperwork! *I izhu panyatna.*' Even a hedgehog could get it.

Olga bristled. She loved proverbs in general, and indeed specialised in making them up, but this was one she had always cordially despised. 'Why bring hedgehogs into it?' she said crossly. 'They're far cleverer than people make out!'

Zemsky shrugged, but Vassily held up a hand and shot Olga a quick look of reproof, as if to say, *Not now, Olga*, then turned back to Zemsky and said: 'Paperwork? You mean – records?'

'Precisely. I've called up the archive people in Moscow to dig up what they can on this sorry lot' – jerking a thumb behind him at the carriage – 'and see if there are any interesting titbits to chew over. Financial indiscretions, criminal charges . . . Who knows? There might even be some unorthodox political affiliations. You know what these bloody artists are like, always jumping on some namby-pamby bandwagon! They'll get back to us later today or early tomorrow, they say.'

Olga raised her eyebrows. 'That's quick.'

'We can move a bit faster than the Trans-Siberian when we want to, my dear,' replied Zemsky.

'That reminds me, sir,' said Vassily, with the faint air of one eager to please. 'We got Larissa's phone records back – Larissa Lazarov, that is, the woman who died under the train.'

'I'm not likely to forget that, am I, Marushkin?' said Zemsky, rolling his eyes and pulling a thumb across his throat. 'Go on.'

'Well, it backed up what she said about making phone calls the day she died – but there was nothing suspicious about any of them. They were all to friends and family back in Volgograd. We called them up to check – she was just telling them about the play, they said, and how she was scared for what might happen next.'

'And with good reason,' muttered Olga.

'Well, that's no good to man or beast, Marushkin,' said Zemsky. 'Go and find me something to work with! I'm heading back to Tayga now, but Davidov's happy to stay, *pravil'nyy*, Timofei? That's settled, then,' he went on, without waiting for a response from Davidov. 'Pushkin can carry on bringing food over for the luvvies? Great. Give me a call, then, Marushkin, when you have anything worth my time – something a hedgehog could understand, *nyet*? Good. *Da svidania!*'

Olga arrived at Café Astana not long after Zemsky had taken his leave, bidding farewell to a bored Timofei Davidov and promising to return with lunch supplies later that day. Vassily walked with her some of the way before peeling off to head back to the police station, but his company left something to be desired on that particular Saturday morning. He was very tired, for one thing, with thick dark bags under his eyes – burning the midnight oil over the case, thought Olga, with a pang of jealousy at the thought of Rozalina bringing him trays of tea and snacks to get him through the night. Then she gave herself a wry little smile: more likely it would have been the other way round, with the hard-working sergeant pressed into filling her hot-water bottles and massaging her feet until she drifted into a pampered, untroubled sleep. But apart from the tiredness,

Vassily was clearly troubled and preoccupied, and no doubt rankled by Captain Zemsky's unwanted and disruptive involvement in the case.

Olga ventured a gambit on the topic as they walked back past the empty seating stand.

'Not the easiest case you've ever worked, Vassily,' she said, softening her words with a smile.

He looked up as if surprised. 'What? Oh, the case – yes, it's a puzzler, all right. Reminds me of the Ivanov murder, back in Novosibirsk.' And he told her about a man who had been killed inside his city-centre apartment at three in the afternoon, while his cleaner was working inside the place and moving from room to room, only to discover his body in the bath with a knife through the heart.

'That took us a while to work out, I can tell you,' he said, the old familiar smile breaking across his stubble-clad chin and working its way up to the wrinkles around his eyes. 'But it ended up being very like this case and our mysterious double Rasputin. It was the cleaner, of course – or, rather, the cleaners . . .'

'He had two cleaners?' said Olga, impressed at this display of big-city wealth.

Vassily laughed. 'No, no – only one, but there was a killer there, too, disguised as the cleaner. It was an incredibly good disguise, too, so as long as he kept away from Mila Kurnovsky – that was her name – there was no way the man would notice, until it was too late. We only worked it out because a kid across the way happened to have been given a new camera for Christmas, and had taken photos of both going into the flat at different times.'

'Sounds useful,' said Olga. 'Shame we don't have CCTV on every corner of Roslazny.'

'That's not a bad idea, actually,' said Vassily. 'I mean, the way things have gone since I got here – three waves of murder, and two mini crime-sprees . . . As if I haven't got enough to deal with at home!'

Vassily's eyes had once more assumed the rather dejected air with which he had set out, and Olga had a strong sense that it was his home life, not the case, that had made him so miserable. He wouldn't say any more, though, beyond a vague reference to Kliment staying out too late, and he set off towards the police station with a rather disconsolate wave of a large, calloused hand and a few muttered words about seeing her again at lunch.

Vassily's mood was catching, and Olga pushed through the Café Astana door in a rather glum mood. Rozalina or no Rozalina, she still cared greatly about him, and seeing him like this was difficult to accept. And why was Kliment staying out late? It was troubling, indeed, for such a thoroughly good young man, but what could she do? Nothing much, she told herself, as she walked up to Odrosov's scantily stocked grocery shelves and scanned fruitlessly for the items Anna had asked her to buy. No: there was nothing at all she could do.

'Don't look for anything there, Olga,' called Nikolai Popov from the bar. 'Igor's stopped placing orders for a bit.'

'No, no,' said Koptev Alexeyev, the mechanic. 'All the food's been stolen! It's the crime wave, you know.'

'That sounds about right,' said Fyodor Katin, who was slowly making his way through a plate of pickled gherkins – one of the few delicacies Odrosov appeared still to have in stock. 'The till was robbed yesterday, did you hear?'

'It's only justice,' said Popov, with a bark of a laugh. 'Igor's been robbing us for years.'

'And now he's calling in all his tabs,' said Alexeyev, with an aggrieved air. 'I haven't got that kind of money lying around!'

'But what about his new vodka franchise?' said Olga. 'I thought he was rolling in money – didn't he have a heap of down-payments from his investors?'

'Ah, well, now,' said Popov, tapping the side of his stubby nose, 'that's what we all thought, too. But Svetlana told me—'

'What did she tell you?' said Igor Odrosov, striding out of the back kitchen with a tea-towel on his shoulder and a look of thunder on his face.

'Ah, Igor,' said Popov, flashing a smile at him. 'We were just saying that Svetlana was telling me how she made the gherkins taste so good – *da,* Fyodor?'

'Yes, yes, that's right,' said Fyodor, loyally, after chewing and swallowing a particularly tough specimen with some difficulty. 'The best anywhere in Roslazny!'

'Damn sight better than the rubbish Pushkin serves at the Red Star, anyway,' said Igor, somewhat mollified. 'No offence intended, Olga,' he added.

'And none taken, Igor,' she replied, raising her hands in negation. 'The Red Star's nothing to do with me – though you'd better watch out,' she added, nodding at the nearly empty shelves to her left. 'My father's operation seems better supplied than yours, just at the moment.'

'It's the cost-of-living crisis, Olga!' Igor cried angrily. 'I can't spend any more roubles at these prices – not till the vodka money comes in. Oh, shut up, Nikolai,' he went on. 'It's only a matter of time!'

Popov responded with scepticism, agitating Odrosov yet further, and prompting Fyodor and Alexeyev to pitch in with their points of view, until Olga realised that any more conversation had become impossible. She reached into first one pocket and then, with a sigh of irritation, into the other, and dropped a handful of rouble notes onto the counter in exchange for the few items she had been able to find, and then, with a backward nod at the men, she gathered up her bag and made for the exit, accompanied by the continued sound of loud debate.

She stepped outside and closed the door behind her with a sigh of relief. Men were like children sometimes, she thought: best in small doses. But there was no time to lose herself in philosophical speculation, for she had a hedgehog to attend to – and not just any hedgehog, but Dmitri the white-breasted Siberian hedgehog, who had been her constant companion through all the vicissitudes of that most trying year, and (alongside Anna Kabalevsky and Ekaterina Chezhekhov) the most faithful friend of all her wide acquaintance. Olga had recently moved Dmitri back into her rail-side hut following a number of unfortunate incidents involving Anna's shoes, one of Anna's very few worldly weaknesses being a fondness for wildly impractical heels – and now that Olga had been removed from the daily cares of track maintenance by Boris Andreyev's decision to second her to the police force, she had to make dedicated trips to the hut to make sure that Dmitri was warm, safe and well fed.

It wasn't really that much of a chore, though, thought Olga, as she walked down the path from Roslazny to the tracks, and then along the final section that wound its way to the hut, a faded green Russian Railways outpost amid the endless encroachments of the Siberian *taiga*. She loved the hut, after all, with its familiar sights, scents and sounds, and she loved even more the little snufflings of Dmitri as he emerged from his pile of discarded tea-towels to eat whatever morsels Olga had to bestow on him on that particular day – a small bag of meal-worms, perhaps, or some earwigs sourced from the storerooms of Nikolai Popov. Then Olga would light up the stove while Dmitri fed himself from a little silver bowl, getting some heat into the room before she left again, locking the door carefully behind her to make sure he would stay put.

Today, however, the door was already ajar when she got to the hut – she must have left too hurriedly the day before, and turned the key in the lock before the latch had closed, locking it open instead of shut. With a rapidly beating heart she pushed inside and made straight for Dmitri's tea-towels, but the little makeshift bed was cold and empty, and there were no prickles to be seen anywhere in the hut. Olga cast around the hut, rapidly inspecting all the hiding-places that could feasibly fit a hedgehog, but encountering nothing except a rapidly mounting sense of dread within her chest. Had they come so far together for it to finish like this, with her poor little Dmitri ending up as nothing more than a tasty snack for some wandering fox or badger?

She rushed outside and looked left, right, forwards and backwards, running around the back of the hut and then to the front again, but there was no Dmitri in sight. She dropped to the ground, rejecting as utterly irrelevant the suggestion told to her by an inner voice that she would look ridiculous in so doing, and inspected the ground outside the hut as if she might find little hedgehog-shaped footprints – and much to her astonishment, she did. Or, at least, she thought she found something that looked like a tiny pawprint in the mud, with a swirling, worm-like shape traced next to it as if a diminutive tail had moved across the print after the paw had left it behind – a tail rather like a hedgehog's, she said to herself – and there was another print, and another, and another, all moving south-east, in the direction of Tayga.

Olga set off at a run, moving fast along the tracks and scanning left as she went, in case Dmitri had got somehow got himself stranded on the rails – the possibility made her feel sick. But there was no sign of him, and no more footprints to see in this drier ground. Still she ran on, always onward, looking around her, into the woods, and even across the tracks to the other side – but there was no little shuffling body to see, only empty space carpeted with dead leaves, cast-off bits of wire, and aggregate.

Soon she came to the siding that peeled off the main line towards the Murder Express, sitting motionless on the rails like a comatose leviathan, with only the generator smoke to convey any signs of life. No doubt the guests, or rather suspects, were reclining on their bunks and trying to sleep off the after-effects of Mikhail Pushkin's cuisine – but maybe, thought Olga, with a hint of desperate hope, just maybe someone there had happened to glance out of a window when Dmitri went past, and could give her a clue as to his current whereabouts.

It wasn't much to go on, but it was something to cling to, nonetheless, and Olga ran along the trackside grass towards the train, with the aim of clambering up the nearest ladder and rousing Davidov to question the actors on this latest and most pressing matter. She had almost drawn close to the rearmost carriage when – to her unbounded relief and delight – she caught sight of Dmitri at last, waddling along in his characteristic manner and trailing half an old tea-towel by one of his prickles, as if he hadn't fully persuaded himself to say farewell to Olga's carefully curated surrounds.

'Oh, Dmitri-*dimi-detka*,' she crooned, dropping to her knees by the track and scooping him into her arms with as much care – perhaps even more – as she accorded to Anna's youngest, baby Ilya. 'Oh, you naughty, naughty hedgehog,' she whispered, 'and there I was, defending you to that nasty Captain Zemsky, and saying hedgehogs were so clever! And now see how silly you've made me look! Oh, you naughty, naughty hedgehog,' she went on, still whispering into his tiny ears – and a few seconds later she was glad she had spoken quietly, because she heard something then that otherwise she might never have heard at all.

'Nonsense, Agapa.' A voice came to her ears – floating down, she realised, from an open window at the rear of the carriage. 'We just have to hold our nerve, that's all, my darling, and then we'll be free, and out of all this, and able to carry on doing what we love for ever.'

'You don't understand, Ilya,' came Agapa's voice in response, as quiet and controlled as Ilya's, but perfectly audible to Olga in the still morning air, and with a sense of menace that sent a shiver across her skin despite the relatively mild November temperature. 'If they find out the names, we'll lose it all! Are you ready to lose it all, *darling*?'

'We wouldn't necessarily lose it *all*,' replied Ilya, in a tone that brought him vividly to Olga's mind: the high, domed forehead, the aquiline nose, the poetic eyes marred only by the air of permanent fussiness that he seemed determined to adopt, as if contradiction were the essence of artistic beauty.

'We'd never act again,' hissed Agapa. 'Is that what you want – confined to prison? No more vodka – no more champagne? Never doing or seeing anything wonderful, ever again? No, no – we've come too far to risk that.'

'Agapa, my dear,' said Ilya, 'I think we should guard our tongues. Walls have ears, you know – and so do windows.' His voice had become steadily louder, and now a hand reached up and pulled the window firmly closed. Olga thought she heard a muttered exclamation from inside before Agapa was cut off – something like *Guard your own tongue* – and then there were only muffled sounds like people speaking behind a dividing wall, and the faint snuffling of Dmitri as he lay in her arms. Presently a light breeze blew up, and shifted among the trees behind the train with sylvan whispers – but Olga didn't notice. Her eyes were turned inwards, and her mind was racing as she tried to understand the meaning of the Putyatins' conversation. Hidden names – a threat of prison – the risk of losing it all . . . No: it was too much for her to grasp just at that moment, with the trauma of losing Dmitri so recently behind her. She needed another pair of ears to listen with her again, so she got silently to her feet and walked off in the direction of Roslazny once more, to see where Vassily might be found.

Olga was sure of one thing, however, as sure as she'd ever been of anything: the Putyatins were concealing something, and something extremely important at that. Vassily could help her uncover it, she was sure, if he wasn't too distracted by Rozalina. But there was one more thing she was sure of, too, and she told it to Dmitri as she carried him along.

'They say hedgehogs are stupid, don't they?' she said, into his ears, while softly stroking his brown-furred head. 'But it was you who found it all out, wasn't it, Dmitri-*dimi-detka*? And I'd like to see Captain Zemsky take issue with *that*!'

Her face turned from affection to righteous anger and she marched on, on, ever on.

9

The Reluctant Thief

'And? What happened?' said Ekaterina Chezhekhov, impatiently. 'What did Vassily do? What did the Putyatins say?'

'Oh, it was the same story all over again,' said Olga, plumping herself down on the platform bench at Tayga station with more than a touch of weariness. 'Well, not the same story precisely, I suppose, because this time it was about something different – this time it was about an overheard conversation, instead of who put antifreeze into Rodion's dinner, or why someone sounding like Sonia Alikovsky was seen buying detergent when she couldn't possibly have been anywhere but with Agapa and Ilya, or how it's possible that there were two Panteleimons in the Red Star at the same time. This time it was none of those, but, oh, Ekaterina, it was just the same!'

'So – as soon as you and Vassily started asking questions, you found they all had perfect excuses?' said Ekaterina, sitting down beside her and lighting a cigarette that she'd plucked from the tray she wore around her shoulders.

'Well, we prefer to use the term "alibi",' said Olga, 'but yes, yes, exactly that. Ilya and Agapa had a perfectly logical explanation for what they'd said, though I can't say it was very respectable . . .'

'Excellent,' muttered Ekaterina, inhaling deeply and with relish. 'Go on!'

'Well, you remember they said they were worried about us uncovering some names – and that they'd never act again if we did? That they'd go to prison? Oh, Ekaterina,' Olga went on, her brow wrinkling with annoyance, 'they were just exaggerating, in typical actor style . . . It was just a piece of theatrics they didn't want uncovered, for fear of damaging their reputation.'

'All right, but what did they actually do?'

'It wasn't much, really,' said Olga. 'They just did a couple of practice runs for the Murder Express under assumed names – two different troupes in two different parts of the country.'

Ekaterina threw her a sideways glance. 'That's it?'

'As far as I could tell. I mean, neither of them went especially well, from what they said. They dragged in Yegor Shulgin to substantiate it all – turns out he'd been with them for the second.'

'Yegor Shulgin? Remind me which one he is.'

'He's a glorified secretary, though you'd think he was director-in-chief the way he tells it,' replied Olga. 'Wears thick glasses and frumpy clothes, and runs all the behind-the-scenes stuff – gives the actors cues if they forget their lines, organises the samovar for tea, all that kind of thing. Anyway, he backed up the Putyatins – told us they'd sworn him to secrecy, that they'd never play the Bolshoi again if people knew they were doing little plays in the back end of nowhere . . . And *that*, of course, is as bad as prison, to anyone who loves a big stage! Egomaniacs, the lot of them.'

'But aren't they famous, these two – the, what is it, Putyins? Wouldn't they be recognised doing these other troupes anyway?'

'Putyatins. They're famous, in a way, but not to people like you and me – more to theatre buffs, literary types, people like that.'

Ekaterina bristled. 'I'm very fancy, thank you very much, Olga Pushkin! I've been to more nightclubs and casinos than you can shake a diamond ring at. Besides, what about the Murder Express? The Putyatins didn't mind putting their names all over that. I don't see the difference.'

'That's what Vassily said. He asked them what was different – and they said, "The train, Inspector, the train! The P36 steam engine, the specially modified period carriages, the lavish costumes and scenes . . ." There was all the difference in the world, they said, Inspector, between a well-funded theatrical spectacle and the two-bit shows they'd put on as rehearsals in the provinces. "You must always rehearse everything, Inspector," said Agapa. "*Everything*."'

'Inspector?'

'Oh, yes, the actors are hopeless at ranks. Kept calling Vassily an inspector and Davidov a commissioner . . . It would have been funny, if it hadn't been for the lot of them making us look like idiots. Thank you,' she said, almost crossly, as Ekaterina passed her a lit cigarette and fired up another for herself. 'I do need something to take the edge off, and I wouldn't be surprised if Vassily did, too.'

'That poor man – an impossible case, and with Rozalina to deal with, too,' said Ekaterina, who had, of course, been kept fully abreast of proceedings at the Roslazny police station.

'The worst thing was that Captain Zemsky was there, too – that fool Timofei Davidov insisted on calling him back for the questioning. To be fair, he was only following Zemsky's own instructions, but I know Vassily was embarrassed. No – worse than that, mortified. It's been thing after thing after thing, and nothing to show for it. I think he's worried he'll lose the Roslazny command. Though there was one thing—'

'What?'

'Well, I'm sure it was nothing – or maybe I'm not so sure. It's just – well, the first practice run the Putyatins organised took place near St Petersburg. At Kommunar, to the south of the city. They all agreed on that, so that all seems quite straightforward. And Agapa said the second had been in another place, some nowhere village near Izhevsk – but when we spoke to Yegor separately, it seemed to me that he was going to say somewhere else. It was almost as if he'd forgotten his lines – and since he's the one who provides the clues, there was nobody to prompt him.'

'Can't Vassily check out their stories, see if Agapa's telling the truth?'

'He's going to – but Ilya warned it would be a waste of time, since almost nobody came to the performances. Nobody would remember them, he said, and that was the biggest injury of all. I honestly thought he was going to start weeping.'

Ekaterina rolled her eyes. 'If anyone's got reason to weep, it's you. First Rozalina came back, and then the threat to your hut – and now Boris Andreyev has you running around helping Vassily just because Zemsky says so, and at the same time threatening to turf you out into the mud. And then there's your book—'

'Yes, yes, thank you, Ekaterina,' said Olga. 'Yes, there's a lot going on. And don't forget all the thefts around Roslazny, too, that Vassily can't seem to stop – and my father's new enterprise, which is putting poor Odrosov out of business. And then there's Kliment . . . I can't put my finger on it, but I'm not happy about him. Something's happening, I'm sure of it. Maybe it's Rozalina.'

'Rozalina?'

'Well, yes,' she said. 'I mean, I know she's meant to be his mother, and all that, but sometimes I wonder—'

'Wait, Olga,' interrupted Ekaterina, 'isn't that one of the actors from the Murder Express? Across the tracks, there – by the lost luggage? That woman – Sonia something – Sonia Alikovsky . . . But aren't they all meant to be locked up in the train?'

'Yes, they were,' said Olga, 'until Agapa Putyatin persuaded Davidov to lend her his phone. Said she wanted to text her daughter that she was well, and not to worry. Of course, she hasn't got any children, but Davidov forgot that, didn't he?'

'I'm surprised he doesn't forget his own name, most days.'

'And then Agapa called some of her high-up friends in Kemerovo, with the result that the troupe had to be released or Mayor Nazarov would want to know why.'

'Nazarov? Up in Kemerovo?'

Ekaterina whistled as Olga nodded in confirmation.

'Vassily didn't have a choice, then,' said Ekaterina.

'Not even Zemsky did,' said Olga, taking one last drag of her cigarette before dropping it and grinding it out under the heel of her boot. 'They have some important friends, the Putyatins. That's how they got the funding, I suppose.'

'Maybe,' said Ekaterina, finishing her cigarette in turn. 'Or maybe they're up to their eyes in debt, and betting it all on one last throw of the dice! I never met anyone in showbusiness who wasn't down to their last kopek. And what's more, I—'

But what was more was destined to remain a matter for conjecture, for at that moment Boris Andreyev, Olga's superior in name if not in nature, emerged from the office across the track. Olga instantly looked down and away, but Andreyev caught sight of her nonetheless.

'Pushkin,' he called, beckoning her over with a wave of his hand.

Olga sighed. 'Well, I'll see you again, Ekaterina.'

Ekaterina nodded, while plucking another cigarette from her tray and putting it to her lips. 'Don't do anything I wouldn't do, Olga! And keep your chin up. I'll have my ears open this end, and who knows what Vassily might turn up? You'll get there.'

'Maybe one day,' said Olga, grimly. 'Maybe. I'm coming, sir,' she called across the track, before jumping to the ballast and picking her way across the rails. 'I'm coming.'

'Sorry, Olga – say that again,' said Dr Zinovev, turning his eyes towards her briefly, and then back towards the road.

'Oh, it's nothing,' she said, glancing back at him. 'I was just saying that Boris – oh, it really is nothing. Forget it.'

And it *was* nothing, she thought, turning to look out of the mud-spattered window of Zinovev's battered Haval – or, at least, it was nothing new: just Boris being Boris, as people said around Tayga. He had merely reminded her that her hut was under threat, and had shown her some technology catalogues he'd been looking at – catalogues that specialised in drones adapted for industrial applications, he noted, with an unpleasant grin, adding that he expected a rep to come and demonstrate a couple in the coming days. And after that, he'd made it very clear to Olga that her future depended in large part upon making progress with the case.

'I've got high-ups breathing down my neck, *da*? We need to make this go away, and fast – express service, not rackety local train, got it?'

Olga hadn't replied, having decided to give Andreyev the same silent treatment that she'd trialled upon the suspects. The results were gratifying, his face getting progressively redder and redder, but (as she reluctantly acknowledged) probably counter-productive in the longer term. In the end he had resorted to restating his points in a rather more aggressive manner, before throwing the door open and inviting her to leave.

An unpleasant meeting, but then again, most meetings with Boris Andreyev were quite unpleasant. So, it was nothing new – but that didn't explain why Zinovev hadn't been listening to her. He'd seemed distracted since they'd bumped into each other on the platform at Tayga, the doctor almost knocking her to the ground while looking elsewhere, then barely meeting her eyes when he realised who she was. He was awaiting a shipment by train, he told her, but it hadn't arrived. To make up for walking into her, he offered her a lift home, as he was going that way – but he'd said Suranovo rather than Roslazny. Once Olga had established that he was really going to Roslazny, she accepted with alacrity, having resigned herself to walking the three miles home in the chill, damp air – but another delay ensued while Zinovev tried to remember where he'd parked his car. And then, once they were installed in their seats and heading to Roslazny, he barely seemed able to concentrate on what Olga was saying. Admittedly, she had been talking about Andreyev, not the most thrilling of topics at the best of times – but, still, she wasn't used to the doctor zoning out like that.

He wasn't looking that well either, she realised. He had always been slender, but now he was positively gaunt, his red-rimmed eyes glowering like twin fires above cheekbones that pushed like blades against his papery skin. He looked so unwell, in fact – so sick and hollowed-out – that she had almost hesitated to get into the car with him. She couldn't say why, exactly, just a shiver of discomfort that she dismissed as soon as she felt it. Zinovev was a known quantity, after all – a devoted medic who stopped at nothing to help his patients, regardless of cost or labour. But clearly he was not a well man, and perhaps some evolutionary mechanism warned her his sickness might be catching.

What was it Fyodor Katin had taken to saying, whenever Zinovev came into view – 'Physician, heal thyself'? Something like that. Perhaps it was true that doctors always neglected their health, just as mechanics – like Roslazny's own Koptev Alexeyev – tended to have the dirtiest, rustiest cars. Of course, Fyodor had his own axe to grind, since Zinovev was the leading competitor for the affections of Anna Kabalevsky. But that didn't mean he was wrong, either. Zinovev was clearly working too hard, or worrying himself into the ground about something, or both.

Olga opened her lips to ask the doctor what was bothering him, having first checked that the road ahead was clear – but then Zinovev spoke: 'How's the case?' he said. 'Any closer to finding the killer – or killers?'

'I can't really discuss it,' she said. 'It's an ongoing investigation.'

And then, feeling that this was perhaps a little brusque, and also remembering that she had just shared a lot of details with Ekaterina, she added: 'I'm sorry, Yury Sergeiivich, but I've been seconded to the police – you know how it is. Same with doctors and their patients, I imagine – confidentiality, and all that. But I suppose I could say – I suppose I could tell you that it's been pretty tough going. You could guess that, anyway, from the lack of announcements . . . I actually came into Tayga today to get away for a bit, to catch up with Ekaterina Chezhekhov and maybe find some perspective on what's going on, as well as giving Vassily a break.'

'And did you find it?' said Zinovev, turning to her and rapping out the words in a harsh, unmodulated tone. 'Your fresh perspective?'

Olga laughed. 'Well, yes and no, I suppose,' she replied. 'Ekaterina always has a fresh take on things – but today it was really just a case of smoking a couple of cigarettes and trying to relax a little. Look out!'

Zinovev had carried on gazing at her with his hot, watery eyes, almost driving into an oncoming lorry as a result.

'Sorry, Olga,' he said, after a minute. 'I'm not feeling quite myself. It's the clinics – we're pretty much out of runway, and I can't find money anywhere . . . In fact, I – I think I won't pop round to yours after all. I'd planned to come and see Anna,' he went on, 'as it's been a while, but – but no, I don't think I will.'

'I'd try and get some rest, Yury,' replied Olga, putting a hand on his arm. 'I think you've been overdoing it, haven't you?'

He nodded without speaking, and Olga was sure – from a rapid sideways glance – that his eyes had added an extra tint of teardrops to their hot surface. He dropped Olga at her chosen location, Café Astana, without speaking much more, and sped off with a hurried wave, the scruffy Haval squeaking and rattling as he went. Olga looked after him for a long moment, wondering what on earth was eating him. It cleared the way for Fyodor, of course, if Zinovev couldn't even bring himself to visit Anna – and Olga's sympathies lay with the Dreamer despite all his ridiculous idiosyncrasies. But that didn't mean she wished ill to Zinovev, and it was with a pensive look that she turned towards the café.

Then she stopped, and looked back at the rear of Zinovev's car as it disappeared around the corner. It had just occurred to her that she didn't know how the troupe got to and from Tayga. There was no public transport, of course, and hadn't been since the last state-funded bus had juddered to a halt after the *sozhkhov* shut down. Did they use taxis, perhaps, as they had on the day Rodion Rultava had been murdered, or was that just a last-minute solution in light of the circumstances? Taxis weren't cheap, with prices the way they were. Her brow wrinkled as she thought about the troupe's finances, and the seemingly deep pockets that allowed for hotels, cars and takeaway food, not to mention the lavishly appointed train, the hire of the seating for the audience, and the publicity splashed all over Tayga and elsewhere.

She turned back towards the café again. She would speak to Vassily when she saw him the next day, and suggest they dig a little deeper into the troupe's finances. Where there's gold, there's also dirt, she said to herself, smiling with delight, then digging into her handbag, and scribbling down the words on a scrap of paper. It was always worth writing down any new proverbs that came to mind, for she could fill her masterpieces with them and become part of the Russian language for ever.

She pushed open the café door with the smile still lingering on her lips, but it soon vanished when she saw the scene inside. The café walls, which until now had been festooned with Igor's Kazakh space memorabilia, were almost bare, with lighter patches showing where this poster or that mission badge had been nailed up ten or twenty years ago. There was a pile of materials on the biggest table in the restaurant – the long rectangular one bearing marks from many years of over-enthusiastic dining – and several men gathered around it, mostly very pale and mostly dressed in black. Igor stood behind the table with a clipboard and a carrier bag of roubles, from which he fished dog-eared notes for change as the men handed him fistfuls of money and tucked the coveted trinkets under their arms. He was doing brisk business, but how could he sell off all his most beloved possessions like this? He was nodding and smiling, and pointing to this and that piece of kitsch, but Olga thought she could see a glint of moisture in his eyes, like a man bidding farewell to a favourite son.

She walked up to the bar, where Igor's daughter, Svetlana, was polishing a glass with unusual assiduity and cheerfulness.

'What's going on?' said Olga.

'What?'

'What's going on with your father?' she said, with a touch more emphasis.

'Oh, he's selling off all his space tat. Should've cut out the middleman, I told him, and just turf it straight into the bin.'

'Yes, Svetlana,' said Olga, forcing herself to be patient, 'I can see he's selling it off – but why?'

'Oh, it's that vodka deal of his,' she replied, quite airily. 'The Rocket Fuel thing, *da*? Well, the fool went out and spent a heap of money on the strength of it, didn't he, and now the franchise cash seems to have disappeared.'

'How serious is it?'

'I don't know,' she said.

'But aren't you worried about your job?'

Svetlana laughed, then wiped the rim of the glass on her leather miniskirt and replaced it on the shelf. 'Don't worry about me, Olga Pushkin – I've got bigger fish to fry than some part-time job pouring drinks for broken-down has-beens.'

'What bigger fish?'

'That would be telling,' she said, tapping her nose and wincing as the gesture shifted her latest nose-ring. 'But put it this way – nobody upstages me, *da*? Nobody!'

She smiled at Olga and walked into the kitchen, leaving Olga more than a little puzzled. What could have made Svetlana so happy? And what could have gone so wrong with Igor's vodka deal?

'It's the cat meat,' said Fyodor Katin, making her jump.

'Oh, Fyodor!' she cried. 'You shouldn't sneak up to people like that.'

'It's not me who's been sneaking up to people,' he said, plumping himself down on the stool next to her and removing his fur hat to reveal a tangled mat of hair. 'These robberies are still going on, you know, and I think they're getting more desperate – I heard old Nadya Popov had her handbag snatched yesterday.'

'She'd probably be more upset to hear you calling her old,' said Olga. 'Anyway, what was it you were saying about the Red Star?'

'Well, who's got a motive to put Igor out of business? The

local health authorities, that's who . . . He's always escaped them so far, but I wouldn't put it past them to have found out about the offer, and got in touch with the franchise people just to spite Igor.'

Olga stared at him. 'Do you really think that's it?'

'I wouldn't be surprised,' said Fyodor, following Olga's example and pouring himself a shot of vodka. 'What?' he went on, smiling at her. 'I know people call me the Dreamer, but I've got more than clouds between my ears!'

'Is anyone serving here?' said a third voice, and Olga turned to see Yegor Shulgin, the troupe's cue-master and secretary, standing behind them.

'Er – well, we are, I suppose,' said Olga. 'Vodka? Here you are.'

'There's a stool, if you want it,' said Fyodor.

'Thank you,' said Yegor, taking off his glasses and rubbing his eyes.

'So – back in Roslazny,' said Olga. 'I'd have thought you might want to get away, after all that's happened.'

'Well, we've got a rehearsal starting later on,' explained Yegor, replacing his glasses. 'But in any case I like these local places. The real backbone of Siberia, I always think!'

'Not for long,' muttered Fyodor, jerking a thumb at Igor and his gaggle of space enthusiasts. 'That's the boss selling off the family silver to survive.'

'Oh dear, dear, dear,' said Yegor, frowning. 'That would be such a shame. I don't care for the other place at all, at all.'

'I'll drink to that,' said Olga, drily, pouring another shot for them all after they had drunk. 'So – another rehearsal. But who have you got to replace—'

She stopped speaking as she realised who the troupe had found to replace Larissa Lazarov: it was Svetlana Odrosov, of course! *Nobody upstages me* . . . Of course Svetlana had a kind of obvious attractiveness, but still Olga couldn't help but feel a pang of jealousy. Didn't they realise she was an author and a fellow explorer of literary worlds? Didn't they know that she understood words in a way that others didn't?

She struggled to suppress the unworthy feelings that envy prompted, only to experience its barbed claws a second time in as many minutes.

'They nearly persuaded Anna,' said Fyodor. 'Didn't you, Yegor?'

'Anna – Anna Kabalevsky? *My* Anna?' said Olga.

Yegor smiled at her. 'Yes, that's right – we thought she had the kind of appeal that would suit the role of a nurse. And we've had great success with Lev, who's taken to the colonel's role just splendidly – splendidly. I couldn't have done it better myself.'

'But she turned it down,' said Fyodor, with a touch – Olga thought – of pride. 'She said she didn't think she could do the role justice, and that it was too out of character.'

'We tried to explain that that could be a good thing,' simpered Yegor, putting a hand on Olga's arm, 'and that actors didn't actually have to be like the characters they play, but she didn't quite grasp it. Bless! Oh – here is the good lady now, and her dear, *dear* children.'

The doorbell had indeed tinkled, and Olga turned to see Anna entering with her brood, her face sequentially lighting up as she saw Olga, smiling politely as she saw Yegor, and blushing as she saw Fyodor.

'Come and have some Rocket Fuel, Anna,' said Olga, whose

feelings of jealousy had disappeared at the sight of her friend's face and the goodness it radiated, like warmth from a hearth. 'We're serving ourselves today.'

'Well, just a quick one, Olga,' said Anna, in a slightly harried tone. 'I've got to take Boris into Tayga in a minute – Nonna's driving me – and I was hoping you'd be here so I could ask you to look after Ilya and Gyorgy.'

'Of course,' began Olga, but Fyodor had also begun to speak.

'We'll both do it,' said Fyodor, smiling awkwardly at her. 'With pleasure.'

'Oh, thank you, Fyodor,' she said, beaming back at him. 'It's so good of you!'

I also said I'd do it, said Olga to herself, but looking affectionately at them both. Yegor also smiled, and took off his glasses again to clean them, but dropped them on the floor – upon which Gyorgy immediately picked them up and put them on, dancing around the café with glee and calling, 'I'm a superhero! I'm a superhero!' before evading Anna's clutches and darting to the door, opening it and shouting, 'Look! Look! It's Popov! It's Popov!'

Finally, and with Fyodor's help, Gyorgy was retrieved, severely chastened, and made to return the glasses to a somewhat red-faced Yegor, who had not taken particularly kindly to the childish excursion. Anna and Olga took this as a cue to make a move, and with Fyodor's help they walked out of the café, leaving Yegor sipping another vodka at the counter, and walking past Popov as he shuffled at last towards the door.

'Watch it,' he said, standing unnecessarily aside to allow the children to pass. 'It's bad enough around here, with all these thieves and pickpockets, without a pack of young hooligans tearing around the place!'

'Oh, come on, Nikolai,' said Fyodor. 'They're just being children.'

'It's serve-yourself inside,' said Olga, who knew how to cheer Popov up.

'Now that's the good news I've been waiting for,' said the butcher, visibly brightening. 'Good day to you all! Odrosov's going to rue the day he diddled me over those dog steaks . . .'

An hour or so later, Olga was gazing out of her bedroom window with Dmitri snuffling in her arms. He had been confined to quarters since his escapade by the tracks, which, as Olga knew, could very well have seen him come to as sticky an end as Larissa Lazarov. And, besides, she told herself with the most sternness she could muster, Dmitri might soon be living at the house full-time anyway, since the hut would no longer be hers to call her own.

She caressed his prickles and looked out at the damp, grey-lit garden, wondering when, when, when the snow would return . . . She longed for it as a desert-dweller yearned for rain, or a sailor for a glimpse of verdant land, imagining the sibilant hiss of countless snowflakes covering each house, each garden, each run-down, dilapidated shamble of a human being with a pristine and virginal dressing. And the village could do with being covered up . . . Everything was falling apart, and she stared into the sky as if her very yearning could chill the air till the longed-for snow came and blanketed everything into forgetfulness.

She would particularly like to forget her latest call with Maxim Gusev, her editor at Lyapunov Books, who had become quite shirty when she pressed him about marketing plans to address the challenge posed by Inessa Ignatyev's *All on the Line*.

'It's in hand, Olga – I told you this already,' he'd barked down the line. 'I can't do any work when I'm on the phone, *da*? So these conversations don't help things to move any faster.'

'You've said it's in hand, yes – but *what* is in hand? You haven't given me any details!'

'Olga, relax – relax! You'll hear more in due course. As soon as I have details to share, you'll be the first to know. And for now, like I say – relax!'

The phone call had, of course, been anything but relaxing, and Olga had needed quite a few minutes of slow breathing, Dmitri in hand, to achieve that result after Maxim had hung up. Consequently, when her ancient Nokia mobile lit up again on the windowsill a few minutes later, she hesitated to pick it up. What could it be but more bad news? When did she ever receive anything else, by phone or letter or conversation?

It rang off, but lit up again a few minutes later. Olga sighed, put Dmitri down on the carpet, and bent to pick it up.

'Ekaterina!' she said. 'This is a nice surprise. I thought—'

But Ekaterina spoke across her. 'Listen, Olga,' she said, 'you need to get down to the police station to see Vassily.'

'Vassily? The police station? But why—'

Ekaterina cut her off again. 'I'm sorry, Olga, but I don't have a lot of time,' she went on, breathlessly. 'Pavel called again and, well, we might be heading to the Tayga Hotel soon.'

Olga rolled her eyes. Yet another romantic assignation! What was Ekaterina's secret? Olga loved her, of course, but often wondered how her colourful outfits, rackety headscarves, garish handbags and partially dyed hair managed to win her so many admirers among the male sex.

'OK, OK,' she said. 'I get it! But what should I talk to Vassily about?'

'*Cars*,' she said. 'I found out from – well, from another gentleman of my acquaintance, everything still amicable, that the troupe's been getting around in two hired cars, an Opel and a Lada Riva. No big deal, I know – but here's the thing: one of the cars has been seen at the Tayga Hospital.'

Olga pursed her lips. 'So – visiting sick children, maybe? Don't actors do that kind of thing?'

'At night? And three nights in a row, a week before the Murder Express started performing?'

'A week before? Your man's sure? Well, maybe one of the actors was sick.'

'No, he checked with the registrar. None of the people we know was treated as a patient.'

'So – what, then? Why do you think Vassily needs to know?'

'I don't know,' admitted Ekaterina. 'But it's strange, isn't it? Could be that somebody in the troupe already knew someone in the region, maybe? It might give you a motive to work with, at last! Oh, Olga, I've felt so bad about you! You have so much to deal with, and everything bad seems to land on your plate. I just hoped – I just hoped this might help. But now I really have to go. Send my love to Vassily!'

'I will—' began Olga, but Ekaterina had already rung off. She gazed out of the window and sighed again. It didn't seem so very much to go on, after all, but it was kind of Ekaterina to have thought of her, all the same. And Olga was pleased, in a way, that this new lead related to the troupe's transport, a topic that had occurred to her only a little earlier. And who knew what might solve a case? More had been made of less, she knew – or, at least, it had in the TV shows she liked to watch in the slow afternoons when her duty rota had allocated her some rare time off. She had once seen Colonel Stepan Grigorovich Babanin, her favourite small-screen detective, commit three murderous sisters to long prison sentences on the sole basis of a discarded piece of banana skin. So perhaps Vassily could do something with the car-hire business, after all. And, besides, it was time she caught up with him again. She would have done before, she knew, if there had been only two human inhabitants at the police station, instead of three or four or five, she thought, reluctantly including Vassily's ferret, Rasputin, and Rozalina's Sputnik in the count.

She bent down to retrieve Dmitri from the corner under her wardrobe and glanced in the mirror, before putting Dmitri down again and darting to the little table that served as her make-up counter. Then, blemishes fixed, she hooked her puffed outdoor jacket with a spare finger and walked through to the living room, where Pasha was entertaining Anna's boys with an energetic game of hide-and-seek while Anna paid a quick visit to Nonna.

'Pasha, I'm leaving Dmitri in his box again,' she called, over the noise. 'I'll be back in an hour or two.'

'Very good,' said Pasha, with the air of a subordinate receiving his orders. 'Wait – are you off to see Vassily?'

'How did you guess?' Olga felt the blood rushing to her cheeks in its usual perfidious manner.

'Well – the make-up, I suppose,' said Pasha, his voice muffled by the lithe form of Boris, who had chosen that moment to leap upon his head.

'Can't I decide to look nice when I go out and about any more? It's nothing to do with Vassily,' she said, a little more vehemently than she'd intended.

'*Da, da*,' he replied, grinning. 'Here,' he added, reaching out a hand and throwing Olga's fur hat towards her. 'Have a good time – and keep an eye open on your way. We don't want you ending up like Nadya Popov, with your handbag snatched.'

There wasn't much chance of that, thought Olga, as she left the house and closed the door behind her. Nadya was a slow-moving target if ever there was one, and with luridly coloured handbags that were as good as a bullseye to any half-motivated mugger. Olga, by contrast, walked quickly from the force of long habit, and if she even carried a handbag – which she did less than half of the time – it tended to be the utilitarian, Soviet-looking one she'd bought from a car-boot salesman one day on the outskirts of Tayga. What was more, Olga prided herself on wielding a strong fist when she had to – and she *had* had to far too often, that particular year. No: it would be a brave thief who chose to target her, she told herself, as she walked through the garden and out onto the path that led north towards Vassily and the police station.

Was it her imagination, though, or did she hear quiet footsteps behind her, as she passed by the old bathhouses? She stopped and turned, but there was nobody there. It must have been her imagination, she told herself, or maybe the echo of her own footsteps gathered by the surrounding ruins and thrown back to deceive her listening ears. She tutted, and turned to move forwards once more – but, again, she seemed to hear something apart from the sound of her own winter boots squelching on the muddy path, damp, uneven, and stubbly with struggling bits of vegetation. The sound wasn't behind her any more, though, but to the side – and as she realised this she looked up and saw a figure dressed all in black, with a balaclava over their face and dark rubber-soled shoes at top and bottom, advancing towards her with a raised arm.

She started, and screamed, and as she did so her fur hat came off, revealing her hair and face to her attacker. She backed away from him, or her, and fell as she did so, tumbling down onto a half-fallen wall and bruising her legs, but raising her arms to defend herself, determined not to yield anything without a fight – but to her astonishment the attacker backed away, staring at her with uncertain eyes, taking first one step, then another away from her, before taking to their heels and sprinting down the path, around the corner and out of sight. Olga stared after the disappearing figure in astonishment – astonishment and bewilderment, but also a touch of unease: hadn't that head, only partially disguised by a balaclava, looked somehow familiar?

10

Agent Provocateur

'Olga – what happened? Are you all right?'

Vassily knew her, she thought, as he reached out a hand and guided her into the station. Oh, yes, he knew her well, to see with one rapid glance that something had indeed happened to her – something disturbing – something alarming.

'Here – have a seat,' he said, pulling one of the rickety wooden chairs out from its place by the wall, and tipping it sideways so the papers on top tumbled to the floor. 'Rozalina?' he called, down the corridor that led to the cells and the warmest part of the police station in winter. 'Do we have any tea on the go?'

'*Nyet*,' came the dispiriting, disinterested answer, and so, with no sign of Rozalina making any effort to make some, Vassily busied himself with the little stove and saucepan he kept on the reception desk, which was soon hissing and bubbling industriously. Then he offered Olga a cigarette, lit one for himself, and sat down next to her.

'So – tell me,' he said. 'What happened? You look white as snow.'

'Snow? I wish it would,' she said, before telling him about her unexpected black-clad assailant and his or her equally unexpected retreat.

'They knew you, then,' said Vassily, taking a deep draw on his Belamorkanal cigarette and gazing ahead with pensive eyes. 'They knew you, and decided not to escape with your handbag in tow – either because they saw someone else coming down the path' – Olga shook her head mutely – 'or because they were worried you'd recognise them if they stayed any longer.'

Olga said nothing, and Vassily continued, after a pause: 'There was nothing distinctive about their clothing, or their walk, or even the shape of their head – nothing that rang a bell?'

'No bells,' she said, after a moment.

'Well . . .' he said, looking at her for a minute. 'Well . . . Oh, the water's ready. Here,' he said, pouring the water into a mug with a teabag sitting in it. 'Here's some tea. It's raspberry – Rozalina's favourite. I hope that's all right?'

'It's fine, Vassily,' she said, despite an initial desire to contradict and overrule – a desire born from an instinctive reluctance to enjoy anything that Rozalina enjoyed. As a matter of fact, though, she shared Rozalina's love of raspberry tea, in large part because it reminded Olga of beloved, half-remembered, long-distant visits to Astrazov to the north of Tomsk, when she would wander down the overgrown paths around the old Lodge, walking hand in hand with her mother Tatiana and plucking raspberries as they went until she could eat no more of the little fruits, at once heavy-laden with moisture and strangely dry to her young, questing fingertips.

The Lodge had long since passed out of her mother's family's hands, and since Tatiana had been born on the wrong side of the aristocratic blanket there had never been much hope of getting it back – but now, sipping the hot raspberry tea and wrapping herself in one of the rather threadbare blankets draped over the backs of the police-station chairs, she could almost imagine herself back there, exploring hidden byways along which the young Lichnovsky counts and countesses, Tatiana's forebears, had run long ago before the bloodshed came.

'Yes, yes, it's fine,' she said, her eyes far-off and unseeing, but Vassily had no such memories to distract him, and was all business with regard to the Roslazny robberies and the Murder Express murders. 'Kliment's out, I suppose?'

'Yes, yes – he's with some schoolfriends somewhere, over Tayga way, I think,' said Vassily, vaguely. 'But we can't have respectable Roslaznyans being attacked as they go about their lawful business,' he said, gesturing at Olga as he spoke.

'So – I'm respectable, am I?' she said quickly. 'Dowdy, you mean – or even frumpy? Dull, staid, boring, predictable? Is that what you mean, Vassily – is it?'

He stared at her in horror until he saw the smile in her eyes, upon which he, too, allowed a smile to crease the stern lines of his current expression.

'All right, all right – so maybe respectable was the wrong word, but you know what I mean. Everyone loves you, Olga – well, everyone except your father and his cronies – so if even *you* are being attacked . . . But leaving that aside for now, there's also our beloved gaggle of thespians and their apparent addiction to homicide. And as it happens I've got quite a lot to tell you – in fact, I was about to come out and find you! Wasn't I, *dorogoy*?' he added to Rozalina, who had just appeared in the reception area, clad in a pink faux-fur dressing-gown that Olga might well have hesitated to wear in company.

Rozalina nodded at Olga, but didn't trouble to force a smile onto her face, which was plastered – Olga noted – in an even thicker layer of make-up than usual. How did she afford it? Olga could barely stump up for concealer and foundation from the cheapest shop in Tayga, the way prices were going – but then again, she had never had a husband to keep satisfied and interested, and maybe that was just what you did, when you were married. So, really, who was she to judge?

Regardless of make-up, she did feel able to judge Rozalina for her consistent unfriendliness towards her, as if she regarded her as a genuine threat to her happiness with Vassily – her happiness, or whatever she called it: they didn't seem particularly happy to Olga. Or, more accurately, Rozalina seemed quite content to be waited on hand and foot by Vassily, while he seemed willing to do anything for his long-lost wife merely on the basis that she was, well, his long-lost wife.

Just now, for instance, he jumped to his feet to find the items for which she had left her comfortable bed in the lattermost prison cell. And once he'd found the hairbrush, straighteners and hairspray for her – buried for some reason under Vassily's casework files – she turned with barely a nod of thanks and walked back towards the cells, her feet shuffling along the uneven floor in shiny pink slippers and her faux-fur dressing-gown sliding along the narrow passageway like some giant insect returning to its lair.

He seemed unperturbed, though, as he returned to his seat and wrinkled his brow. 'Where was I?' he said. 'Oh, yes – the Murder Express! Well, it turns out that a few things have been bubbling away since we last saw each other – bubbling away, and maybe even boiling over, like an unwatched samovar.'

And he told her then of the news he'd had from a couple of far-off rural stations not unlike Roslazny, but much farther west – places like Kommunar near St Petersburg, and Severnyy near Izhevsk, from which reports had come of odd circumstances surrounding theatrical performances, and incongruous events that jarred with the highly respectable public profiles of Agapa and Ilya Putyatin.

'There's that word again, Vassily,' said Olga.

'What – respectable?' Vassily laughed. 'Well, they are very respectable, in the acting world, but that just makes it all the more strange. Setting up in such off-beat locations, with such small audiences – and then the death to follow . . .'

'A *death*? You mean, before they came to Roslazny?'

'Yes – a drowning, in fact, though it was an accident. I've got the report to prove it,' he added, picking up one of the files that had concealed Rozalina's salon products from view. 'And I can't see anything to link the death to either of the Putyatins, or to Yegor, who was with them for the last tour before this, as you know. It was a straightforward suicide, as far as I can make out: one of the actresses had been passed over for the lead, and so took matters into her own hands. I mean that quite literally: she tied a mud-weight around her waist and jumped overboard between performances.'

'Overboard?'

'Yes – didn't I say? The performances near Izhevsk took

place on an old houseboat, on the Izhevskiy Prud – a large pond, or lake, really, just to the west of the city.'

'She drowned . . . What was it Ilya Putyatin said, Vassily? That the biggest injury of all was nobody remembering their performances . . . Could he really have meant that? That an actress – what was her name?'

Vassily glanced down at one of the files lying on the reception desk. 'Kira Obnizov,' he replied.

'Could he really have meant that the theatrical failure of some obscure play was a bigger problem than the drowning of Kira Obnizov? Doesn't that point to a fairly staggering level of heartlessness?'

'Maybe,' said Vassily, nodding to concede the point. 'But it's hardly proof of any wrongdoing, is it? The coroner seemed quite happy on the point of it being a suicide instead of a murder. He wrote there was no sign of any foul play, even though – just as with Rodion – there was no note.'

'Well, there wouldn't be any sign of foul play, would there? I mean, think of it, Vassily. A young actress – Kira was young, I suppose?'

'Twenty-four.'

'There you are, then. A young actress, impressionable, keen to get on in her career – and a powerful older man like Ilya Putyatin, a famous actor and director, offering her personal tuition and assistance . . . Maybe things get a little out of hand, and they start an affair – but it's awkward, and he tries to back out. She threatens him! And then he becomes the peacemaker, offers her flowers and compliments, and one more acting lesson, too – he wraps a rope around her waist, to help her prepare for a difficult scene in the play, he says, but then he throws the mud-weight out of the houseboat door, pulling her down after him, down, down, down until her hair floats up around her like a halo and she is gone. And, hey presto, Ilya Putyatin's problems are gone, too.'

She stopped then, smiling with satisfaction as she saw Vassily staring at her, open-mouthed in astonishment.

'Olga!' he breathed. 'How did you think all that up?'

'It's easy,' she said. 'Or, at least, it's easy if you're a writer. Very hard otherwise.'

'Well, I hope you never take to crime,' he said, still gazing at her in admiration, 'or we'll all be sunk. Only – I'm sorry to pour cold water on your theories, Olga, but Ilya Putyatin couldn't have done any of that. He's got a rock-solid alibi for the day Kira Obnizov died – the coroner made a special note of it. Maybe he suspected him, too . . .'

'Must've been an unusually intelligent coroner,' said Olga. 'But I wasn't really being serious, you know. I've no idea what happened to Kira, any more than you do. But it seems odd to me that any up-and-coming actress with a role in a troupe led by the Putyatins would choose to kill herself, and in such a horrible manner too. But there's something even odder than that, which is—'

'Which is that the Putyatins didn't mention this to us in the first place,' said Vassily. 'I agree – it's odd. It's more than odd, in fact, though I suppose it's natural enough, from another point of view, that they would try to cover up a previous theatrical disaster when a whole new one is just getting off the ground. Might make them look suspicious, when in reality they had nothing to do with it at all, last time around . . . Well, anyway, it's obvious we need to talk to them again, and sooner rather than later.

'And then there's the car-hire business, and those evening visits to the Tayga Hospital,' went on Vassily, standing up and walking over to the window where, by stooping low, he could survey the stretch of narrow road that led to the crossroads near Café Astana. He seemed to be looking for someone, thought Olga, but apparently they were nowhere to be seen, for then he frowned and resumed his normal height. 'We need to find out which actors were visiting there, and why.'

'It does seem odd that they would visit at night,' acknowledged Olga. 'And speaking of the hospital, there's also Dr Zinovev to talk about . . .'

'Zinovev? What's he got to do with it?'

Olga told him then of her strange journey back to Roslazny from Tayga with the doctor, who seemed to have abandoned his initially promising courtship of Anna Kabalevsky, leaving the field clear for his erstwhile rival, Fyodor Katin.

'It's not that I wanted him to win and Fyodor to lose,' said Olga. 'It's just that – well, I don't know what, exactly. But I don't like seeing the doctor like that. He seemed – well, he seemed desperate, really, and like a man running out of time, or running out of something, anyway. And I just wondered—'

'Yes?'

'Well – Agapa and Ilya aren't getting any younger, are they?' said Olga. 'Maybe it was one of them who was visiting the hospital, or both. It would make sense for them to be in the area earlier than the rest of the troupe, as they're in charge . . . Could Zinovev have been giving them some special treatments – cheap drugs on the side, or something illegal like that? Or some emergency procedure they didn't want their theatrical friends knowing about, thinking they'd abandon the troupe and go elsewhere if they thought Agapa and Ilya were on the way out? And maybe—'

'Maybe Zinovev's feeling guilty, since he's a good man and devoted to his poorest patients, as we know – and yet here he is catering to the rich and privileged?' said Vassily, to an answering nod from Olga. 'Well, maybe – maybe. It might be we need to have a word with the good doctor, too, though I can't see how any of this could relate to the murders on the Murder Express. In fact, it's almost the opposite – it could be Agapa and Ilya desperately trying to keep themselves going for the actors' benefit, rather than trying to bump them off.'

Olga nodded, trying to hide her irritation at Vassily killing off yet another possible route to motive for their frustratingly iron-clad group of suspects. No sooner did one potential source of guilt surface than powerful counterweights emerged to topple the latest explanation from its pedestal, and there they were, all over again. It was almost as if some dark mastermind were playing them all like puppets from behind the scenery, standing to one side of the trees along the siding, or beyond the great wheels and connecting-rods of the P36, wreathed in steam-clouds and plotting murder, watching them with eyes that kindled with reflected sparks and the red glow of the fire-box. And who better to direct a performance than a director? she asked herself. Who more qualified, who more experienced, than the Putyatins? Agapa, with her steely-eyed determination to impose her will on her troupe, and Ilya, with his fussy, soft-spoken demeanour, perhaps the perfect disguise for a mind obsessed not with reviews and matinees but with cold-blooded murder . . .

'We need to speak to Yegor Shulgin again, too,' said Vassily, interrupting her racing thoughts, 'since he was with them at

Izhevsk, and also didn't trouble to mention anything about poor Kira's death.'

'So – new interviews with the Putyatins, Yegor and Zinovev,' said Olga. 'That's plenty to be getting on with!'

'I'd better see what the schedule is for today,' said Vassily. 'With the Murder Express, I mean – I think they're still planning to keep going, so there might be a rehearsal in Roslazny where we can get all three of them at once. And I'll drop a line to the hospital and see where Zinovev is. And— Oh, yes, Rozalina, what can I do for you?'

Vassily's tone switched suddenly from hard-nosed business to sickly sweet sentiment upon the reappearance of Rozalina from the cells, clad as before in faux-fur dressing-gown and oversize pink slippers.

'Oh, nothing much, Vassily,' she said, with an insouciant air. 'Only that there aren't any snacks – nothing important! I mean, nothing important, if you think it's fine for your wife to starve away in the course of a day, while you busy yourself with more important things.'

Vassily glanced at Olga, then back to Rozalina. 'Oh – aren't there any biscuits in the tin by Rasputin's cage?'

'Our dear son has eaten all those, and he gave the crumbs to Rasputin, didn't he?' said Rozalina, in tones just as sickly as Vassily's.

'Well, I'll try to pick something up later,' he said. 'I'll be going by Café Astana anyway to get to the train. We've got more interviews to do, and— Oh, hang on. Yes? Marushkin here.'

Vassily's walkie-talkie had crackled into life. He put it to his ear and moved away, first to the edge of the reception area and then, to Olga's horror, out of the station altogether, barging aside the door with his free hand, then motioning to Olga to stay put, before pulling it shut behind him, leaving Olga and Rozalina looking at each other in what fast became – from Olga's side at least – a rather uncomfortable silence.

'So – you're still working with my husband,' said Rozalina at last, sliding into a chair across from Olga and smoothing her dressing-gown with fingers that each boasted a long, shiny purple nail.

'Yes,' said Olga, who couldn't think of anything to add.

'Must be a nice situation for you.'

'Well – not particularly, to be honest. I mean, I'm only doing it because my boss is making me.'

'But you've worked with him before? Vassily, I mean – he told me so.'

'That was different,' said Olga, quickly. 'That was before – before—'

'Before I came back,' said Rozalina, looking directly at her. 'That's what you mean? Before I came back, and when Vassily was free.'

'Oh, well, I mean—'

But Rozalina leaned forward. 'Vassily's mine,' she hissed. 'Mine and mine alone – understand? I know you think you're better than everyone, Olga Pushkin, but I know all about you. I know about Mongolia, and how you sneaked your way out of that exchange programme. I know about your stupid little hedgehog, and your ridiculous book, and your brother. I know your hut's under threat, too – probably they took a look at your latest medical and thought you weren't going to last. Oh, yes, I know it all. And so you see,' she went on, getting to her feet, 'I'd recommend you stay away from Vassily, and Kliment, and me, and Sputnik – from all of us! Though come to think of it, Rasputin might be different – Rasputin you could take. That's about your level! Ha. Yes, that's about where you fit – looking after a mangy old ferret.'

With one last look of pure contempt, Rozalina walked off towards the cells, leaving Olga sitting staring after her. In part of her mind she wondered how Vassily could ever have married somebody so desperately unpleasant, so horrible – so *awful* – and how that union could have produced such a wonderful boy as Kliment. She also asked herself how Rozalina could possibly know so much about her . . . Married couples talked, she knew, and told each other most things under the sun, but that didn't stop it feeling like a betrayal of sorts for Vassily to have passed on so much private information. It reminded Olga of Polina Klemovsky, the very unpleasant and irredeemably nosy engineer who had taken Olga's place on the Mongolian exchange, to Polina's great displeasure. But another question also came to mind: how was it that Rozalina's eyes, which she had just seen closer than ever, looked so different from the wrinkled old photograph Vassily had had pinned up in the back office since Olga had known him? A face could change, and other things, too, if you took into account the terrible treatment that people traffickers all too often meted out to their victims, beatings included – but *eyes*? Weren't they the windows to the soul? And if they were, did Vassily realise what kind of soul they could let out upon the world?

Kliment had not returned by the time Olga and Vassily left the police station a little later, though Olga thought she caught a glimpse of a young figure in the distance as they turned to leave. There wasn't time to discuss Vassily's son, however, or even his wife, who, to Olga's relief, had taken herself back to her cells immediately following their traumatic conversation. The reason for this was Captain Zemsky, whose call to Vassily had been filled with reproaches, timelines and elaborate swear-words, leaving him in little doubt that if he didn't get his bloody arse in gear, as Zemsky put it, he'd soon be directing traffic in downtown Tomsk with Junior Sergeant Timofei Davidov. Vassily's face, upon his return, was at once pale and determined, and he had wasted no time on pleasantries.

'Right – get your things,' he snapped. 'We're going to speak to the Murder Express people right now.'

'There won't be much time before the performance,' she replied, glancing down at the screen of her aged Nokia.

'I don't give a damn,' he said, grabbing his coat and notebook as if they had personally offended him, and marching out of the door so that Olga had to scurry after him, her own coat hooked precariously over a finger.

He didn't take any prisoners at the Murder Express, either, stalking down the track towards the rear of the train and banging on the door of the second carriage until an angry face poked out.

'What is it – what is it?' cried Agapa Putyatin, looking down with eyes of thunder. 'Oh, it's you. We are rehearsing, you know – or trying to . . . These new people: I'm at my wits' end.'

'Good morning, Sergeant,' said Yegor Shulgin, peering around Agapa and nodding at Vassily and Olga. 'I'm afraid it *is* rather trying today – a challenge to get Svetlana up to speed with the lines. And even Lev still struggles at times, days later . . .'

'Well, he is a railway engineer by trade,' pointed out Olga, slightly irritated by Yegor's tone.

'Barely even that, if you ask us,' said Vadim Lilov, the P36 fireman, who had come from the far side of the tracks with some tools in hand.

'I don't know, Vad,' said a coal-stained Simeon Zarubin, the driver. 'He's always spouting a heap of made-up rubbish, so what's the difference?'

'How dare you compare—' began Yegor, but Vassily spoke across him.

'Listen, Dama Putyatin,' said Vassily, who – Olga could see – was becoming annoyed at the impromptu social gathering that had emerged. 'We need to have a quick word, I'm afraid, with, well, with a small number of your crew.'

'Crew?' she said, brushing a strand of blonde hair back behind her ear, and smoothing the folds of her silken tsarina dress. 'It's not a *crew*, Inspector. We are on a train, yes, but in this case appearances are wholly deceiving: the true heart and soul of this vehicle lies not in its mechanical appurtenances, but in the artistic work we achieve upon its humble floor.'

Ilya Putyatin now made an appearance, peering around the side of Agapa and adding his two kopeks' worth.

'If you must use a collective, Colonel,' he said, in his slightly high-pitched, fussy voice, 'you might use troupe, or company – or even ensemble. I hope that is helpful?'

Vassily nodded, clearly trying to retain some vestige of patience, and forced a smile onto his face. 'Very helpful indeed,

Gospodin Putyatin. But now I really must insist that we have a quick conversation with you and Dama Putyatin – and Yegor, too, please. In the first carriage, perhaps? We'll walk down now.'

'D'you want us?' said Simeon Zarubin, scratching his nose with a sooty glove and smearing black dust even more liberally around his face. 'Only we've got to fire up again—'

'No, no, no,' said Vassily. 'No, thank you. Just the crew – the troupe, I mean.'

'Could be confusing, that,' grumbled Vadim Lilov, as the railwaymen picked up their tools again and walked off towards the engine, where Lev's replacement, Yefim, was leaning on the ledge at the side of the cab. 'No consideration, some people – no consideration at all!'

The carriage wall had not yet been raised for the performance, so the interior was pleasantly warm after the growing chill of the November day. Olga and Vassily found seats, as before, from the collection of old-fashioned Victorian chairs dotted around the room, then Vassily called down the corridor for the Putyatins and Yegor Shulgin to join them.

'It'll put them at their ease to see them all together,' explained Vassily, 'partly because they're so worried about their precious rehearsal, and it'll be quicker to do things that way – but also because they'll think they can rely on each other to provide the answers to tricky questions. But I'll see what we can do about that.'

The Putyatins came in with Yegor following, tripping over the wooden divider between the carriages so that he nearly measured his length on the floor.

'Careful, careful,' snapped Agapa, as he brushed past her voluminous skirts. 'This is real silk, you know! If I've told you once I've told you a thousand times you'd never have made it on the stage, Yegor.'

'I have other skills, don't forget,' he said, with a touch of sulkiness.

'Oh, yes, indeed,' said Ilya, archly. 'Where would we be without your support?'

'You've worked together before, of course,' said Vassily, as if remembering this for the first time. 'But things didn't go very smoothly last time, either, did they? What was her name, now – the actress who drowned? Kira something?'

He turned to Olga, as if he now couldn't remember her surname.

'Kira Obnizov,' she said, quietly, watching the actors' faces. Ilya's lips tightened, she noticed, and Yegor had gone pale – but Agapa hadn't changed at all, staring at them with the same immovable mask that she must have used on countless occasions on stage and on screen, a shield behind which to protect her innermost thoughts and feelings.

But then the mask shifted, disintegrating into an expression of fulsome sympathy, and with eyes so marked with sorrow that Olga would not have been surprised to see her shed a tear.

'Kira! Dear, dear Kira . . . If ever there was a casting decision we could take again, that would be it. To think that such a young, such a pretty girl could drown herself over such a little thing as the lead role in one of our humble productions . . .'

'It simply never occurred to us, Chief Inspector,' said Ilya, hand over his heart. 'How could it? I mean, we had seen disappointment before – disillusionment, even, and perhaps a degree of reproach directed towards ourselves – but nothing of that kind.'

'She was already unbalanced before we met her, I think,' put in Yegor Shulgin, shaking his head. 'A paragraph short of a sentence, if you take my meaning. No – a sentence short of a paragraph.'

'Maybe so,' said Vassily. 'But what I want to know is this: why did none of you mention Kira before?'

Agapa made to speak, but Yegor cleared his throat and got there first.

'It's like this, Sergeant,' he said, leaning forward in his chair. 'We would, of course, have mentioned Kira before now – but with poor Rodion dying so unexpectedly, and then dear, dear Larissa after him . . . Well, you can understand that it could put us in rather a difficult position, can't you? Isn't that right, Agapa, *dorogoy*?'

'More difficult than the position you're in now?' growled Vassily, suddenly putting aside his affable manner. 'Obstructing a police homicide investigation by concealing relevant facts – that's a pretty tricky situation to be in, believe me!'

'Ah, well, you see, Lieutenant,' said Ilya, swallowing hard, 'I think what Yegor here means to say is—'

'It wasn't a relevant fact,' rapped out Agapa, between thinly stretched lips. 'It was a terrible, a shameful thing to happen – but it had nothing to do with us! If we'd told you, you might have arrested us there and then, under suspicion of some bizarre liking for doing away with our actors – by far our most precious resource! I – we – judged it better to let you get on with the only investigation that really mattered: the death of our beloved Rodion, and then our equally beloved Larissa. I still can't quite believe it's happened, and nor can I believe,' she went on, 'that you've made so little progress. I find it hard to sleep at night

– no, impossible, ever since you locked us into this very train, cheek by jowl, perhaps, with the murderer himself.'

She shivered, drawing her silk scarf closer around her shoulders, and accepting the half-hearted embrace offered by Ilya, who draped his arm around her on top of her expensive finery.

But then she lifted her head and stared at Vassily in such an imperious manner that Olga found herself believing that here indeed was a Romanov, born again among them, and instructing some manager of serfs upon the proper mode of behaviour on a great estate in the days before the Bolsheviks came.

'I won't forget this, Marushkin,' she said – and Olga noted the bare surname, devoid of surrounding ornamentation. 'No, I won't forget it; and I've got some friends in high places, you know. Oh, yes, I can make your life a misery . . . I've held off till now, apart from getting us out of captivity on the train, because you're a good man, I think, doing a good job, on the whole. But don't push me too far – don't come to me with old stories, trying to pin retrospective guilt on me, like a Moscow detective in the pay of the oligarchs! What happened in Izhevsk has nothing to do with what's going on here – that much I can tell you. And now you must excuse me – you must excuse all of us, even Yegor. We have still a few final pages to go through in our rehearsal, and God knows whether Svetlana will remember the peroration from her scene with Colonel Glazunov . . . And Lev Myatlev's no Rodion Rultava. But time, tide and matinees wait for no woman – so you'll excuse us, Inspector? We can go?'

Vassily nodded, but didn't speak – he merely swept one of his large, beet-farmer hands towards the door in mute permission, upon which the three thespians – or, rather, two thespians and their bearer of lines – got up, nodded stiffly and left the carriage.

'Vassily,' hissed Olga, as the door closed behind them, 'don't you think you let them off a little easily? We didn't ask about the hospital visits.'

Vassily scratched his head, but didn't reply immediately: he was still watching the door that led to the second carriage, as if its reverberations might lend some further clue to the mysteries they had yet to plumb.

'Well – no, no, I don't think so,' he said at last, his fingers still buried in his thick mane of tousled black hair. 'We weren't going to get much further than that, really, I don't think – not just now, with the performance around the corner. We'll ask about the hospital visits later, build up a full picture of who arrived in the area, and when. But for now I learned something useful, at least: Agapa, not Ilya, is really in charge—'

'I could have told you that much,' muttered Olga.

'And something else occurred to me, too, about Agapa's friends in high places. Did you ever come across people in high places who didn't know how to get their hands dirty in Russia?'

'Still, that doesn't mean the Putyatins had anything to do with Kira Obnizov's death.'

'Of course it doesn't – but it does mean they play for high stakes. And when people playing for high stakes start to lose, they'll do anything to turn things around. Anything . . . Maybe even murder.'

'Murder,' mused Olga, 'and with Yegor as their loyal henchman . . .'

But Vassily laughed. 'Yegor Shulgin? I'd hardly trust him to feed me my breakfast, never mind a line in a play.'

Whatever Yegor's shortcomings in conversation, he certainly helped the troupe to make rapid progress in their rehearsal, which resumed as soon as Olga and Vassily could be ushered from the first carriage and its improvised stage. Vassily and Olga sat in the stand opposite and watched as the cast made their way through the trickiest scenes – mostly those involving Svetlana Odrosov and Lev Myatlev – with a lot of shouting from Agapa and even some red-faced, raised-voice interventions from the usually patient Ilya Putyatin, but mostly guided back to the right path by the instructions that Yegor called from behind the carriage door. The minutes soon ticked by, and it wasn't long before the matinee performance was only a quarter of an hour distant.

'Pan! Pan!' came a voice towards Olga and Vassily, startling them from the rather vacant doze into which they had fallen in the course of the rehearsal. It was Yegor's voice, realised Olga, as she looked up to see Panteleimon Pomelov dropping to the ground from the carriage and dashing towards them across the gravel and grass that separated track from stand. Behind him, gesturing at him with jerky movements of a clipboard, stood a cross-looking Yegor Shulgin.

'Oh, ignore that old woman,' said Panteleimon, cheerfully, as he reached them. 'He'd regiment your teeth if he could! He's just on a power trip because he's in charge of the rehearsal running order. Anyway, I didn't come to bellyache about him, or any of the others, though I could, believe me . . . No, I came because I've thought of something quite important. You remember Rodion's black book? Where he wrote down all his little thoughts and observations, all that, and how you were all so keen to find it? Well, I know where it is. You can see— Oh, what is it now, Ilya?'

'Well, Panteleimon,' said Ilya, in his fussy voice, having walked slowly across to them after Panteleimon had jumped to earth from the carriage. 'If you don't come now, we will certainly be in arrears, with regard to the timing of the performance. And given all that's happened, and the somewhat precarious nature of audience loyalty, I trust you'll agree that—'

'Oh, fine, fine,' said Panteleimon, a little testily, rolling his eyes at Vassily and Olga. 'Well, listen, I suppose I can tell you later on. Just keep your eyes open for me, all right? And break a leg. No, wait – that's me!'

Vassily called to him to wait, but the actor had turned already, and was racing back to the carriage as quickly as he had left it.

'Infuriating, isn't it?' said Ilya, in one of the most human expressions to which Olga had yet heard him give voice. 'But I suppose that's the artistic temperament. And now I had better go too, especially as I move rather more slowly than some of these young Turks . . . Enjoy the show, Colonel and – and Miss.'

'Miss?' snorted Olga. 'I do wish people would stop calling me *devushka* . . .'

'Never mind that,' said Vassily, gazing after Panteleimon with an almost hungry look upon his face. 'Damn that Ilya! Just when we were about to get somewhere . . . That Pomelov idiot must have remembered something important, but nowhere near as important as a murder investigation, oh dear me no – because of course a *performance* is about to take place, and nothing matters more than that!'

'Sarcasm doesn't suit you, Vassily,' said Olga, settling into her seat and waiting for the curtain – or rather the carriage-side

– to rise. 'And neither does impatience! We'll just catch up with Pan after the show.'

'We'd better,' rumbled Vassily in response, sitting back, folding his arms and glancing from side to side at the slowly arriving crowd, with an expression of deep displeasure. 'We'd better, after having to sit through this lot all over again, except with worse actors.'

As it happened, however, Vassily's wait was rather shorter than the entire play. The troupe had just got to the part where the tsar, having been caught flirting with Sonia Alikovsky's character Sophie Buxhoeveden, sends for Rasputin in search of man-to-man advice on how to cope with such matters of the heart – only for a long pause to ensue, with no Rasputin forthcoming. Prompted by whispered instructions from Yegor Shulgin, Ilya Putyatin, playing the tsar, repeated his line, but Panteleimon Pomelov was nowhere to be seen.

Yegor now stuck his head through the gap that led to the second carriage, prompting titters from the capacity crowd that had filled the stand – a witness to the free publicity generated by the murders, thought Olga, since the play had been going for some days, and by now (she thought) the novelty would otherwise have worn off a little.

'Look, the tsar's had another lovechild,' called one wit from the audience.

'No wonder he kept him well-hidden . . . Look at those glasses,' said another, prompting another cross look from Yegor, and a rapid removal of his head from view.

But then came another sound entirely: a shriek of fear and shock that seemed to come from the far side of the train. This time Yegor walked bodily onto the stage and peered across into the stand.

'Sergeant Marushkin!' he called. 'Come quickly, please – right away.'

Vassily glanced at Olga, and together they rose without a word, picked their way out of the stand to a rising murmur of speculation from those they left behind, and clambered onto the stage to meet Yegor.

'It's Pan,' he whispered. 'Out the back – by the tracks.'

'He's not – he's not—' Olga couldn't bring herself to say the words she feared.

'I don't think so,' said Yegor, glancing backwards at the actors. 'But come quickly – we need to get him to Tayga, to be sure he's safe.'

Vassily bundled Yegor out of the way and pushed through to the join between the first and second carriages where, he knew, there was a gap that led out onto the track on either side. He jumped to earth on the far side, and gestured to Olga to do the same.

Then he bent down, seeing a long, thin form laid out by the wheels of the first carriage. It was Panteleimon, his face both ashen and crimson, spattered with blood from a deep wound on his forehead.

His eyes were open, and he looked towards them as they approached. 'Va-Vassily,' he said, or rather croaked. Then he looked down at his right hand, which – Olga now saw – was clutching something odd-looking, something that seemed to shimmer in his grasp, or shift as her own perspective moved.

Then she gasped: he was holding hair, she realised, human hair, and not his own.

Panteleimon saw her gaze move, and nodded. 'A-A-Agapa,' he said at last. 'Agapa . . . No . . .'

But his eyes rolled up into his head, and then he shuddered. He spoke no more.

11
Behind the Curtain

'It *wasn't* Agapa,' said Olga. 'That's what Pan was trying to say.'

'Seems that way,' said Vassily, staring somewhat crossly at the inert figure lying next to them, as if he could will him into wakefulness with baleful looks alone. In Vassily's hands lay the strands of blond hair that Panteleimon Pomelov had clutched as he descended into oblivion, but their silvery sheen – so reminiscent of Agapa Putyatin's handsome mane – did not seem to bring him the satisfaction one might expect a policeman to exhibit at the acquisition of a decisive clue.

'No: it can't have been her,' he went on, recalling his rapid inspection of Agapa's hair after Panteleimon was attacked, only to find a pristine, delicately coiffed head with no hint of even a single hair out of place, let alone a handful of plucked locks that would have caused some degree of anguish to the person whose head had surrendered them.

'Then who?' asked Olga, for the tenth time. 'Whose hair is it?'

'If we knew that,' said Vassily, turning the hair over in his hands, 'we'd know everything.'

Then he frowned. 'What's this?' he said, holding up a strand for closer inspection.

'What is it?' said Olga.

'Nothing,' sighed Vassily, after a moment. 'Just a bit of dirt, or soot, that's all.'

Soon after this, Dr Zinovev confirmed that Panteleimon Pomelov had received a serious head injury, and that he was likely to remain unconscious for some time to come.

'It could be a day, or it could be longer,' Zinovev said, leaning against the doorpost and passing a hand over his unshaven chin. 'It's hard to say.'

'And there's no way to bring him round sooner?' Vassily asked; but Zinovev bristled in response.

'Absolutely not,' he snapped. 'You want me to stick some adrenaline into his heart, something like that? This isn't a battlefield, Vassily Marushkin, to talk of such things!'

'Of course, Doctor,' Vassily said, glancing at Olga. 'We're happy to bow to your expert opinion. But while we have you here, perhaps we could have a quick conversation about another matter?'

Zinovev started, staring at Vassily with tired, hot-looking eyes. 'Another matter? Relating to what?'

'Oh, it's nothing – just filling in some of the gaps in the murder investigations,' replied Vassily. 'I understand that' – he glanced at his notebook as if refreshing his memory – 'I understand that some of the actors came to see you before the performances started.'

'Came to see *me*?' The stubble on Zinovev's chin looked darker still against his rapidly paling skin, and Olga glanced at Vassily with admiration: they hadn't known for certain that any of the actors had come to see him personally, of course, but only that they had come to the hospital. But Zinovev was the most experienced physician at Tayga, and it was a good guess that he would have been involved – a very good guess indeed, and seemingly confirmed by the guilty pallor that had spread across his face.

Then Zinovev seemed to pull himself up a little taller, and responded, in a more confident tone, 'Are you sure, Vassily? I think I'd remember that . . . Why don't we look at the records?'

'We know the records don't show anything,' said Vassily. 'We checked earlier. But we know, too, that things happen off the books – and often for good reason. You've looked after Anna Kabalevsky enough times, and turned a blind eye to help her out, haven't you?'

Zinovev's eyes quivered, as if Olga had touched upon the key to his heart, and suddenly Olga wondered if he might begin to weep.

'Look, Yury,' she said, in a soft, gentle voice, 'we don't want to get you into trouble, or anything like that. We just need to know everything that happened before the murders – to get a full picture of what everyone was doing, and why. Maybe then we can get a sense of why Pan ended up holding some strange hair – don't you want to help us work it out? Don't we owe it to the victims, those poor actors who've lost their lives?'

But Olga saw that she had gone too far, as Zinovev returned to his blustering tone.

'Don't lecture me about people losing their lives,' he snapped. 'I see that every day here, while others walk about at leisure. And I resent being questioned like this – and especially by you, Olga Pushkin. I thought we were friends. And I thought you worked for Russian Railways, not for the police! I haven't seen anyone unusual at the hospital – but why don't you run along and ask your precious actors if you're so convinced they were here? I won't stop you.'

He left them then, stalking out of the room without looking back, and leaving Olga shaking her head at Vassily. 'I don't know what's come over him,' she said, 'but he's not the same man he was even a month ago. Did you see his nails? Bitten to the quick. And his shirt – it's the same one he was wearing last time I saw him.'

'Something's not quite right,' agreed Vassily. 'We'll have to dig a little deeper, it seems – but let's leave that for another day. We'd better get back to the train and speak to the actors – assuming they're all still alive, of course.'

They were all still alive, but far from happy. Olga and Vassily arrived at the Murder Express to hear raised voices, and specifically Junior Sergeant Timofei Davidov in a shrill exchange with Agapa Putyatin and Yegor Shulgin.

'You can't keep us here,' Yegor was saying. 'We're victims just as much as Pan and the rest!'

'I agree,' said Agapa. 'It's a gross abuse of power to keep innocent actors confined on a rackety old train—'

'Oh, steady on,' protested Lev Myatlev, but to no avail.

'A rackety old train with a killer on the loose!' went on Agapa. 'Where's your superior officer – the superintendent?'

Vassily flashed a humourless smile at Olga and climbed the steps to the second carriage.

'It's senior sergeant, for the hundredth time,' he said loudly, walking into the melee as silence fell around him. Following in his footsteps, Olga saw that Timofei had allowed the troupe out of their individual compartments, and that all of them – Yegor Shulgin, the Putyatins, Lev Myatlev, Svetlana Odrosov and

Sonia Alikovsky – had now seated themselves in varying positions around the dressing-tables that occupied the far end of the carriage, beyond the half-length corridor along which the individual compartments were arrayed. Olga had the strange feeling that she and Vassily had intruded upon a scene from a private performance, in which Timofei Davidov stood in the role of a supplicant, while Agapa Putyatin and Yegor Shulgin played stern reprovers.

'Now that Davidov's superior officer is here, we can get on with things,' went on Vassily, walking down the corridor towards the open seating area at the end. 'I was going to speak to you individually, but I might as well just ask you all together.'

'Ask us what?' said Svetlana, in her usual tone of slightly bored resentment.

'Actually, you're off the hook, Svetlana,' said Vassily, 'since I know you were already here in Roslazny when the performers began to arrive. But for all the rest – when exactly did you get to the area, and how? Train, bus, car, bicycle – what?'

He opened his notebook and began writing down their answers, starting with Sonia Alikovsky's statement that she had arrived in Tayga two days before the start of rehearsals. 'Well, three days, really,' she said, smoothing down a lapel. 'But as I got in after midnight, I don't really know what you'd prefer to write down.'

'Three it is,' said Vassily, glancing at Olga. 'Gospodin Putyatin and Dama Putyatin – I suppose you arrived together?'

He made his way around the circle, building up a picture of the actors' arrival in the region until it became clear that only three of them could have visited the hospital in Tayga on the days the car was seen there: Sonia Alikovsky, Agapa Putyatin and Ilya Putyatin.

'Thank you, everyone,' said Vassily. 'And just one more thing,' he went on, still looking down at his notebook. 'Which of Sonia, Agapa and Ilya was paying night-time visits to the hospital in Tayga?'

Watching those three closely, Olga saw a range of expressions appear on their faces: surprise for Sonia, cold impassivity for Agapa, and a hint of anxiety for Ilya. But then a fourth face stepped into view, blocking her gaze as if to protect those behind him.

'How dare you question these – these *highly esteemed* actors like this?' said Yegor Shulgin, eyes glittering crossly behind his glasses. 'It's disgraceful. Don't you know that medical details are highly confidential? How can you expect them to divulge this information in front of a' – he glanced sideways at Svetlana Odrosov and Lev Myatlev – 'in front of a *mixed* company like this?'

'Who are you calling mixed?' cried Svetlana Odrosov, smoothing down the hem of her leather miniskirt, while Lev Myatlev flashed a quick and highly offensive gesture in Yegor's direction. But Vassily replied before Yegor could say any more.

'Sit down, *grazhdanin*,' he said, with an unmistakable ring of authority. 'Did I say I wanted to know details of medical consultations? No, I did not. In fact, I'm asking precisely because there is no record of any of the Murder Express actors having come into contact with any personnel at the hospital – none whatsoever. And so my question is this: what else could members of this troupe have been doing there? You realise, I suppose, that hospitals have a great deal of expensive equipment on the premises, not to mention drugs that – in the right hands – can go for tens of thousands of roubles . . . But, of course, it would make sense to sell whatever was obtained in a different *oblast*, hundreds or thousands of miles away – and who better to transport them than a travelling troupe with extensive baggage and lots of places to hide things that need to be hidden?'

'Oh, for shame – for shame!' said Ilya Putyatin, holding up his hands in protest at the thought of such activities – but again Yegor sought to come to the rescue.

'What nonsense,' he said. 'We only employ people of the highest moral calibre! Those visits must have been to set up our meetings with the children. You are aware, Sergeant, that we always do charity work, wherever we go? Am I right, Agapa, Ilya?'

'Quite right, Yegor,' said Agapa, breaking her cold mask with a smile – though a smile of a rather glacial character that did not quite reach her eyes. 'But, of course, we didn't want to disturb any of the good doctors and nurses in their vital work. So we merely found a way to let ourselves in and see for ourselves the conditions in which we would need to do our work. We do see acting as work, you know, whatever the public might think.'

'You went in unannounced to look at the children's ward, three nights in a row?' said Vassily, incredulously.

'We always prepare well for events, and do the very best job we can,' replied Agapa, coolly. 'Unlike the police in this . . .' she paused, and hissed over her front teeth as if searching for a word capable of describing Roslazny and its surrounds '. . . in this *charming* backwater, who seem incapable of conducting a simple murder inquiry with any effectiveness whatsoever!'

But Yegor finished his sentence. 'So we can't understand why you are badgering us like this, Sergeant, when the killer remains abroad, unobserved, and – as like as not – ready to kill again.'

'Well . . .' said Vassily, eyeing him doubtfully. 'Well . . .' he said again, but then said nothing more, and Olga realised he was trying their old tactic of the silent treatment in case anyone with a guilty conscience might speak up and incriminate themselves. This time the results were disappointing: for once the actors refrained from talking, contenting themselves with standing or sitting and mutely staring at Vassily until he began to feel pressure to speak.

'Well,' he said again, 'perhaps we'll leave it there for now – in terms of questions, at least. But I must ask you to stay on board until we have completed a further search of the train.'

'Another search?' said Lev Myatlev, somewhat incredulously. 'You've been through the whole thing already.'

'Maybe,' said Vassily, 'but we might be looking for something a little different this time. And now, if you don't mind, I'll ask you to stay where you are while Olga and I move along the carriages and the engine.'

'You'll find nothing on that engine, that I can guarantee you,' broke in Lev once more, with the ardour of a man defending his first love. 'That thing is spotless – spotless!'

'I'll be the judge of that,' said Vassily. 'Olga?' he added, jerking his head backwards to the far end of the carriage where Timofei Davidov was keeping watch, stuffing his hands into his armpits for a trace of elusive warmth in the dank November air.

'Come up here, will you, Davidov, and make sure everyone stays where they are now?' called Vassily. 'Thanks. Right, Olga.

Let's go compartment by compartment, and remember: it's not murder weapons we're looking for, but clothes, make-up and wigs.'

A little earlier, Vassily and Olga had agreed, during the drive from Tayga to Roslazny, that they needed to shift their attention away from obviously incriminating materials like knives and poisons, focusing instead on the accoutrements of theatrical display. That way, they thought, they might get on the trail of the mysterious person who had assumed the disguise of at least three people in the troupe – Sonia Alikovsky; Panteleimon Pomelov, if Lev Myatlev was to be believed, and Agapa Putyatin, if Panteleimon was to be believed – and possibly others, whose impersonations had yet to be documented. So Vassily had come up with the idea of carrying out a renewed search of the Murder Express, starting with the compartments in the second carriage before moving on to the first and the P36, though Vassily held out little hope for this. 'It's an engine,' he said, shrugging. 'It's full of pipes and steam and rods. Where are they going to hide anything? At least, where are they going to hide something you wouldn't be risking your life to retrieve? But we'd better search it, all the same. I can just imagine Zemsky's face when he found out I hadn't . . . Best to cover all bases and hope for the best.'

Hoping for the best was a good philosophy, but in this case it didn't make any difference to the end result, which was a resounding blank across both carriages and the engine.

'Damn,' said Vassily, with feeling, as he sank onto one of the dainty chairs in the first carriage. 'I really thought we might find something to work with – something to point the way. Can you believe it's half a week since Rodion was killed, and we've still got nothing concrete? I'd give my right arm for one speck of dust – for one – for—'

'Vassily?' said Olga. 'What's wrong?' He had come to a halt in the middle of his sentence, staring ahead at the movable wall as if it were a cinema screen playing out images visible to him alone.

'A speck of dust,' he said again, with a wondering tone. Then, without another word, he jumped to his feet and ran towards the door that led out of the first carriage and down onto the tracks via a small ladder.

'Vassily!' called Olga, running after him in bewilderment – but when she poked her head out into the cool air, he was nowhere to be seen. Tutting, she followed his footsteps down the ladder and onto the ground, then looked around for him on every side. He was nowhere to be seen.

'Up here,' called a muffled voice, making Olga jump – and she started again when she did look up, seeing Vassily's face, now covered from ear to ear in black coal dust, appear over the steep side of the P36's tender.

'Vassily Marushkin,' she said, 'what on earth are you doing up there?'

But he only grinned in response.

'And it was all thanks to that little speck of black dirt on the wig,' went on Vassily, sitting down on the creaky little chair in the first carriage and sloughing off coal dust from his trousers. 'I suddenly remembered how steam engines work, and that there were ten tons of coal within a few feet of us.'

'I still don't really understand,' said Olga. 'How could anyone put a box – no, a damn *cupboard* – inside a giant heap of coal and not expect it to be discovered?'

Clambering up after Vassily, Olga had seen him scraping lumps of coal off the top of a long, slender box that had been buried just under the surface. Vassily had already opened one of the narrow doors on top of the box, showing a melee of clothes, wigs and accessories, like handbags and belts. She even saw a couple of large pairs of high-heeled boots. After a few minutes of further clearing, he sat back, panting, and looked at their haul: a complete set of outfits for the impersonation of each and every member of the Murder Express, from Ilya Putyatin's Goethe-like halo of ringed grey hair to Sonia Alikovsky's rather regrettable taste in leopard-print trousers.

'I suppose it would have been found quite quickly, in the normal run of things,' said Vassily. 'The coal would have been used up, the box would have sunk to the bottom, and probably someone would have seen it when they stopped at a hopper to fill up again. But the train wasn't moving around much – just a couple of quick maintenance trips down the line to Tayga – so the coal stayed more or less where it was. And whoever was using it could pop out whenever they wanted to look like someone else . . . All they'd need would be a bucket of water to wash their hands, and there's always water around a steam engine. Shame there's no clue as to which of them had the bright idea of stowing disguises in a P36 tender.'

'We could look at all their clothes, see if there's any streaks of black dust,' suggested Olga – but Vassily shook his head.

'Anyone this clever would make sure they never had anything visible on them,' he said. 'There was only a single speck of dust on that wig, remember? Probably they've got some overalls stashed in a bush somewhere, to throw over their outfit whenever they needed to access it. Actually, that's an idea – let's have a look later.'

'It's likely to be a man, though, isn't it?' said Olga, after a minute. 'I mean, the thing itself weighs a ton,' she added, regarding the slender, coal-stained box that now lay on the floorboards in front of them, 'and it must have been a nightmare to put it under all that coal in the first place.'

'I suppose so,' said Vassily, 'though I'm surprised to hear you say so, Olga! You should never underestimate what a woman can do when she has to – or have you forgotten Ivanka Kozar, or Nevena Komarov? And what about Polina Klemovsky?'

'Don't,' said Olga, shivering at the thought of Polina and her fierce, bespectacled glare. 'I'm not likely to forget any of those women, or what they were capable of, any time soon – but, still, I really don't think a woman on her own could lift that thing up onto the tender and hide it under half a ton of coal.'

'Not on her own, maybe,' said Vassily, glancing at his reflection in a small table mirror and wetting his fingers to remove a particularly large smear of dust from his cheek. 'But people have accomplices, don't forget. And . . .'

Vassily paused, looking up at the door that led to the second carriage.

'And what?' said Olga. 'What is it?'

'Oh, nothing,' said Vassily, though his frown told a different story. 'I thought I saw something – just a shadow, hovering around the window. But I'm sure it's nothing. Still, maybe it's worth . . .'

He didn't finish his sentence, but got up and walked quickly to the door, bending to the small (and rather dirty) pane that looked onto the join between the carriages and, beyond, the doorway to the second carriage.

'No, nothing there,' he said, returning to his seat. 'I could've sworn there was something, but I must be more tired than I think. It hasn't been easy, with Rozalina and Kliment . . . Anyway, what was I saying?'

'Something about accomplices.'

'Oh, yes,' said Vassily, sitting forward so that his chair gave another warning creak. 'We can't rule it out, can we? But the problem is, what can we rule in? The solution could be right in front of us, only we can't see it. We could walk right up to the guilty party and engage her – or him – in conversation, and laugh and joke, and be none the wiser that they were a ruthless killer. And—'

But this time Vassily's flow was curtailed not by his suspicion of a shadow hovering by the carriage door but by Olga, who shushed him with a finger and closed her eyes tight. Vassily had seen her do this before, usually when she was struck by a bookish idea or some writerly sentence or proverb that she wished to preserve for posterity, which she would then scribble down on the nearest piece of scrap paper or even, in one memorable episode witnessed by Vassily and Fyodor Katin, an obscure corner of kitchen wall in the house she shared with Anna Kabalevsky and her brother Pasha. But he had yet to see her abstract herself in such a way while working with him on an investigation, rather than some future masterpiece destined for shelves across the nation. When she spoke, however, he realised why – for here was an idea whose inspiration was at least as much literary as legal.

'You're right, Vassily,' she breathed, gazing at him with eyes half closed in concentration, 'you're absolutely right . . . The solution could be right in front of us: that was what you said. And what did Pan say about Rodion Rultava's little black book, before he was attacked – do you remember? *I think I know where it is. You can see* – and then he was interrupted. But I think I know what he was going to say. He was going to say, *You can see it in front of you now, right there on the stage.*'

'What?' cried Vassily, looking around him. 'Where?'

'There,' said Olga, lifting her hand and pointing towards a small pile of books on a low bookshelf towards the back of the stage, to the side of the tsarina's dressing-table with its china bowl and jug. 'There, in plain sight.'

She got up and, with the certainty of a sleepwalker, she moved towards the shelf with her eyes fixed on dog-eared copies of *The Idiot*, on one side and *Lolita* on the other. Olga tutted, thinking that the troupe could at least have confined themselves to books that had been published when the tsar was still alive – but her literary indignation occupied only a quarter of her mind, for the rest was focused on the slim black volume that lay between them. She reached out a hand, then a finger, and slid the book diagonally outwards until she could see the cover. There was nothing printed on the outside, but when she picked it up and opened it she saw a name written on the first page. She turned the book in her hands to show to Vassily.

'Rodion Rultava,' he read, in hushed tones. 'Olga, you're a genius!'

As soon as they had found the book, she and Vassily assembled all the candlesticks and gas lights they could find in the carriage, and brought them together on the drawing-room table to shed as much light as possible on the little book and its reams of spidery hand-writing. Most of Rodion's diary covered things that had happened long before the Murder Express, of course, but they read through it, all the same, in case anything might emerge that informed later events. This turned out to be a fruitless and tiring exercise, as Rodion had been a prolific diarist – this diary, they worked out from some of the scribbled remarks, was the third he had used that year alone. No event or conversation, it seemed, was too trivial for him to record, and Olga and Vassily soon became experts in the day-to-day trivia of a life lived precariously on the boards in Russia. And even when they finally arrived at the events leading up to the Murder Express and its arrival in the siding near Roslazny, Rodion had still tended to prefer quantity over quality, drowning even the most perfunctory of happenings with a welter of unnecessary description.

'These actors,' Olga muttered, wiping her streaming eyes. 'They don't stint on words.'

'No, but look at his last entry,' Vassily said, putting his finger on a line that included the familiar letters of Tayga. 'He's finally got down to brass tacks – he's talking about the dinner they had at the hotel in Tayga, the night before he died. And he says – let me see – ah, yes: he says he was worried about the cold, and asked Reception for extra blankets, and then he was annoyed because he missed the arrival of the takeaway, and thought Pan would steal his bao buns. Now – why does that ring a bell?'

Olga gasped, making Vassily jump. 'Yegor!' she said. 'Yegor Shulgin!'

'What about him?'

'Well, he told us it was him who asked for the extra blankets, didn't he? But it wasn't him at all, if Rodion's right – it was Rodion!'

'But what does it matter?' said Vassily. 'Maybe Yegor saw him asking for blankets and did the same thing later on. Birds of a feather, and all that.'

'No, no, you don't understand,' said Olga. 'Yegor told us that *he* was actually asking for blankets when the food arrived . . . Surely Rodion would have written it down, if they'd both done it at the same time.'

'No, no, you're right, of course,' said Vassily, staring into the distance with unfocused eyes. 'And surely Rodion would have had no reason to lie to his own diary – a document he presumably thought nobody else would ever read. But that means—'

'It means that Yegor Shulgin told us something other than the plain truth,' said Olga. 'And – and—'

Her heart seemed to slow, and even to stop altogether, as she remembered what Larissa Lazarov had said about the takeaway food the troupe had ordered into the hotel in Tayga, the food that, combined with the poisonous antifreeze, had caused Rodion's death hours later – throwaway words, really, but words that assumed a sinister and devilish hue in light of what had happened since: *Who answered the door and took it in? Oh, I can't remember. Yegor, I suppose, as he ordered it. Yes, I think it was probably him. Or – maybe it was Rodion? It could have been him . . .*

Rodion – *it could have been . . .* But in fact it really could *not* have been, if his diary was to be believed – and as Vassily said, there were no good reasons to disbelieve it.

And hadn't there been a master of disguise hanging around the troupe all this time, stalking them with impunity, camouflaged in the clothes, the hair, the very personas of those whom the murderer had sought to destroy, and all too often with success?

Yegor had ordered the food, but maybe – said Larissa – Rodion had taken it in at the front door. But by his own account, he was simultaneously at the reception desk in search of additional warmth . . .

Unless, of course, someone *else* had played Rodion at the front door . . . Someone capable of playing any of the actors at will, in fact – someone capable of creating expert costumes, someone who knew and could reproduce each and every fashion weakness, verbal tic, facial expression and skin tone, accent and characteristic saying of all their colleagues, from the troupe's grand chatelaine Agapa Putyatin to the recently joined substitute, Svetlana Odrosov . . . Someone in the background, perhaps, but keenly observing, watching, absorbing everything and missing nothing – watching and waiting, waiting for their opportunity to strike when it was least expected, and in the garb of another . . .

The hairs rose on the back of her neck as she pictured the killer to herself, a kind of dark genius whose dramatic gifts had been distorted beyond all recognition, serving only as a means to evil ends – but then her forehead wrinkled, and she tilted her head sideways as if better to bring to mind some faintly remembered words that Yegor had once said to them.

Vassily – yes, Vassily – had asked him if he'd never wanted to be an actor, and what had he replied?

Oh, yes, Olga remembered now. He'd replied that his mother

had told him he could have been an actor, and a great one. But Yegor had decided his talents lay in another direction . . . Could that direction still have been acting, but a different kind of acting – assuming the role of others in everyday life?

His eyes had been glowing in the early winter light, Olga remembered, sharp and clear and light brown, like autumn leaves – but then she sucked in her breath, and again tilted her head: there was something there, wasn't there? Something important – something about his eyes . . .

Of course: his glasses! His glasses were as thick as the end of a beer bottle, so how had Olga been able to see his eyes so clearly? Olga had known others with thick glasses, like her classmate Anastas Belyaev at the Irkutsk Institute of Railway Engineering's satellite college at Tayga, whose glasses had been the subject of many an unfortunate remark by Olga's less sensitive colleagues. Anastas had since invested in contact lenses, and had progressed well up the railway drivers' career ladder – but at that time his eyes had been visible only through a glass miasma that had made Olga feel as if she were swimming underwater every time she looked at him. But she had seen Yegor's eyes with all the clarity of a high-resolution photograph.

And Gyorgy . . . Anna's son Gyorgy had stolen Yegor's glasses and put them on, hadn't he, dashing out of the Café Astana door and calling out that Nikolai Popov was coming – but Popov had been in the distance then, and Gyorgy shouldn't have been able to see the door in front of him if he were wearing Yegor's thick glasses, far less a rotund butcher slowly making his way to the café for his daily vodka, or four?

No: the glasses were fake, thought Olga. They were as much a lie as what Yegor had told them about the night of the takeaway in Tayga. One lie, and then another, and perhaps a whole personality made up of a fabric of lies . . .

'What is it, Olga?' said Vassily, who had been watching her curiously, clearly trying to guess what thoughts could be racing through her mind.

'It's Yegor,' she said, with sudden certainty. 'It's Yegor – his glasses are fake, I've just realised. Gyorgy put them on and could see for miles. And he's been pretending about everything all this time . . . It must have been him who put Rodion's book on the stage after the train was searched again, as a finger up to everyone! Arrogance again – and didn't Yegor stoop over Rodion's body when he died? Maybe he took it then . . . Rodion probably had it on him at all times. And – and – and it must have been Yegor who pretended to be Sonia Alikovsky to get the antifreeze, then dressed up as Rodion to put it into the takeaway when it arrived, with a handful of something else, I suppose, to disguise the taste – and it must have been him, too, who played Pan in the crowded room, gambling that nobody would notice, that he was clever enough to get away with it. Oh, I think he's a mass of conceit, a colossal ego masquerading as a humble assistant! Maybe Yegor drowned Kira Obnizov, too, back in Severnyy, back in Izhevsk, and the Putyatins have been protecting him – but either way, I'm sure it's him, Vassily! Who better to learn about costumes and make-up than a behind-the-scenes specialist at a travelling circus?'

'But – but why?' said Vassily. 'Why would he kill all those people?'

'I – I . . .' Olga paused. 'I don't know,' she admitted. 'Maybe Rodion and Larissa got on to his MO, you know, his modus operandi,' she went on, glad to have an opportunity to display once more the fruits of afternoons spent watching detective programmes, 'and realised he'd done bad things while disguised as other people. And then they had to go before they revealed his secrets . . . But listen: we'll never know if you don't arrest him now, Vassily! Quick – we'd better get to him before anything else happens. I don't even trust locked doors around here any more.'

Vassily looked at her, frowning. He wasn't sure that he fully followed Olga's train of thought, but it was true that Yegor had lied to them, and it sounded like it was also true that his glasses were fake – and it was certainly very suspicious to wear fake glasses. And it was true that Yegor had bent over Rodion's body on stage, affording him the opportunity, if he had quick enough fingers, of filching the diary and putting it into his own pocket.

'Well, all right,' he said at last, getting up and gesturing at the coal-stained box of costumes. 'We'll bring him in, and see how he reacts to the sight of that.'

He walked over to the door, turned the key in the lock – they were taking no chances, on that particular night – and called down the corridor to Junior Sergeant Timofei Davidov, who was standing at the far end of the second carriage, smoking and keeping watch.

'Bring Yegor Shulgin to us, would you, Davidov?' called Vassily. 'Just a few questions.'

'Yes, sir,' said Timofei, his voice muffled by the scarf he wore high around his neck. 'Just one second – better drop this cigarette out of doors.'

'Hurry up, then,' said Vassily, rolling his eyes at Olga, and watching as Timofei stepped out of view. They heard the door opening, and steps as he walked down the ladder, but then – nothing.

'Davidov?' called Vassily. 'Davidov?'

Finally, swearing under his breath, Vassily stalked down the corridor of the second carriage, past the compartments into which the actors had been locked earlier, and looked out of the open door – but of Timofei Davidov there was no sign.

Olga grasped Vassily's arm.

'Vassily – check Yegor's cabin,' she said.

Vassily wheeled to look at her, then grasped a ring of keys from his pocket and rushed to one of the doors. He unlocked it and flung it open, and there on the bunk was Timofei Davidov, gagged and bound, in his underwear alone. There was a pile of clothes on the floor, which looked to Olga like Yegor Shulgin's – but of Yegor himself there was no sign whatsoever.

'We should've known, Vassily,' said Olga, as they got hurriedly into Vassily's Volvo estate. 'We should've *known* . . . All this time, there's been someone hovering in the background, adopting disguises at will – so why would it be any different at the end of everything?'

'I only hope this *is* the end,' muttered Vassily, getting the engine going after several attempts, then putting the car into first and accelerating away from the police station with a screech of protesting rubber. 'I've never had such a difficult case – more false starts than this bloody car.'

'But that's why we should've known,' insisted Olga, as Vassily navigated the narrow bends that threaded through the village, before turning onto the narrow road that led to Tayga. 'It was because of Yegor. *He* was the one hovering in the background, so anonymous and unobtrusive that you'd hardly remember he was there – which was just as well, for his purposes, because he could then be there as someone else – as Rodion, as Pan, as Agapa, and who knows how many of the others? Oh, how could we have missed that? It's always the one you least suspect!'

'Is it?' said Vassily, glancing at her briefly in amusement. 'Is it always the one you least suspect?'

'Well,' said Olga, 'maybe not *always* . . . But maybe it always is, when it comes to dealing with actors. They're all so – so extreme, aren't they? Almost like caricatures of themselves, cobbled together in some badly written play. So the only one who *isn't* like that, the only one who doesn't constantly preen and parade and pontificate, was maybe always a good candidate for guilt, if only we'd thought things through enough.'

'Don't forget what his mother said about him being a great actor,' said Vassily, hanging onto the steering wheel as he nearly skidded around the corner that led into the outskirts of Tayga.

'Yes, but I don't think he could have been,' said Olga. 'He always gets sayings wrong, have you noticed? He says things like – oh, I don't know – a bird in the bush is worth two in the hand, things like that. So maybe . . .'

She paused, her eyes sparkling as her imagination began to take over. 'So maybe that's what this is all about – he *knows* he can't be an actor, that he could never have made it on the stage, so he set out to create a different career for himself in acting. Yes, and – and what he does now, serving as a glorified PA and general dogsbody, gives him perfect opportunities to take his revenge on the career that rejected him.'

'You mean he specifically set out to become, oh, whatever his job is, so that he can literally kill off actors one by one?'

Olga lifted her hands. 'I don't know – but I can't think of any other reason for what's happened, can you? And don't forget poor Kira Obnizov, back in Severnyy – maybe she was his first, the time when he finally moved beyond inner resentment to outer evil.'

Vassily nodded as he swung the car onto the road that led off Kirova Prospekt, running a short distance southwards until it terminated at the Tayga railway station. 'Well, you might have found a motive, Olga – though we'll only know if we catch him, I guess. So first of all, I hope you're right about the railway.'

Back in Roslazny, Olga had practically insisted that they head straight to Tayga on Yegor's heels, arguing that a man like him, soft and unused to Siberian conditions, would never make for the surrounding countryside – that he would either try to steal a car or head straight for the nearest transport terminal, and that since there were very few cars in Roslazny, and no buses to speak of in the region, that was bound to mean the Tayga railway station, which he could almost have reached by now on foot. Vassily had muttered something about the risk of yet more disguises and deceptions, but he hadn't been able fundamentally to challenge any of Olga's reasoning, and so they had set off towards the police station in Vassily's rusty but serviceable Volvo 240.

Like many journeys, however, the setting-off was more hopeful than the arriving; and when they skidded to a halt in front of the railway station and took in their surroundings it was hard to believe that they would catch their prey after all. The Trans-Siberian had just come in – Olga could see glimpses of its familiar livery through the windows and doors of the pale-green station building – and there was a flood of passengers, crew and vendors in front of the station building and on the bridges and platforms beyond. Yegor Shulgin, dressed as Timofei Davidov, could disappear in the crowd, and then disappear for good.

'We've got to think like him,' said Olga, putting her fingertips against her forehead. 'We've got to think like him, just like we did when we figured out where Rodion's diary was.'

'Just like *you* did, you mean,' said Vassily, but Olga wasn't listening.

'He'll think we'll expect him to discard his uniform and get another disguise,' she said, speaking slowly, with her eyes closed. 'He'll think we won't expect him to be in plain view, but instead scurrying along behind bunkers of grit and bits of equipment and street stalls, hiding at every opportunity. And so – and so—'

'And so?' said Vassily, after a minute, tapping the steering wheel in his anxiety to get out and upon Yegor's trail.

'I've got it,' said Olga. 'He'll be at the café bar – not at the front, that would be too obvious in his uniform. But round the side, behind the back of that staircase that leads up into the first floor. He won't have his cap on, and he'll have ruffled up his hair from behind – so all you'll see will be a man in some kind of uniform, relaxing after a long shift with a coffee and a few *pelmeni*. But it will be him – and when he sees us come and go, he'll wait till the next train's about to leave, and dash onboard, and we'll never see him again. Come, Vassily – come! Let's go and see if I'm right!'

As it happened, Olga was wrong, but only in one respect: he was drinking tea instead of coffee.

'Yegor Shulgin,' said Vassily, loudly, as Olga covered his other side to prevent any dash for freedom. 'I am arresting you for the murders of Rodion Rultava and Larissa Lazarov, and for the attempted murder of Panteleimon Pomelov.'

As Vassily read Yegor his rights, Olga watched him closely, seeing little emotion apart from the initial pallor arising from the shock of his final discovery. When Vassily finished speaking, Yegor took his glasses from his pocket and put them back on his face, blinking as if they were a strong prescription instead of – as Olga had guessed – simple, transparent plastic.

'Take me away, then, Sergeant,' he said at last. 'My conscience is quite clear.'

12

Red Souls

'His conscience may be clear, but nothing else is,' said Vassily the next day, addressing Captain Zemsky, who was sitting opposite Vassily in the Roslazny police station, smoking one of Vassily's Belamorkanal cigarettes and sipping a glass of vodka that Kliment had poured a few minutes earlier.

'Ye-es,' murmured Zemsky, narrowing his eyes and gazing at the cloud of smoke he had just exhaled. 'Yes, it's about as clear as a pea-souper rolling down the Moskva in June – but at least you got your man, Marushkin. At least you got your man. And not before time!'

Junior Sergeant Timofei Davidov laughed nervously, as if Zemsky had cracked a joke, then lapsed into silence when Zemsky darted him a look. Vassily suppressed a smile: Davidov was still very much in the captain's bad books, having allowed himself to be knocked out, disrobed, and tied up by Yegor Shulgin on the Murder Express the day before.

'Always assuming, of course, that we *did* get our man,' said Olga.

'You don't think Shulgin's guilty?' cried Zemsky, scattering ash from his cigarette as he leaned forward on his seat.

'You don't think he did for Rultava and Lazarov and nearly that ridiculous creature in the hospital, too – what's his name, Marushkin?'

'Panteleimon Pomelov, sir,' said Vassily. 'He played Rasputin in the play and—'

'Ha ha, yes,' chuckled Zemsky, sitting back again and winking at Olga. 'The long-haired troublemaker, *nyet*? The one who got knocked out by a woman in her fifties.'

'Well, it was really Yegor Shulgin disguised as Agapa Putyatin,' began Vassily, but Zemsky cut across him again.

'Details, Marushkin, details! Don't bore me with the details. And the same goes for you and your doubts, Pushkin,' he added, pointing his cigarette at Olga. 'I've got enough to deal with, believe me, with half of Kemerovo breathing down my neck to get the plays back on . . . Those Putyatins have some serious clout. The last thing I need is anything that might rock the boat. So if you've got any doubts, keep 'em to yourself! Am I right, my dear?' he added, beaming at Rozalina Marushkin as she walked into the office, looking, Olga had to admit, almost charming, in a rough-edged kind of way.

'Whatever you say, Captain,' she said, flashing a dazzling smile of her own – a smile of the kind, Olga thought, that she very rarely bestowed on Vassily or anyone else. Then she turned on her (very high) heel and called through to the reception area behind her, 'Kliment! Kliment – ah, there you are. More vodka and gherkins for the captain!'

Kliment hurried through at Rozalina's bidding, and dutifully topped up Zemsky's glass, did the same for Vassily and Davidov, then plucked gherkins from a glass jar and laid them on a plate. He still looked anxious and drawn, thought Olga, as if he wasn't getting enough food or sleep, or both – like Dr Zinovev, but what could Kliment have to deal with that could compare to the cares of an overworked, underpaid medic? Kliment also seemed unwilling to catch Olga's gaze, darting around the office and then rushing out again without having looked directly at her once. Rozalina's handiwork again, thought Olga. She could just imagine her words: *Don't talk to that woman – don't even look at her! She wants to take your father away from us, and we can't let that happen, can we?*

Olga watched her leave the office without regret, and Vassily, she noticed, seemed to relax a little as she clacked away down the passage that led back to Reception.

'To be honest, Captain, it's not just Olga who's got doubts,' said Vassily. 'I mean, Shulgin hardly seems the murdering type. He didn't even seem to have much of a motive, or one that we could discover, anyway . . . He just rolled over and nodded when Olga suggested some possible rationales to him. I think he'd have agreed to anything at all – he didn't seem to care.'

Vassily didn't look at Olga when he was saying this, but Olga took no comfort in that. She knew why his gaze stayed elsewhere: it was because he was angry with her: she had broken her own rules on the importance of silence. Rather than let Yegor Shulgin speak for himself, she had pressed him to respond to her own theories about his motives, asking him whether he had killed the actors because they'd discovered some nefarious act he'd undertaken while in disguise, or because he was out to wreak revenge on the profession in general.

In response, Yegor had merely nodded, then confirmed that both were true – that he *had* done bad things while in disguise, and been discovered, but that he was also out to get his own back on the profession that had excluded him. It was all far too pat, too neat, to satisfy Vassily or anyone else, and he bitterly – and obviously – regretted the opportunity, now gone without hope of recall, to let Yegor stew in his own juice for a while and perhaps yield something more authentic and truthful. Olga had been lucky, in Vassily's view, that Zemsky had not been there, or she would have found herself summarily ejected from her secondment, or worse; and even as things were, a certain degree of massaging had been required for the official report of Yegor's arrest and initial interview to avoid Olga becoming the target of the captain's ire.

As it was, however, Zemsky was blissfully unaware of this particular back story, and seemed positively relaxed about the whole affair.

'He didn't care, did he? That makes two of us. He confessed to the murders, didn't he? His DNA was all over those costumes, wasn't it? And he's in a prison cell in Tayga, isn't he? Well, that's good enough for me, Marushkin – and it should be good enough for you, too. You've solved a murder case, man – and a pretty high-profile one at that! Kemerovo are pleased – but there's no rest for the weary, don't forget. You've still got a spate of low-end crime in Roslazny, *da*? No *banya* for you just yet.'

Zemsky knew, of course, that there were no *banya*s in Roslazny these days. Once, long ago in the days of the tsars, there had been several, and you couldn't walk far down the village pathways without encountering a long, low, log-built sauna with aromatic smoke blooming from a short chimney – but when the state farm was established it came with a public bathhouse, and the old buildings fell into disrepair. Now the *sozhkhov* had gone, there was nothing left at all – but Olga had been to *banya*s in other places, and knew what it was like to sit in a *predbannik* relaxation room sipping fermented *kvass* before a gentle massage with eucalyptus and juniper twigs. *Pomylsya*, they said in Siberia, *budto zanovo rodilsya* – washed and born again. She began to imagine what it would be like to build a *banya* with Vassily, and what it would be like to wash next to him, and to be born again into a new life – perhaps to give birth to a new life – but then she closed her eyes and made herself think of something else. Her cheeks were hot and glowing, she realised – and, besides, Vassily wasn't hers to do anything with, except the sharing of a neighbourly glass of vodka at Café Astana, and the solving of the occasional crime or two. It was virtue that was called for, not vivid imaginings.

But that was exactly what troubled her about Yegor Shulgin: virtue, or rather the air of virtue that he had adopted in all his dealings with the police following his arrest, as if he had at last accomplished some weighty task whose completion satisfied a long-desired yearning. As he had said himself, his conscience was clear – and it really seemed to Olga that this strange man, this rather anonymous-looking person, whose face and body could so easily adopt the appearance of another's, believed he had done nothing wrong in murdering two, and nearly three, of his colleagues in the Murder Express. He wouldn't respond to questions or elaborate on his motives. He just stared at them through his clear Perspex glasses, unblinking and unconcerned, as if they were passing the time together in a dentist's waiting room. They had packed him off to a cell in the Tayga police station to await transfer to Kemerovo for processing, and he had walked blithely away with Timofei Davidov, like a man heading to the shops on a Saturday afternoon.

Olga found it all utterly inexplicable, and couldn't avoid the feeling that Yegor was so satisfied with himself because he thought he really *had* done something good. He had the air not of a murderer but of a martyr dying for some unknown but laudable cause.

'Oh, *yes*, Olga,' Anna Kabalevsky had said later that day, when Olga had told her this thought at dinner, sitting at their narrow table with its patchwork of too-small plastic tablecloths. 'That's just what the great saints did, going to their deaths with the certainty of divine reward. They sacrificed themselves for God.'

That was all very well, thought Olga, as she went to bed that night. Yes, that was all very well, but what could Yegor Shulgin be sacrificing himself for? It didn't make any sense. Didn't most martyrs *want* the world to know what they were giving themselves up for? If the world didn't know, what was the point of the martyrdom? She leaned over to her bedside lamp and clicked her room into a darkness that matched her bewildered thoughts.

Things were no clearer the day after, either, when Olga walked to Café Astana to find a village awash with rumours of dark events in Tayga.

'The doctor's under investigation,' said Nikolai Popov, nodding at Olga as she took a seat at the bar.

'Which one?' she said.

'Zinovev, of course,' said Fyodor Katin, sitting on the other side of Olga and looking sternly ahead as if trying to resist the temptation to gloat at his rival's misfortune. 'Who else?'

'Under investigation for what?' said Olga.

'They don't know, Olga!' said Igor Odrosov from behind the

bar, in decidedly grumpy tones. 'Nobody knows what's around the corner, do they? You might think you can spend whatever you like, for once, because you've got a vodka franchise coming in – but no, no, no! Don't ever think you can rely on what people say. You can't trust anyone, these days. You can't even trust your own daughter, who's stopped showing up for work because her head's been turned by some rubbishy play – like some customers I could mention, who've taken to eating at Mikhail's bloody Red Star. Red Star? Dead from food poisoning, more like, *da*, Nikolai?'

But Popov only shrugged, prompting Odrosov to flash a particularly unpleasant gesture in his direction and retreat towards the sanctuary of his kitchen, leaving only the dangling threads of a beaded curtain clattering behind him.

Popov turned to Olga and grinned. 'Can't be too easy on him – eh, Fyodor? Need to keep him desperate, push those premium meat prices up and up . . .'

'Premium?' scoffed Fyodor. 'Cats and dogs and horses?'

'I'm surprised you've got time to hang around here, Fyodor,' said Olga, quickly, forestalling the tediously predictable riposte from Popov. 'Aren't you busy with rehearsals, like half the village, these days?'

Like Svetlana Odrosov, and Lev Myatlev before her, Fyodor Katin had been pressed into service as a behind-the-scenes replacement for the departed Yegor Shulgin, just as Koptev Alexeyev, the village's resident mechanic, had been co-opted by Agapa Putyatin as a stand-in Rasputin for as long as Panteleimon Pomelov continued to occupy his hospital bed in Tayga.

'Of course we're busy,' said Fyodor, with the air of a much-in-demand Muscovite star being pressed on his schedule by an importunate journalist. 'But the work is so demanding, so *intense*, that we have to have time off. And you know, Olga,' he said, leaning a little closer to her so that Popov could not hear, 'I do wonder, sometimes, about these theatrical types. I mean, nobody loves literature – drama, and prose, and poetry, and everything – more than I do, but as I say, I do wonder . . .'

'What do you wonder about, Fyodor?' said Olga, looking affectionately at him, and thinking how *real* he was compared to Yegor Shulgin – how honest and authentic, down to the genuine super-strength glasses, lank hair and threadbare outfits that would never be admitted onto even the humblest of provincial stages.

'Well, it's Agapa, you see,' he said. 'Agapa Putyatin,' he clarified, as if Agapa alone was a kind of secret keyword known only to those within the theatrical inner circle. 'She came yesterday morning to ask me about taking Yegor's place, which was pretty quick work, considering everything that was going on. But she didn't seem particularly relieved about Yegor being uncovered as a murderer. She seemed . . .'

'She seemed – what?'

'Well, anxious, really,' said Fyodor. 'Yes – anxious, as if there was some bigger problem that still remained unresolved.'

Olga sat in silence for a moment, staring down into her glass of blue-tinged Rocket Fuel. Finally she opened her lips to speak, but Fyodor got there first.

'There was something else, too,' he said. 'Something Sonia Alikovsky told me she'd heard Agapa saying to Ilya. Ilya Putyatin, I mean – our director.'

Olga rolled her eyes. 'Yes, thank you, Fyodor – but what did Agapa say to Ilya Putyatin, the director?'

'Well, it was a couple of days before Yegor was arrested, she said. She was smoking by the tracks and heard footsteps coming along the other side of the train – the side towards Tayga. They were talking quietly, and Sonia couldn't hear them. So then she— You won't tell her I told you, will you, Olga? There is such a thing as troupe loyalty, you know. Good. Well, she tiptoed quietly down to the gap between the two carriages, so she could hear a little better. And she heard Ilya telling Agapa that they couldn't go on, not with a killer on the scene. But then Agapa said, no, not at all – that it was better to have a murderer in the region – that nothing could be better, in fact, in light of the Murder Express. Ilya said something back to Agapa, in quite a heated tone, said Sonia, but by now they had walked past the gap in the carriage and she could hear no more.'

'Agapa said it was *better* to have a killer about?'

'Yes, I suppose because it keeps the audiences coming in, for curiosity's sake. That's certainly true – but I have to say it's made me hesitate a little, when it comes to my new career. After all, if the second-in-command is rubbing her hands together at the thought of her actors being bumped off in exchange for ticket sales, I'm not sure it's going to be a good fit. It might be something that looks good in principle, but less good in theory. I mean – good in practice, but not in theory. No . . .'

Olga smiled as Fyodor rambled on, reflecting that he did, after all, share a few characteristics with Yegor Shulgin. But Fyodor had a heart that was filled with goodness, and that made all the difference, thought Olga Pushkin.

After she left the café, Olga wandered down to her little railside hut to see if anything needed doing on the maintenance side. During her secondment, the Tayga depot had been charged with the upkeep of her hut, as well as all the track duties that usually fell to Olga – but she was well acquainted with all the characters at the depot, and was fairly certain that little or nothing would have been done in the several days since she had last been there. And therein lay the problem – for if the Tayga depot people hadn't needed to come out and do Olga's work very often, didn't that imply that Olga's work didn't really need doing at all?

Olga shook her head as she turned the last corner on the path that led to the hut, emerging from the gloom of the overhanging boughs into the comparative brightness of the long clearing through which ran the main line – comparative only, for while the grey, low-hanging cloud shed more light than the dark green trees, it was still a leaden, heavy kind of light, at once darker than the glittering cold sunlight of high-pressure days in winter and lighter-hued than the clouds that shed snowflakes by the countless million. Olga stopped, looked up and sighed, longing once more for the snow's return, or even a brilliant frost under a wintry sun – anything but this drear, drab and dingy procession of damp, low-hanging clouds.

She continued staring upwards for a moment longer, like a fervent believer hoping for a sign from Heaven, but nothing new was forthcoming – only more of the same, day after day the same with no knight in armour upon the horizon to relieve the tedium, no Vassily Marushkin or any other man to sweep her off her feet and away, far, far away from Roslazny and its monotonous surrounds.

She sighed again, and walked on towards her hut, reminding herself that there was a time, not so long ago, when she had been delighted to secure her future in Roslazny – when she'd been overjoyed to pack Polina Klemovsky off to Mongolia in her place and return to her house, her hut and her hedgehog in peace. But that had been when Vassily was still free, or at least, if not quite free, open to negotiation on the matter. But all that had changed when Rozalina had tottered onto the scene with yappy little Sputnik in her arms, and now everything was different. Vassily was no longer hers, and even his son, Kliment, seemed altered, transformed by his mother's presence into a nervy, ill-nourished creature ready to jump at his own shadow. No, the situation was transformed, and all that had once seemed to thrill and tingle with imminent change had turned dowdy and over-familiar again, robbed of its fleeting sheen of all-promising magic and revealed for what it had been all along: the humdrum furniture of a humdrum life. But at least she still had two havens to call her own: the house she shared with Anna Kabalevsky and Pasha, and the hut she shared with Dmitri, or used to, at any rate, until he had made his bold, near-suicidal bid for freedom, and was obliged to be returned to the safety of the house.

Yes, the hut was a haven, and— But what was that Olga could see draped over the door, and around the gables, painted in a faded lime-green crossed with white? She saw yellow-and-black tape, of the kind she'd seen wrapped around live wires, or across sensitive parts of a crime scene – and on the door she saw something nailed to its surface, a laminated notice in plain black and white, whose headline text she could read as she drew near.

SCHEDULED FOR DEMOLITION. DO NOT ENTER.

With a racing heart, Olga pushed aside the tape, ripped off the paper, and barged open the door, dropping into the threadbare armchair beside the bookshelf and breathlessly reading the text below the catastrophic title. *Inefficiencies in network maintenance,* she read, *system-wide need to maximise return-on-investment . . . New technologies becoming available to replace human operators . . .*

She threw aside the paper in disgust without reading to the end. She didn't need to: it was painfully obvious that Boris Andreyev had followed through on his threat at last, long after Olga had outwitted him regarding the plan to send her to Mongolia. Revenge, it seemed, really was a dish best served cold.

Olga jumped to her feet and strode to the desk to pick up her walkie-talkie. He wasn't going to get away with this, she told herself – he hadn't got rid of her last time, and he wouldn't be able to this time, either! She'd show him that railwaywomen are made of sterner stuff than he supposed. She'd show him!

But then she put down the walkie-talkie and slumped back into her armchair. What was the point, after all? She had miraculously outwitted Boris Andreyev last time and sent Polina off to Ulaanbaatar in Olga's place – but that was just it. Miracles, like lightning, didn't strike twice. There would be no second delivery of manna from Heaven, no new intervention from sources divine and unexpected. This time, there would be only the drabness of defeat, the tedious, heart-breaking task of emptying the hut where she had nurtured so many dreams. Now the time for dreaming was over. Now harsh daylight had broken in, and Olga was awake, and all the soft blandishments of the night had vanished, leaving only harsh reality behind.

She looked up, out of the little window across from the armchair, and found a dull comfort in the cold grey picture framed there, with stark, leafless branches reaching over the empty track, lifting and falling in the soft November breeze. She gazed, and breathed, and let the world fall away. She would let herself dream one more time in the little hut, bringing her mother to mind – yes, Tatiana, and her far-off childhood in the Lodge at Astrazov, the fairy dwelling in the woods where the Lichnovsky counts and countesses had holidayed, until time and the Bolsheviks had thinned them out, killing them off one by one and leaving, in the end, only Tatiana and Lubov, the housekeeper, alive to remember them. But Mikhail, Olga's father, had stolen Tatiana from Astrazov, leaving Lubov alone amid the dwindling light under the trees until she, too, disappeared, like the Lichnovskys before her, and was gone.

Olga carried on looking out but with eyes that now went beyond what she could see, as if there were some kinder, gentler world beyond where her tears would be recorded and balanced by some sort of redress, where suffering and sorrow were just one side of a fairer coin. But she shook her head, for she was not Anna Kabalevsky, to believe such things. For Olga, there was only this world, rent as it was with evil and misery and the needless shedding of innocent blood. There was only the hut, the window and the bare-branched trees beyond, sighing in the breeze like Olga's steady breathing, and like her doing nothing more than staying rooted to a single place. For now, that was enough, she thought, as her eyes slowly closed in sleep. That was enough for trees and branches and heartbroken railway engineers without a hut to call their own. That was enough.

The light had already begun to fade by the time Olga came out of her hut, draping a thick grey blanket over the dark green of the trees overhead, and turning the railway clearing into a long, dark space like the nave of some ruined cathedral. In some part of her mind, she recognised that the scene was far from beautiful, objectively speaking – there were too many rusty signal boxes and rotting sleepers for that. But every inch of it was precious to her, and she turned away with a half-choked sob rising in her throat, as if she were tearing herself away from a much-loved friend after a too-short reunion.

She took a slightly longer path home so she could avoid walking past the Red Star, though she could hear its clientele in the clear evening air, singing raucous songs that floated across to her with unpleasant clarity and volume. She even thought she could distinguish her father's booming voice amid the melee, though it could just as well have been his partner in crime, old man Solotov. But however much she hated them both, she had to admit that they – and their associate, Olga's Aunt Zia – had made quite a splash on the Roslazny scene. And now, with Odrosov facing bankruptcy on account of vodka-franchising money that had never arrived, the Red Star looked set to dominate Roslaznyan café society for years or decades to come. They'd certainly made the most of Odrosov's well-timed downfall, that was for sure.

Olga frowned. It had been *very* well-timed, hadn't it? Almost *too* well timed: as if maybe Mikhail and Vladimir had put their heads together and plotted a way to bring Odrosov down at the same time as they launched their own enterprise.

It couldn't be, surely – could it? Olga had spent part of the afternoon reading Gogol's *Dead Souls*, one of the books that her mother Tatiana had bought her on a long-ago visit to Tomsk State University, and her mind was filled with the scurrilous schemes dreamed up by Pavel Ivanovich Chichikov upon his travels. Maybe Mikhail and old man Solotov were up to something similar – she wouldn't put it past them, and—

But who was this, driving along in the evening without headlights, she asked herself, hearing the distant sounds of a car bumping over one of the paths that wound through and round the village like haphazard veins and muddy capillaries? The car drew nearer, and she saw it was a Lada Riva, painted in what looked like some light colour – blue, maybe, or pale green. And then she frowned: hadn't the troupe hired a Lada Riva to ferry the actors from Tayga to Roslazny, and to pay clandestine visits to the hospital, too?

She ducked behind a nearby tree, a stunted birch that had grown half-heartedly out of one of the many ruins that dotted the village, and watched as the car drove by within a hundred feet or so, passing by the old bathhouse that had replaced Roslazny's *banya*s, moving on in the direction of the track – and more specifically in the direction of the siding where the Murder Express still waited on its steel-rimmed wheels, tens of immobile tons pressing the track to earth, and the rails yet holding them upwards in defiance. A light flickered on inside the car – a mobile phone, perhaps, or a torch – and flickered off again, but not before Olga had seen two people: someone at the wheel, a woman, she thought, and another in the passenger seat, sitting forward as if willing the car and its cargo (for Olga had caught a fleeting glimpse of bulky items in the back seat) to move more quickly, more surely over the darkened road in front of it. But how could they drive any faster than they already were? As it was, they were taking serious risks to both their car and their health, since the potholes in Roslazny's roads and pathways were as numerous as they were wide and deep.

But why was the car driving without headlights? Olga could have understood it if it had been one of Koptev Alexeyev's special deals, but the troupe had hired their Lada from a hire-car operator in Tayga, with a moderately aged but still comfortable Opel. Even in Siberia, hire cars had to undergo frequent checks, so Olga found it hard to believe that the car's headlights had packed up of their own accord. The driver must have chosen not to use them, but again, why? And where was everyone? wondered Olga, looking around her and seeing empty pathways on all sides. Early evening was usually a relatively busy time in Roslazny, with people taking to the pathways to visit friends after the day's work, or heading to Café Astana – or, these days, to the Red Star – to buy food or drink vodka or both. But tonight the village seemed deserted or, rather, already concentrated indoors at the Red Star, from which Olga heard ever louder, ever more inappropriate singing above the noise of the Lada's puttering engine as it headed onwards on unknown errands.

Where was Vassily when you needed him? thought Olga, but then she tutted at herself. Who needed Vassily when she had her own two feet beneath her, two eyes to look around her and nothing left to lose ahead of her? Vassily was probably celebrating the end of the case with Rozalina and Kliment at the station, or maybe at Café Astana, ordering plate after plate of Odrosov's greasy *pelmeni*, and washing the indeterminate meat down with gulps of Rocket Fuel. No, she didn't need him, she thought: she'd had her own way of dealing with things before Vassily arrived, and now that Rozalina had taken him away, she would just have to return to her old habits and approaches – which in this particular case meant charging after the unlit car as fast as possible to see what on earth it was up to. And if someone had appeared after all in the deserted streets of Roslazny, and asked her why she had decided to investigate the car, she would have had nothing to say but the following: *I don't know, but I'm still not happy with what's happened. I'm still not happy with the end of the case. Yegor Shulgin killed those actors, yes, but why? And why did he say his conscience was clear? Something doesn't add up – and I mean to get to the bottom of it.*

She set off at a jog, running after the car as if she were a bloodhound following the acrid cloud of blue-grey exhaust. In a moment, though, her pace slowed and her brows clouded. There had been something familiar about the figure in the front seat – hadn't there? Something in the way they sat, or rather perched, leaning hungrily forward as if desperate to will the Lada on to its destination. Where had she seen that figure before? It was somewhere outside Roslazny, she thought – and that probably meant Tayga, for Olga rarely had time to go much farther. And she was sure that the strand of memory the shadowy figure had plucked was something out of the usual routine – something beyond her habitual stops at the depot and on the platforms at the railway station. No: it had been a dark place, she thought, a dark and narrow place, so that the figure had appeared to her in similar lighting as it did now. A dark and narrow place . . . Where might fit that description in Tayga, beyond the mind of Boris Andreyev?

Olga gasped as her own mind supplied the necessary answers at last. Of course! It had been the alleyway that led from the railway station up towards the café where she had had her memorable meeting with Slava Sergeivich Kirillov, the so-called counsellor who had stripped her of a thousand roubles in exchange for nothing much, before everything had happened with the Murder Express – before she had even seen Inessa Ignatyev's *All on the Line*.

Olga had walked up in the growing darkness, she recalled, and seen two people talking, a woman and a man, as in the Lada just now. They'd been talking quietly together, before bringing their conversation to an end when they heard Olga approaching. Olga thought she had seen them exchange something – the woman had handed an item to the man, a small object, maybe an envelope. Then the woman had stalked off up the pathway ahead of Olga, rapidly disappearing, while the man had glanced in her direction before pulling up his collar, pulling down his fur hat, and shuffling past her with averted eyes, but with the same sense of suppressed urgency that had brought him to mind when Olga saw the Lada. It was as if his desires were stronger than his ability to carry them out. And he had reminded her of someone she knew, she was sure of it. She had stood there, watching him until he, too, vanished from sight, but the faint note of familiarity failed to blossom into definite recognition. After a while Olga had turned and walked on to her unpromising rendezvous.

But now she had a chance to find out who the man had been, and the woman – assuming she was the same woman she'd seen in the Tayga alleyway. Olga turned and headed decisively towards the tracks, the same direction the car had taken in its unlit journeying. She could still hear its engine running softly, and its suspension creaking as its wheels navigated the unforgiving Roslazny potholes, bumping and swaying as it made its way to the edge of the village. It would have to stop there, Olga knew, so presumably there would be a chance to see them getting out of the car, and perhaps identifying at last the mysterious figures from Tayga – so she hurried onwards, moving from doorway to doorway and tree to tree, always poised to duck behind a useful piece of street furniture if the car suddenly turned around, or if some other person appeared on the scene. But the car kept moving onwards, and nobody else appeared, until at last Olga saw a red glow appearing on trees near the track – the car's brake lights, of course, which could not easily be switched off. So they had stopped, probably in the little clearing Olga had in mind, marking the end of the path and the beginning of Russian Railways territory.

Olga turned her head and scanned first to her left, and then to the right, looking down the path that led back to Roslazny – had she heard a noise, a faint rustle of fabric brushing past a wall? But she saw nothing, and a moment later a soft breeze came, lifting the boughs and sending a whispering noise to her ears. That must have been what she heard, she told herself – but not entirely convincingly.

Partially reassured, she turned back towards the track and moved forward again, picking her way yet more carefully now to avoid loose twigs, or anything else that might reveal her presence to the Lada's passengers. Foot by foot, yard by yard, she moved closer, closer, ever closer, skirting the last trees, tumbledown walls and rusted bits of farm machinery until at last she caught sight of the Lada. It was parked where she'd imagined, close to the edge of the tracks and near the large birch that dominated the clearing, and whose leaves formed a thick carpet underfoot. The car's engine was still running, but all the doors were open, including the boot, and figures were moving around the vehicle – *three* figures, she realised, not just two: there was a third person, an older man by the look of things, who was standing next to the woman while the first man, the one she had seen bending forwards in the passenger seat, bent to the car boot and began pulling out something heavy.

He cursed softly: the object seemed to be stuck. He called to the others, who came round to the back of the car. The older man fished something out of a pocket, and fumbled with it until a strong beam of light arched up into the night. The woman swore loudly, and grabbed the torch from the man's hand – but not before Olga had seen her face, and the face of the first man, the passenger she had seen in the Lada earlier. And she gasped as she did so, for she was looking at the face of Dr Yury Sergeiivich Zinovev from the Tayga Hospital, and beside him Agapa Putyatin, de facto director of the Murder Express.

'What was that?' said Zinovev, standing and looking in Olga's direction.

'Probably nothing,' said Agapa. 'A fox, or something – the place is overrun with vermin.'

Nevertheless, they stood and watched for several minutes longer, until, seemingly satisfied, they turned back to what they had been doing before, joined by the third figure, the hapless torch-waver, whom Olga now identified by his movements as Ilya Putyatin, Agapa's husband. She smiled a thin, humourless smile as she watched them, for each person was playing the role in which she would have cast them in whatever hidden work they were carrying out: Agapa directing operations, crossly but effectively; the weary, selfless doctor doing her bidding without sparing himself; and Ilya dancing uselessly around the edge, offering irrelevant comments in his high, fussy voice, but doing little to help.

But then her smile disappeared, and did not soon return: she had seen what it was they were getting out of the car boot, and what it was that Ilya now began to extract from the back seat of the car. The large, shapeless mass that Olga had seen dimly by the light of a fleeting glow was now revealed as a long object wrapped in bed sheets, and tied at the top and bottom with some kind of cord. There was a round shape at the top, and then two longer, narrower shapes visible to the sides, and two more at the bottom. It was clearly heavy: Ilya struggled to lift it on his own, and had to call Zinovev to help him, causing the doctor to drop his own, similar, object and rush to the older man's side. Of course it was heavy, thought Olga: it was a dead body, after all. Yes, a dead body: one of two that they had stuffed into the car and driven to Roslazny, presumably from Tayga.

Had they driven all the way from Tayga without lights, wondered Olga – but then she stopped herself. She was in some kind of shock, she realised, and her mind was trying to cope with the horrifying sights in front of her eyes by deflecting onto other, less worrisome, thoughts. But there was no time for that: she had to stay focused, and be a useful witness to what was happening in front of her eyes. She had to observe and remember every detail: Vassily would want to know later, and Zemsky. But she spared herself time for a fierce jet of satisfaction. She had been right about Yegor Shulgin or, rather, she had been right that Yegor Shulgin was not the whole story. Something else, something bigger, had been going on behind the scenes, behind the theatrical curtain that the Murder Express had draped over Roslazny this past week, and now Olga would rip it from its fastenings to reveal whatever terrors might lie behind.

The trio finally succeeded in dragging the bodies from the car, and then set themselves to carrying them down towards the P36 and the Murder Express, the two men addressing the task by each taking one end of a body, which sagged horribly in the middle, and walking with difficulty along the uneven ground and then the gravel track that led towards the train. Having left one body, they came back for the other, and repeated the process, with Agapa looking around to check that nobody was coming, then following the men down towards the Murder Express.

Olga, too, checked that nobody could see her, and then – when a minute or two had elapsed – forced herself to step out from her hiding-place behind the birch and follow their footsteps to the Murder Express. Forced herself, because it went against every grain of common sense to put herself deliberately in the way of danger – especially when she had already escaped so many perilous situations that year, for one reason and another, and by good fortune as much as by design. But there was nobody else to follow Agapa, Ilya and Zinovev – nobody else to see what was going on.

Or was there? She looked again over her shoulder, troubled by the faint sibilant hiss she had heard behind her a few minutes ago, and remembering the lithe figure, clad all in black, that she had seen in Roslazny all too recently. But there was nothing to be seen, only the far-off remains of ruined houses and spindly, bare-branched trees, disappearing now into the twilight gloom, and unpopulated by anything save the sad emptiness of neglect.

What was it that Slava Kirillov had said, back in Tayga? *Toughen up! Do your work without complaining, like a soldier!* Kirillov was an idiot, that much was certain – but perhaps in this case he was right. Olga compressed her lips together, drew in a deep breath, and set off towards the Murder Express. It was down to her, once more, to find out what was really going on behind the scenes.

She crept down the pathway, taking care to avoid stepping on the gravel that had been scattered somewhat carelessly over the uneven ground, and peering ahead in case the trio had made an unexpected stop – but no: they kept going with the second body, until they had deposited it in the same place as the first, by the foot of the ladder that led into one of the carriages. It was the second carriage, Olga saw – the one with the compartments that Vassily had used as impromptu cells, and with the small dressing area at the end.

Then they bent to the bodies and, to Olga's horror, began to unwind the sheets from them, peeling off the white fabric until what lay beneath was revealed. She tried to tear her eyes away, but couldn't at first, mesmerised by what she was witnessing, the gradual unveiling of two people who until recently had been alive, who had breathed just as she did, but who now were stilled in death. One was a man and one a woman, both in their sixties, thought Olga, and dressed in drab, everyday clothes – presumably the outfits in which they had been brought to hospital in their last illnesses. Olga choked a sob into silence, but felt her heart lurch all the same with sorrow: she didn't recognise the faces, she hadn't known them, but they were people nonetheless, with parents, grandparents, siblings, cousins, uncles, aunts, friends, associates, enemies and acquaintances, likes and dislikes, favourite places and dishes . . . How precious is each individual life, thought Olga, and how recklessly the world deals with them, as if they were pennies cast unwanted from a discarded purse.

She looked away in revulsion, feeling waves of hatred leaping up in her chest against the Putyatins, who no doubt were behind the scheme, whatever it was, and for Zinovev, the so-called good doctor, who was helping them, and who had no doubt arranged for the bodies to be brought from the hospital morgue. Where else could you find readily available corpses on demand? Yes, yes, she thought, her mind racing – Agapa was the woman she had seen in the alleyway with Zinovev, and that was what they must have been arranging: the delivery of two dead bodies a week or so from then. But *why*? What was the point of stowing two corpses in the Murder Express, just as Yegor had hidden his costumes in the P36 tender? Could it be some terrible PR stunt, making a splash in the dramatic world with real dead bodies serving as props? But Olga no sooner voiced the idea in her mind than she rejected it as too crazy, too outlandish, for even Russia to tolerate. Things were bad, but they weren't that bad – yet. She needed to learn more, to find out why they had brought two dead people from Tayga to Roslazny.

She watched as they finished unwrapping the bodies and began lifting them into the train, first one and then the other. When the last of them disappeared – Zinovev taking the dead man's feet and lifting them into the carriage, with the Putyatins going ahead of him – she walked stealthily down the last part of the track until she reached the carriage. The ladder was short, only three rungs and then the wooden step, with a dip in the middle where countless feet had worn it away over the years – it was small, but it looked enormous to her then, a leap into the unknown, and maybe mortal peril. But she glanced around her again, and saw no Vassily Marushkin, no Fyodor Katin or Nikolai Popov, no kindly or homely faces coming towards her with helpful hands. There was only her: it was down to Olga Pushkin, soon-to-be-retired railway engineer, second class, to take care of things once more.

She stepped forward, slowly, quietly, and lifted her hands to the rails: they felt cold to the touch, bringing those gaping dead faces to mind, but she shook off the thought and pulled herself up nonetheless. One step was done, then another, and a third, and then her boot made contact with the wooden step, and she was inside. She moved forward slowly, almost an inch at a time, taking care lest her jacket brush against the wooden wall with the same hissing noise she'd heard behind her earlier, and her ears primed to listen, almost aching with the effort to pick up useful noise.

She heard bumping then, and a crash, as if someone had knocked a heavy object against a door.

'*Careful*,' hissed Agapa Putyatin. 'We don't want any damage, remember? The doctor managed to get them to us in good condition. Now keep them that way!'

'Yes, dear,' said Ilya, quietly and clearly – thought Olga – trying to keep his patience. 'I'm doing my best, but the – ah – gentleman is rather heavy.'

'He ate too much *kurnik* for his last meal, that's all,' said Agapa. 'Just get your hands under his arms and onto the bed. Where's Zinovev?'

'Dealing with the woman,' said Ilya.

'Taking his time,' muttered Agapa, between deep breaths – clearly she, too, was finding the man hard to move. 'What about the other stuff?'

'The – ah – *kindling*?' said Ilya. 'It's under the bed in Svetlana's compartment.'

'Why hers? I thought we agreed on Lev's. Ah, there you are, Zinovev.'

'I think she smokes more,' said Ilya. 'Bad for the health, isn't it, Doctor?'

But Zinovev was clearly in no mood for conversation, and only grunted in response – concentrating instead, it seemed, on manoeuvring the second body. A door opened – she could hear its hinges creaking – then banged against a wall. Was Zinovev putting the body into one of the compartments? Again Olga forced herself to move, this time inching closer to the edge of the wall so she could see what he was doing. She pushed the smallest possible sliver of her face around the corner, and saw Zinovev's back disappearing into one of the compartments – Agapa's, she thought, and just down from this, along the corridor, she saw that the door to Ilya's room was also open.

She moved back around the corner into safety, breathing quickly but silently. So they had brought the bodies to put into their own compartments – but why? And what had Ilya meant by kindling – was he planning to start a campfire? And why in Svetlana's compartment – and why did it matter that she smoked more than Lev, or indeed more than just about anyone in Roslazny or its immediate surrounds?

Olga leaned her head back against the wall, her mind teeming with new and terrible suspicions. Agapa and Ilya were no longer young, she thought – their glittering careers were nearly over. There would be no more TV premieres, no more first nights at the Bolshoi, no more lucrative directorships at this or that provincial theatre . . . How were they going to provide for their retirement? Thespians were hardly known for their financial acumen. Maybe they'd realised they would run out of savings quickly, and cast around for an alternative plan. And maybe – maybe that woman who had drowned, Kira Obnizov, had stumbled across it, somehow, and so had had to be silenced. It wasn't that she'd been having an affair with Ilya, but rather that she'd discovered all too much about his affairs . . .

But Yegor Shulgin had been there too, reflected Olga. Yegor Shulgin had also been aboard the houseboat on the Izhevskiy Prud where Kira had drowned, and maybe that wasn't a coincidence. Could he have had something to do with her death, too? What was it he'd said when they arrested him? *My conscience is clear* . . . Had he been killing people off because they, too, suspected the Putyatins? He had often mentioned his mother, how much he missed her – it would be easy enough, wouldn't it, for those affections, those emotions and feelings to be transferred to Agapa instead? She was about the right age to have been his mother, though she would probably shriek in horror to hear somebody say so. If Yegor thought he'd been defending a stand-in for his own mother, then that would make it easier to do anything – anything at all – with a clear conscience.

And the bodies . . . Olga frowned, struggling to recover a memory from earlier that same day – something she'd seen that now seemed relevant, somehow, to the Murder Express. Something in her house, perhaps, or Café Astana . . . *Or her hut*. Yes, yes, she had it now – it was her ancient, dog-eared copy of Gogol's *Dead Souls*, and the memories it had brought to mind of Pavel Ivanovich Chichikov and his picaresque wanderings in search of landowners willing to surrender to him their dead souls – listings of serfs who had passed away, but whose persons could still be counted to Chichikov's credit in some imaginary estate, and used for prestige and as collateral against enormous loans. The bodies that Zinovev had provided were of older people, and of a man and a woman, too. And the kindling . . . If the train were to catch fire, say, then it would be difficult to identify the bodies – difficult or, if the Putyatins had taken the trouble to get rid of their dental records beforehand, impossible. Then Ilya and Agapa would be 'dead souls', leaving them free to flee with their crimes unpunished.

So they wanted to fake their own deaths, thought Olga. But why start the fire in Svetlana's compartment? Why not start it in one of their own, so that it seemed they had dropped a cigarette, not Svetlana? Unless – unless—

Olga gasped, and flung a gloved hand over her mouth as if she could retract the sound. She stood absolutely still, listening in case enquiring footsteps came down the corridor to discover her standing there – but all was quiet. She relaxed a little, and returned to her train of thought. Of course: they wanted to kill them all at once. That was why there were only two bodies! Two to stand in for Agapa and Ilya; the rest of the troupe would provide their own corpses, delivering them into the Putyatins' grip by walking onboard of their own free will. Then they would be locked into their compartments, and the fire would be triggered, and the Murder Express would end in screams and agony.

But how would this help the Putyatins provide for their retirement? They would be dead, technically, so how could they benefit financially – assuming, of course, that Olga was right about their motive, but she could think of no other. What if they had taken out life insurance, and left arrangements so that the proceeds would devolve to some last remaining relative – and what if *that* relative was themselves a fiction, some persona created by the ever-creative actors to occupy the needed legal role and nothing more? Then, after a suitable time had elapsed, that 'person' – with all the relevant officials receiving the appropriate bribe, of course – could transfer the money to an anonymous bank account, and the Putyatins could sail off into the sunset. And meanwhile the good Dr Zinovev, having provided the bodies for (no doubt) an appropriately sizeable fee, could return to his work at the hospital with enough cash to keep his clinics going – though with no clearer a conscience than Yegor Shulgin's. And Anna Kabalevsky . . . Olga closed her eyes at the thought that Anna had once considered Zinovev in a romantic light.

Suddenly a voice broke through her reflections.

'You insufferable busybody,' cried Zinovev, his snarling face inches from her own. 'Why can't you just leave things alone? Now you'll regret it – but not for long,' he added, grabbing her arm roughly.

Olga stared at him in terror, seeing murderousness written in his eyes – a murderousness born of long, unbearable days of stress, exhaustion and desperation, she instinctively knew, but no less dangerous for all that. She reached behind her for the rail that ran up alongside the ladder, as if she might pull herself backwards to safety, but her glove slipped on the metal, polished as it had been by many thousands of hands, and she lurched forwards into Zinovev's grip.

But then Olga started backwards as something flew past her face towards Zinovev, sparking a cry of pain and loosening his grip on Olga's arm. Olga jumped backwards, staring at Zinovev in horror – for a long, slender piece of metal like a javelin was lodged in the doctor's shoulder, already rimmed with a patch of dark crimson that spread ominously down his shirt.

'Olga, quick!' cried a voice from outside. She looked down and saw the same lithe figure she had seen before, clad all in black even to the extent of a balaclava, standing now by the ladder and gesturing furiously to her. 'Jump down – now!'

She did as she was told, moving as if in a dream and with legs that felt like rubber, but reaching for the rails and feeling their reassuring solidity as she dropped down the steps onto the ground. The figure pushed past her and pulled the carriage door closed, then quickly wrapped a chain around the handles and tied as much of a knot as was possible with the thick chain, then ran to the far end of the carriage and did the same with the other door, repeating the process for the first carriage, which of course had a connecting door to the second. Zinovev and the Putyatins appeared at the windows, trying to heave the door open, then doing the same for all the other doors, but with no success.

In the meantime, Olga half expected the figure, having added vigilante policing to its roster of extra-legal activity, to run off into the night and disappear once more – but to her surprise it came sloping towards her. She began to inch backwards. She had no idea who it really was, after all, and perhaps she had jumped from the frying pan into the fire. But then she stopped, realising that the figure was walking in rather a bashful manner, exactly like a child who knew he had to admit to some wrongdoing but was reluctant to get it over with.

The figure reached her, and after a moment pulled off the balaclava.

'*Kliment*,' gasped Olga, realising with a rush of mental energy that it was his round head that had sparked the sense of recognition previously. 'What on earth are you doing here?'

'I'm sorry, Olga,' said Kliment, gazing at her with doleful eyes. 'I can explain everything . . .'

'Kliment!' shouted another voice, and Olga turned to see Vassily Marushkin running into the clearing by the train, and behind him Fyodor Katin, Anna Kabalevsky, Svetlana Odrosov, and several other villagers. 'Kliment,' said Vassily again, this time with more than a touch of anger. 'What the hell are you doing in that outfit? Don't tell me it's been you all this time – don't tell me—'

But Olga cut him off. 'Not now, Vassily – he can explain everything later, I'm sure. The thing you need to know now is that Kliment just saved my life. It's Zinovev, and the Putyatins – we've locked them in now. Well, Kliment did – I'll explain later. But they were going to burn the train with the actors in, and fake their deaths! Or— Well, that's what I think, anyway.'

'Zinovev?' cried Anna Kabalevsky, her eyes round with shock.

'Burn *me*?' cried Svetlana Odrosov, her eyes narrowed with indignation. 'Burn *this*?' she added, gesturing at her newest leather miniskirt.

'Look, Vassily, we can sort out all the details later. But you've got to get Davidov down from Tayga, and Zemsky, too – then arrest the Putyatins and Zinovev, and take them in for questioning. There's been murder done on their account, I'm sure of it, and more to come.'

'Look!' cried Fyodor Katin, pointing at the second carriage, where a thin tongue of flame had begun to flicker out of a join between two planks of varnished wood.

'Who's that – Zinovev?' said Kliment, looking up at one of the doors on the first carriage. The doctor's face was pressed up against the window, and illuminated on one side by an angry orange glow – and suddenly Olga realised that the fire had already spread far more quickly than they had realised.

'Unlock the doors,' shouted Kliment. 'I mean, undo the knots in the chains – I did them! Quick!'

With Vassily's help they had soon loosened the chains that had locked the doors, but they couldn't pull them open to allow Zinovev and the Putyatins to escape.

'It's the fire,' shouted Fyodor. 'The carriages are warping.'

'No,' replied Vassily. 'They've locked them from inside – look!'

Olga looked where he had pointed, and saw the square bar of metal that meant a closed lock. 'Then we can't get them out!' she cried.

'We're going to try, all the same,' said Vassily, and reaching into his pocket he pulled out a weighty torch with which he smashed the small window over the door. Seeing this, others did the same on the three other doors, and tried to reach in to unlock them – but they were beaten back by the fiery gusts that swept out of the carriages. Even Vassily gave up, recognising that he, too, would soon perish if he tried anything else. The Putyatins had disappeared from view, though Olga thought she heard a distant cry – but Zinovev stayed longest, pressing his face against a compartment window as if he could escape the inferno that was sweeping through the carriage. He saved his last look for Anna, a glance of piercing sorrow and sadness for what might have been, if there were no clinics to pay for, or sick people to heal – but then he toppled downwards at last. For a moment, his hand stayed firm against the dirty glass pane, skin pressed into whiteness, but then it peeled away and was lost.

13

Of Rogues and Rozalina

'So he's confessed now, has he? Again?'

Olga was sitting in the police station across from Vassily, in the old familiar seat in front of the fire and its missing tiles.

'He did,' confirmed Vassily. 'It was pretty easy, once we knew what angle to use.'

'Agapa?'

'Agapa,' he replied. 'He even admitted to murdering Kira Obnizov, when we started talking about Agapa Putyatin . . . Kira had got on to the Putyatins, just as Rodion Rultava and Larissa Lazarov had – just like you guessed! Rodion *was* talking about them, on the phone in the village that time you overheard him, before everything started – and it *was* Yegor slinking along the hedge and listening to him: he said as much to me. It had happened before, said Rodion – he knew that the Putyatins were dangerous, that they'd struck before and might strike again. That's why he said, "Agapa," as he lay dying . . . What was it Agapa said to me? *You must rehearse everything, Inspector* – and so they had. Only Kira got on to them, and then Rodion – but Yegor was watching, watching and waiting . . . As soon as a threat emerged to Agapa, they all had to go, one way or another – a costume would come out of the box, and soon a body would go into another kind of box . . . And of course Agapa was quite relaxed about Kira Obnizov's death, and the deaths of Rodion and Larissa, because she had had nothing to do with any of it! Yes, Yegor was half in love with Agapa, I think – though it was complicated, because he saw her as some kind of replacement mother, too. Just like you thought, Olga – though how you worked it out, I've no idea!'

'Well, I know what it's like to wish your mother back,' said Olga, softly. 'I suppose I felt sorry for Yegor, just a little, despite everything he'd done. He was just so desperate to protect Agapa, whatever the cost.'

'I can tell you who doesn't feel sorry for him at all,' said Vassily, wryly, 'and that's Panteleimon Pomelov.'

'To be fair, Yegor basically put him into a coma for several days,' said Olga.

'True,' said Vassily. 'And in disguise, too . . . Yegor's mother was right, all along: he was a great actor, in a way. And loyal to a fault.'

'His loyalty wouldn't have saved him, if he'd been on the train when the fire went up. They were going to torch the lot.'

Vassily nodded. 'They'd prepared it all so well – even to the extent of paying for free drinks for all at Café Astana and the Red Star, so they could get a clear run through the village with the Lada. And if you hadn't happened to fall asleep in your hut, and miss the whole shindig, they'd probably have got away with the whole thing – Zinovev, too.'

'Oh, don't mention his name,' said Olga. 'It breaks my heart. I know he was working with would-be murderers, but he was a good man, really. All that work he did for the community . . . I mean, he *did* give those dead bodies to the Putyatins, which wasn't ideal – but I know he only did it to get money for his clinics, and for his patients . . . He'd run out of money at last. Even selling his house wasn't enough to keep everything afloat . . . Anna's very upset about it – she can't talk about him at all. There was a time when she saw herself with him, I know – but sometimes we only see what we want to see.'

Vassily lifted his eyes and looked at her. 'Maybe now at last Anna can have some happiness in her life.'

'Maybe,' said Olga. 'Maybe, when some time has passed. But you can't force the heart to do your bidding. Believe me, I know.'

Vassily dropped his gaze back to the flames, and nodded slowly without speaking.

After a moment Olga breathed in loudly, as if signalling a change of subject, and said: 'And what about Kliment? Is he still locked in the cell?'

'Of course he is,' said Vassily, crossly. 'And no visitors allowed! I had no choice but to arrest him, finding him in disguise like that, as if he was some kind of Yegor Shulgin copycat trying to impersonate a cat-burglar. I just can't believe he's been going around stealing things and selling them on in Tayga. A policeman's son! I'm the laughing-stock of the whole *oblast*.'

'But I still don't understand why he would do that,' said Olga. 'What does he need money for? Has he been buying things – new clothes, shoes, video games, cigarettes, vodka?'

'No, no,' said Vassily. 'Not as far as I know, anyway. He's got everything he needs – I've seen to that, as far as I can on what the government pays me. It isn't much, God knows.'

Olga reached forward and put her hand on Vassily's arm. 'You do everything a father could, Vassily Marushkin,' she said gently. But she removed her hand quickly at the sound of approaching footsteps – Rozalina's, of course, since Kliment was confined to his cell. But to Olga's relief the footsteps receded again, as if Vassily's wife had heard them talking and decided that she didn't want to taunt Olga that day.

'I try, Olga,' said Vassily, looking into the fire. 'I try – but what can I do, when he behaves like this? It's bad enough having all these deaths in my own village, but now I have to deal with a petty thief in my own family, too? I just can't get through to Kliment, these days – it's like some curtain has fallen between us, and we can't hear or see each other.'

Olga thought she knew what the curtain was, but she tried to steer the conversation away from what was obviously a painful topic. 'At least we've found out how Agapa and Ilya managed to control everything in their favour – the Murder Express licences and permissions, the siding and the seating stand, all provided courtesy of Arkady Nazarov.'

As the Mayor of Kemerovo, the capital of the *oblast*, Nazarov was technically Vassily's boss, as well as the boss of every other public servant in the region. That included Boris Andreyev, Olga's superior at the Tayga depot. But Agapa and Ilya had somehow come across some extremely compromising photographs of Nazarov consorting with some presumably well-paid employees who were providing wholly illegal services in a range of glamorous locations.

'Well, it's hardly surprising, is it?' said Vassily. 'I mean, you know what the high-ups are like—'

'No, Marushkin,' boomed a voice, as Captain Zemsky

barged open the station door and stalked in. 'Tell us: what are the high-ups like?'

'Captain,' said Vassily, taking a minute – like Olga – to recover from the shock of his superior's sudden entrance. 'I wasn't talking about you, of course, sir – I was really referring to people like Nazarov, up in Kemerovo.'

'That *pridurok*?' cried Zemsky. 'Oh, he won't be there for long. I've heard things that would make your hair stand on end, and they won't stand for it – not even in Siberia! Give him a few weeks, and that'll be it.'

'Shame,' said Vassily, glancing at the brown envelope they'd found in a secret compartment at the bottom of Agapa's suitcase in the hotel at Tayga. 'Those photographs could have been useful.'

'I could have got my hut back,' joked Olga, but Zemsky turned to her with a serious look.

'What hut?' he said. So Olga told him and, to her astonishment, he seemed to get quite worked up on her behalf. 'So you've been in this hut for years, keeping our passengers safe, and now these idiots want to replace you with *drones*? No, no – this can't stand. Marushkin, give me that envelope – it contains the photos?'

'Well, yes,' admitted Vassily, 'but I was going to enter them into the archives. It's a chain-of-evidence thing, and—'

'*Yerunda*,' cut in Zemsky, almost rudely – or, at least, Olga would have thought so, were Zemsky not seeming to take her side. 'Never mind all that. I can bring them back later, if you like. But as it happens I'm going to Kemerovo tomorrow to see our good mayor, and I might – I just might – take these with me. And then, Dama Pushkin,' he added, looking at Olga, 'you just might find yourself facing a pleasant change of circumstances.' With that, he walked out of the door as suddenly as he had arrived and was gone.

Olga looked at Vassily, feeling dazed and breathless.

'Could he really do that?' she asked. 'Could he really get my hut back?'

'Well, it's like I always say,' said Vassily. 'With Zemsky, you never know! You just never know.'

Olga had wanted to see Kliment, but Vassily's ban made that impossible. She'd barely seen Kliment, in fact, since he'd saved her from an unknown fate at Zinovev's hands. Seeing his son standing by the burning train, dressed from head to toe in clandestine black, Vassily had instantly hauled him away to the police station, almost before Olga had had time to shout a few words of thanks to him – and there he had stayed ever since, while Vassily scrambled to finish the Putyatin paperwork so he could begin digging into what Kliment had got up to. Like Vassily, Olga was completely at sea when it came to Kliment's motivations, and she was keen to talk to him and find out more about how he'd come to be near the Murder Express at the vital moment – but Rozalina was still down in that part of the police station, and since Olga had no desire to battle past that particular gatekeeper, she placed the meeting in her 'to do' file.

It had grown quite large: Olga had been so completely taken up with the Murder Express that other tasks had, of necessity, slipped down the priority list. Among other things, she wanted to find out more about the vodka franchise scheme that had filled Igor Odrosov with such vaunting ambition that he had more or less bankrupted himself. But before that she had to say goodbye to the last surviving members of the troupe, who had organised farewell drinks at Café Astana with the P36 crew.

'*Za zdorov'ye!*' cried Panteleimon Pomelov.

'*Dolgoy zhizni!*' cried Sonia Alikovsky, standing next to him, and lifting her little vodka glass to toast the company, made up of Igor's regulars: Fyodor Katin, Nikolai Popov, Alexeyev the mechanic, Nonna the chamber-maid, and the other diehards who had resolutely stuck by Café Astana despite all the enticements of the Red Star, along with Simeon Zarubin the driver, Vadim Lilov the fireman, and, of course, Lev Myatlev, the engineer-turned-leading-man, with Lev's replacement, Yefim Burtsov, who was looking around him with the dazed air of a man who wasn't quite sure what he'd got himself into.

'You'll be glad to see the back of this place,' muttered Popov, addressing the actors, but to Olga's surprise Panteleimon disagreed.

'Not entirely,' he said. 'I mean, yes, we've had a terrible time. But some good things, at least, have come out of the Murder Express. *Da*, Sonia?' And he leaned over and kissed her, to applause from most of those present.

Olga was surprised: Sonia was quite a bit older than Panteleimon, and had a sharp, brittle quality that was quite at odds with his relaxed and easy-going demeanour. But then she looked more closely at Sonia, who was gazing at him with pure affection in her eyes, and saw a softness there that she had missed before. Maybe she was just another woman who'd been treated badly by the world, and who kept her shield up as a result. And Olga knew a bit about that, too.

Before Panteleimon left he gave her a present – something that seemed worthless, at first glance, but which proved highly valuable to Igor Odrosov and the village at large.

'Some old woman dropped this,' he said, handing her a piece of paper. 'She had a red coat on – I was about to catch up with her and give it back to her, but then Sonia appeared, and I got distracted – can't imagine why,' he added, giving Sonia a playful nudge, and returning her affectionate look with interest. 'Anyway, maybe you know who it is. It might be important.'

Olga looked down at the piece of paper, which turned out to be a flyer for a vodka-franchise scheme. *Allow us to invest in you*, it said, in large red font across the top of the page. *You won't be sorry when we scale your brand across the whole of Russia!* And so it went on, extolling the virtues of the scheme and how it would inevitably make the fame and fortune of every single subscriber in a matter of weeks or, at most, months.

She nodded at Panteleimon and stuffed it into her pocket as if it were of little importance, but her heart was beating rapidly once more: she happened to know the old woman in the red coat, and – more important still – she had just discovered what had happened to Igor Odrosov and Café Astana.

'Thank you, Pan,' she said, squeezing his arm, and meaning it. 'Thank you, oh, thank you!'

All sorts of people are getting their comeuppance, thought Olga later that day, and their little world was all the better for it. Things could always be made better, she thought, if lots of people did lots of small things to make them so. It was only daunting when you looked at everything at once.

No sooner had she realised that it was her own Aunt Zia, in her favourite red coat, who had dropped the phoney flyer than the whole scheme appeared before her mind's eye as if by magic. It wasn't the health authorities, as Fyodor had thought. Of course it wasn't! No, the vodka franchise scheme had been no more than moonshine: it had been dreamed up by old man Solotov and her father Mikhail, no doubt with Zia's willing connivance, to get Igor Odrosov to over-extend his finances and go out of business. Then it would be easy for the Red Star to swoop in and hoover up the clientele, quickly achieving total domination in the Roslazny catering and general supplies market. It was brilliant, Olga had to admit – terrible, but brilliant – and Igor had fallen for it hook, line and sinker.

Olga knew where Zia kept the spare key to her home, the pale-green house at the centre of the village, and it didn't take her long – having first ascertained that Zia was out – to get inside and find a small stash of the fake marketing materials, flyers and posters and brochures, that they had fed to Igor like bait to a hungry fish. Olga gathered up a collection of these, and made her way to the Red Star, where she had the satisfaction of seeing her father's face turn a deadly white upon her appearance.

'I'm not asking you to shut down,' she said, dropping the materials on the counter into a puddle of spilled beer. 'You've got a right to run a business, the same as Igor. But I know all about the scheme – I know everything, and I've kept a few of these for insurance – so I can shut you down any time I choose. But, like I say, I don't want to shut you down. All I want is for you to return the money to Igor. All of it – every last kopek.

You can pretend the scheme made a mistake, that he's not suitable for investment – whatever you like. I don't care. But give him the money back, and help him track down the men who bought his space memorabilia, or you'll be getting a call from Kemerovo. Yes – I've got a direct line to the mayor. Or didn't you know that?'

Olga marched out of the door again with a satisfied look on her face, but she made herself wait until she turned the corner before whooping aloud with joy. Finally she had got one over on her father and done someone else a good turn into the bargain. It was like Christmas had come early. But then she looked up and her smile faded as she saw just the same leaden sky as she'd seen for months, with never a snowflake in sight.

Olga decided to make her way to the police station and tell Vassily what she had just accomplished – always assuming, of course, that there was a way to do so without meeting the dreaded Rozalina. And she also wanted to talk to Kliment, as soon as possible, but again without Rozalina's presence. And then an idea occurred to her: she could approach the police station from the opposite direction, from the north-east – that would bring her by the cells first, and from her own experience of incarceration earlier in the year, Olga knew there was a window above the cells that was often left open, just a little. If she went by, and walked carefully, she might be able to gauge whether Rozalina was with Kliment or not – and if not, she might be able to get into the station and down to the cells to speak to him without Rozalina realising at all.

It was a good plan, but like most plans it didn't long survive contact with reality. As soon as she drew near to the cell window, walking as quietly as ever she had by the Murder Express, she heard Rozalina speaking, and Kliment's soft voice in response. That was that, she thought – there was no chance of catching Kliment alone. But then she heard something more important still. It was something Kliment was saying, the words sounding strange and incongruous coming from his lips.

'It's a bit dangerous, Mama,' he said. 'Someone might see you.'

'Don't worry about that,' she said, dismissively. 'Just tell me where it is!'

'It would be easier to show you,' said Kliment. 'Tayga's quite difficult until you know all the backstreets.'

'Well, that would be just lovely, wouldn't it, *dorogoy*?' said Rozalina, with a grating, sarcastic tone that set Olga's teeth on edge. 'Only you're locked in the cell!'

'Not for ever,' he said. 'I'll be out soon, and then—'

'Soon's no good,' replied Rozalina. 'I need it now.'

'But what for?' said Kliment. 'Papa can give us everything we need, and—'

Rozalina spoke across him again, this time with a brusque bark of a laugh. 'Your papa? No, no, Kliment – he can't give me everything *I* need. That's why I've been asking you to help me. And you've done very well – until you let yourself be captured. And for what? To act as the hero for some nobody who works for the railways?'

'I wish you wouldn't talk about Olga like that, Mama,' muttered Kliment. 'You know how much it upsets me.'

'*Da, da*,' she said. Olga imagined her waving a hand in dismissal. '*This* upsets you, *that* upsets me – but as long as I get my money, I don't care too much, do I, little boy? No. I don't really care at all.'

Olga had heard enough, and with tightly compressed lips she stalked around to the front entrance and told Vassily exactly what she had just heard.

'It was Rozalina all along, Vassily!' she cried, pointing towards the cells, and turning to look in that direction as the sound of angrily clacking high heels came to her ears, accompanied by an angry yapping. 'It was you, all along,' she said again, as Rozalina came into view, marching into the reception area just as quickly as Olga had marched into the station, and accompanied by her little dog Sputnik, which was barking as usual in its shrill, rather irritating tones. 'You made Kliment dress up in black and go around the place, stealing things from people, and then – what? Sell them for cash in Tayga, and stash the money somewhere until you could pick it up, and blow it in the boutiques and hair salons! I remember what he asked Vassily – people do bad things for good reasons, don't they, he said. But I didn't realise he meant himself.'

'Ha!' said Rozalina. 'As if! Though it wouldn't do you any harm to get your hair seen to – or buy some new clothes. Where'd you get that outfit? Charity shop?'

'Never mind my clothes – what about Kliment? What about your own son? You just barged into Roslazny, not caring about any of us, and doing everything you could to make a nuisance of yourself. You've imposed on poor Vassily's kindness as well as Kliment's, and as for me, you've hated me from the start, just because Vassily and I have worked together! You've told me I'm useless, that I'm not even fit to do my job! And I—'

She paused, looking from left to right as her mind raced.

'You what?' said Rozalina, rudely, after a moment.

'You knew about my medical,' said Olga, slowly, wonderingly, as she processed what this could mean.

'What?'

'My medical,' said Olga again. 'My medical report – you've seen it, or at least you've been told about it by someone who has. But nobody sees those apart from the human-resources people up in Kemerovo. Nobody except for . . . Unless . . . unless . . .'

A memory of a woman, short and broadly built, with thick glasses like Yegor Shulgin and yellow wooden clogs on her feet, had come unbidden to mind – a woman named Polina Klemovsky, who had gone to Ulaanbaatar in Olga's place, and had sworn undying revenge on her and Vassily as a result. Polina had seen Olga's medical: she'd read it, with a lot of Olga's other paperwork, when left unattended in Olga's hut one day. And now a horrible suspicion dawned on her, a suspicion that soon turned into ice-cold certainty.

'You're not Rozalina,' she said.

'Olga, stop!' cried Vassily. 'I know you're upset, but—'

'Vassily, *this isn't Rozalina*,' said Olga. 'I just heard her talking to Kliment in a way no mother should talk to a son. I recorded it, actually. Listen!' And she dug out her phone and played back the recording she had made as insurance, crackly and distant but clearly audible, nonetheless.

'So I needed a bit of extra cash,' said Rozalina, airily, after the recording was finished. 'So what? Vassily doesn't make enough to keep a pig in comfort!'

'But you didn't get a job to earn it, did you?' said Olga. 'No. You forced Kliment out in the cold to steal and beg and borrow, threatening our friends and neighbours to make a few extra roubles! But that's not even the worst thing you've done. The worst thing you've done is to come here at Polina's bidding – I suppose you're a friend of hers, or a minion, at least, who happened to look a bit like that old picture of Rozalina that Vassily has up. Yes: you could pass for her, at a push, with enough stories about beatings and bad treatment . . . You've come here at her bidding and made Vassily think he's got his wife back. And then I heard you on the phone, asking someone, "Is it safe?" – that was after Rodion died. I think it was Polina on the other end, wasn't it? You suddenly got cold feet when people started dying. So you're a coward, as well as an imposter, a pretender – an *actor*,' she finished, imbuing the word with all the contempt she felt for some of the specimens of that profession she had recently encountered.

There was a silence after this, in which Vassily stared at Rozalina – or the woman who claimed to be Rozalina – in horror, and while Rozalina herself stared back at him in defiance.

'Rozalina,' he said at last, but tentatively, wonderingly, as if beginning to detach the person from the name, the denoter from the denoted. 'Can this be true? Are you really not my wife? I mean, I know you look a little different, but I thought – the beatings – but maybe after all . . . Your eyes – your eyes aren't quite the same, but I thought all the hardship – the separation from me and Kliment – but – but—'

'Oh, but, but, but!' sneered Rozalina. 'So you've worked it out at last, have you? Well, I've had some fun, playing with you idiots – a heap of country bumpkins, just like Polina said! And your precious son the biggest bumpkin of all. But at least I've had free board and lodging for a while, and that's not to be sniffed at, even in surroundings like this. It's a hard world out there, you know.'

She bent down and picked up her dog. 'Come on then, Sputnik,' she said. 'It's time for us to hit the road.'

'You can't just – leave,' said Vassily, slowly. 'You've probably committed several crimes – impersonation, incitement to criminal activity, and—'

'Oh, come off it, Marushkin!' she cried, an unpleasant smile appearing on her lips. 'Your son's just been arrested – by you – for theft and for selling stolen goods. Are you really going to tell everyone that you were taken in by a fake wife, too? That really would finish you off! And now, if you don't mind, I'll get my things together and be on my way. No, don't worry about driving me to the station! I'll just call a taxi. I've still got some of Kliment's money left!'

Olga reached out a restraining hand to Vassily's arm, as Rozalina, or the woman who had pretended to be Rozalina, walked off to collect her belongings, with Sputnik yapping happily after her.

'Let her go, Vassily,' she said softly. 'It's not worth it – *she*'s not worth it. You're better off without her – you and Kliment. Only – only – only I'm so sorry that you had to go through it all.'

He nodded, not speaking, just staring after the woman he had thought was his wife – staring with eyes that laid bare the terrible weight of betrayal.

'I – I can stay, if you like,' she added. 'Until she goes.'

'Thanks, Olga,' he said quietly, turning away as if he were addressing the wall instead of her. 'But I'd rather be alone, if you don't mind. Just me and Kliment. We've got some talking to do.'

Olga nodded, slowly: how could she disagree? She bent and picked up her handbag, nodded slowly once more, and placed a hand on Vassily's shoulder. He didn't move, so she slowly took her hand away. Then she turned, and walked to the door, and left, fading into the failing light and disappearing from view, leaving Vassily still standing, motionless, staring at the unanswering wall.

14

Long-Promised Road

'So – you can keep your hut?' said Pasha, cradling Dmitri in his hands, and leaning back in his armchair. 'And Boris – Boris is really off to Mongolia, like Polina?'

'So it seems,' said Olga, laughing and sitting back in her chair, then leaning forward again and plucking one of Pasha's cigarettes from the packet of Cosmos that lay next to him on the patched-up fabric with his Zippo lighter.

'I thought you were giving up?'

'I'm celebrating,' she protested, lighting the cigarette with a flourish and throwing the Zippo back onto his chair. 'It's not every day you can overrule the foreman of Tayga depot – or, at least, get him overruled by somebody higher up and sent abroad. There's no more talk of some stupid drones flying up and down the track, as if they could replace what I do – as if a flying camera could make up for decades of training and experience!'

'*Da, da*,' said Pasha, who had heard this many times before. 'But I still don't quite understand what happened.'

'It's like I said,' Olga went on, inhaling and then exhaling with relish. 'It was down to Zemsky – he knew all about Boris, it seems, from his informants at the Tayga depot, and once he'd decided he wanted to reward me for helping with the Putyatin case, it didn't take him long to sort out what to do. It was easy, in the end. You remember that Boris was organising demonstrations from the drone operators – the idiots he wanted to replace me with? Well, he just handed them a few thousand roubles from the police budget, and got them to livestream footage of Boris engaging in certain illegal activities by the track.'

'What activities?'

Olga laughed again. 'That was the funny thing,' she said. 'You remember the Putyatins were seen down at the hospital, and we wondered – briefly – if they might be using the Murder Express as cover for drug-smuggling? Well, Zemsky happened to know that Boris was doing exactly that. And after that, it was child's play – route the drones over the tracks at just the right time, and get the footage to Boris's superiors up at Russian Railways in Kemerovo with a suggestion for a resolution in Polina Klemovsky's clog-steps – and then, as Popov would say, Bogdan's your uncle!'

'So his own idea was his downfall? That's some kind of justice,' said Pasha, with an approving smile.

'It's *poetic* justice, to be precise,' said Olga. 'Yes, I've got my hut back, and Boris is history. Zemsky says he'd be surprised if he got back to Russia in less than ten years.'

'Could be worse fates, these days,' muttered Pasha.

But Olga continued regardless. 'Anyway, that's not all there is to celebrate, Pasha! We've got the Murder Express business all cleared up, and Igor's back in business at Café Astana, too – not to mention my discovery of the so-called Rozalina's true identity.'

'True, true – you've done very well, Olga, but there are broken eggs for the omelettes, *nyet*? Vassily, deprived of his wife for a second time, and' – he lowered his voice and jerked his head towards Anna's bedroom – 'and Anna has lost Zinovev.'

'I know,' said Olga, as her triumphant smile faded. 'I haven't even seen Vassily since Rozalina, or whatever her name really was, went away – more than three days now. And as for Anna . . .'

Her voice faded, and she shook her head, thinking of how her friend had looked in the days after the death of Zinovev: pale, and drawn, thin, too, hardly touching the extravagant dinners that she and Pasha had put together in an effort to bring her out of her grief. And Pasha, she knew, was also struggling, however much he put a brave face on things – struggling because he felt Anna's sorrows as if they were his own, and because of his own challenges: the perpetual, useless search for useful employment, for companionship, for love. And above all hung the ashen clouds of war, and the shame Pasha felt over his ex-comrades, and how powerless he was to do anything, as a disgraced ex-private with nothing to his name but the record of a dishonourable discharge. To Olga, looking back, Pasha's release now had the character of a miraculous escape, for without it he, too, like hundreds of thousands of others beside him, would be facing an impossible choice: try to murder those ahead of him, or face being murdered by those behind him. But, nonetheless, she knew he was in anguish about it, and she suffered with him, too.

She turned to look out of the window, the unremitting grey clouds rolling slowly overhead and letting fall thin streaks of rain that spread themselves upon the glass and ran down, only to be replaced by more raindrops, numberless, like soldiers on a battlefield, and as quickly vanishing from sight and memory. She exhaled, slowly, creating her own grey clouds, and wishing, wishing, wishing that the winter proper would arrive at last. Then, at least, she could pretend it was the year before, that things were as they had been before Vassily returned, before Bogdan Kabalevsky left, before Pasha was discharged, before Ivanka Kozar and Anatoly Glazkov and Grigor Babikov and Polina Klemovsky and Nevena Komarov and all the things that had happened to her in this most tumultuous of years. She looked, and wished, and waited, but only rain fell from the heavy-laden clouds, and nothing changed, save the drops that fell from the branches and were straight away renewed.

A faint sound came to her ears, a sound of men's voices. The sound grew louder, and she sighed: she was in no mood for visitors. But then she stirred, and got up, and ran to the window, peering out to confirm what she had already guessed.

'Pasha,' she said excitedly. 'Pasha, it's Sasha – Sasha Tsaritsyn! He's got Fyodor with him.'

Pasha looked up at her with glowing eyes. He and Sasha had known each other for years, ever since Sasha had sat with Olga in the little schoolhouse in Roslazny, and they had seen each other again in the autumn, after the unpleasantness with Polina Klemovsky – whom Sasha had helped them to dispatch to Mongolia. Pasha had hoped that their old friendship might have developed into something more – but then Sasha had gone back to Kemerovo, where he worked as a journalist, and things had gone quiet again, as they did when two people who were interested in each other had heavy commitments in different places. Pasha had accepted this with equanimity, as he accepted everything, but Olga knew he had longed for something different – and now here was Sasha once more, walking through the door with the same lank hair, faded leather jacket, and wide, toothy grin.

The grin was a little more forced than usual, though, thought Olga – and wasn't his face rather thinner than before, stretched and taut like Anna's, as if he was under some terrific strain?

But Fyodor gave her little time for reflection, announcing with great enthusiasm how he had met Sasha at Café Astana, and how he had immediately brought him over to see Pasha and Anna and Olga. Fyodor's booming phrases summoned Anna from her room, and she came through into the living room accompanied by her three boys, so that the quiet scene Olga had shared with Pasha moments before seemed like a week ago.

'What's all this, Fyodor?' said Anna. 'What brings you to our door, shouting like this and waking up my children?' But she had leavened her words with the beginnings of a smile.

'We've got a plan,' said Fyodor, his eyes gleaming. 'We've got a plan to do something – right, Sasha? And we thought – well, we thought Pasha might like to join us!'

'That's right,' said Sasha. 'We've got a plan to do something about this terrible war.'

'Well, sit down, sit down,' said Olga, shooing them towards the sofa and armchairs with her hands, then bustling into the kitchen to make tea. 'So tell us,' she called through the small open window that led through into the living room. 'What's this wonderful plan?'

So Sasha told them how he had started working with families of soldiers in Kemerovo, soldiers who had been sent to the front – and how he had started to hear rumours of soldiers who had deserted before they got there, jumping out of trains or fighting their way out of barracks, desperate to avoid fighting for a cause they didn't believe in – to avoid fighting for a cause that didn't even exist in the first place.

'Many of them get away abroad,' said Sasha, sitting forward in his seat, his mug of tea untouched, 'though some don't, and are sent back to the front to die – and for what? For nothing.'

'No argument there,' muttered Pasha, drinking deep from his own mug.

'But what about the families they leave behind?' put in Fyodor, who – Olga could tell – had been itching to speak this whole time. 'They're ignored by the state, wages left unpaid, castigated by those around them . . .'

'There's nobody to help them,' said Sasha, 'nobody at all. There isn't even a register to record who they are. Or, at least—'

'At least there wasn't till now,' said Fyodor, reaching over and thumping Sasha's leather bag. 'But Sasha here has started to put one together, based on his own research in Kemerovo and elsewhere.'

'Yes – and we want your help, Pasha,' said Sasha, turning to Olga's brother and tapping him on the knee. 'You're an ex-soldier, after all – you know how the army works! You can help us understand how and why soldiers desert, how to find out where they've gone, what they need to survive, what they want for their families back home . . .'

Pasha shook his head doubtfully. 'I don't know,' he said. 'If I'd been a military policeman, maybe – I was only a private, remember? That's all I know.'

'That's enough,' said Sasha, while Fyodor nodded enthusiastically. 'Most of the soldiers deserting *are* privates! Will you come and join us, Pasha? We don't have much money, just some funds I managed to siphon off from the paper's investigative unit. But it's enough for a flat in Kemerovo, and we can build from there. Only – only it might be dangerous. Nobody wants us digging into this kind of thing, and least of all right now. I can't promise it'll be smooth sailing.'

Pasha looked at him, and then at Anna. 'The thing is, Sasha, I've got to stay and help Anna. The children aren't easy – and that's important work, too.'

'Of course it is, Pasha,' said Sasha, earnestly. 'But don't you see? There are other children, too – families of men who've had to leave their homes, their motherland, so they don't have to fight for a cause they don't believe in – for a cause few of us would believe in, if we weren't spoon-fed lies all day long. All wars are evil, aren't they? But needless wars are the most evil wars of all . . .'

'Peace with honour,' said Fyodor, quietly. 'That's the aim of all politics, or it should be, anyhow. But what we're doing now . . . There's no peace, and there's no honour, either. We've got to do something about it – and we want you to help, Pasha. We *need* you to help.'

'Are – are you going too, then, Fyodor?' put in Anna, her voice gentle and melodious after the loud talking of the men. 'You're going off to Kemerovo?'

Olga looked at her, seeing two things: the renewal of interest in life, in love, in happiness that Fyodor represented after Zinovev; and the introduction of a new anxiety, at the thought of him going into danger of any kind – and on this point Olga knew how she felt, for they had only got Pasha back this year, and now he might be off again, and into greater danger than he had ever faced before.

'Will you go, Pasha?' she said.

Pasha looked at Anna, who looked back at him with tears in her eyes, but who nodded all the same. 'Of course you must go,' she said. 'You've helped me so much, all year, and we'll miss you terribly – but there are so many mothers, and wives, and sisters, and cousins, and aunts, and friends, who have lost their own, and who also need help. Of course you must go. And you too, Fyodor,' she added, turning to him. 'Only – only come back, won't you? Come back, before the end of the year?'

Before the end of the year, thought Olga, as the men took their leave later that day, after a long dinner that she wished could have continued for ever, so that none of them would ever have to go. But the food had been eaten, morsel by morsel and plate by plate, and the glasses had been emptied, one by one, and at last, like all things under the sun, the dinner came to an end, and it was time to say farewell. So soon they had lost them: just this morning she had sat talking with Pasha as if he would be there for ever, and now he was gone again, and Fyodor too, the Dreamer, whose dreams he now would make a reality at last. So soon: but were they not just sharing in the fate of so many women in Russia, now and in history, whose men were torn from them because of the whims of those on high? Perhaps there was a kind of virtue in sharing in that suffering, a kind of elevation or nobility, the chance to say that she, too, knew what it was to sit at home in peace, and wish she were somewhere – anywhere – else.

The door closed, and the footsteps died away into the quiet of the November night – and then there was silence. Or not quite silence, for Olga could hear the faint sound of singing. Anna had retreated, red-eyed, to her bedroom with her children

– perhaps she was singing them a lullaby, Olga thought. But when she went closer to Anna's door, she realised she was not. She was singing 'Katyusha', a song they had learned in school together, a song from the Soviet times when men's lives were worth less than thistledown, less even than now. She leaned against the doorpost and listened, allowing her eyes to fill with tears at last, now that they were gone; and under her breath she sang along to the sad, beautiful song and its wistful words.

Rastsvetali iabloni I grushi –
Apple and pear trees were blooming,
Mist flowing on the river.
Katyusha was on the bank,
The steep and lofty side.

She was walking, singing a song
Of a grey steppe eagle,
About her true love,
Whose letters she was keeping.

Oh, you song! Little song of a maiden,
Head for the bright sun,
And the soldier on the far-away border,
Bringing news from Katyusha.

Let him remember an ordinary girl,
And hear how she sings –
Let him preserve the Motherland,
As Katyusha preserves their love.

'I can't tell you, Olga!' said Ekaterina, her voice crackly and distorted down the line.

'But why not?' said Olga, then tutting as she realised Ekaterina couldn't hear her: the reception had always been terrible at her little rail-side hut. She got out of the chair, walked across the hut, and stepped out into the chilled, late-November air. 'Can you hear me now?' she said, holding her lips close to the microphone of her ancient Nokia.

'Yes,' said Ekaterina.

'I was saying, why can't you tell me?'

'Well, you – you might not approve.'

'That's never stopped you before!' said Olga. And it was true: Olga had frequently disagreed with the romantic life-choices made by her dearest friend, Ekaterina Chezhekhov, but that had never had the slightest impact on those choices, whether it was regarding Konstantin Babanin, the travelling fridge salesman from Nizhny Novgorod, or Dmitri Volkov, the business ethics 'expert' from Suranovo who had tried to sell Olga life insurance off the books.

'No, it's never stopped you,' she went on. 'But I thought Pavel Veselov was the one for you – didn't you say that? That he was everything you'd ever wanted?'

'Well, yes,' said Ekaterina, after a pause – a pause, Olga knew, occupied by the process of first extracting and then lighting a cigarette from one of the packets she was meant to be selling. 'But then Pavel went off with Mila Obolensky – you know, that tramp with the ginger hair, who works in purchasing?

But I'm better off. Good riddance, is what I say – the rubbish took itself out!'

'But who replaced him?' said Olga, plaintively. 'That's what I want to know.'

'Well, if you really *must*,' said Ekaterina, the reluctance plain in her voice, 'it's Slava Kirillov. You know, your counsellor.'

Olga's mouth gaped. Slava Sergeivich Kirillov, the camouflage-clad counsellor – *that* was who Ekaterina saw as a fit replacement for the much-lauded Pavel Veselov!

'Olga?' came Ekaterina's voice. 'You still there?'

'Yes, yes,' she said. 'Well, there's no—' Olga stopped herself just in time: she'd been about to say *There's no accounting for taste*, but that wouldn't do at all. 'I mean, there's no reason why you'd be so reluctant to tell me that, is there? Slava is . . . Well, he's a fine – a fine figure of a man,' she said at last.

'Well, yes, I suppose he is,' said Ekaterina. 'It's just – well, he's a counsellor, you know? He's got qualifications – he's a businessman in his own right. I didn't want you thinking I was getting ideas above my station.'

Olga's mouth gaped again: Slava Kirillov, above Ekaterina's station? It was very much the other way around, but she had no wish to rain on her friend's happiness. 'No, no,' she said. 'Not at all, Ekaterina! He's – he's a good catch. And you've got to seize your opportunities when they come along. You've got to catch the best catch you can!'

She hung up a little later, went back inside, and sat down in her chair, wondering what she, Olga Pushkin, could possibly hope to catch. Vassily had swum beyond her reach once more, this time not because of Rozalina's return but because of her departure, the bitterness of disappointed hopes seeming to seal his heart off once and for all. And Olga could hardly blame him for that: Rozalina had not only taken him in, after all, playing upon his desperate desire to see what he wanted to believe, but had also manipulated Vassily's dear son Kliment – who suffered from exactly the same weakness – into the desperation of criminality, pushing him into a course of action that had ended in the brutal finality of a key turning in the lock of a cell in the Roslazny police station. 'Rozalina', whatever her name was, had relied on the Russian male tendency to brush over problems rather than talk about them with each other, and she had not relied upon this in vain: Vassily and Kliment could have solved each other's doubts in moments, had they troubled to talk about them, but instead they had carried on, unspeaking, to the brink of disaster. No: it was eminently understandable that Vassily should turn his back on relationships, after spending more than a decade searching for his lost wife, only to be taken in at last by a convincing but duplicitous deceiver.

But who else could she think of other than Vassily, stuck in Roslazny day in, day out, with only Tayga and Suranovo – hardly Moscow and St Petersburg – to widen the candidate pool? It's not as if Koptev Alexeyev or any of the others in Roslazny or Tayga was worth considering. And, besides, she didn't want anyone else. That was the problem: Vassily Marushkin had spoiled other men for her. And if Vassily had given up on love, if Vassily could hardly bring himself to speak to her, or even nod at her in the street, where did that leave her?

No: the most she could hope for, in these later days, was to catch her breath, once in a while, between the business of her timetable at the hut – now happily restored to her – and the extra housework and childcare at home, now that Pasha had gone off with Sasha Tsaritsyn and Fyodor Katin. They heard from them, every day or two, with breathless tales of this or that family they had helped, or a deserter they had sent money to in some remote location at the ends of the earth, or a vital message given to a loved one before they passed away. It was all important, vital work, but she missed Pasha's kindly, gentle humour and endless strength. She even missed Fyodor Katin's endless pontificating and remorseless piling-up of new ideas and manifestos for the reform of Russia – schemes that, however much they were needed, never seemed to amount to anything that real people could put into practice.

His latest scheme, for example, had been to agitate for a new agrarian revolution. 'We're only three meals from regime change, Olga – did you know that?' he'd said to her, the week before he left with Pasha. 'If the workers in the fields downed tools, and the lorry drivers, too, and all the people who bring us our food, there'd be a new government in the Kremlin within twenty-four hours. It's like – it's like –' his eyes had glowed behind his dirty, genuinely thick glasses as he searched for the right metaphor within the jumbled thoughts in his mind '– it's like we're all candles, heated in one way, and bending in that direction, weakened by the flame. But what if you removed the flame? We could burn strong and bright, too. Things could change, Olga! Things could change.'

But could they, really? As the years went by, Olga became more and more resigned to the thought that, actually, they couldn't – that it was best just to await events, to be borne along on the tide of history and surrender all thoughts of agency or will. Take her book, for example: a couple of weeks ago, she had burned with the desire to find out what had happened, and how

Inessa Ignatyev had mysteriously come up with the same idea as Olga, and somehow rushed it out into the world before her own precious masterwork had even left the printing presses . . . Nothing had seemed more important, for a little while. But then the Murder Express had clanked into the siding at Roslazny, and Rodion had died, and Larissa, and then Dr Zinovev and the Putyatins; and with all that death had come a certain resignation, a quiet and calm acceptance that things weren't controllable by any individual, and that there were more important things than literary careers, after all.

What did it matter, when all was said and done, if her books sat at the backs of shelves, neglected, before being carted off into storage, or to be pulped, while Inessa Ingatyev's poor-quality knock-off flew off the shelves and into bags? Inessa Ignatyev was already a celebrity, of a sort, and that was how books were sold, these days – or so Maxim had told her, anyway. How could Olga compete with a TV journalist, whose face was already recognised by tens or even hundreds of thousands of people? How many people knew Olga's face, by contrast? A couple of hundred, maybe, if you included the railway workers who rattled past her hut on shunters or maintenance trains or even the Trans-Siberian, leaning out of the dusty windows to wave a gloved hand at her, before pushing on to the far ends of the earth, to Ulan Ude, past the upper reaches of Outer Mongolia and into Ulaanbaatar, then down to Beijing and beyond, or staying north, following the line until it reached Vladivostok at last, and was at an end. A couple of hundred people, and maybe a tenth of those read books, or fewer: twenty books she could sell, perhaps, with any certainty. As for the rest, all those unknown people who would wander into bookshops off Red Square or Nevsky

Prospekt, they would just buy Inessa Ignatyev's book, wouldn't they, and Olga would never be any the wiser? She would be none the wiser, until her sales figures arrived from Lyapunov Books, and she realised that the print run would not be renewed.

She sighed, glancing across at her little stove, merry with bright red and orange flames, and reflected that she might as well have thrown her manuscript in there to begin with, cutting out the middleman, as Svetlana Odrosov had suggested for her father's space memorabilia. There would be no glorious entry to Tomsk State University, she realised – no sudden access of wealth to solve all her problems, and Anna's, too – no dramatic resignation from Russian Railways, as she moved on to pursue her long-lived dream of studying Russian literature and writing, at last, something her mother Tatiana might have read and been proud of, had she lived.

But then Olga smiled a sad, sweet smile, remembering a saying of her mother's. 'The sole purpose of life is to serve humanity,' she'd often said, quoting Leo Tolstoy – and who could really disagree, if they stopped to think about it? Olga had wanted to serve humanity by writing great books, by swaying humanity into goodness by the sheer force of her inspiration and the beauty of her prose – but perhaps that wasn't her destiny, after all. Anna and the boys were human beings, weren't they? Couldn't Olga serve humanity just as well by keeping a roof over their heads, and putting food in their mouths? She thought Tolstoy would have approved of that, and her mother too. Kindness, after all, was the only star worth steering by.

The stars: how long it had been since she had seen them, glittering into twinkling life in the chilled air above the faded roof of her hut, or over the straggly trees and bushes of the garden by their house. How long it had been since she had stepped out in frosty air, drinking in the ice-cold freshness as if it were some revitalising liquid and she a traveller in arid places, staring upwards at the countless dots of brilliant, distant light, a speckled canopy of unimaginable beauty whose obscuring by streetlights in far-off cities she could only imagine with pity.

Night was beginning to fall: would there be any clear skies tonight, she wondered, or would it be the same endless curtain of grey rainclouds?

She got up again, and walked to the door – but then she stopped, and sniffed around her like a bloodhound. What was that she could smell? There was a faint fragrance in the air, infinitely desired and half forgotten in its absence, but now tantalising her with the scent for which she had waited, in patience and impatience, for so long – the perfume that spoke of white flecks dancing in the sky, and seemed itself to sit lightly upon the air: the mark of *snow*.

She threw open the door and rushed outside, and there she saw, with a joy almost beyond words, the beginnings of a snow-shower coming from the heavens, bringing with it the subtle sound of hissing that spoke of a desire fulfilled, the replacement of the muddy earth with a blanket pure, untouched, continuous, complete. She stood by her hut and leaned back until she was gazing straight up at the sky, the spiralling snowflakes invisible against the backdrop of the clouds, perceptible only as pinpricks of cold moisture upon her upturned face. She threw her arms wide as if she could embrace the sky, as if she could somehow express the relief she felt at the snow's return, as if its thistledown weight were all she needed to cover her sorrow with a new disguise.

'Olga?' said a tentative voice, and Olga spun round, cheeks burning with embarrassment.

'Oh, Vassily,' she said. 'You made me jump! I was just – I was just – I was just stretching after a long shift! You know how it is. And – Kliment?' she added, with joy. 'You're out of prison at last?'

Kliment nodded shyly at her, and Vassily explained how Zemsky had taken a more understanding approach to Kliment's criminal spree, once Vassily had communicated what had happened with Rozalina.

'He told me to open the cell and get my boy out,' Vassily said, looking at Kliment with so much affection that Olga thought a tear might almost come to his eye. 'I never would have predicted he'd react like that but, you know, that's—'

'That's Zemsky,' finished Olga, smiling at him. But then he smiled back, an unexpectedly dazzling grin, and Olga tutted to herself as she felt her heart turning over. Damn Vassily! Why did he have to come traipsing down here, interrupting her at an embarrassing moment, and making her feel things she definitely did not want to feel, in light of everything that had happened? She was delighted to see Kliment free, of course – she had still to thank him properly for saving her life – but she would have much preferred to thank him by himself. It would have been less confusing, she thought, to see the son without the father.

There the son was, however, and the job still needed to be done, so she stammered her gratitude in stumbling words, making a blushing Kliment – if anything – more embarrassed than she had been earlier.

'Are you out for a walk?' Olga ventured, after the resulting silence threatened to grow awkward. 'You've got good timing

– look at the snow! How I've longed for it! But why are you walking down this way? Don't tell me you're going back to the crime scene again?'

Kliment cleared his throat, and looked at Vassily. Then he nodded over his shoulder, and for good measure jerked his thumb behind him – it looked to Olga like some kind of clumsy, pre-agreed signal – until Vassily broke into a smile and nodded back at him, upon which Kliment, his cheeks now burning with an intensity to match Olga's, flashed a nervous grin at Olga and turned away, walking back towards the village and soon disappearing behind a growing white curtain of swaying snowflakes.

Vassily watched him go, and turned to Olga with a smile – the kind of smile Olga hadn't seen on his face for quite some time, and one she couldn't help but return, despite her reluctance to allow herself to show (or feel) any emotion whatsoever.

He didn't speak at first, and once more she felt compelled to break the silence – like a suspect under investigation, she reflected, but without being able to prevent the impulse.

'What is it, Vassily?' she said. 'What can I do for you?'

But he only stood there, watching her, standing and breathing, breathing and standing and smiling.

'Vassily?' she said again, but this time with a choked-off sob in her voice, for he had stopped smiling at her now, and was looking straight into her eyes, his solemn gaze interrupted only by twirling flecks of whiteness that pirouetted in the light breezes that played along the tracks.

'Olga,' he said, stepping towards her, and reaching a hand out to hers: it was warm in the cold air.

'Olga,' he said again, this time lifting his other hand to her cheek.

'Vassily,' she said, softly, almost faintly, for her knees felt weak beneath her. 'What are you doing?'

'What I should have done a long time ago, Olga,' he said, stepping yet closer. 'I've come to my senses at last, and let her go – Rozalina, I mean. She's lost to me, and gone for ever into the darkness of Russia, and it's terrible – it breaks my heart. I wish for Kliment's sake that I could have found her, but she's gone, swallowed up like so many others. I mourn her, and always will. But somehow I've got to let it all heal again – not by taking in some horrible imposter, but by doing just one more thing.'

'One more thing?'

He nodded. 'Just a simple thing,' he said. 'I only want to ask you one question.'

'What is it, Vassily?' she said, gazing into his eyes: they glowed with reflected brightness from the hut, its door still standing open and letting the lamplight flow steadily outwards, like a lighthouse in a sea of infinite white.

'What are you doing for dinner?'

'You mean – tonight? Well, nothing, I suppose – nothing special, anyway.'

'So – you can come and eat with me?'

'With you?'

'With me, and with Kliment,' he said, smiling again. 'Who else is there?'

And then, when she didn't reply, he continued: 'So, what do you think, Olga? Will you come and have dinner with us? Unless – unless you'd rather do something else?'

She looked up at him, seeing his tousled black hair under his fur hat, tilted at an angle as usual; and his kind eyes gazing back at her, deep-set like hers in his weather-beaten, beet-farmer's face; his hands, so large and powerful but now at rest, one holding hers and the other cradling her cheek, warming it against the chill wind; and beyond him the snow itself, whirling around them with abandon and dressing them in endless profusion, like confetti thrown ahead of time, or a blessing given in the form of flowers, set against the old, familiar, beloved sight of her little hut, the stove warm within, and resting on it the bubbling samovar, and beneath it the little pile of tea-towels where Dmitri, forgiven at last, was buried in warm oblivion.

'Oh, no, Vassily,' she said at last. 'Dinner would be lovely – no, lovely isn't enough . . . Not nearly enough. It would be wonderful, truly wonderful – the most wonderful thing in the world.'

Author's Note and Acknowledgements

In the first Olga Pushkin novel, *Death on the Trans-Siberian Express*, I describe Olga as follows: 'Her cheeks were broad, her nose stolid and wind-raw, her eyes deep-set and wary and wise. She had a face like Russia.'

Russia, wary and wise? The book came out in November 2021, and three months later this description had already aged like milk. The ink had hardly dried on my signed copies when Russian wisdom seemed a distant memory. It was war without the peace, and crime without the punishment; dead souls in deadly earnest.

As the Russian tanks mobilised, I was finishing the second, *Blood on the Siberian Snow* – and the pall of war has hung over the entirety of the current book, from conception to drafting to completion. 'Russian literature [consists in] the phenomenal coruscations of the souls of quite ordinary people,' wrote D. H. Lawrence – but what happens when those same people enact a genocidal attack upon a neighbouring state? What new ethical duties might this impose upon those writing about Russian society?

One literary response could be self-censorship – disengaging from Russia and writing instead about other places closer to home, a stance illustrated by Elizabeth Gilbert's decision to pull her Siberia-set novel, *The Snow Forest*. After all, 'writing what you know' has never been more popular. Sally Rooney recently declared that she couldn't imagine writing fiction set elsewhere than her native Ireland, prompting John Banville to remark that 'writers in Ireland now seem just to be writing about their immediate lives and the lives of their friends'. I also have Irish roots – so on this logic I should have abandoned Moscow for Monaghan, and Tomsk for Tipperary.

Not everyone agrees, however. Nobel Laureate Kazuo Ishiguro described this approach as 'the most stupid thing I ever heard . . . It encourages people to write a dull autobiography. It's the reverse of firing the imagination'. And perhaps there is still something to be said for writing that moves beyond the narrow confines of our own experience – for attempts to engage, however inadequately, with cultures and languages emphatically not our own. As Northrop Frye put it, 'literature speaks the language of the imagination'.

Ethically, too, I felt obliged to continue engaging with Russia in this third novel in the series, or rather the people of Russia as I had encountered them on my own travels. As I noted at the end of *Blood on the Siberian Snow*, Olga Pushkin was inspired by a real-life Olga who I met in July 2015, in a second-class compartment on the Trans-Siberian Railway between Nizhny Novgorod and Kirov. It was her face and name that came to mind when I had the idea for *Death on the Trans-Siberian Express*, walking my baby daughter Acacia to sleep one New Year's Eve – Olga's, and all the others we met on the tracks and elsewhere, offering us welcome, hospitality and their own versions of Rocket Fuel vodka, and supplanting stereotypes with the hope of a kinder future. And perhaps writing about Russia as it could be might help to efface the Russia that currently is. Perhaps, contra Sartre, essence could still precede existence in some productive way.

Nevertheless, settling the *why* still leaves the *how* – how best to engage, that is, with a dictatorial society drenched with propaganda. A good place to start is by engaging directly with state action on the page, writing novels that deliberately foreground formal and informal politics and their complex entanglements with social dynamics. (If this is the starting point, perhaps the endpoint should be more writers in politics. There are plenty of fabulists at Westminster, after all – so why not add some professionals into the mix?)

Another starting point could be past literary engagements with despotism, such as Thomas Mann's modernist masterpiece and partial allegory of Nazi Germany, *Doktor Faustus*. Mann emphasises personal culpability in Faustian downfalls; for example, the devil is literally in the details of the composer Adrian Leverkühn's self-impelled descent into the perceived creative freedom of Nietzschean insanity, rather than existing as some external driving force that can serve (like NATO for Russia) as a scapegoat for all ills. Likewise, the narrator, Serenus Zeitblom, is complicit in his friend's fate, standing in for the 'serene' lip-service paid to humanitarian ideals even while societies fall into the chill totalitarian grip. Alongside culpability and complicity, Mann also adds another 'c': the disastrous consequences of dealing with the devil (however interpreted). Leverkühn suffers a final and irrevocable collapse into delirium, leaving Zeitblom to relate the cataclysm engulfing Germany as the Allies advance in 'devastating liberation'.

And yet, and yet – there is one fourth, final 'c' that Mann leaves in the text, a literal note of consolation, the high 'G' with which Leverkühn's last work, *Dr. Fausti Weheklag*, concludes: a reedy yet tangible symbol of grace, standing 'als ein Licht in der Nacht' (as a light in the night). By the end of the book, the no-longer-serene Zeitblom recognises the catastrophic outcome of Germany's embrace of Nazism, and in his anguished doubts that Germany 'could ever in future dare open its mouth on humane matters' we perceive the only grounds upon which this situation could ever come to pass (as indeed it has). 'The blood-drenched state . . . that carried the masses along on a surge of ecstatic happiness', in Zeitblom's apt phrase, does not last for ever. Perhaps we can still hope that wisdom might return to a post-war Russia, and even find there a society at last willing to be, in Leverkühn's words, 'on familiar terms with humanity'.

As always, I must thank my editor, Krystyna Green, and my agent, Bill Goodall, for their encouragement and insight throughout the latest process, alongside Jess Gulliver, Hazel Orme and Amanda Keats at Constable/Little, Brown. I must also thank my father John, my sister Sinéad, and my friends Andrew, Catherine and Peter for their continued and spirited support along the way. My son Irah, who was several months old when I began the book, was perhaps of less direct assistance, although his sleep schedule – or rather lack-of-sleep schedule – certainly helped to concentrate the mind. Last of all, but not least of all, my wife Claire has read every word I have ever written about Olga, joining me on her odyssey down the endless rails and offering humour, shrewdness and wisdom along the way.

And what of Olga Pushkin herself and her real-life counterpart, somewhere in deepest Russia, in Perm or Krasnoyarsk or Kirov? Perhaps they are still journeying onwards, as I wrote in *Death on the Trans-Siberian Express*, day in, day out, regardless of drunken fathers or chauvinist foremen. The tracks lie always before them, the horizon forever receding. Maybe one day they will reach it. Maybe one day.

CRIME AND THRILLER FAN?

CHECK OUT THECRIMEVAULT.COM

The online home of exceptional crime fiction

KEEP YOURSELF IN SUSPENSE

Sign up to our newsletter for regular recommendations, competitions and exclusives at **www.thecrimevault.com/connect**

Follow us

@TheCrimeVault

/TheCrimeVault

for all the latest news